Reckmire Marsh

Reckmire Marsh

Sara Hylton

St. Martin's Press
New York

Library of Congress Cataloging-in-Publication Data
Hylton, Sara.
    Reckmire Marsh / Sara Hylton.
        p.   cm.
    ISBN 0-312-13595-5
    1. World War, 1939-1945—England—Fiction.
I. Title.
PR6058.Y63R43   1995
823'.914—dc20   95-31034
                                                     CIP

First published in Great Britain by Judy Piatkus Limited

First U.S. Edition: October 1995
10 9 8 7 6 5 4 3 2 1

Reckmire Marsh

Prologue

I loved Genoa from the sea. It has a majesty denied it in the maze of narrow streets surrounding the great avenue that ran downhill to the harbour, but from the sea, Genoa was sublime. Castles stood on rolling hills, bell towers and turrets gleamed ethereal in the setting sun, and as I hurried alone along the harbour wall the ocean-going ships in the big harbour were lighting up like palaces.

I had been cautioned not to be away too long, but I felt a pressing need to walk in the freshening wind that swept in from the sea and walked quickly in the direction of the city lights. On the broad avenue there were cafes, theatres and great shops, brilliantly lit and busy with people, but I headed for the narrow streets behind which were a treasure trove of antiquities.

I paused at a shop window attractively dressed, neither a jumble nor pretentious, and here were old brocades, intricate brooches and buckles, glass-topped tables, carved ivories and marbles. A stack of malacca canes leaned idly against a gilt table leg and in one corner a bronze statue of an ancient Roman soldier driving four horses that pulled his chariot took pride of place. My eyes moved upwards and then I felt the cry being dragged from me as my eyes were rivetted on a small picture above the bronze.

I was trembling, and for a moment I had to press my face against the cool glass of the window and a passer-by paused to ask if I was ill. I knew that I had to look at the picture, confident that when I held it in my hands it would look entirely different. A trick of the light, no more than

1

that had made it familiar, and I deliberately did not look at it again when I walked into the shop.

Behind the counter a small hunchbacked man stood like an ugly old gnome protecting his treasures and I was aware that my voice trembled when I asked if I might see the picture. It took some time for him to clamber over the bric-à-brac, then hé was dusting the picture gently before he handed it over the counter.

It was old, the glass discoloured, the gilt frame scratched and in need of repair, but in my hands the picture came to life and I could see the coarse dune grass stirring in the breeze, see the waves tinged with the colours of the setting sun come tumbling in across the sand, and feel the sudden pain of the sharp cruel rocks cutting into my hands as my eyes looked upwards towards the house standing lonely and timeless on the point.

The shopkeeper was looking at me curiously, and with a sudden lift of his hands he said, 'The picture is old, the artist unknown, but I have better pictures than this, pictures of Italy. That is not Italy.'

'No. But I know this place.'

'You do, Signora? Do you wish to buy it?'

'How much are you asking for it?'

His manner changed from casual indifference to assurance. 'I can see the picture is important to you, Signora, I give you special price.'

The figure he quoted was ridiculous as I knew it would be, and putting the picture down on the counter I said gently, 'It is too much, Signor. The picture needs restoring, and as you say the artist is unknown.'

'Please, Signora, let us discuss it. I have had the picture a long time, I have forgotten how I came by it, but to you it is important. See, I want you to have it, I give you very spécial price.'

He scribbled the price on a piece of paper and pushed it across the counter, then he stood back looking at me expectantly.

'It is still very expensive,' I said quietly.

'But if you do not take it you will regret it, and if you come back for it the picture might have gone.'

2

'I doubt that very much if you have had it for such a very long time.'

He sighed. 'Very well then, for you, Signora, I will take off one third. I have made you a gift of the picture, do you not agree?'

I nodded. 'You will take a cheque, Signor. I had not thought to be buying anything this evening.'

He nodded, and watched while I made out the cheque. He took it from me and his face lit up with pleasure at my signature, then he made a great play of wrapping up the picture and handing to me across the counter.

For a long time I kept the purchase of that picture to myself, but when I was alone I stared at it long and earnestly. It seemed to me that fate had directed my steps to that small shop in Genoa, made me look in that particular window where the picture was waiting for me.

It seems strange after long years of closing my heart and my mind to memories of Reckmire that it should now figure so prominently in my dreams, but every night I am there where the salt marshes stretch from the river's estuary to the point on which the house stands and where the rolling Atlantic pounds relentlessly on the rocks below.

I loved those marshes which presented a wonderland for birds of all description, but especially sea birds and geese flying inland from their summer nesting grounds in Iceland to make their winter home in the shadow of the fells. Now day after day I remember it, the narrow road of sorts that cuts through the marshlands, a road that becomes completely covered when the tide rushes in, and woe betide any unfortunate traveller who tries to beat the tide on that lonely stretch.

It seems now that I have always known that rambling marsh and the haunting cries of the gulls, just as those living in its shadow have always known the great stone house standing high on its rocky crag. I only knew Reckmire as a joy during my girlhood, a lonely house surrounded by gardens in which clusters of thrift bloomed profusely in the spring.

Those old careless summers did not condition me for the heartache that came later, and even now when the years have brought a serenity which often eluded me during those other years when joy and anguish were so miserably intermingled, I have become obsessed with heart-searching and the feeling that it could all have been so very different.

I wish I could have loved my mother more, understood her better, never perhaps gone to Reckmire so that the past would not be torturing me now. Was there something more in Paul that I never found, never fully tried to find, and would my darling Robin be with me still if I had taken the trouble to search for it?

I have been happy in this laughing land where tall dark cypresses have replaced the conifers of my youth and where the sun shines down on red-roofed old towns and dreaming cities. Here with those I love I had thought the past was over and done with and my heart was ready to welcome joy again. Now, staring at the picture in my hands, I realise that running away is not the answer.

It will take courage to go back to the marshes alone but this is something I must do. I have to face my past, lay my ghosts. It can no longer be swept away like fallen leaves, for the past has shaped the present and will shape the future. There are voices clamouring to be heard, and I pray that I may be given the strength and maturity to face them alone.

I saw sorrow and acceptance in the faces of those I left behind. They know that I love them and will return to them but they also know they have no place in the world I am returning to. The plane soared higher so that now all I can see through the windows are sunlit clouds drifting like snow fields and the domes and spires of Florence sweltering in the heat of the noonday sun are far below.

It is fifteen years since I walked across the sands at Reckmire with the tears streaming down my face and the cries of the gulls mewling in my ears. What will my thoughts be when I see those sands again?

Book I

Chapter One

To fully understand everything that came later it is necessary to go right back to the beginning, so I am going back to that small village in Surrey where my mother's parents lived.

My grandfather, John Edward Fowler, was a Chartered Accountant with his own practice, a lucrative one, in the town of Godalming. They lived in a half-timbered pseudo-Tudor house at the top of a tree-lined lane in the company of similar houses. Houses with nice gardens, shaded lawns and summer houses.

My mother, Linda, was their only daughter whom they spoiled and cossetted from the day she was born. From early photographs I have seen of her she was a small pretty child with soft brown hair and wide-spaced brown eyes, always pristine neat and sure of herself. I am not like her in any way, neither in looks nor disposition.

Because my father spent most of his life abroad on Government business mother and I spent a great deal of my early youth living with my grandparents. Mother maintained that it was disruptive for a child to be shifted about like a parcel and no doubt when I was older and in school she would decide to travel with my father and live overseas. In the meantime I only saw Father when he came on leave to The Cedars, the name of Grandfather's house in Surrey.

Life was very orderly. Every morning we watched Grandfather setting out for his office, carrying his rolled umbrella and briefcase, dark-suited and bowler-hatted, escorted to the gate by Grandmother who stood there until he turned the bend at the end of the lane. Most mornings Mother and I went with her to the shops in the village, and in the afternoons when it was fine I was sent to play in the garden, and when it was chilly I was allowed to take my toys into the summerhouse from where I could watch grandmother's guests arriving for her bridge afternoons. In winter I sat in the kitchen watching Mrs Prothero, our daily, setting out Grandmother's best china and trays of tiny sandwiches and cakes. I liked Mrs Prothero who invariably produced a bar of chocolate for me and I got the pick of the cakes.

At the weekend the four of us would set out in Grandfather's Morris Cowley to drive along the leafy lanes of Surrey. We would stop for tea at some country tea shop and perhaps wander around the gardens of a stately home. For two weeks in the summer we would all drive up to Warwickshire where Grandmother's sister lived. I could never understand why there was a nursery at the top of their stone house furnished with shelves filled with books, a large grey rocking horse and a cupboard filled with toys.

I was not allowed to play with them or even touch them, and when I screamed with temper at being chastised for climbing on board the rocking horse, Mother patiently explained that everything in the room once belonged to her cousin Harry who had been drowned in the sea at Great Yarmouth.

Tears rolled helplessly down her cheeks as she told me and later I learned that my mother had been with him in the sea on the day it happened.

That accounted for the fact that my mother hated the sea and was the reason why we never visited my other grandparents who lived in a house standing on a cliff top overlooking the Atlantic and a desolate stretch of marshland they called Reckmire.

They called to see us just once when I was four. They had been spending some time with my father in Brussels and had promised him that they would break their journey north in order to see us. They arrived just before lunch in a very large car and we ate our lunch on the terrace because it was a hot July day.

I'd sat in the kitchen with Mrs Prothero most of the morning watching her prepare lunch. Grandmother had paid us several visits to see that everything was going to plan and Mrs Prothero complained heatedly, 'I wish she'd stay out of the kitchen and let me get on with it. You'd think the King and Queen was coming. What are they like these grandparents of yours, Joanna?'

'I don't know, I can't remember.'

'Well, she keeps on tellin' me they're gentry. I 'ave to say Sir Robert if I speaks to your grandfather and Milady if I speaks to her. What will you call them, love?'

'Mother says I must call them Grandma and Grandpa.'

At that moment Mother came into the kitchen. 'Time to get changed, Joanna,' she said, and for what seemed ages I was forced to stand still in my bedroom while she changed her mind several times about the dress I should wear, and the hair-ribbon I should wear with it.

Grandma, Lady Albemarle, was tall and slender. She had dark blue eyes and fair hair and was beautifully dressed in blue with furs around her shoulders. Grandpa too was tall, and he made a fuss of me. They came with presents for all of us and were quick to compliment Mrs Prothero on the excellence of her lunch. I saw Grandpa press something into her hand and later when they had gone Grandmother admonished her that she should not have accepted anything, she was amply paid for everything she did.

After lunch I walked with Grandma around the gardens, answering her many questions on what I did with my time, which toys I had and which books I liked to read. She was so nice I soon began to feel at ease with her, then she started to tell me about Reckmire, the marshes and the long stretch of beach over which the unpredictable Atlantic thundered.

'You would love it, Joanna,' she said gently. 'Someday you should come and spend some time with us when my other grandchildren are there. It will be nice to have you all together.'

I listened to her eagerly but I knew even then that if my mother had anything to do with it we would never go there. When Grandma repeated her invitation to Mother and my grandparents later, Mother simply sat there with a set expression on her face, that closed-in, defiant expression which I had come to know so well.

Other people speak of their mothers with joy and undisguised admiration. How I envy them and wish with all my heart that I could follow their example.

I learned not to speak about the sea or the marshes because any mention of them made her angry. I asked my father about them when he came home on leave and he described them in detail, his eyes warm with memories, delighted that I seemed anxious to know things about the way he had spent his youth. But when Mother came into the room he quickly changed the subject; not, however, before she had heard some of his story.

I remember her face, cold, with thin pinched lips, and the raw accusation in her eyes. 'I don't want you filling Joanna's head with talk of Reckmire, Robert, I never intend to take her there.'

'But she would love it, darling.'

'What has that got to do with it? I should hate it, and she does happen to be my daughter. You know how I hate the sea and everything connected with it.'

'They are my parents, Linda, I feel very guilty that we don't see much of them.'

'Well, you're abroad most of the time, they know that.'

'They also know that I get fairly generous leave.'

'I'm not stopping you going, Robert, and if they want to see Joanna they can visit here anytime – my parents have told them to – and I don't mind if they spend a holiday with us just so long as it isn't near the coast.'

'I just think sometimes it would be nice to see my two sisters and their children. They're Joanna's cousins and she's never met them.'

'I don't want to talk about it any more, Robert, you know how I feel. I've grown up with it and it's never going to go away.'

'I was always brought up to face my fears,' Father said evenly.

I watched her face crumple into tears. It was her final ploy and my father crossed the room to comfort her, his face filled with remorse.

10

We did not go to Reckmire. Instead we rented a cottage in the Cotswolds and at the beginning of September I went to my first school at the corner of the road.

It was run by a Miss Pemberton and four assistant teachers and it had a good reputation for girls between the ages of four and ten. The school was housed in a large brick house where Miss Pemberton lived with her invalid mother. Generally she took around sixty to seventy girls.

For the first few months I was happy. For the first time I had friends of my own age. I was invited to birthday parties and summer picnics, but when Miss Pemberton decided all her girls should have swimming lessons my mother refused to give her permission.

I remember sitting miserably silent while my mother explained her reasons for her refusal. The death of her cousin in the sea, her aversion to water sports and the fact that I was delicate. I was not delicate, but she was so adamant Miss Pemberton retired with good grace and when the others went for swimming lessons I was left behind to read and pore over my books.

From being a popular girl I rapidly became unpopular. They called me spoilt, a namby-pamby whose mother wouldn't let her do anything which had an element of risk attached to it. They stopped inviting me to parties and when I cried bitterly Mother merely said, 'They're evidently not very nice girls, Joanna. On Saturday we'll go to the shops and have tea in that new cafe in the high street, I'm sure you'll like that much better.'

I heard Mrs Prothero chatting to the daily woman from next-door. 'Poor little mite,' she said, 'she's so lonely. All this cossettin's goin' to ruin her life.'

When our next-door neighbour repeated those sentiments to Grandmother, my mother was so furious Mrs Prothero was subjected to a severe scolding for gossiping to neighbours and the outcome was that she left in a temper, but not before she accused my mother of spoiling my childhood and the rest of my life if she didn't watch it.

How I used to pray that things would change. I wanted my father to come home so that I could persuade him to allow me to have swimming lessons but I had little hope

11

that he would do anything to upset Mother. Fate did take a hand however when Grandmother was taken ill at one of her bridge parties and had to be brought home.

I watched Mother fussing over her where she sat panting in her chair, her face a peculiar red colour, her eyes staring wildly. The doctor said she had had a mild heart attack and gave her an injection, after which she slept and looked more like my grandmother. In the night however she had another heart attack and in the morning Mother came to tell me tearfully that my grandmother was dead.

I wept over her. I had loved her, she was part of my childhood, and she was the first person close to me who had died. Father came home for her funeral and because Mother was so distraught there was no opportunity for me to ask him about my swimming lessons.

For the first few months after her death Grandfather seemed miserably unhappy, then time began to erase the sorrow and he started to go out again. Much to Mother's dismay he took up golf and joined the local golf club, then he too started to play bridge and when Mother broached the subject of summer holidays he informed us that it was his intention to go on a bridge holiday with three other people. These were Mr and Mrs Cahill from across the way and a Mrs Bolton we had never heard of.

After he returned he brought Mrs Bolton to meet us and the atmosphere was noticeably cool. She was a smartly dressed lady with silver hair who brought with her her Golden Labrador called Honey. I loved him on sight, even when Mother said she didn't like large animals and Honey was shut away in the kitchen until it was time for Mrs Bolton to leave.

I liked her, I thought she was nice, and anybody who loved Honey must be nice I told myself. Mother and Grandfather had words and there were long silences over the dinner table and sometimes they didn't speak for hours. The outcome was that Grandfather said he intended to marry Mrs Bolton, and since we were living in his house if Mother and Mrs Bolton couldn't get on we should have to look around for somewhere else to live.

Mother wept, reminding him that Grandmother had only

been in her grave for ten months and that she was his only daughter. Grandfather sulked, and then Father came home to deliver his bombshell.

The Government was sending him to the Far East where he would be expected to remain for several years. He had a month's leave in which to sort out his affairs before leaving for Singapore and Grandfather missed no chance to tell my mother that it was her duty to go with him.

I was made the reason why she couldn't go. She had no desire to live in the Far East, I would have nowhere to live in England since Grandfather had stated his intention of remarrying, and I needed her more than anybody. That was when Father appealed to his parents and suddenly they were there. Grandpa said very little but Grandma was quick to inform Mother that it was time she realised she was a wife as well as a mother. Her place was with my father in Singapore, my place was here in England where I should receive my education.

With four people ranged against her Mother was forced to capitulate and in that month it seemed my entire life changed. Grandfather and Mrs Bolton were married and went off on their honeymoon leaving mother to pack everything she thought essential to her life in Singapore. I was enrolled into a boarding school which Grandma said she had had good reports of in Harrogate, in distant Yorkshire which I had never visited, and in the school holidays I was to stay with various relatives, Grandfather and Mrs Bolton, Aunt Marcia, father's sister whom I had never met and who lived in Somerset, and Grandpa and Grandma at Reckmire.

This last decision brought on an angry scene between my parents, but it was Grandpa Albemarle who determined the issue by saying Mother was spoilt and foolish and it was high time she grew up.

Suddenly girls who had ignored my existence for months started to fuss over me. Once more I was invited to birthday parties, all of which I acknowledged calmly but made the excuse that I was helping my mother to pack or wished to spend more time with my father.

Grandfather Fowler and my new grandmother came back from their honeymoon and at the end of the month we

13

saw my parents depart for Singapore. Mother was pale and tearful, I promised to write to them often and then I returned joyfully with grandfather and Mrs Bolton, now Mrs Fowler, to their house in Godalming and to Honey.

For those few remaining weeks I was happy. I took Honey for long walks and played with him in the garden. My new grandmother was easy-going. She made few demands on my time and laid down no restrictions. As long as they had their bridge evenings and dinners at the Golf Club she was happy, and I no longer had Mother's restricting presence to find fault with the things that made me happy.

At the end of August my Albemarle grandparents appeared with the intention of taking me to my new school in Harrogate.

I was introduced to Yorkshire on a cool windy day when the dark Pennine Hills loomed forbidding and stark in the distance and the landscape changed from leafy lanes and gentle meandering rivers to stretches of wild sweeping moorland and forests of dark evergreens, to wide turbulent rivers and sudden shafts of sunlight illuminating limestone crags.

I was informed that Harrogate was a Spa Town frequently visited by royalty and with connections with the Princess Royal who lived close by at Harwood House. I saw it as a town with wide tree-lined avenues, grey stone buildings and sweeping lawns, a place of some elegance, and as we drove up the long drive to the school doors this too was set amidst green lawns and where great oaks were already shedding their leaves.

We were received in the friendliest fashion by the head-mistress, a tall silver-haired woman who smiled down at me and asked if I had any questions to ask.

'Shall I be given swimming lessons?' was my first and most vital question at which my grandparents smiled and Miss Evesham, for that was my new headmistress's name, said, 'But of course, Joanna. We have a swimming pool here at the school and you will receive lessons several times during the week. You want to learn how to swim, don't you?'

'Oh, yes. Yes I do,' I answered eagerly, and when Miss Evesham looked at my grandma curiously she was quick to

14

explain that Mother hadn't been in favour of it because of an early tragedy.

I went with them to their car and they both embraced me warmly, then Grandma said, 'At Christmastime you are going to stay with your grandfather in Surrey, but in the summer you will come to us. You will love Reckmire then and you will meet your cousins and their friends.'

That was the time I longed for, even over Christmas when I had Honey and was living in surroundings with which I was familiar. I did not miss my father, after all he had been away from us for so long, but I missed my mother. I imagined her small figure and her face with its tight-lipped smile, in my room, on the stairs or when I played with Honey in the garden. I could sense her disapproval when my shoes were dirty and my hair untidy, I stayed away from the swimming baths even though I could now quite easily swim a length, and when Honey leapt into the kitchen with light-hearted abandon I found myself cautioning him gently as though she could know even though she was far away.

There was one place where I would not see her or sense her presence, one place that she hated and where she would never follow me, and that was Reckmire. In eight months' time I would be there and joy filled my heart at the prospect, joy with no hint of fear.

Chapter Two

I began to think the summer would never come. I listened to the other girls talking about their holidays by the sea and for the first time I could think about it without feeling guilty.

It was August at last, a warm cloudless August, and immediately breakfast was over I was outdoors, my eyes straining at the procession of cars coming through the gates and along the drive. Miss Evesham laughed at my excitement, saying, 'You can't expect them to be here yet, Joanna, most of these people only live a few miles away. Your grandfather has to drive from the West Coast.'

All sorts of uncertainties crossed my mind. Suppose they'd forgotten, or perhaps one of them was ill. Perhaps they didn't want me, or worse still, my mother had forbidden them to invite me. By the time I recognised Grandpa's car I was panic-stricken and ran with tear-filled eyes along the grass that verged the drive.

I stopped in my headlong flight when the car stopped and then my grandma was out of the car, saying anxiously, 'Good heavens, child, what is the matter? I told you we would be here.'

She put her arms around me and held me close, and the relief was so great it felt as though a great stone had been lifted from my shoulders. Impatiently I waited while they spoke to one or two of my teachers and then Grandma was saying, 'I shall sit in the back, you shall sit with Grandpa and he will explain to you where we are and what you will see.'

I shall never forget that journey. My mother had always led

me to believe that the north of England was a dismal place, wild and wind-swept, where the towns were buried under a forest of mill chimneys and the people spoke a strange dialect she had had great difficulty in understanding.

Now I was discovering a new and exciting beauty, a thing of coarse waving grass and tints of heather, ancient priories, Norman castles and rivers that flowed through sleepy villages warm with Pennine stone. We called for afternoon tea at a small teashop in the middle of a rambling high street where ducks splashed joyfully in a stream that ran the length of the street and where old men sat dozing under the branches of a giant yew tree.

I revelled in the taste of home-baked scones and strawberry jam, saving the last one for the ducks who squabbled noisily for the last crumb, then we were driving through the Trough of Bowland on our way to the sea. Grandpa brought the car to a standstill high up on the narrow winding road and said, 'Look straight ahead, Joanna, tell me what you see.'

I stared ahead at range of hills, hazy blue in the distance, and beyond the forest stretches of pastureland and a large town with its church spires and towers.

'Well,' he prompted gently.

'I can see the hills and town. I can see the meadows and the road that runs towards them.' My voice faltered. I was unsure what else I was expected to see.

'Those are the lakeland fells,' he said. 'We have just crossed the Pennines and that town you can see is the City of Lancaster. Look beyond it, Joanna, what do you see there?'

'Something long and shining — a river?'

'No, my dear, that is the sea, the Irish Sea to be precise. When the day is very clear it is possible to see the Isle of Man and the Mountains of Mourn from here, but not today, I'm afraid.'

'Is that where we are going, on to the sea?'

'Yes, and very soon you will see how the scenery changes and the winds from the sea change the land.'

I came to know what he meant as we drove onwards towards the coast. Now the trees became stunted and leaned away from the sea as if it threatened them. It was a place of narrow lanes and stone bridges, wide tumbling rivers where men stood in the shallows holding long fishing rods, and then when the meadowland petered out I could smell the salt marshes and we were driving through a wrought iron gate which stood open and a small child playing in the garden of the stone lodge house waved to us gaily.

The long drive led on through pastureland and Grandpa pointed out a herd of deer grazing peacefully under the trees. We came at last to a high stone wall and on the other side to gardens beautifully laid out in front of a large stone house whose small-paned windows shone golden in the sunlight. Two gardeners working on the paths touched their caps respectfully then we were stopping before the imposing entrance to the house and almost immediately the door opened and a man accompanied by a young servant girl ran down the steps to meet us.

My cases were taken from the car and the girl smiled at me shyly. Grandma said, 'This is Jennie, Joanna. She will be looking after you and Gabriella and will take you to your room. She will help you to unpack and put your clothes away, and then she will bring you down to the drawing room. You will meet some of the others before dinner but I doubt if they will all have arrived yet.'

I was too shy at that moment to ask who I would meet, and Jennie was waiting for me to go with her into the house.

When I crossed the hall I could only think that most of Grandfather Fowler's house would have fitted into it quite easily, and then we were mounting the shallow staircase to the realms above. Sunlight slanted through the tall windows on to the polished floor of the hall and the rich rugs and polished furniture. Some of the windows had stained glass coats-of-arms in them and I promised that I would take a closer look at the suits of armour whenever I got the chance.

Jennie smiled down at me and I whispered, 'It's so big, I'll never find my way around.'

'That you will, Miss Joanna, but it'll take time. It took me ages. I kept gettin' lost and one or another of 'em 'ad to come and find me.'

'Do you live here?' I asked her curiously.

'I do now. I came on a month's trial last year and they must 'ave bin satisfied with me because I was promoted to under 'ousemaid. Now I've bin asked to look after you and Miss Gabriella 'til you goes back.'

'Who do I have to meet in the drawing room?'

'I think some of 'em 'ave gone out, it's such a lovely day. I expect they'll be back afore you gets downstairs. There's Miss Corallie, your aunt ... but I keep forgettin', she's now the Contessa Flamouri ... and her husband, the Conte. Miss Gabriella is their daughter, your cousin. Then there's Mrs Manderville and her husband, your Aunt Marcia and Uncle Edward. They came yesterday. Their son Master Robin and his friend are arrivin' sometime tomorrow.'

'I see,' I said doubtfully.

''Ave you never met any of 'em afore?'

'No. We lived in the south with my grandparents.'

'And you never visited?'

'No. Mother didn't like the sea.'

'Is that so? Well, you get plenty o' sea around 'ere. I was born in the village and I've known the sea and the marshes all mi life. When you knows 'em like I do, you can take 'em or leave 'em.'

'I suppose so.'

'You 'ave yer bath, Miss Joanna, and I'll unpack for ye, then we'll 'ave a think about what you want to wear.'

'I've only got cotton dresses and one silk one that I've had a long time.'

'Well, we'll think about it. Now see if you likes your bedroom.'

I stared around me with wide enchanted eyes. The bedroom was beautiful, delicate pink walls and rose-patterned curtains and bedspread. There was a deep pile pink carpet on the floor and a white sheepskin rug near the bed.

'The bathroom's through there,' said Jennie, 'and just as pretty as the bedroom. Go take a look.'

She was right. A pink bathroom with soft pink and grey towels, a pink carpet on the floor, and it was filled with the scent of roses.

'Do you 'ave a dressing gown, Miss Joanna?' Jennie called from the bedroom.

'Yes, a pale blue one on top of my suitcase.'

'We'll 'ave to get you a pink one to match the bathroom, won't we? 'Ere you are, love, when you've 'ad your bath I'll be all unpacked.'

As I lay luxuriating in my bath I thought about my bedroom at Grandfather Fowler's. It had been a dear little room with sprigged muslin curtains at the windows and a deep pink bedspread on the bed but it was not to be compared with the luxury I now found myself in. Mother had always been finicky about the niceties, pretty china and silver cake stands, silver cutlery and cruets, and equally meticulous about my choosing my companions wisely from girls in similar situations to myself, girls whose mothers she knew and whose fathers were in good positions. So why had she never wanted to come to Reckmire?'

Grandmother Fowler had never tired to telling her friends that Father's father had been knighted for services to the Crown and Mother had sat besides her gently smiling. Was there something else that had kept her away besides that old story of the little boy drowned in the sea? Perhaps they hadn't been nice to her, perhaps they wouldn't be nice to me. My grandparents were kind, but what about the others, Aunt Marcia and Aunt Corallie, and what about Gabriella who was half-Italian and Robin who was coming tomorrow?

By the time I had had my bath and donned my robe I was plagued by uncertainties. Jennie had left with my suitcases but I could see that all my belongings had been put away neatly in the drawers and in the wardrobe. Miserably I went to stare through the window. It overlooked the gardens and the long drive and I felt a vague feeling of disappointment. I had been so sure I would be able to see the sea.

I could see that the gardeners had moved into another part of the garden and stood watching them weeding the flower beds, then just as I was about to turn away I saw a car approaching the house along the drive. Curiously I watched its progress until it came to rest alongside Grandpa's in front of the house, then a man and a woman emerged from it and my heart lifted at the sight of a spaniel scampering ahead of them into the house.

I had only seen the top of their heads. The woman was wearing a cotton skirt and bright green blouse and the man too had been dressed informally. I wondered if they were family or guests. I decided to get dressed, choosing the blue cotton dress I always felt comfortable in.

I was brushing my hair when there was a light tap on my door and immediately it opened to admit the woman I had seen alighting from the car. She was pretty with soft brown hair and light blue eyes, and was smiling in the friendliest fashion.

'Hello, Joanna,' she said gently, 'I've been waiting such a long time to meet you. I'm your Aunt Marcia, Robin's mother. I've come to take you downstairs so that you can meet my husband, your Uncle Edward, and have a look round the place. We've plenty of time before dinner.'

When I smiled shyly she said, 'I hope you like your room, Joanna? Mother was very uncertain where to put you, but your mother preferred this room to any of the others. How is she?'

'Very well, thank you. Why did she like this room best?'

'Well, it's away from the sea. She hated to hear it, particularly at night, but from this room you can only hear the wind in the trees and the birds singing.'

She stood with the door open waiting for me to follow her, and at that moment I offered no criticism of the room they had chosen for me. When I saw the sea for myself I would know where I wanted to be.

My uncle smiled at me genially and I liked him instantly. Together they escorted me through the rooms of the house. In the large dining room the long table was already set for the evening meal, and along its length it gleamed with sparkling silver and cut glass. In the centre stood a large bowl of red roses and there was room for twelve people around it.

I stared at it, and Aunt Marcia said quickly, 'There are only ten of us dining this evening, Joanna, my son and his friend are not arriving until tomorrow.'

I was taken into the billiard room and the library, the conservatory and the morning room, and then Aunt Marcia took me into the kitchen to meet the servants.

A large woman sat at the table drinking tea. She wore a white starched cap on her head and a voluminous white apron. Her round fresh country face dimpled into smiles when she looked at me.

'This is Cook, Joanna,' my aunt explained. 'Her name is Mrs Atkins but I think she prefers to be called Cook.'

Three girls appeared round the table, one of them Jennie, and the other two were introduced as Gladys and Dora. They all smiled at me and Jennie said pertly, 'Did you see where I put everythin', Miss Joanna?'

'Oh, yes, Jennie, thank you.'

When we left the kitchen Aunt Marcia said, 'Now we'll go into the drawing room and from the windows there you will be able to see the sea. It's such a beautiful day, Joanna, you are seeing it at its best, all blue and peaceful.'

My grandparents sat together on a couch near the fireplace and when we entered the room Grandma put down the book she had been reading and looked straight at my aunt before she looked at me. There was doubt and uncertainty in her look but Aunt Marcia was smiling cheerfully and I could feel Grandma visibly relaxing. Grandpa, after favouring me with a swift smile, returned to his newspaper.

Below me were cliffs that reached down to a small landing stage, where a boat was moored. Beyond stretched the sea, calm and gentle, blue waves rolling against the cliffs, and when I looked out to where the point stretched in a long craggy arm, there stood a tall white lighthouse. There were steps leading down from the gardens to the landing stage and beyond a rocky path leading to the point, but I saw no sign of the marshes spoken of so often by my father.

Aunt Marcia must have seen the puzzlement on my face because she prompted gently, 'You seem surprised, Joanna. It isn't what you expected, is it?'

'No. I thought there would be marshes.'

'I can see your father has told you something about it. Come with me to the turret room and I will show you the marsh.'

I followed her out of the room and across the hall into an eight-sided room which jutted out from the corner of the house. The room was unfurnished except for a small chest of drawers and a dark carved chair in the window. It was carpeted with a dark red carpet but there were no curtains at the leaded windows and curiously I went to peer through them at the long stretch of marshland with its coarse waving grass. Here there were dunes as far as I could see, and the sand was smooth and golden where it reached the sea.

It was bare and stark and beautiful. In that first moment I wanted to run along that golden sand towards the sea tumbling gently along its length but Aunt Marcia was saying, 'The marsh is called Reckmire, Joanna, and it is by no means as peaceful and safe as it seems. The tide when it comes in is treacherous because it is unpredictable and we would prefer it if you didn't wander along the beach there alone. None of the village children play there. Anyone who has been brought up in this area holds Reckmire in some respect.'

I listened to her words but I knew that sooner or later I had to venture on to the beach below me. My courage demanded it, if only to prove to my absent mother that this was how she should have faced her own fears years before.

As we crossed the hall to go back to the drawing room the door opened and a girl a little older than I entered in the company of a man and woman. The woman was beautiful, tall and slender with red-gold hair and blue eyes, and elegantly dressed. The man was older with silver-grey hair and a tanned serious face. The girl was pretty. Her dark hair hung in waves on to her shoulders and my first impression was that she could never allow the silk dress she was wearing and the pale shoes to become soiled as mine often were.

She eyed me curiously, unsmiling, but the woman came forward immediately, her face alight with laughter. 'So at last we get to meet, Joanna. Mother was right. You are a young edition of me, far more than Gabriella is going to be. I am your Aunt Corallie and this is my husband Rinaldo and daughter Gabriella.'

Her husband took my hand gravely and bowed over it, and I looked up into a remote handsome face and liked what I saw. Aunt Corallie was busy pulling Gabriella forward, saying, 'Now come along, you two, we'd all like you to be

23

good friends even though you're probably not the least bit alike. How is your mother, Joanna?'

'She's very well, Aunt Corallie. She's with my father in Singapore.'

'We know that, dear, otherwise you'd never be here. Run along upstairs, you two, the old nursery is up there. You might as well get used to the lay-out of the house, Joanna.'

'I've taken Joanna round the house, Corallie. I thought she was a little old to find anything interesting in the nursery.'

'Oh, well, she should have seen it years ago like the others did. How many are we for dinner this evening?'

'Ten, I believe. Mother has invited the Harveys.'

'I wonder why? He never has any conversation and she's only interested in church bazaars and dog shows.'

Gabriella stood holding the door open waiting for me so I hurried forward dutifully. We climbed the stairs in silence since she made no effort to converse with me and I didn't know what to say. The nursery was a large room overlooking the gardens at the back of the house. There were long shelves filled with books and glass-fronted cupboards stacked with toys and soft cuddly animals. A large grey rocking horse stood in the centre of the room and in the corner a huge globe of the world. Enchanted, I walked round the room expecting Gabriella to walk with me, but instead she stood by the bookshelves so that I began to feel forgotten.

'Can we come up here whenever we like?' I asked her, more as a way of opening a conversation than from any real desire to know.

She looked surprised. Her eyes, I saw, were beautiful, brown and velvety with long curving lashes that swept against her cheek. Without a second thought I whispered softly, 'You are beautiful, Gabriella, I wish I was like you.'

For the first time she smiled. 'You'll soon get bored playing up here on your own, Joanna, unless you like being on your own?'

'I've become used to it,' I answered. 'I won't be now if there's two of us.'

'I have things I like to do. I like to paint and read, I don't like people to chatter to me when I'm working.'

24

'Couldn't I watch?'

'You'll find other things to do. After all, you've only just got here.'

'Mother said you were half-Italian but you speak English better than I do.'

'My mother is English, I was brought up to speak both English and Italian. When I go back to school in the autumn I shall learn to speak German.'

I looked at her with admiration. At the same time it was evident to me that I would not find the friend I longed for in Gabriella and my thoughts turned to Robin and his friend who were arriving tomorrow.

My earlier thoughts on the subject were borne out starkly over the evening that followed.

I changed into my one silk dress and wished fervently that I looked more grown up when Gabriella appeared in a long full-skirted dress that made her look very adult. She wore her long dark hair twisted intricately on top of her small regal head and even Grandma said somewhat disapprovingly, 'You look very pretty, Gabriella, but there wasn't any reason to dress for dinner tonight.'

Aunt Corallie laughed. 'Oh Mother, she's fifteen now. Time to look a little grown up, I think.'

With some asperity Aunt Marcia said, 'You're trying to look eighteen again and your daughter is trying to look very adult. Thank goodness I don't have this sort of trouble with Robin.'

'Well, of course not, darling, but you'll find that Robin is very intrigued with the way Gabriella is growing up!'

We all took our places at the dining table and I was glad that I was placed next to Aunt Marcia and opposite Mrs Harvey who was a large smiling woman who seemed more intent on seeing that her husband ate and drank sparingly than on any of the conversation going on around her.

'Didn't you say that Robin was bringing Paul Cheviot again?' Aunt Corallie asked. 'Doesn't Robin ever go to stay with his family?'

'He's been several times,' Aunt Marcia replied shortly.

'I found him a very handsome boy,' Aunt Corallie went on, 'handsome and strangely brooding. Not at all the sort

25

of boy I would have thought Robin would have chosen as a friend.'

'Robin feels rather sorry for him. Paul doesn't get on with his father who is something of a despot, and he never talks about his mother. Edward thinks she's probably a pale, self-effacing little woman who daren't say boo to a goose. I'm not so sure.'

'What exactly do you mean by that?' Aunt Corallie asked.

'The boy isn't timid, if anything he's too assertive, and Robin tells me he's quite fearless as a sportsman. He plays rugger, sails, hunts with his father and approves of blood sports. A shy timid mother would surely have had some tender influence on him.'

'I had a cousin like that,' Mrs Harvey surprised everybody by joining in the conversation. 'His father was a terrible man and his wife was frightened out of her wits by him. Both their children took after their father. One of them drank himself to death at twenty-four, the other disappeared when he was nineteen and none of us have seen top nor tail of him since.'

'Paul has always been quite charming to me,' Grandma said stoutly. 'He talks to me and escorts me round the gardens. He thanks me warmly for inviting him here.'

'Well, of course he does, Mother,' Aunt Corallie said. 'You treat him like another grandson. The awful part would be if he didn't talk to you.'

By this time I'd begun to speculate about Robin's friend Paul and wasn't exactly looking forward to meeting him.

'So your folks are in the Far East, young lady?' Mr Harvey began.

'Yes, Singapore.'

'And you'll be going out to see them no doubt?'

'I don't know.'

'I wonder how Linda'll like Singapore,' Aunt Corallie said dryly. 'If ever there was a suburbanite it was her.'

I saw the warning glance that Grandma conferred on her, but unabashed Aunt Corallie went on: 'I was absolutely amazed when Robert persuaded her to go. He's been unable to have his way about everything else.'

'You were friends at school,' Grandma said mildly.

Not really. I'd say I was least friends with Linda than any other girl in the school. I felt sorry for her when her mother was ill and her father took her away to recuperate. She'd nowhere to go in the school holidays and Reckmire was always open house. A little like Robin's Paul perhaps.'

'Little thinking that she'd captivate Robert and end up being your sister-in-law,' Uncle Edward said with a smile.

'How true.'

'Didn't you like my mother?' I surprised myself by asking.

After a brief silence it was Grandma who answered me. 'Of course we liked your mother, dear, we simply wish we might have seen more of you. There were times when it seemed my son and his family would forget us.'

'Father talked about you, about the house and the marsh. I always wished we could come here.'

'But your mother wouldn't allow it?' Aunt Corallie prompted.

'No.'

I was dismally aware of the tension round the table. It was an unspoken condemnation of my mother and what she stood for, and I felt again that sickening antipathy towards her that was to colour my life.

It was Grandma who changed the subject and for the remainder of the meal they talked about local issues and people I did not know. Later Gabriella sat at the piano and played beautifully while her parents sat at a small card table playing cribbage. Grandma worked on her needlepoint and Aunt Marcia read while the other four played bridge.

At half-past nine Jennie came in with cocoa for me and Grandma said it was time for me to go to bed. She came with me to my bedroom after the others had wished me good-night, and stayed until I was undressed and in bed.

'I expect you're sleepy, Joanna. It's been a long day for you,' she said gently. 'I'll leave the bedside light on for you in case you wish to read for a while.'

I smiled. I was not allowed to read in bed at Grandfather Fowler's house, Mother said it was bad for my eyes, but I waited until she had closed the door quietly behind her before I got out of bed and went to stare through the window. A pale crescent moon shone in the sky, illuminating the trees along the drive, and there was a soft wind rustling through the leaves. In the distance I could see lights and hear the distant barking of dogs. I strained with my ears for the sound of the sea but I couldn't distinguish it from the sound of the wind and reluctantly I returned to my bed.

For many years I had yearned to visit Reckmire and the marshes, now I had arrived and the first day was almost over. In the morning I vowed I would face the sea. It held fears for me, fears that had been instilled into me from my earliest childhood. I would not run away. I would make myself walk along the edge of the waves where the outgoing tide had left shells and brown seaweed, I would listen to the gulls and breathe in the salty breeze, and in doing so I would lay the ghosts that had tormented my mother, and to a lesser degree myself.

Chapter Three

There was no sun on the following morning. Instead the sky was a dull leaden grey and in the gardens below my window the flowers drooped dejectedly.

Over breakfast there were arguments. Aunt Corallie and her husband were intent on driving up to Cartmel where there was racing. Grandpa was interested but thought the day would be stormy. Grandma said she definitely would not go, particularly as Robin and his friend were arriving, and Aunt Marcia and Uncle Tom were visiting friends in the area.

'What about you two?' Grandma said, meaning Gabriella and me, but Gabriella was quick to say she had to practise her music and I was equally quick to say that I would explore the house and the gardens.

'Don't venture too far,' Grandma said. 'It isn't a nice day and it could well rain. There'll be plenty of time to explore the beaches on a better day.'

I was glad when they all departed. Gabriella was busily playing scales and arpeggios which I had no interest in listening to and Grandma was at her desk writing letters. I spent the morning exploring the house. It was much larger than I had thought and I marvelled that on one side of the house the windows looked upon lush gardens and grassland while on the other only rocks and clumps of thrift met my gaze.

I loved the turret room best, but the view from it was very different from the one I had seen the day before. Now the sea rolled and seethed in a grey stormy mass and the long stretch of beach and dunes looked lonely and unwelcoming.

Only Grandma and I sat down to lunch. She explained that Gabriella had developed a headache and was resting in her room. When I didn't comment, she said, 'She does suffer from headaches, I do hope it has nothing to do with her eyes.'

'What time is Robin arriving?' I asked.

'Some time this afternoon, Joanna. What are you going to do?'

'Perhaps I'll read.'

'I'm sure that's a good idea, it looks far too stormy to venture out.'

She saw me settled in the morning room with a book on my knee and a few minutes later I watched her leave the house and walk towards the car. A dark-clad chauffeur opened the door for her and I guessed they were driving into Lancaster to meet Robin and his friend.

I waited until the car drove out through the gates before I ran upstairs to collect my raincoat, then without being seen I let myself out through the conservatory and towards the steps leading down to the landing stage. A stiff breeze met me as I clambered down, and I could taste the salt on my lips. Above me gulls wheeled in the sky, and the air was filled with their cries.

I could see that the tide was out and the long craggy arm on which the lighthouse stood seemed higher now than it had the day before when the sea had rolled over it. I was able to step down from the rocks on to the sand and could skirt them until before me stretched the beach, dunes and marshes known as Reckmire.

I was enchanted by it all, by the gulls sailing on the wind and the softness of the sand under my shoes. The shoreline was a treasurehouse of seaweed and pebbles. Shells of all shapes and sizes, intricately sculptured, gleaming with mother-of-pearl, smooth as alabaster, stretched as far as I could see, left by the outgoing tide.

How could all this have been denied me all these years? Why had my father allowed my mother to do this to me? Why had it always had to be her way as though there was no other?

30

Shielding my eyes, I looked back at the house standing high on the headland, a great grey house as much a part of the shoreline as the coarse waving grass on the long expanse of dunes.

There was not another living soul on the beach and I amused myself by playing a game with the sea, waiting for each tumbling wave to reach my feet before leaping back. My laughter was lost on the wind.

I walked along picking up shells, absorbed and enchanted, then retraced my steps, noticing that the sea had reached the line of seaweed. I laughed joyously as I had to leap suddenly backward to avoid the ripples as it swept across the sand.

Dimly I became aware of voices shouting to me against the sound of the surf and in some annoyance turned to see two boys waving wildly to me from the edge of the dunes. I thought they were probably village boys and turned haughtily away, then the shouts became louder and, turning, I saw that one of the boys was running towards me, waving his arms.

I stared at him, and as he drew nearer my first impression was that he was beautiful. The sunlight shone on his hair, turning it to gold, and his eyes blazed blue and angry in his tanned face.

'What are you doing here?' he demanded angrily. 'Can't you see the tide is coming in?'

'I know it's coming in,' I answered him shortly. 'I jump back when it reaches my feet.'

'Look behind you, girl. Has nobody ever told you that this beach is dangerous?'

I turned where his finger pointed and then, incredulously, I saw the danger. The sea curved behind me reaching the dunes and was coming towards me in giant glistening waves. In that brief moment I found myself remembering my grandmother's warnings as well as my father's stories of the many dangers, but before I could gather my scattered wits the boy had seized my arm and was propelling me towards the cliffs. I could hear the pounding waves behind me as he ran with me, half dragging my faltering steps to safety and to where his companion waited impassively on top of the dunes.

I looked up to where he stood, taking in his dark eyes

smouldering with resentment, his unspoken contempt for my stupidity, and then the boy who had saved me was hauling me up behind him while the waves lashed furiously against the cliffs, as if to show their frustration at being robbed of their victim.

My rescuer looked down at me ruefully. 'Never do that again,' he admonished me sternly. 'Never take your eyes off the sea for a moment. Surely you must have known the danger.'

'I didn't,' I gasped. 'I thought it would be an awfully long time. It seemed to be coming in so slowly.'

'It comes in very quickly and from an entirely new direction,' he said sternly. 'If you ever come to this beach again, never forget that.'

'Oh, I won't, not ever,' I promised. 'Thank you for saving my life. You've got awfully wet.'

'I'll dry,' he said with a smile, a sudden sweet smile, then gently added, 'No harm done then. You'd better get off home to the village before they start looking for you. Take care.'

There were no words from the other boy. To him I was a nuisance, a silly girl who had put his friend in grave danger. Wordless I watched them walking away from me, chatting amicably together. Already I was forgotten.

'Get back to the village,' he had said, and at that moment I wanted to chase after them in order to tell them that I was Joanna Albemarle and probably had more right to be on that beach than either of them.

I looked back along the sand to see that already the waves had completely covered the place where I had stood and the sea was a terrifying mass of gigantic waves, crashing on the narrowing shore. I let myself in by the wicker gate and crossed the expanse of rockery adorned with thrift and sea-holly through the stone gateway which led into the formal gardens. It seemed that I was entering a different world where peace and tranquillity reigned.

I was glad to reach my room unobserved. My raincoat was saturated with seawater as was the hem of my dress, and I felt suddenly cold.

I took a hot bath after pushing my soiled dress into a

drawer at the bottom of the wardrobe and as I dressed heard the sharp patter of rain on the window pane. The sky outside was dark and leaden and I could hear the sea. I stared miserably through the window and to my surprise saw the two boys climbing over the wall and dropping easily on to the garden path.

My first thought was that they were trespassing, then with sudden and frightening clarity I knew who the boys were: my cousin Robin and his friend. I didn't know which was which, but if they told my grandparents what had happened it was going to be a terrible start to my time at Reckmire.

I would stay in the room, have a headache, anything was better than listening to them telling everybody about the rescue on the beach, looking at the dark cynical face of the boy who had glared at me from the dunes.

I was wishing my room wasn't so cold. The patter of rain had become a downpour and what would I do with myself here alone? Even as I was thinking it there was a tap on the door and Jennie's head appeared round it, her face wearing a bright smile.

'Ah, 'ere you are, Miss Joanna. Your grandmother sent me up to see if you'd got back. She was worried in case you'd got caught in the rain. There's tea in the drawing room and your cousin Robin's arrived.'

'I'm not very hungry,' I stammered uncertainly.

'You will be when you see all the lovely cakes Cook's spent all mornin' makin'. I'll tell the mistress you'll be down right away.'

There was sand in my hair and when I brushed it I could smell salt water and taste it on my lips. How my mother would have frowned at my morning's adventure. I could visualise her small tight-lipped face, hear her voice, exacting and cold. Now there was no escape. I had to go downstairs and face whatever was coming.

My first thought on entering the drawing room was that the two boys had changed their clothes. Now they were wearing formal lounge suits instead of flannels and blazers, and with a smile the boy who had rescued me came forward to meet me.

'So you are cousin Joanna,' he said gently. 'I'm Robin,

33

and I've heard a lot about you without actually meeting you. Come and meet my friend Paul Cheviot.'

I was glad that this was Robin and relieved that he was making no immediate mention of my escapade. Paul Cheviot did not bother to take my hand but merely stared at me long and hard. Grandma sat on the couch and I noticed beside her a pile of photographs. While Jennie poured out the tea, Robin went to hand round the cups.

'You'll be interested in the photographs,' Grandma said, 'I found them all this morning. I expect Robin's seen most of them but they're photographs of your father and the rest of them when they were much younger.'

I went to sit beside her while she showed me pictures of a very much younger Father, gay and laughing with his sisters on the beach, riding their horses, pushing their boats out, and generally having a lot of fun in summers long before I was born.

'Do you have any of my mother?' I asked.

'Well, she only came here a few times, but you'll probably find one or two. Take them all, Joanna, and look through them.'

I found only two. There was one of Mother sitting prim and unsmiling amongst a group of people in the garden. When I passed it across to Grandma she said, 'That is the time Corallie brought her here from school. They were about seventeen. She was such a small pale little girl with very little conversation and I worried about entertaining her. My children seemed to like all the things she didn't like.'

'But she came again?' I prompted.

'Yes. Strangely enough she met Robert at a dance the sister of one of his friends was giving. They knew Linda's parents and I think Robert took her under his wing, she'd known so few people at the dance. He brought her here several weeks later and they got engaged.'

There was so much more but I knew even then that I would never hear of it. I looked down at the second photograph of Mother and Father standing beside an open sports car in front of the house. He stood with his arm around her shoulders, casually dressed, while Mother as always looked neat and pretty in a silk dress and white shoes.

When I handed it to Grandma she said with a smile, 'That was the last time they came here. Your mother didn't like the car unless the hood was up and I lent her a leather coat. Your father sold the car when they got back to Surrey. I don't suppose he ever bought an open car after that.'

I could never remember us having an open car. I had never seen my mother with her hair blown and she disliked casual clothes. Robin came to sit beside me, picking up the photographs and commenting on them.

'What a pity you didn't come here years ago,' he said, smiling. 'My mother missed having your father for holidays here. The only time we ever saw him was when he came to see us during one of his leaves.'

'Don't you live in Somerset?'

'Yes, not far from Minehead, a lovely old place called Dunster.'

'Close to the sea?'

'Why, yes.'

That was why Father had gone alone to see his sister and her family. What a lot I had missed when I could have been making friends with this nice handsome boy who was smiling at me in the friendliest fashion. His friend was watching us from across the room with a frown on his face. I said, 'Your friend doesn't like me, Robin, he does nothing but frown at me.'

He laughed. 'Paul's like that. He has to get to know people and gives the appearance of being very stern.'

He didn't appear very stern a few minutes later when Gabriella came into the room. With Gabriella he was all smiles and affability as he was minutes later when he came to us to hand out scones. Even I was smiled at and Robin said, 'You see, Joanna, he does like you after all. Will you be going out to Singapore to visit your parents?'

'I don't think so. When Father gets leave they'll come to England.'

'To Reckmire?'

'I don't know.'

I knew very well. It would be to Surrey they would go and I would have to join them there. If anybody came to Reckmire it would be Father, and probably alone.

35

I was totally unprepared for the joys the next few days brought. I went fishing with Uncle Edward and Robin, anchored out beyond the lighthouse in the small boat. I distinguished myself by not being seasick and catching three mackerel. Half of my pleasure was derived from the fact that I was not simply near the sea but actually on it, though some of my elation was marred by the memory of Mother's disapproving face and the sound of her voice.

While we fished, Paul and Gabriella played tennis, and then later, to my amazement, Aunt Corallie asked me if I could ride. When I told her I had never had anything to do with horses she said with an incredulous smile, 'You mean to say your father has never suggested a pony? He loved horseriding. Mother couldn't keep him away from the stables. Tomorrow morning, Joanna, you are going to be introduced to the joys of riding a pony along the line of the surf.'

'But isn't the beach dangerous?' I asked.

Before she could reply Paul said sarcastically, 'Only for idiots who don't watch what they're doing.'

'We understand and respect Reckmire,' Aunt Corallie said. 'We know when it is safe and how far to go. I don't suppose you have any riding clothes?'

'No.'

'Well, we'll have a look round. I'm sure there're some that Gabriella has outgrown.'

'Where will I get a pony?' I asked a little fearfully.

'I'll get hold of the local riding stable. I'm sure they'll have something nice and docile for your first time.'

A pair of jodhpurs and a riding hat that had once belonged to Gabriella were found for me and it soon became evident that Aunt Corallie, Gabriella and the two boys were intent on riding also. They were all wearing correct riding clothes and as we walked through the gardens I asked Robin if we had to go to the riding stables for all the horses.

He laughed. 'We have our own in the stables you can see through the trees,' he said. 'There have always been horses at Reckmire. Only yours is coming from the stables in the village.'

When I didn't speak he said gently, 'I say, Joanna, you're

not afraid, are you? We'll all look after you, and I can promise you'll love it.'

I watched them mounting the horses the grooms brought out for them, thinking Aunt Corallie looked particularly splendid on a large black horse that seemed to be doing a great deal of prancing. She laughed down at me. 'Gypsy's restless this morning, he wants to be off. Ah, here we are. Your mount, I think, Joanna.'

A boy was leading a rather large pony through the gate and into the stable yard, a pony who stood obediently still while they saddled him. I went to stroke his dark satiny neck so that he turned his head and gently nuzzled my shoulder.

'His name's Daniel,' the boy said. 'You'll 'andle 'im all right, miss, 'e's a sensible 'orse and likes the sand under 'is 'ooves.'

Robin assisted me into the saddle and I looked down at him. I seemed an awfully long way off the ground but I had no fear of the pony, and as they trouped through the gates he followed the rest of them without any direction from me.

Aunt Corallie's mount was full of high spirits and it took all her concentration to control him as we moved down the drive towards the gates. Out on the village lane that led to the beach we passed a group of young people who stared at us curiously. Robin said, 'You can see the marshes from here, Joanna, there where the trees are stunted — that long wild wilderness of nothing but morass.'

It was only the beginning of an enchanting summer. I was the baby of the group and they set themselves out to entertain me and make me welcome. Even Gabriella suddenly unbent and decided to talk to me, telling me about her home in Tuscany so that I too came to know the golden countryside and red-roofed villages dreaming under the summer sky. And Paul, unexpectedly praising my horsemanship, made me feel like a grateful puppy under the affectionate hand of a master who had hitherto been uncaring.

We were sitting out in the gardens late one afternoon. Robin and Paul had played an energetic game of tennis and now Uncle Edward and Aunt Corallie had joined them. A chill little wind had blown up and when Gabriella shivered Aunt Marcia said, 'I hope you're not catching cold, Gabriella? You should have a cardigan.'

'I've left it on my bed,' she replied, 'I'll go in and get it.'

'I'll get it,' I was quick to say. I liked doing things for Gabriella. And before they could say anything I was running along the path towards the house. I let myself in by the conservatory and had to pass Grandpa's study on my way to the stairs. The door was open and I could hear Grandma speaking. At first I paid no attention then I heard my name and curiosity got the better of me. I stood just beyond the door to listen. Grandma was saying, 'She's loving every minute of it, dear. I'm so relieved. What would we have done with her if she'd been like Linda?'

'What shall we do when they come on leave, or when they come back for good?' Grandpa asked.

'Well, we can only hope they come on leave when she's at school, I can't even think about when they come home for good.'

'I blame Robert as much as I blame his wife. I didn't bring my son up to become subservient to any woman, let alone a bossy little female like Linda. He's better educated, more intelligent, and yet he's allowed her to take over his life completely so that it's always what she wants, and between them the child hasn't got a voice.'

'Surely they've been happy, Bob?'

'Any marriage is happy when one of the partners gets all her own way. Robert's been brainwashed into thinking he'd be selfish to want something different. I've never particularly liked Linda, but I've been disappointed in Robert too.'

'Surely not?'

'Oh, yes, my dear. We're his parents yet he's stayed away because she said so. Stayed away from his sisters too when they used to be such good friends.'

'But now we have Joanna, dear?' Grandma's voice was softly coaxing. I could feel the salty tears on my cheeks before I took to my heels and ran towards the stairs.

For a while I sat on Gabriella's bed, hugging her cardigan. What would happen to me when they came home? Would it be the end to the marshes, an end to the pony I had come to love and this beautiful old house that seemed more like home than Grandfather Fowler's ever had?

I don't know how long I sat there but it was Gabriella, her face concerned, who came in search of her cardigan and to see what had happened to me.

Miserably I told her everything I had overheard and she sat beside me on the bed, her arm around my shoulders.

'You shouldn't be worrying about that now, Joanna, your parents have only just gone. It will be ages before they come back,' she said firmly.

'I know, but they will come back, won't they? I won't let my mother keep me away from Reckmire. I'll fight her all the way, like Grandpa said Father should have done.'

'You may not have to. She'll probably have changed a lot when you next meet. Come along to the terrace, we're having tea out there.'

'They'll see I've been crying.'

'No they won't, and even if they do, tell them some dust got in your eye.'

Nobody noticed. They were laughing and arguing as usual and when Gabriella said she had to go into the village to buy stamps Paul immediately stated he would go with her. I watched them walking across the grass and Aunt Corallie said, 'He's going to miss her when we go back to Italy at the weekend.'

I amused everybody by saying, 'He thinks I'm a bore. When he takes the trouble to be nice to me he's usually sarcastic the next minute. He's never sarcastic with Gabriella.'

'At your age you needn't worry, Joanna,' Aunt Marcia said. 'In another few years you'll be the beautiful Joanna Albemarle and men like Paul will be falling over each other to attract your attention.'

'It might be too late, I'll remember how mean he was to me.'

They all laughed and Robin said, 'He's not the easiest person to understand.'

'Are things no better for him at home?' his mother asked quietly.

'Quite the reverse, I think. His father is a cold autocratic man and his mother seems totally uninterested in anything.'

'She's probably been conditioned into that way of thinking,' Aunt Corallie said. 'With all their money they could have a good life, see the world, live a little, yet there they are in that grim old house on the Yorkshire moors. No wonder Paul loves it here and appreciates a warm family life.'

With the departure of Gabriella and her parents at the weekend I began to feel that my stay at Albemarle was coming to an end. Early in September I was going back to Harrogate and during the first week in September Robin went with his parents to Somerset and Paul to Yorkshire. Now I was alone with my grandparents and yet I was far from lonely. I was confident enough to ride alone and the gulls and the sea were my companions. Even the long stretch of lonely beach gave me pleasure, but I was careful to respect the incoming tide and knew when to retrace my steps towards the safety of the dunes.

'Are you feeling very lonely, Joanna?' Grandma asked me one day and I was quick to reply that I was not.

'I love the sea and the beach,' I told her, 'but nobody ever seems to go there.'

'The villagers think of Reckmire as our beach and they know it to be dangerous. Why not take a look round the village one day? There's a very old Saxon church which is charming, and a few village shops, not very interesting I'm afraid. You have been happy here, haven't you, Joanna?'

'Oh, yes, I have, every minute of every day.'

'And you've been pleased with your bedroom?'

'I was disappointed that I couldn't see the sea from the windows.'

She smiled. 'When you come again I'll see that you have one of the rooms that looks out over Reckmire. We didn't think you would like it, that's why we chose the one you are in.'

'Because my mother didn't like it?'

'Well, yes. Now I know that you are more like your father in the things that give you pleasure.'

Chapter Four

I set out to explore the village the following morning. My grandparents had driven into Kendal and Cook packed a small basket for me with fruit and sandwiches and Grandma gave me some pocket money to spend if I was able to find something to spend it on.

It was a pretty village. The cottages were built in warm tinted stone and the villagers were evidently proud of their gardens. Along the village street ran a shallow brook over which were stone bridges leading into cottage gardens, and outside the church the brook ended in a pond on which various waterfowl swam and squabbled.

A giant yew stood in what I supposed was the village green and on the seat surrounding it sat several old men, chatting and reading their newspapers. They paid no attention to me as I let myself through the lichgate and on to the long church path.

The church was very old and largely covered in Virginia creeper turning red at the ending of the summer. A woman and a little girl were putting flowers on a grave and as I walked towards the church I met the vicar coming down the path, his long black robe flapping round his ankles, a friendly smile on his face.

'If you wish to go inside the church the door is open,' he said.

'Thank you,' I answered, and as I entered the porch I turned to see that he was engaged in conversation with the woman and child. Sunlight slanted through the tall stained glass windows on to the pews and stone floor and three women were busily engaged in setting out flowers, fruit and vegetables at the altar and any other place where there was room. I stopped to watch them at their work, and one of the women turned to say, 'It's the Harvest Festival on Sunday, love. If you want to come you'd best come early, the church'll be full.'

I smiled at her. Grandma had told me that sometimes they attended the village church, but more often than not it was the church in Bleacarn because Grandpa's parents and grandparents were buried there.

I thought this church was far prettier than the much larger church at Bleacarn where the Albemarle vault stood prominently in the churchyard, ornamental and eye-catching in white marble and black granite.

We had gone to pay our respects at the edifice while I had read the names of the many illustrious Albemarles who had gone before, but here in this small village church there was a warmth and friendliness that had been missing at Bleacarn.

I wandered around looking at the plaques on the walls, some in marble others in stone. Most of them commemorated vicars who had once preached in the Church of Saint Agnes, together with local men of some standing. I was surprised to come across one marble plaque to the memory of Admiral Robert Albemarle, benefactor and worshipper, of Reckmire Hall, Reckmire, who had died at sea in 1787, and I determined to ask Grandpa to tell me about him as soon as I arrived back at the house.

I smiled up at a woman decorating the font and she smiled back, saying, 'Are you visitin' these parts, love?'

'Yes. It is a lovely little church, isn't it?'

'Oh, aye, that it is. I was christened 'ere and married 'ere. You seemed very interested in that plaque in memory of the Admiral?'

'Yes, I thought all the Albemarles were buried at Bleacarn.'

'That they are, but the Admiral died at sea and was never brought back. He lived at the big 'ouse on the point so you might say 'e was entitled to be remembered in the village church.'

'Yes, of course.' I smiled at her and let myself out into

the warm morning sunlight. Was my father called Robert after the Admiral, I wondered, a man who loved the sea and died far away from his home so that the sea became his grave? What would he have thought about my father who had allowed his wife to keep him away from it?

I was still pondering as I walked along the village street towards the few shops, a post office and newsagent's, an antique shop and a bakery, all of them across the road from The Flying Horse, the village inn.

I stood looking through the baker's window where a girl about my age was setting out plates filled with scones and currant loaves. When she produced a large tray of rich cream cakes she looked up and smiled. The chocolate eclairs looked particularly tempting and I thought about the money burning a hole in my pocket.

I would go to the park, I decided, and take two of those eclairs to eat there. The bell over the door clanged noisily as I entered the shop but I was not the only customer. A large customer in a floral apron was already at the counter while the woman serving behind it was busy wrapping several brown loaves.

'Will that be all, Mrs Peabody?' she asked, piling them into the deep basket the woman handed over.

'No, I'll 'ave 'alf a dozen scones. Will ye be watchin' the weddin' this afternoon?'

'I doubt I'll 'ave the time. We'll still be open, you know.'

Mrs Peabody was disposed to gossip and I realised I would have to wait. Across the shop the girl smiled at me sympathetically while their customer said, 'I don't 'old with 'im leavin' 'is mother to marry Ted Ormerod's lass. She's educated 'im single-'anded all these years. Wouldn't ye just 'ave thought 'e'd have paid 'er back a bit afore decidin' to get married?'

'Oh, I don't know, Jennie's a nice girl. He could 'ave done a lot worse,' the shopkeeper replied.

'Twenty years 'is mother's bin a widow and 'er son's 'ad the benefit of whatever bit o' money her 'usband left 'er. Now that girl's goin' to get 'er 'ands on it.'

'Isn't that the way of things? Surely she'll be glad 'e's

43

found a nice girl to settle down with?'

'The widow's pension's not much, not like a wage comin' in it isn't. I've better things to do than watch a weddin' I don't particularly approve of,' Mrs Peabody said adamantly and in a voice which brooked no further argument.

I was of the opinion that Mrs Peabody probably spent her life laying down the law on one subject or other and thought it must be wonderful to be so sure about everything and to be always right.

'I'll 'ave a quarter of yer treacle toffee and a quarter of them 'umbugs there,' she continued. 'I see they've got a lot o' visitors at the big 'ouse. I've seen Miss Corallie ridin' through the village once or twice. It was like 'er to marry a foreigner, just as if there wasn't an Englishman good enough for 'er.'

''Ave you seen her 'usband?' the shopkeeper asked.

'No. I've seen the daughter. Pretty she is but foreign-lookin', not like 'er mother at all. My, but she was a flighty, independent chit of a girl, ridin' that big 'orse of 'ers along the beach at Reckmire. Different as chalk and cheese, 'er and 'er sister.'

'Isn't there a son as well as the two girls?'

'Ay, Master Robert we 'ad to call 'im. 'E's not bin seen in the village for years, not since 'e married that girl from the South of England. Quiet shy little thing she were, but those little quiet ones can be cocky when they 'ave a mind ter be.'

The shopkeeper favoured me with a troubled smile so that I murmured that I was in no hurry. I wanted Mrs Peabody to go on, I was learning things about my family I was unlikely to discover from any other source. Nothing loth, she perched herself on the one stool in front of the counter. The small diameter seemed to groan under her bulk but it seemed not to worry her as she said, 'I've 'eard they 'ad a time with 'er the last time 'e brought her up to Albemarle. Didn't want this, didn't want the other. They were right glad when they left at the end o' the week.'

''Ow do ye know all this, Mrs Peabody?' the shopkeeper asked.

'Well, I'm friendly wi Cook, you know, meets 'er at

Chapel and asks 'er round for a cup o' tea. Then there's our Margy married to one o' the grooms. Talk never loses owt, you know.'

At that moment the doorbell clanged again and two women entered the shop, fell walkers from the clothes they were wearing, and reluctantly Mrs Peabody eased herself off the stool and picked up her basket while the shopkeeper asked, 'Will there be anything else, Mrs Peabody?'

'Not that I can think of,' she replied, rummaging in her purse for her money, then picking up her basket she turned and made for the door. Before she reached it however she turned to say, 'Them tinned pears are dearer than the ones I bought fro' Marsdens in the town and they're no better.'

'My husband charges a fair price for everythin' he sells, Mrs Peabody, but I'll tell him what you say.'

'Well, I 'ad to mention it. Money's 'ard to come by these days, we 'ave to look after it.' After which parting salvo she left the shop while the two women smiled in an embarrassed fashion.

The shopkeeper was about to serve me when Mrs Peabody's head appeared round the shop door and above the noise of the clanging bell she said, 'If ye changes yer mind about watchin' Jenny Omerod's weddin' I might change mine and come with you.'

'Oh, I don't think so,' the shopkeeper said. 'I'll be too busy and there's been so much gossip.'

'Aye, well, some folk 'ave nothin' better to do with their time than gossip.'

The door slammed behind her and the shopkeeper said, 'See what the girl wants, Lottie, and I'll serve the ladies.'

The girl came forward with a smile and I asked for the eclairs. After she had put them in a bag for me, she said, 'You'll have to pay my mother, she won't be long.'

'My grandmother said there was a park in the village,' I said to her. 'Is it very far?'

'No, it's at the end of Friar's Lane. But it's not really a park. We calls it the Rec.'

The two women left with their purchases and I went forward to pay for my cakes. The girl's mother smiled at me. 'Are you a stranger in these parts love? I 'eard you

45

askin' our Lottie about the park.'

'I'm visiting relatives.'

'Are you on your own?'

'Yes.'

'Why don't you show her where the park is, Lottie? You've bin a great 'elp in the shop this mornin', it would do you good to get out in the sunshine.'

Lottie seemed unsure. I was quick to urge her to keep me company.

'I can't stay long,' she said firmly, but her mother said sharply, 'Stay as long as you like, Lottie. It's not nice for the girl to go to the park on 'er own, not with all the village lads millin' about and them that cocky and mischievous. And if ye sees our Freda tell 'er to get off 'ome and run some errands for me.'

'I can do them, Mother,' Lottie said eagerly.

'Do as I've told you. She doesn't pull 'er weight around this place. It'll do 'er more good than 'angin' about with those so-called pals of 'ers. 'Ere's a couple of cakes, eat them in the park.'

So we sallied forth out of the shop and along the straggling high street. At first we walked in silence then we became aware of Mrs Peabody standing chatting at one of the cottage doors and after we had walked a little way I turned round to see two pairs of eyes staring after us curiously. Meeting Lottie's gaze we both dissolved into laughter and Lottie said, 'She knows everything and everybody. My father sez she thinks she's allus right and everybody else is wrong.'

'It must be very nice to think like that. Is she always right?'

'I don't know.'

'She seemed to know a lot about the people at Reckmire.'

'Well, she's friendly with the cook and years ago she used to work up there when they had house parties. She's allus goin' on about them, just as if she was invited there instead of working.'

I was thinking about Cook, who ruled over the servants' quarters like a queen, sitting with Mrs Peabody over their teacups and talking endlessly about the family: Aunt Corallie who was beautiful and wild, Aunt Marcia who was calm and gentle, and my father who had brought home his quiet fiancee, disposed to dislike a way of life he had loved and the people who had shared that life.

'Are you visitin these parts then?' Lottie asked shyly.

'Yes, for almost six weeks during my school holidays.'

'Six weeks is an awful long time. We get a month at our school. Where are ye visiting then?'

'My grandparents.'

'And where do they live?'

There was no help for it, and somewhat reluctantly I answered, 'My name is Joanna Albemarle, I'm staying at Reckmire Hall.'

She stared at me incredulously, then said anxiously, 'How awful 'avin' to listen to Mrs Peabody goin' on and on about your family, particularly your mother. My mother'll be that angry when I tell 'er.'

'There's no need for you to tell her.'

'Oh, but there is. She'll ask where you're stayin' and who you are.'

'Well, I don't really mind about Mrs Peabody and she was right about a lot of things. My mother never liked it here and I doubt if she'll ever come again.'

'Why did she let you come then?'

'Because they're in Singapore and I had to go to school in England.'

'Does that mean you'll not see them for years and years?'

'When Father gets leave they'll come back and then I'll probably have to spend a holiday in the South of England. I don't want to talk about it, I love it here. I love Reckmire. I've never been lonely on Reckmire.'

'It's very dangerous. There's people lost their lives there — I'd never go there.'

'Oh, but you must. I go there some time every day and know how to watch for the tides. My cousin Robin has explained them to me, I'm never afraid now.'

Her voice was doubtful. 'I like the sea,' she said cautiously, 'I like the beach down near Bleacarn but I don't like Reckmire. It's wild and sinister and I don't like all those birds shrieking on the marshes.'

47

'You sound like my mother,' I said softly.

'Is that why she wouldn't come 'ere, because she was afraid?'

'Perhaps.'

I didn't want to tell Lottie the long story of mother's cousin and his death in the sea. She would sympathise, understand perhaps, but I had always thought the time for grief should end, and that it should not be made the excuse to shut oneself away from life, particularly when that life was part of another's.

'There are the park gates,' Lottie pointed out, 'at the end of the lane. We can eat our cakes in the shelter near the dovecotes then I'll have to look for our Freda.'

'Is she younger than you?'

'No, three years older. She's not a bit like me.'

'Why is that?'

'She thinks of nothin but bein' 'ere in the park with the village boys. She's always gettin' out of doin' things at home and she doesn't try at school. My mother sez there's nothin' for 'er but to go into service when she leaves.'

I had noticed how Lottie's speech broadened when she was troubled, and she seemed to be very troubled about her elder sister. There was a frown on her pretty face and as we reached the dovecotes we could hear the sound of shouting and laughter from the adjacent playground.

'Would you like to find your sister first?' I asked her.

'I suppose so,' she said. 'You can stay 'ere if you like.'

I didn't. I wanted to see what Freda was like if her escapades troubled her family so much.

Two young women with children were standing near the swings and after collecting a small boy from a wooden roundabout they came towards us and one of them said, 'If you want your Freda, Lottie, she's in the shelter. There's about eight of them, all smokin' their 'eads off.'

Lottie's face flushed ominously and I sensed her acute embarrassment that they had given her that bit of information in front of a stranger.

As we crossed the playground two boys came out of the shelter and one of them called out, 'Yer sister's 'ere, Freda, come to take yer 'ome.'

There were howls of laughter from inside then a girl came out. She was so totally unlike Lottie I stared at her in surprise. She had a shock of bright red hair, but she was pretty in a flamboyant way, pretty and coarse.

'What do you want?' she enquired sharply.

'My mother says yer to go 'ome – she's got some errands she wants you to do.'

'Why couldn't you do 'em then?'

'I promised to walk with a customer to the park.'

'Is this the customer then?' she said, eyeing me disdainfully.

'Yes.'

She looked me over from top to toe before saying, 'I've seen you round the village. I've seen you riding a pony wi' them from the big house. Who are ye?'

'Joanna Albemarle.'

Imitating my accent and my voice she said, 'Joanna Albemarle. My, we are honoured.'

I stared at her levelly and she called: 'Come out. We've got Joanna Albemarle 'ere, and with my sister Lottie too. Say, who's that fella with yer cousin? I could fancy 'im.'

'His name is Paul Cheviot.'

''E's allus with that dark girl. Sweet on 'er is 'e?'

'My cousin Gabriella.'

She shrieked with laughter. 'Gabriella!' she taunted. 'What sort o' name is that? Gabriella Albemarle?'

'No. Gabriella Flamouri.'

They all laughed and one of the boys taunted, 'Is she a gypsy or somethin'?'

'Her father is Italian,' I replied evenly.

I was aware all the time of Lottie's embarrassed face. Suddenly taking hold of my arm, she said, 'Let us go, please. You'd better get off 'ome, our Freda, or you'll 'ave my mother to answer to.'

She drew me away, but as we crossed the playground we were aware of their laughter and one of the boys called out, 'Come again, Joanna, and bring Gabriella with you.'

Lottie was holding my hand, pulling me quickly towards the entrance to the play area, until we were almost running, followed by their laughter.

Only when we were out on to the path that circled the bowling green did she stop to say, 'I hate the park, Joanna. They're always there during school holidays and this part is filled with old people in the afternoons.'

'Where can we go then?' I asked her.

'We can climb up on to the fell, it's nicer there. You get lovely views of the coastline up there and we probably won't meet a soul.'

'Then we'll go there and you can tell me about everything that goes on in the village. My cousins have gone home, there's only me left. It would be so nice to have a friend in the village.'

'I 'elp in the shop a lot, I don't get much time to go out.'

'But not all the time, Lottie. I do so badly need a friend round here.'

''Ow old are you, Joanna?'

'I'm nearly ten,' I answered her, surprised by her question.

'You're the same age as me, but you seem a lot more grown up. I suppose that comes from goin' away to school and livin' somewhere like Reckmire Hall,' she said sagely.

'Oh, Lottie, you are funny. I don't know anything about serving in a shop and waiting on customers. I want to know about you. When you learned to swim, if you have a dog, do your parents like the same sort of things and want to go on the same sort of holidays? Do you have grandparents?'

She stared at me for several minutes before saying, 'What funny questions you want to know. Let's walk towards the fell and I'll tell you.' She was distracted in the next few minutes however when her sister caught up with us and, falling into step beside us, said, 'Don't you be tellin' my mother I've bin smokin'. You'll know about it if you do! What are ye goin' to do with your posh friend then?'

'We're going up on to the fell,' Lottie answered her.

'Not bin invited up to Reckmire for tea then?' she taunted.

When we ignored her she laughed at her own humour, calling out: ''Bye, Joanna, see you soon.'

'She's not allus like that,' Lottie said defensively, 'only when she's been with that crowd.'

50

'I don't mind,' I reassured her. 'Girls can be horrid to each other. I had school friends who fell out with me when I didn't go swimming. They said some unkind things.'

'Can't you swim then?'

'I can now.'

'I could swim when I was four. My father said it was essential. And, yes, we do 'ave a dog, his name's Rex, and two cats, Smiley and Jet. What was it you wanted to know about my parents?'

'Only if they liked the same sort of thing and where you go for holidays.'

'Well, in the summer we goes to my dad's brother's place in Wensleydale. I loves feedin' the chicks and bein' with the animals, but my mother'd rather be with 'er sister in Chester. She likes the shops and the gossip with Aunt Edith.'

My spirits lifted. So families were much the same after all, mothers and fathers did disagree, but in the next moment Lottie said, 'Of course Mother makes the best of the farm, and Father enjoys the museums and the race track in Chester.'

'So in the end you all go somewhere together. You mother doesn't make a thing out of it?'

'Gracious, no. We're a family, aren't we?'

We sat up on the fell in the warm summer sunshine eating the contents of Cook's basket and our cakes and Lottie pointed out various homesteads dotted about the country-side and the river winding placidly on its way to the sea.

'What's it like goin' away to school?' she asked presently.

'I like it there. I've made friends and the teachers are nice,' I answered her.

'I don't think I'd like to go away to school, I'd be missin' the rest of 'em too much. I don't suppose you'll be leavin' when you're fourteen?'

'No, but I'll be happy coming back here year after year, and it would be nice to think I had a friend here.'

'You'll 'ave your family 'ere.'

'I know, and they're all very nice − all except Paul that is. I don't like him much, but then he isn't family.'

'Will you still be comin' 'ere when your folks come back

to live in England?' she asked curiously.

'I don't know. I don't want them to come back, I'd like for them to stay in Singapore for ever. It would be awful to think that I couldn't come back to the Marshes.'

'That's an awful thing to say, Joanna. I'd be heartbroken if my folks went away.'

I didn't speak. It was an awful thing to say because in a strange way I loved them. I loved my father's teasing smile and his calm sweet way of explaining things to me. I just wished I wasn't so exasperated when he allowed my mother to make all the decisions and have all her own way.

Lottie was staring at me curiously. 'You didn't really mean it, did you, Joanna?' she said earnestly.

In an effort to reassure her, I said, 'They've only just gone out there. By the time they get leave I expect I'll be longing to see them.'

'What will you do with the rest of your day?' she asked.

'Can't we spend it up here on the fell?'

'I'd like to but I must get back. If Mother decides she wants to watch Jenny Ormerod's wedding I'll be needed in the shop, our Freda won't be much use and she hates it.'

Reluctantly I returned with her to the shop. On parting she said, 'Why don't you watch the weddin'? I go back to school on Monday but perhaps I'll see you again afore then.'

My face lit up with a smile. 'Oh, yes, Lottie, I would like that very much, perhaps I will watch the wedding.'

When I reached the church I could see that already a small crowd had congregated around the gates and the paths leading up to the church. A long white car bedecked with white satin ribbons stood outside the gates along with the two others which I guessed were for the guests. I stood with the crowd and a stout woman standing besides me said, ''Ere ye are, love. Wait 'til they get outside the gates afore ye throws the confetti. The vicar doesn't like it on the church paths.'

She thrust a large packet of brightly coloured confetti in to my hands and it was then I noticed Mrs Peabody on the other side of the gate, dressed for the occasion in a blue floral dress and a large hat lavishly adorned with blue pansies. There was no sign of Lottie's mother so I could only surmise she had stayed in the shop.

The bride was a large pretty girl in gleaming white satin. She carried a sheath of lilies and her three bridesmaids, who all looked remarkably like her, wore different shades of blue.

Thinking to enlighten me, the woman beside me said, 'Sisters they are, love. Jenny's the eldest.'

I smiled and looked earnestly at the bridegroom. Jenny seemed to tower over him because he was of average height and very slender. He was fair with a long thin face and totally unlike the big laughing girl by his side.

Dutifully I strewed my confetti, careful that it went nowhere near the church gates, and then the bridesmaids and the bride's parents piled into the second car, along with a small bird-like woman I took to be the bridegroom's mother. She seemed totally bewildered by the proceedings, and as I walked away I heard Mrs Peabody proclaim, 'Well, she's got 'im. It's precious little 'is mother'll see of 'im after today.'

As I walked back along the lane towards the gates of the house I couldn't help wondering if that was what they had said when my father married mother. They would have been right about them. I hoped they were all wrong about Jenny Ormerod.

Chapter Five

My parents were coming home for Christmas. For two years I had spent long glorious summers at the house near Reckmire and news of my parents had come in letters; now they were coming on leave and I was glad it was for Christmas instead of in the summer. We were all to meet at Grandfather Fowler's house in Surrey but I was unprepared for the problems their leave created.

I called Grandfather Fowler's wife Mildred, which was her name, and because she wasn't really my grandmother she seemed to prefer it. I arrived in Surrey several days before Christmas and they met my train at the station. I knew immediately that all was not well. During the drive home they chatted normally but when we got inside the house Grandfather said he had something to discuss with me and Mildred said she would help Mrs Prothero who had returned to work for them soon after Mother left for the Far East.

Grandfather had never circled around problems and he didn't do so now. 'Your parents' leave has put us in something of a quandary dear,' he said. 'Mildred and I had booked passage on a ship going out to South Africa. She's wanted to go for a long time to see her son and his wife who live in Cape Town. It seemed like a golden opportunity. The fact that your parents are coming home has rather thrown a spanner into the works.'

'Does that mean that you can't go?' I asked.

'We're going to go. Mildred would be too upset if we had to cancel and your parents didn't give us much notice.

We're leaving Honey with Mrs Prothero and we think you'll be all right here with her and the dog until your parents arrive on Christmas Eve. What do you think, Joanna?' Before I could say anything, however, he went on: 'I'm not sure how your mother'll take to Mrs Prothero. They weren't exactly on friendly terms before she left. You'll help, won't you, dear? Try to tell her how much we'd looked forward to this cruise and how good Mrs Prothero's been to both of us.'

I agreed that I would do my best. It was going to be the strangest Christmas, but there was Honey and three weeks would soon pass.

We watched them depart in a flurry of excitement during the first week of December and I settled down to taking long walks with Honey in the park, and helping Mrs Prothero cope with Christmas shopping and the preparation of Christmas puddings, cakes and mince pies.

My parents arrived on the morning of Christmas Eve and were greeted far too enthusiastically by Honey who was immediately relegated to the kitchen while Mother, pale and languid, sank into an armchair, complaining that she had a headache and that the journey had been horrendous.

I felt sure we would all hear much more about it in due course. In the meantime however Mrs Prothero produced tea and sandwiches and Father sat on the couch with his arm around my shoulders.

We did justice to the sandwiches although Mother didn't eat a crumb, then after a while she opened her eyes and said, 'Where is everybody? I thought Father would be here?'

'They've gone to South Africa for Christmas,' I told them, adopting Grandfather's forthright manner as being the best way to tell them. 'They've gone to see Mildred's son and his family in Cape Town. The voyage was booked in the summer, it was too late to cancel, and they were both looking forward to it.'

By this time Mother was sitting bolt upright in her chair and I read the signs well. Two bright spots of colour burned in her cheeks and her eyes had grown stormy with tears.

'I think that's terrible, Robert,' she protested. 'Evidently Father thinks more of her son whom he's never met than he does of his own daughter.'

'I'm sure he doesn't, Linda. We did rather drop this leave on them without much notice.'

'They were supposed to have Joanna at Christmas. What did they think she would do?'

'They knew we were coming home and that she'd be with us. We'll all have a lovely time won't we, Joanna?' said Father, appealing to me.

From the direction of the kitchen came the loud barking of Honey and Mother said testily, 'I notice she's left that wretched dog here. Father knows I've never liked big animals. He'll have to go into kennels.'

Furiously I cried, 'Oh, no, Mother, that's not fair. I promised to look after him. He's no trouble. We go for long walks and he's only barking because the carol singers are in the road.'

'I want him in kennels first thing in the morning, Robert,' she said adamantly, but for once my father disagreed with her.

'It's Christmas Day, Linda, I doubt if it will be possible.'

'The day after then.'

Jumping to my feet I ran towards the door, turning to say, 'I knew it would be like this, it's always been like this. The marshes, my swimming, now Honey. Why did you have to come home?'

I ran out of the room slamming the door behind me, and found myself facing Mrs Prothero who was standing in the kitchen doorway, her face filled with dismay as she struggled into her coat.

'Where are you going?' I asked in a frightened voice.

'Only down to the shops, love, but I'm not very sure 'ow long I'll be stayin' here. It sounds as if nothing's changed.'

'Oh, please, Mrs Prothero, don't leave again. Help me to keep Honey quiet and out of her way or she'll have him put in kennels. I couldn't bear it. I'd run away, go to Reckmire, if she sends Honey away.'

'Get your coat, love, we'll take Honey with us and stay out of her way until she's got over the journey. Maybe she does have a bad 'ead. They've come an awful long way, and I couldn't stop him barking. What's your father had to say about sending him away?'

56

'She always gets her own way, Mrs Prothero.'

'Perhaps not any more, love. Two years is a long time. Talk to your father when you gets him on his own.'

As we sat down to our evening meal that night I knew that nothing had changed. Mother's first words to Mrs Prothero were: 'When did you come back to work for Father then?'

'Soon after ye went to Singapore,' Mrs Prothero replied sharply.

'I'm surprised he had you back when you were so rude to Mother.'

'I was never rude to your mother, Mrs Albemarle, my quarrel was with you. But if you'd rather I left, I can go today and come back when your father gets home.'

'I can't tell you to go, Mrs Prothero. I take it my father has paid your wages until he comes home?'

'That he has, but I'll not be stayin' where I'm not wanted.'

'Please, Mrs Prothero,' Father said gently, 'my wife is very tired, we've travelled across half the world and the journey wasn't a good one. It's Christmas. Can't we all agree to make it a happy one?'

'I'm willing to do that, sir,' she replied, 'I'm never one to look for trouble.'

'Well then. Do let us get on with our meal, which incidentally, Mrs Prothero, is very good. You've lost none of your skill as a cook.'

Somewhat mollified, she smiled at him, and went quickly back to her kitchen.

'Really, Robert,' Mother said sharply, 'there's no need to fuss her. She'll think she can speak to me any way she likes if you do.'

'We need her, Linda, unless you feel like doing all the shopping as well as the cooking.'

She said nothing, but I saw that she picked at her food, eventually pushing it away half eaten.

When we both stared at the plate, she muttered, 'I'm not hungry. I think I'll go to bed. I'll probably feel much better in the morning.'

Father stood up and went round to her chair. 'I'll bring you something up later on,' he said gently. 'Try to get some sleep. I know you've slept very little during the voyage home.'

At the door she turned to smile at me. 'I'm sorry, Joanna. Tomorrow I'll want to know all about your school, your friends, and your visits to your father's family.'

At that moment Mrs Prothero came to clear the table and Mother said, 'I take it you will be here for Christmas Day?'

'I've left everything ready, Mrs Albemarle. All it needs is cookin'. I'll come in to serve the meal and clear away, and bring our Edie with me to help, but as soon as we've finished I'll be off 'ome. It is Christmas Day, and I 'ave my sister and her 'usband staying with us. I'll be sure to leave out a buffet for your evening meal.'

The dismay on Mother's face was comical but Mrs Prothero hurried to the table and started to collect the dishes and after a few moments Mother said, 'When are you likely to be here again?'

'Well, I'll come in on Friday to whip round the 'ouse and see if ye wants any shopping doing. We're all goin' out on New Year's Eve and again on New Year's Day, then things'll be back to normal, won't they?'

'Were my father and his wife aware of what you intended to do?'

'Bless ye, ma'am, of course they were. I wasn't supposed to be comin' in at all until we heard you'd be at 'ome. I was takin' the dog to my house and Joanna was goin' to her Aunt Marcia's. You comin' 'ome upset the applecart proper.'

'For me too, Mrs Prothero. I expected to find my father here to greet me. I expected to be dining out on Christmas Day with my husband and family, instead of which I am having to cook a meal and clear away after the buffet meal you are proposing to leave. This is anything but the Christmas I was looking forward to.'

Mrs Prothero's face was red and truculent as she faced Mother, but before she could say a word Father intervened. 'I'm sure we shall manage. We'll all lend a hand. Don't you worry, just go off with your family and enjoy yourself.'

'Thank you, sir,' she breathed. 'I'm sorry to be puttin'

you to any inconvenience, but Mr Fowler knew about my sister comin' and since they weren't likely to be 'ere, 'e said I could do what I liked and enjoy miself.'

'Yes, I'm sure he did.'

Without another word she made her escape and then Mother turned on Father angrily. At that moment she reminded me of a small vindictive snake and I recoiled at the venom in her voice.

'You take everybody's side except mine, Robert,' she stormed. 'Your sisters used to make fun of me but you took their part, your mother never liked me but you always believed her instead of me, and you're taking Mrs Prothero's side even though you know I'm worn out after that voyage and my disappointment at Father's absence.'

'You can't expect her to be here all over Christmas, Linda. Besides, she isn't your servant, she works for your father.'

'What has that got to do with it? He's away and we're here.'

'Nothing is going to change things, Linda, so why don't you go to bed and get a good night's sleep? You'll feel differently in the morning, I'm sure.'

'I'll be too busy tomorrow to feel anything!'

Her eyes slid round to me hovering near the table. 'I suppose you'd much rather have gone to Somerset than be here with us?' she accused. 'And what are we going to do with that dog about the place? I won't have him in the kitchen. He'll have to be shut in the summerhouse.'

'I'll take him for a long walk, Mother. Honestly, he won't be in your way,' I cried.

'Your father knows how much I hate large dogs. They always had large dogs at Reckmire, it amused them that I didn't like them.'

There was distaste on Father's face. I could read it clearly but it was lost on Mother who turned on her heel and stormed out of the room, slamming the door behind her.

Father stared after her. It seemed like an age before he turned towards me. He seemed to make an effort to smile in a casual way before saying, 'She's tired, dear. What do you say about taking Honey into the park? Everything will be back to normal tomorrow.'

59

What, I asked myself, did Father regard as normal? Tomorrow was Christmas Day and I had never looked forward to one less.

Honey was consigned to the summerhouse where I took him his dinner and the rubber ball I had bought for him. I helped Mother with the lunch and, true to her word, Mrs Prothero came with her daughter to see that everything was going well and to serve the meal.

She wished us a Merry Christmas and received a perfunctory greeting in return from Mother while Father pressed an envelope into her hand which I felt sure contained a cheque or a sum of money. She thanked him gratefully. After she had gone back to the kitchen Mother said, 'There was no need for that, Robert. I'm sure Father gave her something before they went away, and she's done precious little for us.'

'She's left her family on Christmas Day and she was here to welcome us back. The meal was excellent, darling, you and Joanna have done a very good job with it.'

All it had needed was cooking but I decided to say nothing. I was pleased with the pure silk dressing gown they had brought me from Singapore and Grandfather had left numerous gifts for all of us. Father handed Mother a long narrow velvet box across the dining table and I watched her open it anxiously, waiting for that small shut-in face to smile so that the clouds could lift and dispel the gloom that had seemed to surround us all morning.

She draped the gold bracelet across her wrist, and I jumped to my feet and went round the table to look at it. It was a beautiful thing, intricately worked and studded with milky white opals.

'Well?' Father asked. 'It is the one you admired in the jeweller's, isn't it, Linda?'

'Yes, Robert, it's beautiful. Aren't opals supposed to be unlucky?'

'Only because they chip easily,' he replied evenly. 'They won't be unlucky for you, darling. Here you are, Joanna, what do you think of yours?'

I took hold of the velvet box he handed over and on opening it found a similar bracelet in silver studded with amethysts. My eyes shone with joy. I rushed to throw my arms around him and Mother said quietly, 'It had better go in the safe, Joanna. You won't be able to wear it at school and if you're into all those horsey pursuits at Reckmire you could quite easily lose it there. What have your father's family bought you?'

I ran out into the hall where I had put the parcels from Reckmire into a cupboard under the stairs. There were gifts from all of them for the three of us, and I was so engrossed in mine I paid scant attention to the others until I heard Mother say in some annoyance, 'Really, Robert, I can't think why Corallie sends me a scarf in this vivid pink. She knows I always liked beiges and mossy greens. It does nothing for me at all.'

I looked up to see her draping a large pure silk scarf over her shoulder. It shimmered delicately in colours of pale pink and turquoise, a deeper blue and stronger pink. It was beautiful — so beautiful that I held out my hand to caress the tender silken folds.

'It's lovely,' I murmured.

'Well, of course it's no doubt very expensive and it's probably the sort of thing Corallie would wear. She was always one for colourful flighty things.'

'The colours suit you beautifully,' Father said gently.

'They are colours I don't care for and I don't suppose I'll ever wear it. Marcia's sent me stationery which will come in very useful and your mother as usual has sent me a cheque to buy something for myself. I wonder if Mrs Prothero is still here?'

'I'll go and see,' I offered. At that moment I wanted to get out of the room and into the kitchen where I could hear Mrs Prothero humming to herself. Her daughter Edie was busy at the sink while Mrs Prothero was busy icing a large Christmas cake. She looked up with a smile when I entered the room and took a chair at the kitchen table.

'Opened all your presents then?' she enquired.

'Yes. Did you get some nice things?' I asked her.

'Very nice, but only what I expected. Slippers from my 'usband and chocolates from Edie there. We don't go in for expensive things in our 'ouse, but then I always says it's not the price of the gift, it's the thought behind it.'

I nodded.

'Everything's done for your buffet meal this afternoon, love. All you'll 'ave to do is clear away afterwards. Honey could do with a walk this afternoon.'

'I'll take him,' I said eagerly. 'Mrs Prothero, it's so cold in that summerhouse in the winter, is there a rug he could have?'

'I've taken in an old blanket. I'd have taken him home with me but my sister's brought her fox terrier and she's a bit snappy. If Honey'd have been with me as we'd originally planned she wouldn't have brought her. Everything's changed, hasn't it, love?'

'Yes, Mrs Prothero, everything.'

'Don't worry about Honey, he'll be all right in kennels, they looks after 'em very well. And when it's all over and 'e's back with Mr and Mrs Fowler, 'e'll soon forget.'

'I hope so.'

In my heart I was wishing Mother would forget about sending Honey into kennels, but early on Boxing Day morning something must have disturbed him because he barked loud and long and I heard Mother screaming that he must go.

He went happily enough, no doubt thinking that he was going for a walk, his plumed tail waving gently, his eyes bright with anticipation. It was only when I saw Father coming back alone that I sat at my window and wept. In a corner of the summerhouse his basket stood forlornly and I picked up his blanket and held it in my arms, thinking that it was all I had left of him.

When Mrs Prothero appeared the next morning her first words were, 'Has the dog gone then, love?'

'Yes, yesterday morning. I was wishing he'd be good and not bark but he did and Mother insisted he went.'

'Aye, well, she would, wouldn't she?'

Later in the morning Father ran Mother to the cemetery where she wanted to lay flowers on Grandmother's grave and I heard Mrs Prothero chatting to old Mrs Webster's companion over a cup of tea in the kitchen. I had not meant to eavesdrop, indeed she believed I had gone with them, but

I couldn't help it when I heard my name mentioned.

'That poor child's cried herself to sleep about that dog,' Mrs Prothero said tartly. 'One o' these days there's goin' to be trouble. He'll not stand it forever and neither will Joanna.'

'I always think Mr Albemarle is such a nice gentleman,' Miss Johnson said. 'He always smiles and greets me when we meet on the road and she barely looks at me.'

'Well, like I've allus said, he's the aristocrat, she's a jumped up little madam. I'll be glad when they've gone back and I've no doubt Joanna'll be glad too. They've been invited to the Lesters' party on New Year's Eve but I'll bet *she* doesn't want to go. I wonder what excuse she'll make?'

It was the first I'd heard of it. The Lesters lived at the corner of the road in a large house similar to ours. Mr Lester was a banker, and his wife was into all sorts of activities connected with the local church the golf and tennis club. Mother thought she was pushy, but actually I liked Mrs Lester. She was amusing and friendly and their New Year's Eve party was an annual affair to which they invited all the neighbours.

My grandparents wouldn't have missed it, but Mother had always gone with them reluctantly and was disparaging in her views of it afterwards.

'Perhaps she'll say she can't go because Joanna hasn't been invited,' Miss Johnson volunteered.

'Joanna's been invited. The Lester children are growing up, Daniel's a bit older than Joanna and Alec's a bit younger. They'll both be there so most of the children of a similar age have been invited.'

'They'll have a house full,' Miss Johnson said dryly.

'That won't worry Mrs Lester. She comes from a big family and she knows 'ow to cope. 'Er 'usband and the children will all rally round. It'll be a right shame if Joanna can't be there.'

'Perhaps it's because she was an only child that Mrs Albemarle's so withdrawn. Mrs Webster said both her parents doted on her, and she married well. What do his parents think of her?'

'We seldom sees 'em and she won't go there. She's not even very friendly with his sister who introduced 'em in the first place.'

I had heard enough. Quietly I let myself out of the front door and walked quickly down the drive. I had just reached the gates when Father's car appeared along the road and lowering his window he said, 'Where are you going, Joanna?'

'Just for a walk, Father.'

'Don't be long,' Mother called, 'it's far too cold for walking. I don't want you ill when you have to go back to school.'

'If you wait until I've garaged the car I'll come with you,' Father offered, but Mother immediately squashed that idea.

'I've asked Monica Gilbey and Dorothy Fenton to come round for coffee, Robert, it would be nice if you could be there.'

They drove on, after Father favoured me with a rueful smile.

The women she had mentioned had been at school with Mother and were the only friends who ever came to the house. They were very much like her. They talked about gardens and plants, holidays in Bexley Heath and Ramsgate, and their parents' ailments.

As I walked quickly along the road I prayed silently that we would be able to go to Mrs Lester's party, and as if God was listening to me I met Daniel Lester at the corner of the road.

'All ready for the party, Joanna?' he called out cheerfully.

'I'm not sure if we're coming.'

'Your dad says you are. He met my dad in the newsagent's on Christmas Eve and said you'd be coming.'

I wanted to believe him, but we'd been going to places before and at the last moment Mother had made some excuse or other not to go.

Although I was walking fast I quickly became aware of the cold. My breath froze on the air and I could barely feel my feet and hands even though I wore woollen gloves and sturdy shoes on my feet.

If I caught a chill I would never hear the end of it, so reluctantly I retraced my steps, hoping against hope that the two friends of Mother's would have left the house.

From the hall I heard the tinkling of teacups and women's voices, and as I crossed the hall Mrs Prothero's head appeared round the kitchen door.

'Come in 'ere love,' she called. 'I've got hot mince pies and Christmas cake. You don't want to sit in there listenin' to them.'

The kitchen felt warm and cheerful and I settled down happily at the table where Mrs Prothero had spread out our private feast. She talked about the sort of Christmas they had had, the pantomime they had been to on Boxing Day night, and I laughed at her description of the antics of the comedians on the stage.

I was on my second mince pie when the door opened and Mother stood in the doorway staring at us.

'Really, Joanna,' she said in an exasperated voice, 'what are you doing in here when we have guests? Wash your hands immediately and come into the drawing room. You should have sent her in there, Mrs Prothero.'

She left, closing the door sharply behind her, and Mrs Prothero said quickly, 'You'd best get in there, Joanna. Finish your mince tart first, although there's plenty in there.'

'I'd much rather stay here,' I said angrily.

'I know, love, they'll not have much conversation that'll interest you.'

She was right. After exclaiming on how much I'd grown, inviting my views on the school I attended and wishing me a belated Merry Christmas, their talk returned to the past when they'd all been pupils at Highbank, Miss Eckersley's private school.

Father sat in his chair near the window, a bemused expression on his face. Neither of us need have been there since the three women were totally absorbed in a past in which we had no part.

The remainder of the Christmas holiday passed all too slowly. Father spent most of it on business in London so Mother and I went to the shops. We took tea in tea shops she had delighted in as a girl, and in the afternoons she invited people in for bridge or gossip, neighbours mostly who were all intent on finding out if we intended to attend the Lesters' party on New Year's Eve.

We arrived late and when the party was well under way. There was music and dancing in the drawing room where furniture had been pushed back and the carpet taken up. An extensive buffet supper was laid out in the dining room and the whole house was alive with laughter and colour.

Lights sparkled on the enormous Christmas tree in a corner of the hall, and even Mrs Prothero had been conscripted in to help with the festivities.

When Mother asked how she had managed to escape from her family when she had found it so difficult over Christmas, Mrs Prothero said evenly, 'My sister and her family 'ave gone home and Joe and Edie are helping us in the kitchen. There's plenty for the men to do, stokin' up the fires, fetchin' and carryin' and seein' to the parkin' outside.'

Daniel invited me to dance and all the way round the room I could feel Mother's eyes on us. Daniel was tall and the pimples had long gone so that he was turning out to be quite a handsome boy. He helped me to food from the buffet then excused himself on the grounds that he had promised to dance with his cousin and couldn't get out of it.

I sat on the stairs with his younger brother Alec who obviously wasn't enjoying the party as much as his brother. He was a solemn ginger-haired boy who viewed the proceedings through large horn-rimmed glasses, nursing a dinner plate piled high with food, and when I took my place beside him I discovered he had little conversation. All his interest was centred on his food and I was glad when Daniel came back after his duty dance and sat beside me on the stairs.

'You'll be going back to school soon, Joanna?'

'Yes, at the end of next week.'

'When do your parents go back?'

'In three weeks.'

'Couldn't you have got time off until they went back?'

'I didn't ask, I never thought of it,' I said quickly.

I was glad I hadn't thought about it, and I hoped my

parents wouldn't think about it before it was time for me to return to Harrogate.

'Have you thought what you're going to do when you leave?' he asked.

'No, it's some time off. I don't know where my parents will be, or even where I shall go to live.'

'Where would you like to live?'

'I'm not sure.'

I knew exactly where I wanted to live but I didn't want to tell Daniel Lester in case he told his mother. If Mrs Lester even casually told Mother I loved Reckmire that would be the last I would see of it, I felt sure.

At the end of the following week Father drove me back to Harrogate on a cold grey morning when there was snow in the wind. He was going on to see his parents at Reckmire and had tried to persuade Mother to accompany him but there had been the usual excuses: her hatred of the sea, her state of health, the fact that she had much to do before they returned to the Far East.

He was mainly silent on the journey north, his face pensive, and I too was reluctant to talk. The icy roads required his full attention and the further north we got the more the weather deteriorated so that when we reached Yorkshire it was snowing quite heavily.

We stood at last in the school hall where tiny puddles were forming from our wet shoes and dripping raincoats and Father was telling an anxious headmistress that he would attempt to finish his journey but if it proved impossible would book in at some hotel or other on the way.

He embraced me warmly, looking down at me and saying gently, 'Work hard, Joanna, and we'll write often. Perhaps it won't be quite so long before I get leave again.'

I clung to him with sudden sorrow at his leaving. I loved him. Like me he was trapped in the human bondage that was his marriage and I watched him striding away towards his car with tears streaming down my face.

Chapter Six

I was unprepared for the next time I saw my father. I was fifteen years old and it was summer. I had spent the entire morning up on the fells riding Merlin. He was really Gabriella's horse but I had outgrown the pony and they were not coming to the Hall from Italy this year; instead we were all going to spend three weeks with them in Tuscany.

I had thought my parents would come home on leave after two years elapsed but there had been no mention of it and as I sat on the short moorland grass staring out across the fell towards the sea I could only feel joy in my life as it was at the moment. Two carefree weeks on the marshes followed by that journey into the sunshine of Italy.

There had not been the usual family gathering this year. Robin had gone to stay at Paul Cheviot's house in Yorkshire and I was not sorry. I never quite knew if Paul liked me or not. Lottie said I shouldn't care, Robin obviously liked me which should be enough.

On the day I had taken Lottie home for tea Robin had set himself out to be nice to her, whilst Paul on the other hand had imitated her North Country accent until even Grandma had remonstrated with him. Lottie had a crush on Robin; Paul, with his remote handsome face, merely unsettled her.

Lottie had left school the previous summer and was working in the shop, helping out in the bakery and serving customers. Her sister Freda was in service with old Doctor Stanton and they only saw her on her day off.

I looked forward to those days when I was invited to

tea at the bakery. I felt part of a warm caring family. Lottie's father was a jolly humorous man and her mother plied us with our favourite cakes and pies. Lottie's sister Freda treated me with the same sort of sarcasm that Paul reserved for Lottie. She made me feel uncomfortable with her sly innuendoes about class distinctions and people with too much money.

Making up my mind suddenly, I used a large stone to scramble up on Merlin's back and we set off down the sloping fell at a brisk gallop. I pulled him in sharply when we reached the lane, surprised to see Lottie walking towards me with a smile on her face.

'I saw you comin' up here, Joanna,' she said. 'I've been to put flowers on Grannie's grave. We're not busy today. It's market day in Bleacarn.'

'Do you want to ride him?' I asked, watching the grin spread over her face.

'Not after the last time I don't! I've never bin so scared, and that Paul did nothin' but laugh at me.'

'Never take any notice of him,' I said, 'he laughs at me all the time. I thought I'd ride along the beach. Do you want to come with me?'

'You've got visitors, Joanna. I saw a man drivin' a big car goin' through the gates.'

'It's probably a friend of Grandpa's, nothing to do with me,' I said confidently.

At a walking pace we ambled along the village high street and it was only when we reached the baker's shop that we saw Lottie's mother standing in the window. Seeing us, she came out looking rather flustered.

'You're wanted up at the house, Joanna,' she said sharply. 'Yer grandmother thought you might 'ave been with us. She sent Jennie Lawson down to say if I should see you, would you go back immediately?'

Consternation must have shown in my face because she was quick to say, 'I don't think you need worry, love, nobody's ill. Your father's at the house, Joanna.'

Emotions chased themselves across my mind. Joy at seeing him tempered with reluctance that my time at Reckmire and my long awaited holiday in Italy were threatened. Where was my mother in all this, waiting like some pale threatening ghost to lay waste to all our plans?

Lottie smiled at me ruefully. 'I'll see you soon, Joanna. I 'ope nothin's wrong.'

My heart was racing as we trotted along the road, through the gates and took the long uphill drive to the house. A large dark green car stood outside the front door but I rode round to the stables, leaving Merlin in the care of the groom.

There was not time to change out of my riding clothes. I could hear voices in the morning room. Father sat opposite my grandparents but they all looked up when I entered the room and Father rose to his feet and came to take me in his arms. I stared up into his face apprehensively, but thinking that he looked tanned and well. There was evidently nothing wrong with him and I said falteringly, 'Where's Mother?'

'Come and sit down, Joanna. We have a lot to talk about. Your mother is quite well, she's in Surrey.'

'Have you come to take me back?' I asked desperately.

He shook his head, then said gently, 'You'd hate that, wouldn't you, Joanna?'

I nodded wordlessly, and at that my grandparents stood up and Grandma said, 'You talk to Joanna here, Robert, I have letters to write and your father has to go out anyway.'

I watched them leave the room, aware now that I was going to hear something that would affect my future, and fearful that it could only be detrimental if Mother was in England.

For what seemed an eternity he remained staring down at his hands, clenched together in his lap, then meeting my tortured gaze he reached out and took my hands in his.

'Joanna, I'm sorry,' he said sadly, 'but I think that it is best for you to hear it from me then you can ask your questions and I'll do my best to answer them. Your mother and I have decided to split up. Our marriage hasn't been working for a very long time, we've grown apart and I can't see any future for either of us in staying together. Nobody else is involved and at this stage I can't say if we shall ever divorce. I'm sorry to bring you such sad news at the start of your summer holidays but you had to know. Is there anything you want to ask me?'

70

'Yes. Does it mean that I shall have to live with Mother wherever she is?' I asked fearfully.

'When I am in England you will spend time with me as well as your mother, probably here at Reckmire, but when I am abroad, you will stay with your mother.'

'I see.'

'At the moment she is staying with your grandfather but she is very anxious to find a place of her own. She is looking at flats in Surrey. Very nice flats, Joanna, because of course she will be well provided for, as will you. You will be allowed to finish your education in Harrogate but school holidays will be dictated by wherever I happen to be. Are you terribly shocked by all this, dear?'

'No.'

I was dismally aware of the doubt in his expression, the fear that I was blaming him for the breakdown in his marriage, and I had to dispel it. In a burst of anguish, I said, 'How could you bear it, all those things she didn't like, all those excuses you had to make for her because she disapproved of everything and everybody, even poor Honey? All the things I loved.'

Shadows chased themselves across his face but he had been loyal too long. It was a habit, it had become a way of life, and once again I was aware that the defences were coming up. In desperation I cried, 'Will I have to go to Surrey now, father? We were going to Italy, I want to go to Italy!'

'We are all going to Italy. I want to see your Aunt Corallie and her family and I have several weeks' leave. When I return to Singapore I'll write often, and if I'm still there when you leave school you may be able to come out to me for a spell.'

My eyes sparkled as I said joyfully, 'Oh, yes please, I'd love that.'

'Well, we'll see. The world is changing, Joanna, and I don't like what I hear about in Europe, Germany and Italy. Then in the Far East there is Japan. We can't be sure which way they will jump if there is trouble.'

Untroubled by his fears, I could only think that we were going to Italy. I'd spent weeks reading about the beauty of

71

her countryside, her ageless cities and the warm sun shining down on her vineyards.

It was early-evening when I walked with Lottie across the fell. She listened without speaking while I poured out all the trauma of the afternoon.

Her face remained pensive and for a long time we walked without speaking until at last she said, 'You're goin' to be unhappy bein' with your mother all the time, Joanna. You're goin' to miss the sea and the gulls, you'll hate not comin' here.'

'I know. My father will go away leaving us together, and in the end I'll become somebody else, somebody she wants me to be, liking the things she does, not me at all.'

'Your father and your grandparents'll care Joanna. They won't let it happen.'

'My father'll be at the other side of the world and nobody will know what she's like.'

'Then it'll be up to you, Joanna. You'll 'ave to stop 'er or you'll never make a life for yourself. Do you love 'er at all?'

'Oh, Lottie, I do try. I want to love her, she looks so small and sweet and she's pretty, but just when I'm thinking she's nice she acts like a viper in the things she says. One minute she's cocky and dictatorial, at others she's tearful and badly done to. At those times we've always made a fuss of her and waited for her to become nice again. I'm not surprised Father's ended it. For years I've wondered how he could stand it. Now he's gone and I don't know if I can.'

'Perhaps she'll change now, Joanna? Now that she sees he's gone she won't want to lose you.'

'Perhaps.'

I had little faith that Mother would change, I had little faith in miracles.

I was happy with Father at Reckmire. We sailed the boat and rode across the fells. We walked the length of Reckmire and scrambled over the dunes where we watched the summer tide rolling in across the sand and sat for hours watching the birds flying above their nests across the marshes.

It was out there that I asked him plaintively, 'Did you ever love her?' And he answered reflectively, 'At first I loved her very much. I thought she was gentle and sensitive. I thought time would settle our differences, teach her that there was joy and beauty in the sort of things she had always rejected, but it was never possible.

'She never tried. She never admitted that she could have been wrong. Instead I was the one who changed. I listened to the sometimes harsh things she said about my family, my sisters in particular, and if I saw their imperfections, I closed my eyes to hers. I'm not blaming your mother entirely, it was my fault too. I should have asserted myself, stood up for the things I believed in, but the sulks and tears were too potent. They made a coward of me.'

He did not know how desperately afraid his words made me feel. Would I too become a coward in the face of her intransigence?

I was neither a woman nor a child. The years behind me were few and they had been a hotchpotch of wonder and happiness interspersed with desolation and heart searching. The future was a closed book. My school friends could look forward to long years in the shelter of happy family life. I on the other hand would feel more and more like a parcel to be shuffled around between two parents and two families. When could I ever again expect to feel stability and continuity?

There had been long telephone conversations every evening between my parents but it was only on his last evening at Reckmire that we heard Father's voice raised in protest. When he came back into the room we all looked at him. His face was pale and there was a sense of deep anger about him as he went back to his chair and sat silent, staring into space. Grandma was the first to speak.

'Didn't Linda ask to speak to Joanna?' she asked.

At first he appeared not to hear her, then visibly shaking himself out of his lethargy, said, 'I've told her I'll telephone again later when I've had a chance to discuss things with Joanna.'

'What sort of things?' I murmured anxiously.

'She wants you to go back to London with me, Joanna. She doesn't want you to go to Italy. Your mother thinks your place is at home with her.'

I sat staring at him, visibly shaken. It was Grandma

who said sharply, 'That is totally unreasonable, Robert. This holiday in Italy has been planned for some time and Joanna has been looking forward to it. Whilst you are in this country she has a duty to see as much of you as she possibly can. After the holiday is over, naturally any future holidays will be spent with her mother.'

'That is what I have told Linda. Obviously she doesn't agree.'

I had never in my entire life been more devastated. I had lived and breathed Italy since the day I knew we were going. Now suddenly it was all to be taken away from me, even when my whole world was going to change. In sheer desperation I cried, 'But I must go to Italy! I'll die if I don't go.'

Grandma smiled. 'No, Joanna,' she said gently, 'you won't die, but you may never find it in your heart to forgive your mother for what she is trying to do. Would you like me to speak to her on Joanna's behalf, Robert?'

'No, Mother, it isn't necessary. I shall tell her that I will take Joanna to Surrey on our way back from Italy and leave her there until it is time for her to return to school. By that time Linda may know where she intends to live. In any case, she's been house hunting since the day she got back.'

'What does her father feel about all this?' Grandpa asked, and Father replied, 'We haven't had much chance to talk about it but I don't think Mildred was surprised. If anything she was a little fearful that Linda might be living with them for some time.'

Later that day I heard Father arguing with her on the telephone again, and was miserably aware that I was the cause of their argument. After a while he came into the room, saying tersely, 'Your mother wants to speak to you, Joanna. You know why. I've done all I can, now it's up to you to tell her how important this holiday is to you.'

Her voice was the plaintive little girl's voice I had heard so often over the years.

'Joanna darling,' she began, 'I've so much to tell you and show you. I think I've found a lovely little flat in a darling little village not far from Godalming. It's a first-floor flat with big windows overlooking the park and it's not far from Father's house so we can see him often.

'I've been telling your father about it and that I want you here to help me move and get settled in. You'll love it, Joanna, and I know you're longing to see where you're going to live. Were you very upset at the news of our separation, darling?'

'Yes, Mother. I want to spend as much time with Father as possible, I don't know when I'll see him again.'

'Robert will get plenty of leave, Joanna, and he doesn't have to worry about somewhere to live like we do. You can't have much packing to do and Robert will take you to the train. Father and I will meet you at the other end. All you have to do is tell us which one you are catching.'

'Mother, I'm going to Italy at the end of the week. It's been planned for ages, Aunt Corallie is expecting us and I'm looking forward to it.'

'Well, of course you can't go now, Joanna! Things have changed, even Corallie will be able to see that.'

'Please try to understand, Mother, I have to go and I have to be with Father. I'll come to you as soon as I get back to England, in three weeks.'

'You're selfish, Joanna, just like all your father's family! Selfish and uncaring. Corallie was always like that, but I expected your father to be different. He wasn't. Now I can see that you are just like him. I'm very disappointed in you, Joanna, I would have expected you to want to be with me. A mother should be able to rely on her only daughter when she needs sympathy and comfort.'

I heard the sharp click of the receiver being replaced and could picture her tearful and angry. Grandfather would be fussing around her like an old hen and Mildred would be appalled at yet another scene like so many others.

Father came to put his arm around my shoulders sympathetically. 'We heard all you said to her, Joanna, and you were right to say it. You know that your life too is going to change and if you ever blame her, remember that it is as much my fault as your mother's. I took the line of least resistance. I gave in to her when I should have opposed her. I did it because I believed her to be gentle and fragile and needing compassion. Now I know that she was strong, selfish and often greedy.'

75

I should have been looking forward with joy to going to Italy, now I was obsessed with guilt. I pictured my mother house hunting, furniture moving, overpowered by decorators and carpet fitters. On the evening before we left she telephoned me to say she had been thinking about me and hoped I would enjoy my stay in Italy.

Delighted with her thoughtfulness, I rushed to tell her details of our journey and the clothes I was taking, only to be interrupted by her plaintive voice saying, 'Aren't you in the least bit interested in your new home, Joanna?'

My enthusiasm faltered and then ebbed, and in a small voice I said hesitantly, 'I'm sorry, Mother, yes of course I'm interested, please tell me about it.'

'Well, of course I'm nowhere near straight. There's been so much to do and Father wasn't well so he wasn't much help, and Mildred was off with that dog of hers and only came round in the morning. Just go off and enjoy yourself, dear, I'll be straight before you get back and I'll be longing to see you.'

Instead of returning to the others I ran up to my bedroom where I burst into tears. All joy in the holiday had gone, the guilt was too powerful, and as I sat sobbing in my room I could picture her in her new flat, lonely and tearful, believing that she was unloved by both her husband and her daughter.

I did not hear Father come into my room until I felt his arm around my shoulders, and his voice warm and sympathetic asking, 'What's wrong, Joanna? It's something your mother said, isn't it?'

'I should have gone home, she has so much to do and she's so lonely,' I cried bitterly.

He took both my hands in his, his eyes looking into mine gravely.

'Listen to me, Joanna. You've been happy these few years since your mother and I went out to Singapore and when we come back from Italy it is all going to change. You will spend a lot of time with your mother and it may be that you will not come here for a very long time. You have to learn that she is often wrong in the things she says, that her cries of self-pity are unnecessary and often cruel, and you have to remember that you are an individual with thoughts and longings that are your own and which she has no power to control.

'I am far from blameless in all this. I should have been stronger, I should have seen how things were a long, long time ago, but I lived in a fool's paradise, making excuses for her, taking the line of least resistance. Now you are going to Italy and you are going to love every moment of it. Time enough to think about the future on your way home.'

I smiled tremulously, agreeing with him while silently I felt sure it would not be like that.

Often on that long journey into Italy's sunshine I felt Grandma's eyes on me, searching for the joy she had hoped to see, disappointed that this wonderful treat they were giving me was overshadowed by guilt.

How warm was their welcome into that beautiful villa set high on a hill in the enchanting countryside of Tuscany surrounded by gently rolling hills covered in vines, and where tall stately cypresses thrust their dark leaves towards the heavens.

Chapter Seven

In only a few short days it seemed to me that I had become part of a new and wonderful way of life. A new world had been opened up to me composed of palazzos and piazzas, duomos and castellos, and always to the west there was the enchantment of the long white coast road and to the east the dreaming beauty of the mountains. The sun rose every morning in a blaze of glory and the silver nights were scented with mimosa and filled with the chirping of a host of cicadas.

If I thought of my mother at all it was with amazement that she could have turned her back on such a happy and devoted family. In a few short days Father seemed to have become young again. Tanned by the sun and happy in the bosom of his family, he laughed more than I had ever known him laugh. He and Aunt Corallie resumed their comradeship and Grandma warmed to their banter and light-hearted good humour.

Gabriella seemed to me very grown up. She was beautiful and stylish, and she and her mother delighted in showing me the enchanting shops in Florence where they were eager to see me in the latest Italian fashions. When I remonstrated that Father didn't have nearly enough money to allow such extravagance they both dissolved into laughter, saying that for the first time for years he was not being restrained by anybody telling him the place for money was in the bank and not on the back of his daughter.

The result was that by the end of the first week my wardrobe had almost doubled and Gabriella insisted that

I have my hair styled by her hairdresser. That night when I arrived on the terrace for dinner everybody present applauded.

I was wearing a new pale blue gown which I knew my mother would have considered far too adult and expensive for me, but which brought my father to my side with a strangely sombre expression in his eyes. Then, linking my arm in his, he said gallantly, 'Allow me to escort my very beautiful daughter to the Castello Varasi.'

Gabriella had told me that the Varasi family were their nearest neighbours and when I wanted to know more about them she blushed prettily until Aunt Corallie said in an amused voice, 'Gabriella has told you about their castello and their gardens, she has told you that the Conte Varasi and his Contessa are charming, now ask her to tell you about Carlo who she's been in love with for a very long time.'

'Oh, Mother,' Gabriella said softly, but Aunt Corallie only laughed.

'It's true, darling,' she said. 'Now let me hear you tell Joanna that he is the handsomest, most charming, most wonderful man she will ever meet, because you've been telling us that for ages.'

Everybody laughed, and I felt vaguely sorry for Gabriella to have her admiration for Carlo Varasi made public. Her father put an affectionate arm round her shoulders, saying, 'Carlo has been coming here since he was a small boy, they were playmates before they were friends, and now I very much fear my daughter is in love.'

'Why do you fear it, Rinaldo?' Grandma asked curiously. 'Gabriella is enchanting, surely he can see that?'

'Well, of course,' my uncle said with a smile. 'I fear it because I am jealous of any man who might take my daughter away from me.'

'Oh, Papa,' Gabriella said with a smile, 'Carlo and I are friends, it may be that he will never love me.'

'The writing is on the wall,' her father said, 'and I am not displeased. He is all the things you say he is, handsome, charming, and the Varasis are an old and noble family. Daughters can't always be trusted to bring home a man their parents approve of.'

'Has he a job?' Grandpa asked practically.

'Well, of course, the Varasis have a vast estate to manage but they are also bankers. I have no doubt Carlo will follow his father into the banking profession.'

Grandpa sat back in his chair well pleased, and it was only later when I walked with Gabriella to the cars that I said, 'I thought you might be in love with Paul Cheviot. You were always together.'

'Oh, Paul's all right,' she said airily. 'He was fun to be with when I went to stay with Grandma but I couldn't possibly marry him.'

'Why not?' I persisted. 'I couldn't marry him because I'm not sure I like him, but you got along with him.'

She laughed. 'Oh, Joanna, you are funny,' she said. 'I will have to do more than get along with somebody to think of marrying them. Besides, I couldn't possibly marry Paul and have to live in Yorkshire where his family have woollen mills. It would be far too dreary. And Paul hates his father and hasn't much time for his mother.'

'Has he told you so?'

'Well, of course he has. His father is a terrible man, he has other women all the time, and his mother sounds positively browbeaten.'

'I think Paul can be cruel, he says some awful things to me,' I said shortly.

She laughed. 'If you didn't mind so much he wouldn't say them. You get cross and retaliate. He likes that.'

'Well, thank goodness he won't be coming here,' I said thankfully, but with another laugh she said, 'Actually I think he and Robin are coming here next week for almost three weeks. It will be fun seeing how Paul reacts to Carlo. When he sees I have another friend he may decide to be nicer to you.'

'Second best, you mean?' I said defensively, but by this time we had reached the cars and I was joining my father on the front seat of our tourer.

I was thoughtful on the way to the Castello Varasi and Father said, 'Has something upset you, love, you're in a deep study?'

'Gabriella says Robin and Paul Cheviot are coming here

next week, did you know?' I answered.

'I wasn't sure, does it matter?'

'Paul makes me feel uncomfortable.'

'Why, has he done something to offend you?'

'It's just the way he is. Everybody else likes him, perhaps I imagine it.'

'He'd better not try while I'm there,' he said gallantly. 'Nobody makes my daughter look small.'

I stole a glance at his face. It seemed so young in the moonlight, the lines of care which had always been there had gone. Perhaps thoughtlessly I said, 'I wrote to Mother this morning, I told her how beautiful it was here and what a lovely time we were having. I haven't posted it yet. Is there anything else I should tell her?'

He didn't answer me immediately. Instead a thoughtful frown appeared on his face and it was several minutes before he said, 'Perhaps you shouldn't enthuse too much about our holiday, Joanna. Your mother will be busy setting up the flat and no doubt she'll be resentful.'

'I promised to write. What can I say if I don't tell her about the holiday?'

'Tell her you've been thinking about her. That you hope things are going well and that you are looking forward to seeing her as soon as we arrive back in England.'

'And nothing about the holiday?' I persisted.

'Yes, of course, but not too much,' he replied gently.

'Will you be coming to the flat when we arrive home?' I asked him.

'I shall take you there as soon as we arrive. Mother wants to spend a few days in London, take in a few plays and look at the shops. I will drive them home to Reckmire when I take you back to school.'

'Will you be staying with us?' I asked hopefully.

'No, Joanna. I shall be staying at my club, but I'll see you of course. I thought it might be an idea if I got seats for the theatre for the three of us, before you go back to school. It would be a pleasant way of finishing the holiday. What do you think?'

'Oh, yes please, Father, I would love that. A musical, something everybody wants to see.'

'There's a new Ivor Novello show at the Hippodrome everybody is raving about. How about that?'

'Oh, yes please, that would be perfect.'

There was no more time for conversation because by this time we were driving through vast wrought iron gates and along a long winding drive that led towards the Castello Varasi, and I was sitting on the edge of my seat peering through the windows in an effort not to miss anything.

They came out on to the terrace to meet us, a silver-haired aristocratic-looking man and a tall elegant woman accompanied by a bevy of dogs of all sizes, and then Carlo was there and I was remembering my thoughts the first time I saw Robin running towards me across the sand, that he was beautiful, with the summer sun shining on his blond head and tanned face.

Carlo Varasi was handsome with a beauty totally unlike Robin's. He was tall and graceful, but his hair was blue-black like a raven's wing and when he smiled chiselled lips parted to reveal perfect white teeth, and dark Italian eyes looked down at me with an appraisal that brought the warm blushes to my face.

In other years when I was far away from Tuscany in what seemed like another world I remembered his smile, even when I believed I was in love with somebody else and when my future in a world suddenly gone mad was filled with uncertainties and remembered pain.

In the days that followed Gabriella and Carlo were kind to me. They took me riding through the vineyards and together showed me sites they had always known but which filled me with utter rapture. We stood under the shadow of the cathedral in Orvieto looking out across the rolling hills, and I marvelled at the leaning tower of Pisa which reminded me of a wedding cake and where Carlo bought me a statuette fashioned in Carrara marble depicting two doves, exquisitely carved and delicately pink.

He was a mine of information about the Campanile and the Baptistry which he said was also leaning, explaining that the tilt in the tower was leaning more and more and that if something was not done, in two hundred years it was likely to come crashing down.

I found it hard to believe that that beautiful tower was threatened. Without the tower and the Baptistry there would be no Pisa, but as Carlo explained there were so many wonderful treasures in Italy to be cared for. He told me that every year his father gave vast sums towards the saving of valuable pieces of art, but the government had other things they preferred to spend the money on.

He added this last piece of information with a set expression and I had the distinct impression that he was not in favour of whatever it was the government spent the money on.

In a very short time Gabriella grew tired of looking at buildings and grumbled that she'd been brought up on art galleries and museums. Her father explained patiently that it might be years before I could visit Italy again and I should see as much as possible during my stay. The outcome was that Carlo and I explored the area together but he spent the evenings with Gabriella.

She didn't seem to mind this arrangement. After all, I was a schoolgirl, and she had great faith in her beauty and Carlo's evident admiration.

I fell in love with the Florence that Carlo showed me, a Florence totally different from that I had seen with Aunt Corallie and Gabriella. I felt I was walking through a museum with the blue sky for a ceiling. Florence must surely house the most beautiful things Western civilisation had ever fashioned and I allowed my imagination to picture it during the time of the Renaissance while my head spun with thoughts of Michelangelo and Leonardo.

I pictured Catherine di Medici holding court in her dazzling palazzo and stared with awe at the statue of David with its exquisite proportions and chillingly vain, self-satisfied expression.

I fell in love with Carlo. A schoolgirl crush they would have called it, but there was so much pain in loving him. I became sulky when Aunt Corallie teased me slyly about my blushes whenever he spoke to me, until Grandma told her to stop, and when Gabriella put a possessive arm through his I felt I hated her.

How sad it is that first love is often so painful when it should be tender and filled with joy. I felt like Juliet waiting for her Romeo, except that this Romeo belonged to somebody else and my heart ached with the pain of rejection. Carlo was kind. He must have known how I adored him, and because he was kind our excursions into the city ceased, and now Gabriella came with us as we toured the enchanting countryside.

At the weekend Robin and Paul Cheviot arrived and almost immediately Paul realised that I was besotted with Carlo and derived a great deal of pleasure from it. I thought him insufferable and lost no opportunity of getting back at him when I saw how angry he was when Carlo and Gabriella went off together.

The resentment that flared between us afforded Aunt Corallie and Gabriella some amusement but on the evening before we left, our usual light-hearted conversation over the dinner table turned into something more serious.

During the afternoon Paul and Robin had been into Florence where they had seen groups of people standing sullenly on the pavements watching lines of fascist youths marching through the city streets. Uncle Rinaldo said it was unfortunate that a display of that sort was threatening to destroy a visitor's joy in the city.

Much of their talk was lost on me, but from the seriousness of their expressions I understood that things were happening in Italy that none of them welcomed.

Somehow on that evening something seemed to have gone awry. The men talked about a man called Adolf Hitler in Germany and an Italian called Mussolini and of a world that they feared was changing, and when I looked round the beautiful room and the elegant people sitting round the dining table I felt that I was looking at the scene from a play and we were all actors playing a part.

The ladies drifted away leaving the men to their serious talk and I went out into the garden. It was so warm and a full moon shone, silvering the trees, gleaming fitfully in the pool. I had not been there long when I heard footsteps on the gravel behind me, and turning I saw that it was Carlo stepping out of the shadows to meet me. He smiled, that sweet friendly smile that made a slave of my heart, and I clenched my hands, wishing with all my heart that I could hide my blushing face and the eager puppy look in my eyes.

He must have noticed yet his voice was casual as he said, 'I shan't see you after tonight, Joanna, so I have come to say goodbye. Tomorrow I am going to Rome with my parents to attend a cousin's wedding.'

When I didn't answer him he held out his hand, taking mine and holding it.

'Perhaps you'll come back one day, Joanna,' he said, looking down at me. 'You should go to Rome and Venice. Italy has so many wonderful things to show her visitors. In these last few days you have only just touched the surface.'

I was aware that my voice trembled as I said, 'It may not be possible for me to come for a very long time. My father is going back to the Far East and I shall be living with my mother.'

'Then you must bring your mother. Surely she would love it as you do?'

'I don't know.'

'Perhaps I shall see you at your grandmother's house? I have been invited to visit them with Gabriella and her parents.'

'I doubt if I shall be there. My mother won't go.'

'Then perhaps it really is goodbye,' he said regretfully. He raised my hand to his lips and gently kissed it, then with another smile he turned away. I watched him striding away from me with the sort of misery I had never known before, when suddenly he turned and came back to me. When I stared at him wide-eyed he said, 'Sometimes, Joanna, one has to hold fast to the things one wants from life. You must remember that at those times when you feel alone.'

With another smile he turned to go and this time he did not come back. When I looked back at the house I saw that Paul Cheviot was standing on the terrace and wondered how long he had been there. I turned and walked through the gardens and to my dismay he came after me. I wanted to run but there was nowhere to run to, even though I was hating the thought of his sarcastic humour levelled against a moment that was precious to me.

I ran through the rose gardens towards a small summer-house built like a miniature Greek temple, hoping against hope that he would give up the chase, but the hope was a forlorn one and I stood trembling while he regarded me from the doorway with a half smile on his face.

'Quite a touching little scene, Joanna,' he said softly. 'I shan't say a word but don't be surprised if Carlo isn't entertaining Gabriella with the pathos of your first schoolgirl crush.'

I remained silent, horribly aware of the tears swimming in my eyes and rolling shamefully down my cheeks.

For a long moment he stood looking down at me, then unexpectedly he reached out his hand and brushed the tears from my cheek. For the first time since I had known him his voice was kind as he said, 'Poor Joanna, does it really hurt as much as all that?'

The kindness in his voice made it worse and I turned away angrily while the sobs rose in my throat and went to sit near the window on one of the narrow marble seats. This time he didn't come after me but stood silently regarding me while he waited for the sobs to cease, then with a gentle smile said, 'First love doesn't last, Joanna. You're in love with love, with the moonlight and the beauty of your surroundings. This is a love story that isn't meant to be.'

'I know,' I murmured.

'Then if you know you're halfway there,' he said. 'You'll very soon have other things to think about. A new life with your mother, and the coming to terms with that.'

'What do you know about my mother?' I said, suddenly angry that my future should concern him. My foolish young pride hated the fact that it should be Paul reminding me that the old life was coming to an end, that all too soon I must return to something I had been dreading for all too long.

'I can see that you don't want to discuss your mother with me, and you're quite right, of course, where you go from here is no concern of mine. I should do something about your face, Joanna, unless you want the rest of them to see that you've been crying. I would hate them to think that I had caused the tears.'

He turned and left me, and some time later I returned

unobtrusively to the drawing room where I sat on the window seat listening to the rest of them discussing a Europe they felt was changing.

I was a schoolgirl who couldn't even begin to think that the Italy I had experienced for three enchanted weeks could ever change. I was desperately in love with red-roofed old towns and rivers that turned molten gold in the sunlight, but more than that was the exquisite pain of first love which was powerful enough to shut out everything else.

All I could think of was that the most enchanting time of my life was ending and before me was a future that beckoned nowhere.

Chapter Eight

From our arrival in England everything seemed to happen too quickly. My grandparents went immediately to their London hotel and then Father drove me to Mother's new flat near Godalming. I felt strangely nostalgic as we drove through lanes I remembered vividly from the past, and then we were driving through the open gates towards a large square building which had once been a stockbroker's residence and had now been turned into a block of modern flats.

For a few moments we sat in the car staring up at the windows, each one with its small balcony, and what my father's thoughts were at that moment I could not imagine. He collected my luggage from the boot of the car and we walked together through the large glass doors into a foyer thickly carpeted in a serviceable magenta carpet. A man sat behind a wooden desk in the centre of the hall reading a newspaper spread out in front of him and behind him was a board holding rows of keys and a small telephone switchboard in a corner.

He looked up when we approached the desk and Father said, 'We are here to see Mrs Albemarle.'

'Ah, yes, sir, she said she was expectin' you. First floor, sir, number nine. It's at the front of the house, there's a lift round the corner.'

Father thanked him and then to my amazement Honey bounded out from behind his desk and leapt at me in an endeavour to lick my face. Father laughed and the Commissionaire said, 'My, but the dog knows you, miss, and no mistake. He's always left with me when Mrs Albemarle's folk come visitin'. He is a bit big for the flat but I don't think she's over-fond o' dogs anyway. Now come here, boy, and behave while the young lady and her father go upstairs.'

Taking hold of Honey's collar, he dragged him protesting behind the desk and Father and I went in search of the lift. The sight of Honey had cheered me up considerably. At least I would be able to see something of him.

As we left the lift we surprised Grandfather and Mildred waiting to enter it. The two men shook hands affably and Mildred said to me, 'Did you see Honey, love? I always leave him at the desk.'

'Yes. He knew me Mildred. Can I come round to see him after I get settled in?'

'Of course you can. He's a very well-behaved dog and wouldn't do any harm in the flat but your mother says he's too big and might knock some of her ornaments over. She's expecting you.'

'I hope you're not leaving on our account?' Father said evenly.

'Not at all, my boy,' Grandfather replied, 'but we thought it best for you to be on your own. Are your parents well, Robert?'

'Very well, thank you.'

'And how was Italy? We both love it, don't we, Mildred?'

'Indeed. I for one am hoping we can go back there very soon.'

It was affable and impersonal. I felt it set the scene for my future life with my mother, but Father was saying cheerfully, 'Now then, we want number nine. I suppose it's along this corridor at the front of the house. There'll be a nice view of the park and the high street.'

I could hear the bell tinkling tunefully in the flat behind the door and then Mother was there, holding the door open for us, and we were stepping into a tiny hall with several doors opening from it. All I was aware of was a large display of flowers on a marble hall table, and a pale green carpet and pale green walls.

Mother went to a door at the end of the hall and we followed her into a tastefully decorated lounge that didn't

89

look lived in. It was a chocolate box lounge of pale peach and turquoise, so much I was instantly aware of, and although it was late-August the room seemed surprisingly cool until I realised this was the effect of marble in the fireplace and occasional tables. There was a large bowl of peach roses on a small table near the window and at the long windows themselves hung expensively draped curtains to match the peach carpet on the floor and the turquoise cushions on the sofa and chairs.

I thought longingly of Reckmire that had been beautiful and lived in. A home where this was a showplace, but a showplace without tradition while Reckmire held a tradition that would live on.

Mother enquired politely if we would like tea, and Father answered her too hastily that he had left his parents in London and was expected to join them.

'They didn't wish to see the flat then?' Mother asked.

'They'd had a very long journey. I'm sure they'll be delighted to see it when we call for Joanna to take her back to school.'

'You mean they're staying in London until then?'

'I believe so, unless they change their minds. I shall be busy at the Foreign Office, but I have promised Joanna that on our last evening together I'll get tickets for a show in town. I'd like you to join us, Linda.'

'As well as your parents?'

'Actually I had thought just the three of us.'

'Oh, well, I suppose so. If your parents do decide to come perhaps we could include Father and Mildred as well? What show were you thinking of?'

'I thought the Ivor Novello. The music is good and it's getting rave revues.'

'I prefer a play myself. Musicals are never true to life and I'm a little sick of Ruritanian romances which have been played out.'

'Well, we'll see. I'll be in touch before then, of course.'

For a long moment they stared at each other, then he held out his hand saying, 'Goodbye for now, Linda. I hope you'll be happy here, it all looks very nice. Do you have enough money to pay for it all?'

'Father was very good. He came every day to help me to get straight. Mildred came the odd evening, but she's always tied up with that dog of hers. You were very generous, Robert, and Father bought the curtains and gave me some of the things that had been Mother's.'

She made no effort to go with him to the door but I went, choking back my tears. In the doorway he put his arms around me and I sensed his sadness.

'We'll meet very soon, Joanna,' he said gently. 'I'll get tickets for the Novello show, that's the one you want to see, and you'll soon be getting back to school.'

He said it as if he thought I would be glad to be going back to school, and it was so true. I watched him walk down the corridor on the way to the stairs. As he reached the corner another door opened and an elderly lady accompanied by a small Pekinese came out of her flat. She turned to stare at me and then followed Father towards the stairs.

When I got back to the lounge Mother said, 'Was that Miss Whipple going out? I thought I heard her door.'

'An elderly lady with a white Pekinese?'

'She's very nice really, but she's been asking a lot of questions about me. Where my husband was, why wasn't my daughter here, were we separated? I suppose I'll have to get accustomed to being some sort of curiosity. What was the weather like in Italy? We've had an awful lot of rain.'

I started to tell her then about the scenery, the history, the fun, the closeness of the family, and then in some dismay realised that I shouldn't have been speaking of it at all. I only had to look at her small shut-in face to realise that she didn't want to know. When I paused in my tale, she said icily, 'I suppose Corallie had you round the shops in Florence, making you dissatisfied with the clothes you took from England? Corallie was always the flamboyant one, trying to make everybody else appear plain and uninteresting.'

'Oh, Mother, she's not really like that at all. She's great fun and I love the way she dresses and the way she talks,' I cried in Aunt Corallie's defence.

'You're too young to understand, Joanna. She was the same at school. Corallie always wore the most outrageous evening dresses, flaunted the most suspect boy friends. Of course she would have to marry an Italian, an ordinary Englishman would have been far too ordinary for her.'

'Uncle Rinaldo is nice, I like him, Mother, there's nothing at all flamboyant about him, and Gabriella is lovely.'

'And now you have come back disenchanted with this country and the way we live our lives.'

'But I'm not, Mother, honestly I'm not.' In some desperation I looked wildly round the room. 'I think the flat's lovely. We are going to be happy here, aren't we?'

'I'm perfectly happy here, I'm not sure about you. I'll have to wait and see how Robert's relatives might have changed you, Joanna. I could have a very good social life here. Mrs Rostron on the second floor is rather nice. She's a widow and I've had tea with her once or twice and invited her back here. We've formed a bridge four for two afternoons and we have coffee mornings. You can help me with these, Joanna, they're all waiting to meet you, and you can help me with the refreshments and the entertaining.'

'Yes, Mother, of course.'

'Life is very social. We get invitations to everything Saint Mary's Church is doing, and once a month we have a trip out somewhere, either to the country or to a show in town. I do hope your father gets seats for a decent play, I should have told him which one I wanted to see.'

I stayed silent, hoping against hope that we would be going to see the Ivor Novello musical. There was only just over a week before I would be going back to school but I had no idea how I would fill my days.

On the following morning I accompanied Mother to the shops and we called for coffee at a new cafe in the high street. The afternoon stretched before us and when I suggested that we might go round to Grandfather's she said sharply: 'I don't want you roaming all over the place with that dog of theirs, Joanna. I don't encourage Mildred to bring him round here. After all, this is hardly the place for a lolloping dog of that size. I don't want him on my cushions.'

'Honey is very well-behaved, Mother. The lady down the corridor has a dog and another on the second floor has a spaniel.'

They don't bring them when they call to see me. They

can do what they want in their own homes.'

Mother expected me to enjoy the coffee mornings and bridge afternoons when I helped her with the tiny sandwiches and the making of small exquisite cakes which she did to perfection.

I came to dread those occasions which were more an excuse for local gossip than anything else. Flatmates who did not play bridge were criticised for indulging in other activities, and how alike they all were, those women with marcel waves and crepe-de-chine dresses. They spoke in genteel accents and seemed to me to be set in a time warp of bourgeois respectability. I soon began to realise that they were all unaware that my parents had separated.

Mother talked about Father as though they were still living together although he had to spend some time in London because of his job. She talked about my grandparents with great affection, her father and deceased mother as pillars of the local community and Father's parents as powerful gentry somewhere in the North of England.

When she saw the amazement in my eyes she stared at me sharply and defiantly, cautioning me to say nothing about the real state of our family life to anybody.

They learned about Aunt Corallie, married to an Italian Conte, and their beautiful daughter Gabriella, and Aunt Marcia whose husband owned vast acres in Somerset, ignoring the fact that he was a local farmer, and Robin who was clever and studying at Oxford.

They were impressed but not unduly so, since they all had a similar story to tell, and when they departed I was left wondering how much of what I had heard was really true. Very little if Mother's romancing was anything to go by.

I was happiest walking in the park with Honey whom Mother referred to as 'that wretched dog,' and soon came to realise that although Grandfather was still disposed to spoil his one daughter, his second wife was far from enchanted and came to the flat seldom. Largely because she had to leave Honey at the desk downstairs, but also because she and Mother had little in common.

I waited anxiously for Father to telephone with news about

the show he had promised to book for, and was glad that Mother was out when he did so.

He was pleased that he had been able to get good seats for the Ivor Novello show, but added in the next breath, 'I'm not sure that your mother is going to like it, Joanna, she seemed to prefer a play. But it is the last night we shall spend together for a very long time and I thought the musical would cheer us up.'

When I told Mother about the telephone call she said, 'Did he say if he had booked for the grandparents too?'

'No, Mother, just the three of us.'

'What are we going to see?'

'The Ivor Novello show at The Hippodrome,' I replied with a sinking heart when I saw her expression change from anticipation to sulky indifference.

He came for us late in the afternoon and was offered sherry and her cheek to kiss. Seeing him standing in the middle of the small pretty-pretty room I felt he had no part in it, but never had I loved him more. I felt my heart crying out for all the lost years when he had not seemed to matter, and the long years before us when I would never be quite sure where he might be.

He had brought a spray of orchids for Mother to pin on her dress, and a large box of chocolates. She decided against wearing the orchids because their colour clashed with her dress, instructing me to put them in water instead. She looked pretty in her deep blue silk dress with her short dark hair framing her face. She was wearing the silver fox cape Father had bought her just before they went out to Singapore, and as we left the flat we met Miss Whipple and her dog at the end of the corridor. She smiled, and Mother was quick to say, 'We're going into London to the theatre, Miss Whipple. This is my husband, Robert.'

We had excellent seats in the centre of the dress circle because Father thought I would be able to see better there than in the stalls. All around us was the happy hum of conversation and laughter, and while Father and I chatted Mother stared down at her programme. Then the orchestra started up.

The music was romantic and tuneful. All around us people

were appreciative of the singing and dancing, the exquisite scenery and the tender love story which unfolded. I sat there entranced until slowly I became aware that Mother's face wore that tight-lipped, shut-in expression which said all too plainly that she was not enjoying herself. Father and I joined in enthusiastically with the clapping that went on around us, but Mother sat clutching her box of chocolates and programme. Leaning across, Father said gently, 'Are you not enjoying it, Linda?'

'Well, you know it's not really my sort of show, Robert. The story is trite. A good play would have been far more entertaining.'

'Everybody else seems to be enjoying themselves,' he said quietly.

'Well, of course. They're probably people who like this sort of thing. I don't.'

After that I began to think it was wrong to applaud, wrong to join in the laughter, and wrong to believe in the pathos which changed the story from light-hearted entertainment to heartbreaking sadness.

It was over. People were on their feet applauding rapturously and calling for Ivor Novello. He came to the front of the stage, a handsome, shy man, acknowledging the applause, speaking in a quiet voice and thanking the audience for their acclaim. Then at last the curtain came down and we were leaving our seats. The woman who had been sitting next to Mother stared at her curiously before saying, 'Wasn't it wonderful? Didn't you enjoy it?'

'Yes, thank you, it was very nice,' Mother replied shortly, then shrugging her arms into her furs led the way up the steps and out into the corridor.

I felt exasperated with her. I could read nothing into Father's expression then we were in the late-night traffic heading for home and none of us seemed inclined to talk.

Mother invited him in for coffee but he said hurriedly, 'I don't think so, Linda. I'll be here on Saturday morning to pick Joanna up to take her back to school. I'll have my parents with me.'

'Saturday!' Mother exclaimed. 'Why not Sunday? She isn't due back at school until Monday morning.'

'My parents are anxious to get back and I haven't the time to do two journeys,' he explained patiently.

'So you're taking her to Reckmire before you take her to Harrogate? Really, Robert, surely another day wouldn't have made all that much difference? I'd have thought she'd had enough of Reckmire to last her a lifetime.'

Neither of them were to know that my heart had lifted with joy that at least I would have one whole day near the sea when I had never expected to see it again. I stared at their set faces, Mother's angry and resentful, Father's adamant, and silently I prayed that he would have his way.

She was unable to understand that times had changed, Father had changed. Once her wishes would have been paramount. Now, belatedly, he was insisting on doing things his way and I was left wishing it had all happened a long time ago. Now, sadly, it was all too late.

I listened to her anger against my grandparents, my aunts, and Reckmire which she described as desolate. People must be out of their minds to want to live there. I was glad when I was allowed to go to my bedroom where I could dance joyfully round and think about Saturday.

Neither of us mentioned it. Dutifully I accompanied her to the shops, the library, and helped with refreshments for the coffee mornings. Then Saturday came and I rushed to open the door for Father accompanied by my grandparents.

My mother was polite, my grandparents admired the flat and the view across the park. Father was busy with my luggage and since Mother had made no effort to offer coffee I was glad that their visit was brief.

Grandfather Fowler and Mildred arrived just as we were about to leave and because I had been feeling guilty at leaving Mother alone I was glad to see them. When I went to embrace her I felt her rigidity, that elusive withdrawal that she had always been able to produce when for some reason or other she was displeased with me, and as I turned away I was aware of the compassion in Mildred's eyes.

Mother's unspoken resentment seemed to have put a blight on our journey north. For miles it was taken in silence. My grandparents sat at the back of the car, staring through the window, and Father looked straight ahead, his face pensive, his mind on other things than the morning traffic.

It was only over lunch that our spirits seemed to revive, and as the distance increased so too did our enjoyment of the journey. By the time I was aware of the dark rolling Pennines and the distant view of the Lakeland fells I was sitting forward in my seat with a strange determination not to miss anything of what I considered my last visit to Reckmire. What I was seeing today would have to last.

I had one day to recapture the last lingering joy of a summer that would stay in my mind for a very long time with its first shy flirtation with love although now Italy seemed a distant unsubstantial dream, like my first love and the bitter-sweet pain of remembering Carlo's dark laughing eyes and the smile that had twisted my heart.

On Sunday afternoon I sat on the hillside with Lottie while she listened in silence to my recollection of a summer steeped in sunlight. She was a willing audience. She sat wide-eyed, hugging her knees, enjoying my memory of a land completely alien to her, sympathetic of a precious, gentle love that could have no future, and as we parted on that wind-swept fell overlooking the sea I said nothing of my desolation that we might never meet again.

'Why are you leaving so soon?' she asked. 'I thought we'd be up here all afternoon.'

'This is the only day I have, Lottie, and I have so much to see. You won't come near the marshes and I want to go on to the beach. I'll write to you, Lottie, thank you for being my friend.'

'Will you really write to me? I'm not much good with writin' letters, so don't be upset if you don't get one back.'

I laughed. 'Of course not, but I wish you would.'

'What's to tell you? Nothin' ever 'appens round 'ere. The young folk get married, the old folk die. You don't want to 'ear any of that, I'm sure.'

'Oh, but I do. I want to hear about Mrs Peabody and the other people that come into the shop. I want to hear about your sister and all the silly things she gets up to. If I can write to you about all the things I do at school, you can surely write to tell me about people I know.'

'You'll laugh at my grammar and show the other girls.'

'Oh, Lottie, of course I won't. When Mother writes it'll be all about her bridge parties and coffee mornings. I'll look forward to your letters.'

'Well, we'll see. I'll stay up 'ere and watch you go down the hill. When you gets to the stile you can turn round and wave to me.'

When I reached the stile she was there, waving her hands wildly in the air, then I turned and ran down the road towards Reckmire. Because it was Sunday there were no men working in the gardens and a gentle peace seemed to lie over it, a peace reflected in the sound the sea made as it rippled in silver crescents across the sand.

I thought it was the last time I would walk along the curve of Reckmire, stopping occasionally to pick up some shining pebble or interesting shell. The sound of the surf was in my heart, the smell of the sea a sharp and poignant delight. At last when I climbed up the rocks that led to the house I turned to look back along the beach and found myself remembering how Robin had pulled me back towards the dunes while I could feel the lash of Paul Cheviot's anger and his unspoken contempt at my stupidity.

I could taste the salt on my lips as I turned to walk back to the house, in tears of desolation because I thought it was the last time I would walk along the beach. In this I was wrong.

The talk around the dining table that night was all of separation. My grandparents felt they were losing me as well as my father, and then when they saw that it was upsetting me their talk turned to other things. Their disquiet about the world situation, Hitler and Mussolini, their distrust of a Germany on the march and their fears for Aunt Corallie and her family in Italy. When I thought about that sun-kissed countryside I couldn't reconcile their fears but at that time I was more concerned with my own future and sense of loss than anything that might or might not be happening in far off lands.

It was suggested that I should go to bed early because of my journey back to school the next day and Grandma came into my room to see if I had everything. As she drew the curtains across the window she said, 'It's a full moon, Joanna, one of those beautiful nights when the sea is only a whisper on the breeze. It's hard to think on a night like this that the beach can be a treacherous place or that the sea can become a monster.'

She kissed me goodnight but after she had gone I could only lie sleepless, staring into the darkened room. It was so still it seemed that outside my room there was only an empty void where not even a dog barked. It was as if a giant hand had come down to still the leaves fluttering in the breeze and the gentle breaking of the sea upon the shore.

It was much later when I heard the sound of bedroom doors being opened and closed. The walls were stout and there were no voices to be heard, but still sleep refused to come to me and impatiently I turned on the light beside my bed and picked up a book from my bedside table. I tried reading but the book could not sustain my interest, and at last I got out of bed and padded over to the window. The gardens and rocks were bathed in moonlight and without a second's thought I slipped my feet into my slippers and reached for my dressing gown. Noiselessly I opened the door and without the need for a light made my way to the turret room where I could gaze down upon the entire reach of Reckmire. The sea rolled in in silver crescents along the shore and in the bright moonlight the waving grass on the dunes took on vague silvered shapes that changed constantly with every flickering breeze.

As I stared across the beach I became suddenly aware that a man had stepped out from the shadows and was walking slowly along the sand. He walked with his head down, his hands buried in the pockets of his coat, and seemed to me to be surrounded by a deep and penetrating loneliness. I didn't recognise him at first. It was only when he turned and walked towards the sea that I realised it was my father, and for one blinding moment I was afraid that he was going to keep on walking until the incoming tide engulfed him. Then, slowly, he turned and walked back towards the house.

I did not hesitate. Without a second's thought I was running down the stairs and across the hall, pulling back the bolts on the doors and running wildly across the damp grass to where the rocks led down to the beach.

In the daylight I had been mindful of their slippery smoothness and sudden dangerous crags, but not tonight. It was as though I had charmed feet as I slithered and leapt on to the sand below. Then I was running across the sand with my hair streaming behind me and my voice calling out to him, lost in the wind.

He stood still, staring at me, then I was rushing headlong into his arms and he was smiling, delighted to have me with him regardless of the time and the loneliness of the empty beach.

As we strolled back towards the house he told me that they had both decided that divorce was inevitable but promised always to be there for me, I must never forget that.

Book II

Chapter Nine

I sat with my elbows on the desk, staring out of the window at a cloudless blue sky and a flock of swallows that had come to rest on the top of the school's sports pavilion. Boys in white flannels were busy at the nets and a group of girls carrying tennis racquets passed in front of the window so that the sound of their voices and their laughter came in through the open window.

It was half day closing at the library where I worked part-time. That I worked at all was a concession not easily agreed to by Mother. I had promised my old headmistress that I would write to her as soon as I made up my mind what my future would be. She had encouraged me to go on with my education since my examination results had been very good, but Mother said it was unnecessary. Father was generous with his allowance for both of us, Grandfather Fowler had died eighteen months before leaving her a considerable sum of money, and because she had seen so little of me over the years now was the time for us to be together to enjoy ourselves.

It was an arrangement that stifled me. I had come to realise however that I must be devious in my dealings with Mother. She did not want me to learn to drive, but when Mrs Steven's daughter Alice passed her driving test first time, not to be outdone Mother gave her reluctant permission for me to learn. I was never sure if it was a good idea since now that I too had passed my test we went everywhere together.

The next hurdle was a job. When I trotted out the names of local girls we both knew who were working in the city, going to university, or articled to some firm or other, she became angry. It was only when Mrs Holly's two daughters found part-time jobs, one in a local bank, the other as a doctor's receptionist, that she began to change her mind and think that perhaps it was the done thing.

Mildred decided she would like to live near her sister in Bexhill and to my regret departed with Honey. She and Mother had never been good friends and all we got now was a Christmas card, although I had been told Mildred would always be pleased if I cared to visit her.

The visit would never happen. For one thing Mother wouldn't go to Bexhill, it was on the coast and she disliked Honey, and going without her would cause so much acrimony it wasn't worth it. Nor did I ever write to my headmistress because I knew my news would sadden her and make her think what a terrible waste my education had been.

Father wrote to me, long letters about the Far East which I treasured although he made no mention of leave and if he ever came home didn't come to see us.

My grandparents at Reckmire continued to send expensive Christmas and birthday presents, but I never went to see them because Mother had become extremely good at feigning severe migraines at exactly the right moment.

The job at the library cropped up when one of her friends, whose sister was the librarian, happened to say that they were looking round for a part-time assistant and wondered if I might be interested?

'Oh, I shouldn't think so,' Mother said calmly. 'After all, Joanna doesn't know anything about the library service and she doesn't have to work, you know.'

Mrs Airey helped herself to another sandwich and said, 'My sister would see that she got plenty of training and help. Besides, it's unnatural in this day and age for a girl to stay at home all day with nothing to occupy her mind. Both my girls have been working since they left school and I'm glad not to have them under my feet all day.'

'Oh, Joanna and I are not a bit like that,' Mother exclaimed. 'We like being together. We go to the shops and the theatres. We drive out in the car and we're absolutely never bored.'

Mrs Airey merely sniffed while the other ladies sitting round the table busied themselves with their cards and nothing more was said. The following morning I went to the shops, but I also went to the Public Library and asked to see the librarian.

She was a straightforward middle-aged woman with a sense of humour and a direct approach. She seemed to know all about me and after a few minutes asked pointedly, 'I don't think your mother's keen on the idea of your working, Joanna, does she know you intended to visit us?'

'No. I'll tell her when I get back.'

'We need somebody rather quickly. Miss Pemberton's left us without much notice because her husband's been promoted and they're going to live in the North, and Mr Lathom is very forgetful these days and not very well, I'm afraid. I shall need to know before the weekend, Joanna.'

'I'll tell you tomorrow afternoon, Miss Carson. How many days would I be required to work?'

'All day Saturday and Wednesday, half day Tuesday. I really think we could manage with that.'

'Then I promise faithfully I'll call in tomorrow and let you know. I'm sure Mother will agree.'

I was anything but sure. I feared she would find a hundred and one reasons why I shouldn't work there but I knew for a certainty that I had to grasp this chance with both hands because it was the only crack in a great black wall which could let in the light.

Over tea I listened to the usual gossip about our neighbours and their affairs but when my thoughts were miles away she said sharply, 'I don't think you're even listening to me, Joanna. You were an awful long time at the shops. Who did you meet?'

I made myself reach out calmly for a piece of cake before saying in what I hoped was my normal voice, 'I called at the Public Library, Mother. I wanted to hear a little more about the part-time job Mrs Airey was talking about.'

Her eyes opened wide and the colour rose slowly in her cheeks. I was aware of her mouth becoming tighter and her hand clenching the fork it was holding.

'How very deceitful, Joanna. You evidently knew where

you were going when you went out, why didn't you mention it?'

'I knew you wouldn't like it. I thought you would do everything you could to stop me going.'

'Well, of course I would. You're certainly not cut out to be a librarian. I know Joyce Carson, she's a real blue stocking if ever there was one. She's a typical old maid and has worked in that library as long as I can remember. I don't think I've ever known her have a man friend.'

'I haven't had one either, Mother.'

'Gracious me, Joanna, Janice Carson is three times your age. There's oceans of time for you.'

'Mother, I need a job. It isn't enough to go to the shops, take tea with your friends, drive out into the country. All the girls I was at school with have jobs or are making a career for themselves. I'm every bit as capable as they were.'

I had not raised my voice in argument but had deliberately kept it gentle and reasonable. I quickly became aware that she was determined to be unreasonable.

'I expect most of those girls needed to find work, Joanna,' she said adamantly. 'As you are in the fortunate position of not needing to, it would be very wrong for you to take a job from somebody who might.'

'I might not need it financially Mother, but I do need it from every other viewpoint. I need to use my brain. I need to have something to do, I'm bored with my life. My father would be the first to agree with me.'

'Your father has seen fit to disassociate himself from both of us. His parents and sisters are totally disinterested in what either of us does, so please don't bring in your father as if he was a saint and it is only I who thwart you.'

'What do you expect them to do, Mother? You don't visit them or even correspond with them. It is we who have cut ourselves off, not them.'

'Joanna, I am feeling very tired and can sense one of my bad headaches coming on. I don't want to discuss this any more. Take this job at the library if it is more important than my feelings on the subject, but when you are fed up with it, don't come moaning to me that you've made a mistake.'

She pushed her plate away from her and, holding a

106

handkerchief to her brow, left the table and went to her room. Once I would have followed her, fussed round her, making her drinks and bringing her tablets, but there had been too many such scenes. All my life I had seen Mother holding the rest of us to ransom, first my grandparents when I was a little girl, and then my father. I had witnessed the cossetting, the guilt at having caused her suffering, and then her forgiveness and the capitulation when she deigned to accompany them on some special treat in the car or to the theatre. Now it was my turn, and if there was to be any life for me at all I had to be strong, even if it meant a deterioration in our life together.

I did not see her again until I went into her room much later to see if she wanted anything. She lay with her eyes closed, moaning a little before she said, 'I have a terrible head, Joanna, the worst for some time. I couldn't face anything.'

'Would you like me to send for the doctor, Mother?'

'It wouldn't do any good. I know what has caused it, it's not going to go away while I'm so upset.'

I wished her goodnight and left her alone. I couldn't stand her tears, her drama, the iron will behind that all too fragile exterior. Next morning before she was awake I went to the library and accepted the job.

For days the atmosphere at home was terrible, and then miraculously it changed. She spoke about my employment to her friends as if I was God's gift to the library, as if Miss Carson couldn't live without me, and she fussed over my clothes and her idea that I should look efficient and businesslike.

Those two and a half days a week I spent in the library were a joy. I came to know all those who changed their books there and came every day to pore over the newspapers and magazines. They talked to me about their families and I came to know their preferences and idiosyncrasies, like Mrs Sefton who enjoyed torrid romances and her sister who only read thrillers, and old Mr Jeffries who came out of the way of his wife's coffee mornings and for whom I had a strong fellow feeling.

As I waited for the last customers to leave I stared around

107

me with great affection. It was a light airy library, well-kept and roomy, and there was a large bowl of roses on the desk which Miss Carson had brought in that morning.

I had a selection of books for my mother although she never seemed to have much time for reading and invariably found fault with what I had chosen.

Across the room two schoolboys sat giggling over a book they had taken from the adult section and I could only guess that they had found something riskqué, the contents of which would no doubt be bandied about the school cloakroom later in the afternoon.

Seeing me looking at them, they hastily gathered their belongings together and escaped through the main door, then Mr Jeffries was there, saying, 'I've exhausted the newspapers, Miss, so I'll toddle off home. What are you going to do with your half day?'

'I'm not sure. It's so lovely. We'll probably take a ride into the country.'

'I see you've got your grandfather's car. Does your mother drive?' he asked curiously.

'No. Only me, I'm afraid.'

'So you're the chauffeur then? Your mother's going to miss that when you get yourself a nice boyfriend,' he ended, then with a bright smile was gone.

As I walked home across the park I thought about his words. Other girls I knew went to the tennis club or played golf. They went riding on the downs or to Saturday night hops, but any mention of such activities had always brought on an attack of migraine and the plaintive accusation: 'Joanna, how can you be so selfish? Those girls have fathers and sisters and brothers. We've only got each other. Don't I count for anything?'

So here I was, nearly nineteen years old, with a job that occupied me two and a half days a week, and what other time I had devoted to playing hostess to Mother's friends, driving her into the country, picking her up from the hairdresser's and generally devoting my life to being her companion. It was a prospect that seemed to stretch before me, unchanging and desolate.

She would have spent the morning exchanging gossip with

her friends and now she would be waiting for me with a light lunch and while I ate it would entertain me with all they had talked about. She would be ready for our drive out into the country, and because it was a lovely day she would be wearing a silk dress, a matching hat and gloves, and would encourage me to get out of my business-like attire and into something resembling her own.

There was the sound of laughter from girls playing tennis in the park and outside the flats stood a large removal van. Evidently whoever had bought the flat at the end of the corridor was moving in at last.

I had only just let myself into the hall when Mother opened the lounge door, saying brightly, 'We have visitors, Joanna, aren't you a little late?'

Without answering I followed her into the lounge where I found a woman sitting beside a small coffee table and another younger woman looking through the windows. She turned and immediately I recognised a girl I had gone to school with years before when we lived in Grandfather Fowler's house.

She had always been a pretty girl. Now she was a slender, elegant woman with a worldly poise that made me feel suddenly countrified and gauche. Mother was chattering amiably.

'I've been telling Mrs Chantry and Stella that we were going to take a drive out into the country but they haven't the time to come with us so perhaps we'll cancel it for today, darling. You don't mind, do you?'

'Of course not, Mother. It's awfully nice to see you both again.'

'I've left your lunch in the kitchen, Joanna. We'll all have a nice long chat this afternoon.'

I excused myself while I ate lunch, set out on a plate for me on the small kitchen table, arranged on a flowered tray, prettily, like Mother did everything, even a plate of boiled ham sandwiches and a basket of fresh fruit.

I could hear Mother and Mrs Chantry laughing and chattering in the lounge. While I was clearing away the door opened and Stella came into the kitchen. She perched on the corner of the table while I washed the few dishes, readily taking up a tea towel to dry them.

'Why don't you and I take a nice long walk this afternoon, Joanna? I've been listening to them most of the morning, now I want to talk to you.'

'Didn't Mother have her coffee friends here?'

'All of them. I've been listening to them too. We have to go around four because we're having visitors this evening, but it gives us a couple of hours and there's so much I want to know.'

'I can't think what. Nothing ever happens to me, you've much more to tell me.'

'And I will, every bit of it. You don't need to change, Joanna.'

Mother didn't think our intended walk was a very good idea and it was Stella who stuck to the idea, not me. Mother also deplored the fact that I didn't intend to change into something more fitting. She said working clothes were for working in. After all, I wasn't without prettier things.

Stella said we didn't have a lot of time, so that in the end we escaped into the afternoon sunshine and it felt like a major victory.

'Your mother says you're working part-time at the local library,' Stella began. 'Do you like it there?'

'Yes, I do. I meet people and get to borrow the newest books,' I answered her steadily.

'You've no idea how much I envied you when you went away to that school in Harrogate. I thought the world would be your oyster. You were holidaying with your father's family and we'd all heard they were landed gentry with large estates and oodles and oodles of money. Was any of it true, Joanna?'

'All of it, Stella, only for me it had to end when my parents separated.'

'Why, for heaven's sake? They're still your grandparents surely? Don't you go to see them?'

'No. I used to write to them and they wrote to me. Now it's ages since I heard from them so I don't write any more.'

'And your father?'

'I haven't heard from him either. He always sent me Christmas and birthday presents but he hasn't for some time. Mother has the idea he's met somebody else and is forgetting about us.'

'I always thought your father was a lovely man. I'm sure your mother's wrong about him.'

'I don't see how when he never writes to us.'

'The Far East is a big place. Maybe he's a long way from civilisation, and letters can go astray.'

'Not all of them, Stella, and that doesn't explain why I don't hear from my grandparents,' I replied stolidly. 'Tell me about you, though. Where have you been living and what do you do? I'm sure it's a lot more interesting than anything I can tell you about me.'

'Well, I did awfully well with languages and got a job in Prague at the British Embassy. I got out just before Hitler invaded Czechoslovakia. Then I went to Amsterdam for a while but Europe's heading for trouble, people talk of nothing else, and I really think my days at The Hague are numbered.'

'You mean, there's going to be a war?' I asked sharply.

'That's what everybody I meet seems to think.'

'And we shall be involved?'

'Sure to be.'

'Against Germany?'

'And Italy, unless there's a miracle and suddenly everybody concerned sees sense,' she answered grimly.

It seemed incredible to me that two English girls on a sunny summer's afternoon should be discussing war in lands far away, and yet even in the quiet backwater of my life I had heard the first faint whisperings of dread. Old men studying the newspapers in the reading room of the library, whispering to each other and shaking their heads in doubtful awareness, recalling their memories of the last conflict which I was too young to remember because it had been over two years before I was born.

Suddenly I found myself remembering that summer in Tuscany. Oh, it was impossible to believe that if there was war Carlo would be my enemy, and yet I was unable to discount the memory of those feet marching across the city square and the look of disquiet on Carlo's face.

Stella chatted on about her life, her boyfriends, her

activities, and by the time we had walked back to the flat I saw my life for what it was, a copy of my mother's, but at least she had had the joy of being married to my father and had seen something of the world. She had her memories, even if they now made her bitter. I had no memories to look back on unless it was those few all too short weeks in the marshes and that brief time in Italy.

'What will you do if war comes?' Stella surprised me by asking.

'Do! I don't know. Carry on as usual, I suppose.'

'There'll be no "as usual",' Joanna. You'll be called up like the men, and a part-time job at the library won't get you out of anything.'

I stared at her in surprise. She was smiling at my bewilderment, then with surprising astuteness said, 'It'll get you away from your mother, Joanna, and into the real world. If you ask me, it might not be a bad thing.'

'You talk as though I'm unhappy.'

'My dear girl, you're living in a time warp. Look at you, you're a faithful copy of your mother. Same hair style, same size heels on your shoes, predictable hem line. But you're not really like your mother, Joanna, you're blonde and beautiful, with a figure to drive men wild. We felt sorry for you years ago when she stopped you doing things at school. I'm feeling sorry for you today because you've not been allowed to spread your wings.'

Half angry, and burdened by loyalty to my mother, I bit my lip and stalked on ahead, but she came after me, taking hold of my arm and spinning me round to face her.

'Honestly, Joanna, I'm not being horrible to you, I'm just trying to wake you up. Don't you know that people are gossiping about you? That's why we came today, not because Mother ever had anything in common with your mother but because so many people are sorry for you.'

'Why should they be sorry for me? I'm perfectly happy. And your mother didn't need to put herself out. I think we should go back so that you can both go home.' I said angrily.

'You've every right to be angry, Joanna, how you live your life has nothing to do with me, but I've listened over the years to Mrs Prothero. She came to work for us, you know, still does, and Mildred Fowler was always annoyed about the way your mother treated you. I'm sorry you're angry, I'm an insensitive pig, but I did mean well, Joanna.'

We stared at each other, and I could feel the tears pricking my eyes. Impulsively she put her arms round me.

'Will I never learn to keep my big mouth shut?' she said sharply. 'If your mother sees you've been crying she's sure to want to know why, and things could be difficult.'

Impatiently I wiped my eyes, and Stella reached into her handbag for her powder compact. Reassured at last that I looked presentable, she linked her arm in mine, saying, 'Honestly, Joanna, I'll never mention anything like this again, but we will stay friends, won't we? If I come to live in London we could meet and do a show or something.'

'Yes, that would be nice,' I murmured.

Back in the flat we found Mother and Mrs Chantry sitting over their teacups. I thought Mrs Chantry greeted us with rather too much enthusiasm and that there was a strained look on her face. It was nothing Mother had said, rather the effort of keeping up a conversation that said nothing. I had seen that identical strain on other faces over the years.

Before they left Stella said brightly, 'I've been telling Joanna I'll probably be coming back to England in the not too distant future. If I'm based in London it would be nice to meet and take in a show.'

'Yes, of course, it seems ages since we went to a show in town. We'd like that, wouldn't we, Mrs Chantry?'

'I'm sure these two girls won't want their mothers tagging along. Besides, I get to take in lots of shows with Bernard.'

'You're very fortunate. I don't have a Bernard to escort me to the theatre,' Mother said sharply.

'Then, my dear, you should set your stall out. A little less of the coffee mornings and bridge parties, and a little more of the sports and golf club.'

'I'm perfectly happy with the way things are. I've never been interested in sport and I don't golf,' snapped Mother, but Mrs Chantry, not to be outdone, said evenly, 'Sometimes one has to be interested in all sorts of things to accommodate someone else, my dear. Mrs Atherton wasn't interested in golf before her husband died, then quite suddenly she meets a charming man on holiday who is interested in golf. Now they're married and sailing up the Amazon.'

I wanted to laugh. Stella raised her eyes heavenwards and Mother stood stolidly in the doorway while Mrs Chantry, totally oblivious of her resentment, went gleefully on.

'Why not join St Mary's Dramatic Society, dear? It would give you a wonderful interest and so many eligible men in the town are members. Well, we must go. I've been chattering far too long. Our visitors will have arrived before we get home. It is nice to have met you both again. You must both come round to see us, I'll be in touch.'

Back in the living room Mother said angrily, 'I don't know why they came. Probably to look at the flat and see how I've furnished it then she can report back to all the people we used to know when we lived at Father's. She was friendly with Mildred, you know. I expect Mildred gossipped about me, she was always jealous of me.'

I stared at her in surprise. 'Mother, I don't think Mildred was ever jealous of you. Why should she be? She had everything she wanted, and she was always nice to me.'

'Well, of course she was. It was a front she put up for Father's benefit. She didn't like him giving me presents, or money, and I expect she resented what he left me in his will. Heavens, is it that time? I suppose it's far too late to go out in the car now. She was dying to know what had gone wrong between your father and me, but I was far too wide awake to tell her anything.'

I busied myself with the afternoon tea trolley. I'd heard it all before, Mildred's jealousy, her father's stupidity because he married her, and if she had only known how much I pitied her would it have made any difference.

'What did you two girls talk about?' she asked in an endeavour to break my silence.

'Stella talked about her job abroad and said she might soon be coming back to live in England.'

'Really? Her mother seemed to think it was marvellous for her living abroad, she said nothing about her living here.'

'She had to come out of Prague because the Germans

invaded the country. Now there's great uncertainty in Europe.'

'It'll blow over, it always does. I've no time for all this warmongering, we shouldn't become involved.'

'I wonder if Father will have to come home from the Far East if there's war? We don't even know where he is.'

'And he isn't in the least concerned that we don't know or he'd write!'

'It isn't like him not to. His letters were always full of news — you've no idea how I looked forward to them. It's strange too that Grandma doesn't write. Perhaps she's ill? Why don't we telephone and find out?'

There was sudden alarm in her eyes. She turned towards me from where she was putting crockery away in the kitchen cupboard. 'I don't think that's a good idea at all, Joanna. You wrote to them regularly and they were the ones to stop answering your letters. They were never returned so they must have got them. We do have some pride. I've told you what I think has happened. Your father has found somebody else. After all, there were enough women in the Far East visiting relatives and simply looking for husbands. If he has done, then he and his family probably think it's best for all concerned that they cut themselves off completely.'

Her arguments were always logical and yet I couldn't reconcile them with the warmth I had experienced at Reckmire and the closeness that had existed between members of Father's family.

Chapter Ten

The beginning of 1938 started badly. Mother slipped on the steps of the post office and broke her wrist which meant that more than ever I was at her beck and call. I seemed to have no life of my own although it was a pretty straightforward break and healed after five weeks.

I dropped her off at her coffee mornings and collected her later, and she managed to play bridge when one of the ladies produced a sort of wooden contraption so that she could place her cards in order, sufficient at any rate to enable them to get by. She was impatient with the talk of war and it seemed to be everywhere. Young men were seen about the streets in uniform if they were Territorials, gas masks were issued, and in the evenings we went to ARP lectures. A team of workmen came to dig out an air-raid shelter for the flats and similar shelters were being erected in the parks and back gardens. Mother insisted it was all a storm in a teacup and I remember vividly the day I arrived home from the library to find her waving the evening paper triumphantly in my face.

'What did I tell you!' she exclaimed. 'Mr Chamberlain has come back from Germany with Hitler's promise that there will be peace in our time. He'll be on the news at six o'clock.'

So we listened to the radio, and the following morning it was headline news with pictures of Mr Chamberlain gleefully waving his bit of paper in the faces of a crowd of journalists as he stepped off the plane.

We wanted it to be true, but as if nobody believed it we

went on preparing for war. Children were being sent away from the large cities, barrage balloons were tested in the sky above our heads, and old men studying their newspapers in the reading room were shaking their heads and murmuring together.

Miss Carson put my fears into words by saying, 'I don't know what the situation here will be if war comes, Joanna. The library will stay open as usual but the staff will change. I'm too old for anything else and my mother is an invalid, but the new apprentice will be called up and I don't know what will happen about you as you're only here part-time.'

When I repeated this conversation to Mother she retorted angrily, 'Mrs Carson's no more an invalid than I am. She's well enough to attend everything they have at St Mary's. If she's the excuse to get her daughter off the hook, then the same one should count when it comes to you.'

'Miss Carson is the Librarian, Mother, and she's also well into her fifties. I'm young. If there's a war I should do something.'

'You're just like your father, Joanna. You want to go, don't you? You wouldn't care about leaving me here alone. Anyway, it's all supposition, there isn't going to be a war. Everybody panicking like mad and spending a lot of unnecessary money building shelters nobody will need. There's a run on the shops too, with people rushing to buy groceries and clothes before the stocks run out. I do think we should have a day in London, Joanna. We might get something decent. I met Mrs Chantry coming off the train last Thursday, absolutely armed with parcels from the London shops.'

'Did she say if she had heard from Stella?' I asked her.

'She's living in London now and working at the Foreign Office. She was more concerned with her purchases than her daughter. I really think we'll go up to London on your next day off. We'll give ourselves quite a treat, dear, have afternoon tea at the Dorchester and hope to see some well-known faces.'

Mother was only interested in the shops and I was amazed how easily she could close her eyes to the sandbagged buildings, the newspaper placards proclaiming doom, and the assortment of young men and women wearing service uniform.

She selected a seat in the Dorchester tearoom against the wall from where she had a good view of everybody who came in.

'Mother used to love coming here,' she informed me. 'We saw so many famous actresses and actors as well as politicians. You see, Joanna, how normal everything is with the lights and the tinkling of teacups. Everybody here is looking relaxed and chattering quite normally.'

It was true that people were laughing and chatting together but there was a strange enforced gaiety about their laughter, the gaiety of people standing on the brink of a terrible unknown, and among that crowd of lounge-suited men and elegant women was an unusual preponderance of service men and women. Mother made no comment on the fact as her eyes lingered longingly on the assortment of rich cakes the waiter presented.

As my gaze roved restlessly round the room it suddenly came to rest on two young men in Air Force uniform just rising from their table and walking towards the door. It was many years since I had seen my cousin Robin but there was no mistaking his tall slim figure and bright shining hair before he set on it his peaked officer's cap. As if by unseen hands I was pulled to my feet and Mother looked at me curiously.

'What is it, Joanna?' she asked sharply.

'I'll be back in a moment, Mother, I've seen someone I must speak to.'

Without another word I was hurrying towards the door, relieved to find Robin and his companion standing chatting in the middle of the foyer. Without any hesitation I went towards them, touching Robin gently on his arm and saying, 'I'm so glad to see you. It's Joanna.'

I was aware of it instantly, the first recognition before the shutters came down, then the sudden chill from someone I had always associated with smiling geniality. His companion stood back uncertainly and Robin's brief smile showed an immediate desire to be elsewhere, and quickly.

His voice was too casual as he asked, 'How are you, Joanna?'

118

'I'm very well, Robin, but I want to know about my grandparents. It's so long since I heard from them, from any of them, even my father, and I've thought about Reckmire so many times. Will you tell them you've seen me, that I've asked about them?'

'Why didn't you write to them, Joanna? Why did you suddenly stop?' he said evenly.

I stared at him in amazement. 'But I did write to them, Robin, long letters about what I was doing, where I was going. They never answered them and the last letter came back simply readdressed.'

'When was that?'

'About four months ago.'

'And when did you last hear from them?'

'All of two years ago. I never hear from any of them, not even from my father. Does that mean that they don't live at Reckmire any more?'

My eyes searched his face and found that gradually the hostility left it and instead a strange sort of compassion took its place. His voice too was kinder, more in tune with the voice I remembered which had always spoken to me with the gentlest and friendliest understanding.

'Grandpa had a heart attack about eighteen months ago, Joanna, and at Mother's invitation they went to live in Somerset so that they could both be looked after. He's very much better and they're happy enough in Somerset but they're getting on in years and Grandma is very frail these days. We did have fun at Reckmire, didn't we, Joanna?'

'Oh, yes, Robin. It was wonderful, the happiest time of my life. What is happening to the house now?'

'It still belongs to Grandpa but it's been made into a nursing home for wounded officers, subject to there being a war, of course.'

'Will there be, Robin?'

'I doubt if it can be avoided. Forgive me, Joanna, but this is my friend and brother officer, Flying Officer Peter Davidson. My cousin, Joanna Albemarle.'

'I thought you wanted to go into archeology, Robin? Isn't that why you went up to Oxford?'

'I think there will be a great many of us unable to do

119

what we wanted to do. When I saw that the threat of war was very real, I joined the Air Force.'

Suddenly we all laughed when we realised that Peter Davidson was still holding my hand, and then when I looked across the foyer I saw that Mother stood staring at us before, with grim determination on her face, starting to walk towards us.

'My mother is here, Robin,' I said urgently. 'Perhaps you would like to say hello?'

Immediately I was aware that the shutters had come down again and with unnatural haste he said, 'Actually, Joanna, we were already late for an appointment so if you'll excuse us we really must go. Please give your mother my apologies. Perhaps we'll meet again one day?'

There was dismay on Peter Davidson's face, and sad misgiving on Robin's, all the same in the next moment I was staring after them as they walked out into the warm sunlight of an August day, then beside me I heard Mother ask: 'Who were they, Joanna? How long have you known them?'

Still bemused by the suddenness of their departure, I answered her dully, 'My cousin Robin and his friend.'

'Marcia's boy?'

'Yes, Mother.'

'They quite evidently didn't wish to meet me or they would have stayed a little longer.'

'They had an appointment, Mother. It's a pity I didn't see them earlier,' I answered her.

'I wondered where on earth you had got to. You simply stood up from the table and almost ran across the room. People were staring at you, and you hadn't finished your tea. I told the waiter to take it away, I felt so silly sitting there on my own,' she said petulantly.

'There was no need, Mother, I was coming back to you.'

'Well, we might as well get back now. I've paid the bill and brought out all the parcels. Wasn't that boy in uniform?'

'They both were, Mother, Air Force uniform.'

'Gracious me, I thought he was up at Oxford and too clever for words.'

I was glad that there was little time for conversation as we hunted for a taxi. The train too was full and we were unable to sit together, a situation which left me free to think about the things Robin had told me and to face the terrible thoughts that were hammering at my mind.

Robin's eyes and whole demeanour had been accusing. He believed that I had deliberately set out to forget Reckmire and all those I had known there. Now, those missing letters became an agonising conundrum. Who was to blame? As the train ate up the miles I became more and more afraid of the answer to that question, the only possible answer ...

It was impossible openly to accuse mother of stealing my letters and yet what other answer was there when we were the only two people living in the flat? I looked at her sitting staring demurely out of the window at the speeding countryside. A small dainty figure in a neat navy blue dress with snowy white piqué collar and chic navy blue pillbox hat. Everything about my mother was neat and tidy from her plain navy blue court shoes to her dark shingled hair, but it was a sterile neatness without either tenderness or passion.

Long before we stepped off the train at our local station I had come to realise that I must try to find out what had happened to the missing mail, but I did not have the courage to ask her for the truth. I could not face her anger or her tears of recrimination. I knew I would have to search the flat and if she had destroyed them then there was nothing I could do; at the same time I also knew that my life could not go on in the same vein as before.

I needed to approach my grandparents in Somerset to try to bridge the lost years and in the hope that they might have news of my father, but how could I do this without implicating my mother? I only knew that during the next few days I wanted her out of the house so that I could start my search, afraid of finding what I was looking for yet unable to face the disappointment if I could not.

We had nothing to say to each other as we carried our parcels out to the station yard where I had left the car, and when we arrived at the flat she seemed entirely concerned with her shopping.

'Perhaps I'll go round to see Janice Gerrard,' she said

later. 'I told her we were going to town, she'll be interested to know what we've bought.'

Janice Gerrard lived in one of the bottom flats and I was quick to encourage her to go there and not to hurry back. Even so I waited quite some time until I was sure she had found Janice at home before I started my search.

Methodically I started with all the usual places, hating myself for searching through her wardrobe and dressing-table drawers, exasperated when I found nothing. Where would my mother hide things she did not want me to see?

There were no hidden corners in a modern flat, no cellars or attics, no old furniture with intricate drawers. Her bedroom revealed nothing and I started on the kitchen cupboards with little hope that I would find anything. Then I realised with something like amazement that I had found none of the things Mother would treasure and which I knew she kept religiously from one year to the next. Old birthday cards and postcards, mementoes off wedding and birthday cakes, things she had been sentimental over, every small thing that was part of a memory.

She had kept them in an old hat box which had belonged to Grandmother, and had enjoyed taking them out and brooding over them for as long as I could remember. She would never throw them away, they were part of a past she found infinitely preferable to the present, but where had she found a place for them? There was only one place left: a cupboard in the kitchen over the cooker in which Mother said she'd kept old pans and dishes she would never need to use but which were too good to throw away. I needed to climb up the small stepladder to open the door and at first my heart sank when I saw that indeed there seemed nothing inside but several large pans, a kettle and some earthenware dishes. Gingerly I pulled them out, balancing them precariously at the edge of the cupboard to enable me to look behind, and then I saw it, the dark brown leather of Grandmother's hat box, and for a long moment I stood poised on the top step, afraid to reach into the cupboard to take out what I suspected was there, but more afraid of the disappointment if all the hatbox contained were the mementoes of Mother's lost dreams.

I stood with my ears straining for any sound from the corridor then, making up my mind suddenly, I went to the front door and let down the catch. She had not taken her key so would have to ring the doorbell. There would be sufficient time for me to replace the hatbox and the pans before I let her in.

I opened the box cautiously, and a sudden feeling of shame washed over me when I looked down at a box of iced roses and good luck charms, but having come so far I could not stop. I had to go on taking out birthday cards tied with ribbons, wedding invitations, holiday postcards, and then my heart leapt alarmingly when underneath in a large brown envelope I found letters. At first I stared at them in stupefied anger when I recognised my father's writing on envelopes addressed to me and dated as recently as two months before. There wasn't time to read them then, but my hands were reaching underneath, searching for others and finding them. Letters from Reckmire, from Somerset and from Italy, two years of letters. The pain in my heart brought the scalding tears into my eyes before I replaced them in the box to be read when I could be sure there would be time.

Quickly I replaced everything as I had found it, then I returned to the living room to await her return. I could settle to nothing. I was restless with anger and pain. I wanted to confront her with what I had found but I was not brave enough. She was my mother, I didn't want to despise her, and yet that was what I was doing. I wanted to escape from that flat and go anywhere as long as I was putting distance between us, but that was impossible. Instead I waited for her return and when at last I heard the doorbell I went to open the door with trembling hands and my heart thumping sickeningly in my breast.

She was in high good humour and I was glad that I was not expected to contribute any conversation myself. Janice had been quite envious of Mother's purchases. 'I don't know why,' she added, 'there's no reason why she can't go up to London, her daughter could take her if she got somebody to look after her little girl for the day. Janice is always going on about all her friends and what a good mother-in-law she's got.'

123

'She wanted to know what you'd managed to get. If I'd thought about it I could have taken them to show her. She'll be here for the coffee morning, it's my turn, so I could show them what we've bought then.'

I heard her in her bedroom putting her purchases away, then she was back with a bright smile, saying, 'I told Janice we'd been to the Dorchester for tea and that we'd met your cousin Robin, in Air Force officer's uniform too. She was so envious, Joanna, I felt rather sorry for her so I promised if she wanted to go up to London one day next week I'd go with her. You'll take us to the station, won't you, dear, and pick us up later?'

'Yes, Mother.'

'I'm not sure I shall enjoy it as much as I've enjoyed today, but there are times when one simply has to put oneself out. You're very quiet, Joanna, you're not saying much about the lovely day we've had.'

'I've got a headache, Mother, I think I'll go to bed soon.'

'Well, there are some aspirin in the kitchen cupboard. If I'd known I was going to be on my own I'd have stayed a little longer with Janice. Perhaps I'll give her a ring and go back there.'

'Yes, why don't you?'

Our camaraderie had always been a fragile thing. Now it had gone forever. As I lay sleepless throughout the night I could only think that I had to get away, but when I finally slept, fitfully and restlessly, all I could feel were her small hands clinging mercilessly to me as she begged me with tears streaming down her face not to leave her.

I awoke to rain pattering against the window, and the sound of my mother humming to herself in the kitchen.

I waited impatiently for the day she had chosen to visit London again with her friend. I would be alone for most of it and there was no likelihood that she would disturb me while I read through the missing letters.

How could she have done this to me? For years she had told me she liked to get up early because she slept badly. Now I knew it was so that she could take in the morning post and look through it alone. I thought about all those mornings when I had found her sitting at the breakfast table with the newspaper spread out in front of her and the post on a plate in the centre of the table. My eyes had been drawn to it eagerly, only to be met by the gentle shaking of her head and her voice saying, 'Nothing but circulars, darling, and bills. They seem to have forgotten about you.'

Now I was reading an affectionate letter from my father in distant Singapore and others in which he talked about his life in a land I had only ever dreamt about.

Grandma's letters were filled with warmth. She was interested in all I had been able to tell her in my letters, and I learned about Grandpa's heart attack and their decision to leave Reckmire to live with Aunt Marcia. Then came other letters asking why I had stopped writing, hoping that all was well with us, and begging me to write to them soon. It was when I read these pleas that the angry tears rolled down my cheeks and my entire being became imbued with a devastating anguish.

There were two letters from Italy in which Gabriella brought vividly alive that all too short time I had spent there and once again I found myself aching to see the sunshine and the beauty. She ended her letters with the words, 'Carlo sends you his love as I do', and seeing their two names linked I came to realise that that was how it would be. My young foolish heart had fashioned an impossible dream.

I think the letters which stunned me most was the one from my father in which he said he had opened an account in my name and would continue to add to it at the bank he had used in London. It was for a considerable amount and I squirmed with frustration when I thought how generous I had believed my mother to be when she bought some of my clothes and contributed to my very modest salary.

Why had she been afraid to let me have the use of my own money unless it was to keep me chained to the sort of life she had planned for us?

In all my life I had never felt such anger or such utter helplessness.

Chapter Eleven

My first urge was to write to my grandparents in Somerset
and tell them what had happened, then almost immediately I
realised that I could not do this. Some strange sense of loyalty
would not let me betray my mother. It was not possible to tell
any of them that for months she had hidden my letters so that
I believed they no longer cared about me, and what must my
father think when I had not even bothered to thank him for
his thoughtfulness?

I wanted to confront her with them. I wanted to watch
her face and see it crumple into fear and misery, but that
was one scene I couldn't face. I only knew that it couldn't
go on. I had to get away but at that moment I had no idea
how I could manage it.

I put the letters back where I had found them and then
went out into the warm sunlight because I felt like a caged
animal in the flat. I walked for what seemed miles without
thinking where I was going, and it was a church clock chiming
five o'clock that sent me hurrying back to the flat to pick up
the car.

I saw them walking up the station slope, two happy
shoppers armed with innumerable parcels, chatting happily
together, and when they saw me waiting for them they both
waved. My eyes refused to meet hers, but I took their parcels
and placed them in the boot of the car, then took my place
at the wheel. Mother was chatting like a little bird, about
their day, their lunch, their purchases, and I was glad that
the early-evening traffic required all my attention.

'What did you do with your day, Joanna?' Janice asked.

'You haven't been at the library today, have you?'

'No. I went for a long walk, it's such a beautiful day.'

'It was so hot in London,' Mother said. 'I've bought you something you'll like, Joanna. It is nice isn't it, Janice?'

'Oh, yes, it's lovely. Your mother's so kind to you, Joanna.'

I didn't speak. I kept my eyes rigidly on the road ahead and Janice said quickly, 'I shouldn't chatter while you're trying to concentrate, Joanna,' and Mother said, 'Joanna's a very sweet daughter, she knows she can ask me for anything within reason and I try to give it to her.'

I was glad when we had reached our destination and I was unloading the car and following them into the block of flats.

The long evening stretched in front of me and yet I knew if I suggested going out she would want to know where I was going and if we couldn't go together?

My present proved to be a cream leather handbag which was obviously expensive and which I dutifully admired. I prepared our evening meal while she put away her purchases and as we ate I listened to her describing them happily, ending with, 'Janice bought a summer coat. It wouldn't have been my choice but I didn't wish to influence her at all. Did you like her suit, Joanna? She said it was new.'

'I thought she looked very nice, Mother,' I replied evenly.

'Well, yes, but there again she always goes in for those dingy colours that don't really suit her. You're very quiet, Joanna. I thought you'd have been asking all sorts of questions about our day out.'

'Were there a lot of people in uniform?' I asked curiously.

'Well, yes, and the newspaper placards are stirring it all up again. Why can't they all sit back and enjoy the summer without constantly upsetting people by this talk about war? It seems to me those young people like wearing uniform, but it doesn't bring the war any nearer.'

How could I bear to think about a war? And yet it would be my best chance of getting away from Surrey and changing my life. I told myself that I was being selfish and irresponsible, and yet I couldn't bear to sit looking at her face. Not now when I knew what she had done to me.

We sat together in the sunlit lounge on the morning the Prime Minister told the country we were at war with Germany, and in the stunned silence which followed his announcement I looked across the room at Mother's face, the face of a lost spoilt child.

That same evening, as we were leaving the church hall where a meeting had been called to discuss the war news and how it might affect us, we met the Librarian, Miss Carson, who greeted us with a smile and invited us back to her house for coffee.

'How is your mother, Miss Carson?' Mother asked. 'Doesn't she mind having visitors?'

'She's away with her sister at the moment. It's a nice change for her and she was keen to go.'

'She's fit to travel then?'

'Well, it's a little bit like launching a battle ship but we managed. Aunt Pheobe lives in the country. It would be nice for Mother to stay there for a while, at least until we know what the war is going to do to us.'

'Oh, surely you don't think it's going to change things too drastically? We'll still be needing library books and everybody's saying it won't last beyond Christmas,' Mother said.

I did not miss the look Miss Carson conferred on her, a surprised, pitying look which was echoed in my heart.

I listened to them chatting about familiar things, and some strange urgency prompted me to ask, 'What is going to happen at the Library, Miss Carson? Old Mr Lathom's on the verge of retiring and the two young men will have to go. I was wondering where that left me?'

'Perhaps you'll get Mr Lathom's full-time job, Joanna, but it's more than likely that you'll have to go too. Being a part-time librarian isn't a necessary occupation. I've no doubt we shall soon be informed.'

Mother's dismay would have been comical if it hadn't been so heartfelt. 'Surely you don't mean Joanna will have to join one of the services? That's impossible. I need her at home, I'm far from well and too nervous to live alone. I shall get Doctor Marriot to tell them so if there is any hint that my daughter will have to go. Surely you're not serious, Miss Carson?'

She was quick to disassociate herself from further mention of my possible call up. Instead she changed the subject adroitly to talk of her views on the current influx of novels and recommendations on what she thought Mother would like to read. It was only when we arrived home that Mother said, 'Surely she wasn't serious about your having to leave the library, Joanna, especially about having to join one of the services?'

I reassured her. It was too soon and I couldn't live with the trauma I would have to go through in the waiting period.

I did not have to wait very long. At the end of November I received my call-up papers and my job at the library went to an elderly man who had served in the library service elsewhere and was not too far off retirement.

As for my Mother, the tears flowed and the hysterics. Indeed she worked herself up into such a state our next-door neighbour complained and said it was high time I sent for the doctor.

He turned out to be the junior partner, a young man not long qualified, who viewed my mother's distress with some alarm. He prescribed tranquillisers and advised me that if her distress continued she was well on the way to a nervous breakdown.

I tried to explain about the event that had started it, but the poor man was well and truly frightened and departed after receiving my promise that I would telephone him should she become worse. Instead I telephoned Doctor Marriot whom I had known all my life and he came in the early-evening of the same day.

Her reaction to his visit was far more subdued than it had been for his partner's, and when he left he pulled me gently into the hall and closed the door behind him.

'I've seen it all before, Joanna,' he said calmly. 'Your mother's a silly, spoiled woman who has never grown up. Years ago I told John Fowler that he was making a rod to break his back when he gave that girl of his all her own

129

way. He made a tyrant of her, and now you are going to have to assert yourself. Sometimes one has to be cruel to be kind. If you don't stand up for yourself she could spoil your life.'

'She's not really ill, is she, Doctor Marriot?' I asked anxiously.

'Not she. She's angry and she's frightened, of being alone, of being without a daughter who dances attention on her. When your father left I felt very sorry for you, Joanna, I felt she would take you over body and soul just as she took your father over until he took it into his head to cut and run. Now you're being given an opportunity to do likewise and you have to do it, Joanna. Get as far away as possible, and you'll see Linda will cope, she'll show us all that she's a survivor.'

'The time before I go is going to be dreadful.'

'Yes, I expect it will be. Don't worry, I'll pop round tomorrow and give her a good talking to. So you're going into the Wrens?'

'Yes. I've always loved the sea and I like the uniform. Mother hated the sea, she doesn't know yet that it's the service I want.'

'Your mother's tried to shelter you just as she was sheltered. Doesn't your father encourage you to make a life for yourself every time he writes?'

I smiled. 'I doubt if he would put such thoughts into a letter,' I said softly.

'No, I suppose not. Your mother would probably want to know everything he said. Ah, well, don't worry, Joanna. In a few weeks your entire life will be very different and it's my advice to you to let the past go. There's a great big adventure just around the corner.'

He kept his promise to visit us the next day and I left him talking to Mother in the living room when I left for the library. One or two of her friends came in to change their books and one of them said, 'How will your mother get along without you, Joanna?'

'I'm sure she'll manage very well, Mrs Stepson,' I replied with a smile.

'Well, of course we'll still have our bridge parties and

130

our coffee mornings and we'll no doubt take up some sort of war work at St Mary's. The vicar's organising all sorts of things. There's an Air Force camp not far away. If you joined the RAF it's possible you could end up there.'

As far away as possible, Doctor Marriot had said, and that's how I wanted it to be.

There was an atmosphere throughout the evening but the hysterics had gone to be replaced by silences when she occasionally dabbed at her eyes and treated me to long sighs.

I tried to make conversation by asking if any of her friends had called and telling her that I had seen one or two of them in the library. She sniffed disdainfully. 'Mrs Stepson will take over everything the Vicar starts, she's that sort of woman, and I'm annoyed with Janice. I introduced her to two of my friends in the High Street the other morning and she's invited them round for tea without asking me. It's the last time I ever invite her here when I have guests.'

'I told Janice you didn't feel well, Mother, and she saw the doctor arriving this morning. She probably thought you wouldn't feel well enough to visit,' I replied.

'She could have asked all the same.'

'Please, Mother, try not to fall out with your friends over such small things. You're going to need all of them in the months ahead and looking for slights and jealousies is silly.'

'It's not me who's being silly,' she snapped. 'Really, Joanna, I'd expect you to take my part, not that of some woman who is being mean to me.'

Again there was the long silence, the weary sigh, and in desperation I said, 'It's my half day tomorrow. Suppose we take a run out in the car? We can invite two of your friends to go with us if you like?'

'No. We'll go on our own. When you've gone I shan't know what to do about the car. I don't drive and they're talking about petrol rationing. Perhaps I'd better sell it. You might not want to come back here.'

'That's up to you, Mother. It was Grandfather's car. Why don't you learn to drive it, if only for shopping and visiting friends?'

131

'Your father could have taught me ages ago but he never offered.'

'You never wanted to learn, Mother, and Grandfather didn't exactly encourage you.'

'No. He was always protective, afraid I might have an accident, and your father always liked a fast car. I talked him out of those silly open cars he always had when I first met him, but the big powerful ones were no better. I didn't want to drive any of them.'

In the few days left to us I tried desperately hard to understand her and to love her. She was morose and tearful, and I was glad of the time she spent with her friends and the few days I had left for my job at the library.

On my last day I was touched when Miss Carson presented me with a warm woollen dressing-gown which she hoped I would be able to make use of wherever the Navy decided to send me. Mother made no comment when I showed it to her and I was pleased that she elected to go out on the evening before I left which enabled me to do my packing in peace.

On the following morning I stood outside the flats waiting for the taxi I had ordered to take me to the station. I'd expected tears and much sobbing, but instead her expression had been hard, her face etched in lines of bitterness. I looked up at our window anxiously and raised my hand in farewell as the taxi sped up the curving drive. She was at the window staring down at me, but she neither raised her hand in farewell then nor when we drove away. Instead she continued to stand there until we drove out into the road. It was the ultimate mark of displeasure, that impassive stance which spoke volumes.

Chapter Twelve

The force of the gale hit me like a knife as I stepped down on to a vast expanse of concrete which had once been a play area for the holiday camp which had been taken over by the Admiralty. The rain lashed down, dancing in the puddles that covered the concrete, finding its way inside the upturned collar of my mackintosh, saturating my neck.

There were about twenty of us, wet and miserable and hungry, but inside I glowed with a sense of freedom I hadn't known for some considerable time.

A woman petty officer of ample proportions lined us up in a dismal group, surveying us with weary distaste before barking a command to straighten up, turn right and quick march. The girl beside me muttered, 'I 'ope we're not expected to see much of her. She's got it in for us already.'

I smiled. She'd been in my compartment in the train but we'd been too far apart for conversation, though occasionally she'd smiled and I'd begun to hope that we might be billeted together.

There was no time for conversation, however. We were shepherded into a corrugated iron hut for twelve girls, with narrow beds and tiny lockers, a hut which was evidently heated by a foul-smelling and smoking stove. I had always thought that boarding school had been spartan but this was much worse. But nothing, however dire, could take away the joy of being free from Mother's sulks and tantrums. I was pleased to see that the girl from the train was to occupy the next bed and after telling us to unpack as quickly as possible and stand by our beds, the petty officer departed.

The girl by the next bed grinned cheerfully. 'My name's Sally Spencer,' she said. 'I suppose you can tell by my accent that I'm a Lancashire lass.'

I held out my hand, saying, 'I'm Joanna Albemarle. I do hope we'll be able to stay together.'

'Albemarle's an unusual name. There were Albemarles who lived in a house called Reckmire Hall. I don't suppose you've ever heard of it?'

'Oh, yes, I do know it. It belongs to my grandparents.'

She stared at me curiously before saying, 'I've never seen you around there.'

'I went every summer for several years. I knew Reckmire Marsh and the point. I knew the fells and the park and was friendly with a girl in the village, Lottie, her mother had the baker's shop.'

'I know it. They goes for miles to that shop. I know Freda Felton better than Lottie, she's quite a girl is our Freda, gone into the army she has. If I know 'er she'll 'ave as many soldiers as Montgomerie afore the war's over.'

I laughed, and the girl at the other side of her laughed also. My mother wouldn't have approved of Sally Spencer. She would have regarded her as brash and rather common. I thought she was warm and funny.

We unpacked quickly and put our belongings into the lockers, then dutifully we stood at the ends of our beds and almost immediately the petty officer was back in the company of an officer who eyed us with the same sort of weary acceptance. We were all part of a pattern, call-up girls, miserable and reluctant, cold and hungry, standing rigidly to attention while she informed us where we could find the shower block, the medical block, the hut where we would receive our uniforms, and last of all the Naafi.

We were expected to be in the shower block at six o'clock and lights out by ten and advised that if we wished to ask any questions now was the time. The last remark was greeted by silence, and after giving us a long hard look they both left, closing the door so sharply the entire room was enveloped in a puff of smoke from the dismal-looking stove.

'I wonder if it's like this in all the services?' one of the girls asked sharply.

'Worse, I should think,' said another. 'I only joined the Wrens because they get to wear their own nightclothes and their stockings are decent. You should see the things my sister's expected to wear in the Women's Army.'

Weeks passed. Long days when we went to our beds exhausted, often miserably cold, and the war was at stalemate.

At the end of six months we were all interviewed to decide on our futures. By this time they were well aware of our potentials, our backgrounds and ambitions, and we knew the time was approaching when we would go our separate ways.

'I'm destined for the cookhouse,' Sally informed me cheerfully. 'My mother was a housekeeper for old Mr Grimshaw and my father was his gardener. I was brought up on the estate and helped out in the kitchen when I left school. I've told them all that so no doubt they've earmarked me for somethin' similar. What about you, Joanna?'

'I don't know. My mother never went out to work and my father's employed by the Foreign Office. He's out in Singapore. I worked part-time at the local library. It's anybody's guess what that fits me for.'

'Office work probably, but you can drive, can't you?'

'Yes.'

'Well, that's an accomplishment. They're lookin' for drivers.'

'How do you know?'

'Well, I'm sure they will be. Not many of the girls drive, only you and Sybil Benson. She's 'opin' for a job drivin' some Admiral about.'

We laughed. Sybil had high flung notions about a great many things and wasn't exactly the most popular girl in the group.

I was amazed how much they knew about me. The sort of work my father had done for most of his life, as well as his father before him. The knew that Grandpa had been knighted and that that one of his daughters was married to an Italian. I wasn't quite sure if this would be detrimental considering that we were at war with Italy.

At the end of six months we were given a week's leave and we said our farewells in the knowledge that none of us would be going back there. We were told we would be informed during leave where we would have to report to next, and I headed for home on a spring morning when the trees were bursting into new life with a strange new expectancy in my heart.

Mother was out. The flat stared back at me impersonally with its pretty-pretty living room. There was a bunch of early daffodils on the coffee table but apart from these the room seemed unlived in. I had been unable to write to tell her about my leave because it had been sprung on us at the last moment so I hadn't really expected her to be there to greet me. Nevertheless I felt vaguely lost as I started to unpack and put my things away.

From the front window I was able to stare across the park and partway down the High Street which was busy with morning shoppers. I was struck by the unusual absence of cars along that busy road.

I watched Miss Whipple come along the drive with her white Pekinese, then further down the road I saw Mother walking with another woman and a man, chatting animatedly together. At the gates they stopped and the man handed several of the parcels he had been carrying to the two women and after saying their farewells Mother and her companion came towards the flats while the man continued down the street. I didn't know either of them, but decided to meet Mother at the door rather than surprise her when she entered the flat.

She was alone when she stepped out of the lift, and I went forward quickly to embrace her while she looked at me for several moments in stunned silence before saying, 'Why didn't you let me know you were coming home? How long have you been here?'

'Not long, Mother, I saw you walking along the street.'

'I went to the shops with Mrs Craig, she's new here. Her husband died last year and her daughter's in Australia. The man we were with is Mr Walsh. His wife died just before Christmas. He comes to St Mary's and was kind enough to take us for coffee and carry most of our shopping. If we can get hold of some petrol we could perhaps take the car out this afternoon, it's ages since I went for a drive and it's a lovely day.'

'You didn't sell the car then?'

'Well, no. Mr Walsh has kept his eye on it for me. He understands cars and assures me it's taken no harm over the winter.'

'Hasn't he suggested taking it out, Mother?'

'I couldn't possibly go with him. You know what they're all like here, they'd have had a lot to say, and he's very circumspect.'

'Miss Carson was asking if I'd heard from you lately when I was in the library yesterday. I suppose you'll be going in to see her?'

'I have a week's leave, Mother. I hope to see all the people I know whilst I'm home.'

'You can't possibly spend all your time visiting, Joanna, or you'll have no time to spend with me.'

During the rest of the afternoon I listened to her going on and on about her friends, her activities, and the absence of things in the shops. She asked no questions about my six months as a Wren until we were sitting down to tea when she said, 'You haven't said a word about what you've been doing, Joanna. Have you met some nice girls?'

Some devilment prompted me to say, 'I met a girl from near Reckmire, Mother, Sally Spencer. She knew some of the people I knew. We had a lot to talk about.'

She stared at me without emotion. 'Are her family gentry too, Joanna?'

'Her parents work for Mr Grimshaw. You know, the Grimshaws had that large house on the edge of the fell at the other side of the village?'

'You say they worked there?'

'Yes. Her mother was the cook, her father the gardener.'

Her displeasure was evident, and yet she changed the subject abruptly. She was learning that, just like my father, I was averse to her particular brand of snobbery.

My visit to the library was rushed because Mother had

made plans for us; indeed, as the week progressed she had plans for every moment.

I waited on them at their coffee morning and marvelled that the war seemed not to have touched them. They gossipped about their neighbours, the events at St Mary's, and their only thoughts about the war were centred on the absence of certain things from the shops.

On my last afternoon Mrs Craig and Mr Walsh were invited for tea. Mrs Craig arrived carrying a large volume of snapshots of her daughter's family in Sydney, and Mr Walsh came with a genial smile on his face and a large bunch of spring flowers.

He informed me that Mother had been very lonely but had never complained, a statement I found difficult to believe. He insisted on assisting her with the crockery, the carrying in of cakes and sandwiches, and, after we had eaten, the removal of the debris.

Considering that I was the one who had been away none of them seemed the slightest bit interested in me. Instead they talked about themselves, the vicar's attempts to enroll them on his various committees and the food rationing which was decidedly unfair to those living alone.

In the evening after they had left Mother said tentatively, 'Mr Walsh is very kind, Joanna, he's also very lonely. I hope you don't mind his coming round here for tea now and again?'

'Of course not, Mother, why should I?'

'Well, I don't want you getting the wrong ideas.'

'Mother, you're a free agent, you can do exactly as you please, you know that.'

'Well, I'll be awfully lonely when you've gone. You haven't mentioned your letter.'

'I was expecting it, Mother. It's to tell me where to report and what time.'

I had not thought she would attempt to hide letters from the Admiralty, but had taken the precaution of being up early every morning since my arrival.

I hated not being able to trust her, but I couldn't help it. When my letter arrived it was to inform me that I was to report to a naval base on the east coast of Scotland, a wild lonely coast where the north-east wind swept with all the cruelty of an arctic winter. Here I learned to drive huge lorries and worked on their maintenance, but in the evenings I worked hard over my books and emerged at the end of seven months with a junior commission and a reposting to London.

It was a different world in my new officer's uniform, driving senior naval officers from one conference to another, from the south coast to the Admiralty, and with the posting came a flat owned by the Admiralty in the West End of London which I was to share with another Wren.

It was almost dark when I arrived with my luggage at the flat on the second floor of a large brick house in a fashionable square. There was no response to the doorbell but I was surprised to find that the door opened to my touch. It led into a small square hall, and beyond through an open door I could see a large comfortably furnished room with the glow of firelight reflected on the ceiling.

I called out but there was no reply so I entered the room, leaving my luggage in the hall.

I could hear the sound of running water and when I went through into one of the bedrooms beyond I was faced with chaos. Clothes were strewn across the bed, over the chairs, littering the floor, and I stared around me in dismay. Then from the doorway came a cheerful voice, saying, 'You've arrived then. Golly, I'm sorry the room's such a mess but I've only just come back from leave. This isn't your room by the way, yours is next-door. I'm Jill Preston.'

'I'm Joanna Albemarle,' I said, holding out my hand, then with a smile, 'Do you actually get to wear all these civvy clothes?'

She laughed. 'I was hoping to wear a dress tonight but I've had second thoughts. Everybody will be in uniform. How I was longing to wear this.'

She picked up a scarlet creation from the bed and holding it in front of her whirled round the room, and she was so pretty I could well imagine the impact she would have made amongst those more soberly clad.

'What do you think?' she asked laying the dress back on the bed.

'It depends where you're going,' I answered with a smile.

'Well, some of the girls do wear their civvy clothes but most of them are in uniform. I guess I'll stick to uniform. I've got a date with the most divine man, I love him to death.'

'Is he somebody you're engaged to?'

'Heavens no, I've known him a little while. We were introduced at the Searchlight Club, that's where we're going tonight. I say, he's got a friend with him, somebody on leave, so there'll be three of us. I said I didn't mind, I thought his friend was sure to meet somebody. Why don't you join us?'

'I'm sure his friend would prefer to find his own companion,' I answered.

'Why should he? You're very pretty, and obviously very nice. He'll be delighted I've taken you along. Do come, Joanna, you'll have a wonderful time.'

'What is this Searchlight Club? I've been shut away in Scotland, I don't know anything about the activities here in London.'

'Oh, it's a club somebody dreamed up in a basement under an office block. It's got atmosphere and also a terrific band. They're either too old or too handicapped for the services, but they're wonderful musicians. We all go to enjoy ourselves, simply to escape from this wretched war for an hour or two.'

'What do we do if there's an air-raid?' I asked curiously.

'We stay where we are and hope we're immune. Two nights ago I danced there until the All Clear went and we came out into the dawn, unscathed and smiling. Do say you'll come, Joanna.'

'I'll think about it while I'm unpacking. I travelled overnight from Scotland so I am rather tired.'

'Darling, we're all tired. If you decide not to go it's more than likely that you'll spend the night in an air-raid shelter. You'll sing songs and listen to some idiot threatening gloom and doom and forecasting the end of the world. When do you report for duty?'

'The day after tomorrow.'

'Well then, you've all tomorrow to get over tonight, and you might even be spending it with somebody as wonderful as my date.'

I smiled and started to unpack while she perched on the edge of my bed watching everything I took out of my case.

'What are you expecting from your new job?' she asked idly.

'I don't really know.'

'Well, I'll tell you what you'll get. Ferrying much married Admirals or other ranks around London. Most of them are dour, obsessed with winning the war, wives they seldom see and school fees. Anything remotely close is frowned upon from on high, although you may get the odd rumbustious tar who will pinch your bottom and leer at you through the fog.'

I laughed. 'It sounds as if you might have had one or two of those.'

'Well, I did drive a Rear Admiral down from Arbroath who produced a bottle of whisky at the top of every hill and suggested we drink a toast to freedom. By the time we arrived in London he was very sleepy and very drunk. Needless to say I declined the whisky but laughed all the way home.'

I decided I was going to like Jill. She was someone I needed, someone warm and funny, obviously delighted when I promised to go with her to the Searchlight Club.

There was nothing obvious about the entrance to the Club except a row of steps that led down from street level under a large building, but as we entered a long narrow passage I could hear music and occasional laughter. There were more steps, then at the end of another passage we were entering a large room filled with people. People dancing, people smoking, people talking, and it was dark and misty with cigarette smoke, but through the smoke I could dimly discern a dais on which sat several musicians, and as we circled the floor Jill's eyes were eagerly scanning the room in search of her date.

'I can't see him,' she mumbled, 'perhaps he isn't here yet?'

141

'Can we find somewhere to sit until he comes?' I suggested.

'Yes, over there against the wall, we can see everybody from there.'

A lot of people seemed to know Jill. They made room for us at the table and handed round cigarettes and ordered drinks for us. They were all service men and women, and most of them wore uniform.

There was an anonymity about this collection of men and women in khaki, air force and navy blue. Plain or pretty, handsome or ordinary, uniform was a great leveller. The music was wonderful: sentimental, nostalgic melodies designed to stay in our hearts forever.

I was introduced by my first name and immediately I was chatting to those around me as if I had known them for years, spontaneously and easily, although later I could not even remember what we had said. I was suddenly aware of Jill saying, 'Here they are,' and I looked up to see two figures pushing their way through the crowd and then, incredulously, I was looking up into Robin's face which was staring down at me in amazement.

It was gone in a flash and while Jill stood up to embrace him I was looking at Paul Cheviot in the uniform of an Army Captain.

Room was made for them at the table, and then Robin and Jill were dancing and Paul was saying quietly, 'Well, well, so the fair Joanna has been allowed to enter the real world.'

'I don't know what you mean,' I retorted angrily.

'I rather think you do,' he said evenly. 'I think we're expected to entertain each other. Shall we dance?'

We danced in silence but I was aware of his dark brooding eyes looking down at me curiously. All around me men and women were laughing and chatting to each other normally, and yet I could find no words to say to this man who had always had the power to antagonise me. When my eyes met his he smiled cynically.

'How on earth did you manage to tear yourself away from your mother to become a Wren? I would have thought she'd have been totally opposed to anything concerned with the sea,' he said drily.

142

I didn't answer him. He knew too much about me, my mother's foibles, my sheltered childhood, my parents' separation after which Reckmire saw me no more, and like Robin he probably thought me ungrateful towards grandparents who had made much of me. I was glad when the dance ended and we returned to our table. I was wishing I hadn't come. For one thing I was constantly aware of Robin's eyes on me and between the four of us there was a peculiar feeling of tension.

Others coming into the club informed us that overhead in a clear starlit night German bombers droned, followed by the sickening crunch of falling bombs, but we danced as though danger could not touch us, with a strange arrogance that in the midst of a city under bombardment we were immune, existing in a private world of cigarette smoke, laughter, the wailing of saxophones and urgent fleeting passions.

I danced with a great many men that night, men who flirted and laughed but who could see no further than the present. Men with memories of the horrors they had seen and expected soon to be returning to. And I watched Paul dancing with a succession of girls, aware that they were flattered by his maddening superior smile and a charm that could move from sombre gravity to light-hearted camaraderie. It was much later when I danced with Robin. Then suddenly the music changed and we were waltzing to the slow haunting music of 'Auld Lang Syne', and all around the room only candles flickered and died, and we stood to attention while the National Anthem was played.

It had been romance to a generation crying out for it, desire and regret, coupled with a haunting fear that life as we had known it had gone forever leaving behind nothing but a remembered pain.

The All Clear had already sounded when we walked out into the night. Cheerful farewells were being called and we were joined by others emerging from air-raid shelters and tube stations. People laughing and cheerful with the relief of knowing that they would soon see another dawn breaking over the rooftops of London, but miserably aware of the glow from the night's disasters.

I walked with the crowd, leaving Jill and Robin to follow.

I had not seen Paul leave the club but I thought he would probably be with one of the girls I had seen him dancing with. As I reached the flat people were urging me to return to the club again and then they had gone on, laughing and chattering across the square. The flat felt cold and unwelcoming. A pile of ashes lay in the grate and I went immediately through to my bedroom where I turned on a bar of the electric fire.

In spite of the lateness of the hour and my weariness I felt if Jill was to come through the door at that moment to announce that there was more dancing, more of the crowd, I would quite willingly have gone with her.

I pulled a chair up in front of the fire and sank into it, letting the warmth wash over me. I remember nothing else. It was Jill's alarm clock ringing shrilly in the room next-door that woke me, and almost immediately I was aware of the sound of traffic and rain pattering on the windowpane. I went to pull back the curtains, staring dully at my wristwatch. It was just after eight o'clock and I was still in my uniform.

I heard Jill go into the bathroom so I undressed quickly and shrugged into my dressing-gown, then hurried into the kitchen to make toast and coffee. She came into the kitchen carrying some letters in her hands, and without looking at me sank into a chair and started to open her mail.

She looked so unutterably weary I was prompted to ask, 'Didn't you sleep?'

She lifted her head slowly and eyed me for several minutes in stony silence so that I began to feel uncomfortable. Then, pouring herself a cup of coffee, she said flatly, 'Remind me not to take you along next time I'm meeting some man I fancy.'

I stared at her stupidly. 'I'm sorry, Jill, I don't know what you mean.'

'Oh, come on, Joanna. You and Robin. All those covert glances. He was my date but you danced the last waltz with him, neither of you spared me a thought, and you never even tried to like the friend he brought along.'

I stared at her in amazement. Her face was cold, her entire concentration given over to the toast she was buttering on her plate, and in all her ridiculous accusations the only thing I could find to defend myself on was the last waltz.

'I'm sorry, Jill,' I stammered hesitantly, 'I didn't know it was the last waltz. One minute we were dancing a quickstep, then they were lighting the candles and playing "Auld Lang Syne". You never told me that would happen. I thought I saw you dancing with Paul.'

'You did. He took pity on me when he saw what was happening.'

'Nothing was happening.'

'Well, for your information Robin hasn't promised to telephone me or let me know when he'll be in town again. In my book that's as good as telling me it's over. I don't want to talk about it any more. I don't want to talk to you yet awhile.'

I could feel my face burning with resentment. I wanted to tell her everything but there wasn't time. Instead I said, 'Jill, there isn't time now, and what I have to tell you would take too long. Will you be in tonight?'

'I don't know.'

'Well, whenever we have the time, I'll tell you about Robin and me.'

'So there is more? Last night he wasn't the same Robin I've known for the last fifteen months. He was always so sweet and warm. Last night he was remote, and when he looked at you there was a question in his eyes.'

'Jill, he's my cousin,' I cried.

She stared at me in open-mouthed surprise, then looking at her watch hurriedly she said, 'I have to go. I've no idea when I'll be back, but like you say, we have to talk.'

Without another word she gathered up her shoulder bag and her hat and let herself out of the flat while I sank into a chair at the kitchen table. After a while I could feel my eyes pricking with tears. It was a disastrous start to my time in London but I couldn't see that any action of mine should have changed Robin's feelings for Jill or hers for him.

Chapter Thirteen

For days our conversation was stilted and Jill gave me no opportunity to tell her more about Robin and myself, and then one day there was a new man in her life and she sang about the flat and drooled over bunches of red roses and huge boxes of chocolates.

It was one wind-swept Sunday afternoon when the streets were awash with rain and flashes of lightning spasmodically lit up the room. I was trying to compose a letter to my mother. In her letters she showed little interest in what I was doing, but moaned constantly about food rationing and the blackout. Mr Walsh was a tower of strength, escorting her to and from her bridge parties, seeing that her friends appeared on time and advising them all on all manner of things.

Jill sat curled up in a corner of the sofa, staring into the fire, occasionally dipping into the box of chocolates on the cushion beside her. She always ate her chocolate ration and usually most of mine. The box on the sofa was a bonus from her new Canadian.

Satisfied at last with the contents of my letter, I folded it and was putting it into the envelope when she said, 'I'm over Robin now, Joanna. Why don't you tell me about him?'

'Does that mean that you no longer see him?'

'Oh, well, he's back in East Anglia. I really did love him, you know.'

'You surely didn't stop seeing him because of me?'

'He was going back anyway, but I'm not about to ask you to go dancing with Gerry and me.'

I smiled, and after a few minutes she said, 'Tell me about

it, Joanna. I've always had the feeling there's some deep dark secret in your soul, you never talk about your folks. Your mother only lives in Surrey but you never visit, not even when you have a couple of days off. What's wrong with your family?'

The relief of unburdening myself to Jill was enormous. For one thing she knew none of the people I was talking about, and the sense of disloyalty was not so acute.

She sat in silence while I poured out the wretchedness of my schooldays when I couldn't go swimming with the others and the way I was ostracised as a result. I described my grandparents' house and the marshes at Reckmire, and told her how Robin had dragged me to safety up the cruel rocks.

When I came to my parents' separation it became more difficult, but then came the joy of my visit to Italy and the first faint stirring of a hopeless romance.

It was only when I came to the hidden letters that my voice faltered and a feeling of deep shame swept over me. Not my shame, but shame that I had a mother who would do such a thing. I told her at last, in short halting sentences, how Robin had spoken to me coldly, thinking it was I who had forgotten people I had loved and who had been kind to me.

When the sorry tale was finally told she said nothing for a long time but sat staring into the fire, hugging her knees, and I was dismayed to see that her eyes were filled with tears.

I smiled a little tremulously. 'It's not worth crying over, Jill, but I have to make sure that it can never happen again.'

'You can't go back there, Joanna. You've made the break, now you've got to think about the future. London is full of nice eligible men. You have to find one so that after the war he'll be there to keep you away.'

'I don't think that's the answer,' I replied seriously. 'If I fall in love with somebody then it might be, but not simply to go looking for a substitute for the past. I need to make my peace with my grandparents and find my father.'

We stared at each other across the hearth and our thoughts ran on similar lines. The Japanese bombing of Pearl Harbour had brought America into the war and the talk everywhere

147

was of its effect on Singapore and our territories in the Far East. My father's safety was a constant worry and although I had started to write to the last address I had from him, none of my letters were returned and I received no replies.

'Did you tell Robin about the hidden letters?' Jill asked.

'No. How could I? Besides when I saw him that afternoon in London I wasn't sure, and then when I found what Mother had done I was too ashamed to tell him or anybody else.'

'So Robin knows nothing of all this?'

'He knew that Mother had problems with Father's family. Somehow or other she never fitted in, and because she made her fear of the sea an excuse we never went to Reckmire. I loved it so much, Jill. I came to hate all those years when she'd kept me away, but she is my mother and she needs my loyalty. I don't think she can help the way she is, she's spoilt and demanding, and I feel mean when I stay away when I could so easily go there. It's just that this terrible war came into my life like a friend and I hate having to feel this way.'

'What will you do when your leave comes up? You're due for some pretty soon, aren't you?'

'Yes. I don't know. It's something I shall have to think about.'

I was glad that Jill allowed the matter to drop. In the weeks that followed I was kept busy working long hours at the Admiralty or kicking my heels at some dismal base waiting for an officer I had been detailed to drive back to London. There were nights when we spent long hours in a sleeping bag in some local bomb shelter and I learned that Jill's Canadian had gone the way of Robin and now she seemed entirely besotted with an American she called Hank. He was young and dashing, he was also engaged to be married to a girl back in Boston, but he filled our flat with flowers and it worried me that there could only be heartbreak at the end of it for Jill.

When I said as much to her she said lightly, 'None of us knows what will happen, Joanna. Hitler's got hold of most of Europe, Italy's got the rest, and in the Far East there's Japan sitting like a spider just waiting for us. Nobody can take away what we've had so live for today, I say, let tomorrow take care of itself.'

She grinned at me across the table where we sat over our evening meal.

'How is it that I find all these marvellous men to drive about and you don't?' she demanded.

I grinned back. 'I don't know. I'm not surprised they call it the Senior Service,' I grumbled, 'I only get to meet the old ones. All the young ones must be at sea.'

'Well, I've met some of the young ones. It's because you look so sensible and upper crust, just the sort of girl any Admiral would want to drive him around.'

'You make me sound awfully dull.'

'Not dull, Joanna, but that mother of yours conditioned you into looking too nice, beautiful and sacrosanct. Aloof from ordinary mortals. Come to the club tonight, Hank's out of town and we could go together. There'll be people there we know and lots of men to dance with.'

I agreed to go with her, and as we strolled along the street in the direction of the club she asked quietly, 'Have you decided to go home next week, Joanna?'

'No. I expect I shall, though, I haven't fixed up to do anything else.'

'Have you told your mother you'll be going?'

'No. It doesn't matter if I simply arrive.'

Her face was thoughtful as we walked the rest of the way. It was only later when we sat with our coffee before going to bed that she said, 'It's my birthday on Saturday, Joanna, and Hank is taking me away for a long weekend, somewhere in the country. Are you very shocked?'

'No. Are you very much in love with him?'

'I think so. I like Americans. They're audacious and brash, but they know how to make a girl feel great.'

'And after, when he's gone home, back to her?'

'Oh, Joanna, that's a lifetime away. He may not be going home, she may not be waiting for him, none of us may be going home. Stop thinking about what might be and enjoy what there is. Don't go home on leave, Joanna, find somewhere else to go.'

I could hear her speaking on the telephone when I let myself into the flat several evenings later, and when I entered the room I thought she seemed very pensive as she replaced the receiver.

For a moment I wondered if she had been speaking to Hank, but then she said, 'Hank and I are going out to dinner this evening, Joanna, why don't you go to the club? It's better than going off to the air-raid shelter on your own.'

'I'll think about it. Actually I thought I'd wash my hair, and I might telephone home later on.'

She gave me a long hard look before saying, 'You've decided then?'

'Not definitely.'

'I'm getting some cards already, there's one there from Robin,' she said evenly.

'How nice of him. So you see, he hasn't forgotten you after all,' I replied.

'No. There's nothing sentimental about it. He just says, "Have a happy birthday, love from Robin." The sort of sentiments my brother's expressed.'

'You do have Hank, Jill.'

'Of course. With chocolates and nylons, flowers and perfume, and the weekend to look forward to. It's funny but I was never like this with Robin, I just wanted to see him, wanted to see his smile and the laughter in his eyes. I wanted to hear his voice and see the way his hair shone under the lamplight. Which is love, Joanna? Hank gives me so much. Is it all that I'm in love with and not the man at all?'

How did I know? I had only known shy adolescent love, that first faint blossoming of a passion doomed to fade as quickly as it had blossomed, but I was remembering Robin racing across the beach towards me and my first startling thought that he was beautiful, the most beautiful human being I had ever seen. Somebody who had been a part of that exquisite day when I discovered the gulls and the wind and the urgent sound of the sea.

Jill went off with her American on Saturday morning and I still hadn't made up my mind what to do in the next four days. The flat felt strangely empty without her radio constantly blaring out dance music. After I had washed the breakfast things I stood for a long time staring out of the window, watching the normal life of London pass below me.

Sunlight lit up the square, warm early-October sunlight, and I thought about Mother's flat with its pretty-pretty lounge and the niceties of morning coffee and afternoon tea. Meetings with her friends, her blushing searching for excuses when Mr Walsh came round, and my spirits plummeted in spite of the beautiful sunny day.

I was about to turn away when I saw a small open tourer drawing up in front of the flats and a man wearing Air Force Officer's uniform jump nimbly out of the driver's seat. The sun glinted on his blond hair and he looked up at the windows, shielding his eyes against the light. In that moment my heart missed several beats as I recognised Robin and realised that I would have to tell him that Jill had gone away for the weekend with somebody else.

I waited anxiously for the bell to ring, then there he was, smiling down at me with all his old camaraderie, and then he was in the flat sitting on the arm of the settee and I was stammering an excuse as to why Jill wasn't there.

'I know she isn't here, he said, smiling. 'She's gone into the country for a few days. She told me she was going, and you have four days leave, haven't you?'

'Well, yes. Did Jill tell you?'

'She did. She also told me that you hadn't decided what to do with it.'

'No. I suppose I'll go home.'

'You don't sound very enthusiastic, Joanna.'

'No, I'm not.'

'In that case, why don't you come with me? I've got the car. It's not exactly a pristine model but it belongs to three of us who use it whenever we get leave. We're due for a few days of glorious autumn weather and I have to drive North to Kendal, part holiday, part business. Are you going to join me?'

'Oh, Robin, I'd love to. Are you sure you want to take me when there must be dozens of people you'd rather take?'

He threw back his head and laughed, then catching my look of surprise, sobered up immediately, saying, 'Poor

Joanna, what has happened to all that independence, that sparkle when we put you on that pony and when you stormed back at Paul whenever he made you angry? I'm asking you to go with me because I want you to come, because you love Reckmire and I thought you'd like to see it again.'

'You're going to Reckmire!' I cried hopefully. 'But I thought you said the house was now a nursing home?'

'It is, but there's still a flat on top of the house that the family can use, and I have to see Grandpa's solicitors in Kendal. I can't think why he never changed them when they went to live in Somerset.'

'Do they know you intended to ask me to go with you?'

'They know I was coming to see you. Grandpa had a stroke a few weeks ago and unfortunately hasn't fully recovered. He walks badly and can't use his right arm, and Grandma too is looking very frail these days. He's bothered about his will and I'm going with all sorts of instructions about what he wants to happen when he shuffles off this mortal coil.'

'Oh, Robin, I am sorry, I would so like to see them. Will you tell them how much I've missed them?'

'It seems you have a lot to tell me, Joanna. Between us we should have enough to fill four whole days of each other's company.'

What a joy it was to get out of uniform and into a plain skirt and white silk blouse, with my hair held back by a coloured chiffon scarf and high-heeled court shoes on my feet.

'Better wear a light coat,' Robin advised. 'Unless you would like me to put the hood up?'

'Gracious, no. I want to feel the sun on my face and the wind in my hair.'

'You're not much like your mother, are you? I remember Uncle Bob had to get rid of his tourer because your mother hated it.'

I didn't answer but busied myself shrugging my arms into my camel coat, hoping that Robin wouldn't continue with his talk of the past.

I felt exhilarated with the wind and the speed of the little car when we were at last on the open road. Conversation was not easy above the sound of the engine and the rush of the breeze so we drove mainly in silence, a warm companionable silence, and my heart felt as light as a bird when I thought that ahead of us lay the sea and the long reach of Reckmire Marsh.

We ate our lunch at an inn Robin remembered from the old days, a quaint place of small rooms and dark oak rafters, where the innkeeper's wife apologised profusely because there wasn't a great deal on the menu.

'I can do you potato pie, love, or sausage and mash, but the days o' good caterin' 'ave gone til the war's over,' she said sadly.

We settled for sausage and mash and apple pie to follow, and over our lunch we talked about the family and our days near the marshes.

'I wonder what has happened to Aunt Corallie?' I asked.

'Granny desperately wanted to bring her back to England before the war started but she wouldn't come. She said her place was with her husband but we do wonder what has happened to them and if that beautiful place where they lived still belongs to them.'

'Why did they ever go in with Germany when so many of them loved the British more?'

'Why do we ever do anything, Joanna? Why did your mother keep you away from us and why did you never answer any of our letters?'

He was staring into my eyes, his face grave and perplexed, and hurriedly I said, 'Please, Robin, I don't want to talk about it now but I will tell you soon. When I've gathered up enough courage.'

How wonderful it seemed to be driving along familiar lanes where honeysuckle climbed rampantly over the hedgerows and where the trees leaned awkwardly away from the sea.

When we reached the village's rambling high street that swept downhill towards the church I sat forward in my seat, rewarded by seeing Mrs Peabody standing on her doorstep, arms akimbo, holding forth to three other women one of them leaning on her broom, the other two carrying shopping bags. I laughed joyously. Nothing had changed.

'Do you know them?' Robin asked curiously.

'I know Mrs Peabody, the village gossip.'

153

'Every village has one,' Robin said smiling, and by this time we were passing the church with the towers of Reckmire before us and the vista of the marshes and the blue haze of the sea.

There were no gardeners at work on the formal gardens, but here and there were groups of young officers sitting in the sunlight or sauntering along the paths. Robin's face mirrored my thoughts.

I stood alone in the empty hall waiting for him to come back to me. He had gone in search of someone in authority and I stared disconsolately up the shallow curving staircase, thinking how impersonal it seemed, impersonal and clinical with its faint smell of disinfectant. I could hear the sound of a radio from what had once been the dining room, and faintly, from the drawing room the somewhat inexpert tinkling of the piano.

A young naval officer came out of the library carrying several books and seeing me standing somewhat forlornly in the centre of the hall, said with a smile: 'Have you come to see somebody? Perhaps I can direct you?'

'No, thank you. I'm here with my cousin, he'll be back soon.'

'You're bringing him in? It's a great place, the nursing's superb and I'm glad it's so near the sea. Some of the other chaps aren't so enthusiastic though.'

'Oh, why's that?' I said in some surprise.

'Well, it's a bit of a way out for one thing. Visitors are always grumbling that it's not an easy journey to get here. They should be glad we're so well looked after and enjoy the views from the windows.'

At that moment I could see Robin coming through the door in the company of a plump fresh-faced woman wearing white uniform and my companion said with a smile, 'Here's Matron. You'll find her as enthusiastic about Reckmire as I am.'

He left me and by this time Robin and the Matron had reached me and introductions were being performed.

'Your cousin tells me you'll be stayin' in the flat, Miss Albemarle. I hope you'll be comfortable there. There've been no fires in the place for some time and the rooms could be a trifle musty. I'll have fresh beddin' taken in and one of the orderlies will light fires. I hope you'll both dine here with the rest of us. You'll find it more convenient, I'm sure.'

'Yes, of course,' Robin and I answered together, and he went on, 'I'll get the bags upstairs, Joanna. Perhaps you'd like to have a chat to Matron and look around the house?'

When he'd gone Matron looked at me with a wry smile. 'He's nice,' she commented, 'but then they all are. You'll know this house like the back of your hand?'

'Well, yes. Are you happy here?'

'Ah, to be sure, I love it. It reminds me a lot of the west coast of Ireland where I come from. Couldn't you tell from my accent? Sure and the boys pull my leg over it. Let's take a look around and you can tell me how much it's changed.'

As we passed from room to room I was subjected to a great deal of interest from young men sitting with books on their knees, playing snooker in the billiard room or chatting in the drawing room, most of them wearing some sort of bandage or plaster cast but all of them with a welcoming smile on their face and a degree of curiosity.

'What have you done with the turret room?' I asked her.

'Nothing, love, it's too small for anything really and too far away from anywhere else. Major Carter loves it. He spends most of his time just sittin' there listening to the sea and waiting' for that wife of his.'

The major sat in a comfortable chair facing the door and I wondered if he loved the sea so much why he wasn't looking through the window at the long reach of Reckmire.

As we moved inside the room I soon realised that he was blind when he said hopefully, 'Have you somebody with you Matron?' I stared into eyes that met mine sightlessly. Matron said brightly, 'I've brought you a visitor, Major, Miss Albemarle. This was her grandparents' house. It still is, I suppose.'

Awkwardly he shuffled to his feet, one hand clenched upon his stick, and I went forward to take his outstretched hand.

155

'Please sit down, Major, I hope we're not disturbing you?'
I said quickly.

'Are you ready for your tea then?' Matron asked. 'I'll
leave Miss Albemarle to chat with you and she can look
after you when the tea comes. She can tell you all about
the sea and the rocks round here. It's the sound of the sea
he loves, that's why he's always up here on his own.'

I drew up a chair to sit beside him and from it I could look
across the beach towards the marshes. He said softly, 'You're
looking out of the window at the sea. I wish I could see it –
I have to make do with listening to it. I know when it's angry
and when it's benign like today. You love it too?'

'Oh, yes. When Robin invited me here for the next few
days I was terribly excited. It was the greatest joy of my
life coming back to Reckmire.'

'Robin?'

'My cousin. Like Matron said, this was our grandparents'
house.'

'How wonderful. Is your cousin in the war?'

'Yes. In the Air Force. He's a bomber pilot.'

'And you?'

'I'm in the Wrens. I'm stationed in London, driving
important people from one place to another.'

'London isn't a very safe place to be in these days.'

'No. Most nights there are air-raids and we spend the
night in a shelter or down in one of the tube stations. Life
does go on. Sometimes we dance the night away as if there
was going to be no tomorrow.'

He smiled, and in his smile was sadness and memory,
bitterness and chagrin, and I saw his hand reach out to
grasp an envelope lying on the table beside him.

It was already crumpled as if he had been holding it tightly
for a very long time. He said softly, 'It's from Jackie, my
wife. I was going to ask one of the chaps to read it for
me but I decided against it. I was hoping she'd come this
weekend but I got this letter instead. I didn't want them
feeling sorry for me.'

'Oh, I'm sure they wouldn't. Perhaps something's prevented her from coming? It isn't the easiest place to get to,
I was glad Robin was able to borrow a car.'

156

'Jackie's a dancer in a revue in London. I never got to see it. This happened to me just before I was due for leave.'

'I'm sure she'll come whenever she can.'

'Will you read it for me, Miss Albemarle? Oh, not every word, just the bit where she says when she'll come. You'll probably find most of it far too boring but women are far more sympathetic than men, aren't they?'

'Sometimes,' I answered with a smile.

I took the envelope from his hand and sat staring at it for several moments before taking out the letter. He was leaning forward in his chair, staring at me eagerly, encouragingly.

Although she addressed him as 'Darling Andrew', the letter was short, and it was all about her. What she was doing, who she was meeting, who was seeing the show and how it was received. Only at the end was there any mention of a visit when she wrote: 'I'm all tied up at the moment, darling. I'm sure you realise this and getting to that Godforsaken place is no joke. I'll try to make it soon. All my love, Jackie.'

'Well?' he prompted impatiently.

'The show's a terrific success and as soon as she can get away she will. She's longing to see you and sends you her dearest love.'

He smiled, and I hoped my voice had been convincing. I passed back the letter which he kissed and laid on the table top.

'She's a great girl, you know. She's so beautiful and talented. I've never been able to understand what she could see in a plodding old buffer like me.'

'Have you been married long?' I asked curiously.

'I met her early in the war. In an air-raid shelter, would you believe? I took her home to Devonshire to meet my parents but they didn't get on too well. Dad thought we should wait until after the war and Mother hadn't thought I'd want to marry a showgirl. She'd rather set her heart on a girl I'd known most of my life, the daughter of friends of theirs. Neither of them seemed to understand that the war altered most things. All the old values have gone out of the window. Life's for living, not for waiting.'

When I didn't speak he said quickly, 'I say, I am going

on an awful lot about me. Is there some young fella you're keen on?'

'Nobody special.'

'I'll bet you're pretty though. Come closer, let me see.'

Obediently I moved towards him, and then he reached out his hand so gently it felt like a feather against my face as he followed its contours and the texture of my hair.

'What colour is it?' he asked.

'I'm fair. Blonde, I suppose.'

'And your eyes?'

'Dark blue.'

'You're a beautiful girl. I knew you would be,' he said, smiling.

'How could you know? Actually when I was very young I wished I was like my cousin Gabriella who was half-Italian. She had so much colour she made me feel insipid and drained.'

'Never want to be like somebody else, Joanna, be content to be you. Jackie's a beautiful girl. She has dark red hair and green eyes. I can imagine them even though I shall never see them again.'

His face was sad, reflective, and I could feel the stinging tears in my eyes and was glad he couldn't see them.

At that moment a young wardmaid brought in a tray with tea and biscuits laid out on it and I was glad to have something to do as I busied myself arranging it for him on the small table near his chair.

'We're to have dinner with the rest of you,' I said in an endeavour to take his thoughts away from his wife. 'You'll be there, won't you?'

'Oh, yes. One of the nurses comes for me around six o'clock. Time enough to get spruced up before dinner.'

We finished our tea in companionable silence, then as I collected the tea things together on the tray, he said, 'What sort of a day is it, Joanna? Something tells me it's beautiful, an Indian Summer's day?'

'Oh, yes, that's how it is. How perceptive of you.'

He smiled. 'I imagine what it's like out there. Usually the sea tells me but today it's quiet. I suppose they're sitting outdoors?'

'Yes, a great many of them.'

I took his hand in mine, saying, 'I'll take the tray out with me and I'll look forward to seeing you at dinner.'

'Rather. They'll all be on their best behaviour tonight. It's not often we have a young lady at the dinner table.'

My conversation with Major Carter had unsettled me strangely. I had looked upon this time at Reckmire as a joyous thing, a lull from the storm and a nostalgic venture into the past. I had embraced the war as an escape from a life I resented. Now I was face to face with its cruelty.

Chapter Fourteen

I walked along the reach of Reckmire before dinner, following the line of silver ripples until the beach curved.

I wore my favourite silk dress and when a chill little wind blew up from the sea was glad to retrace my steps towards the house. I saw Robin walking towards me across the sand and in the glamour of his uniform he seemed even more handsome than when I had first seen him. Then he had been a boy, now he was a man, and something strange and haunting about his expression made my heart race suddenly and urgently.

'You look very pretty, Joanna. Is that dress intended to set the dining room alight tonight?'

'I thought I should make an effort,' I replied shyly.

'Quite right too. Apparently we're not to sit together. Matron has placed us at different ends of the table so you'll have to do your best to entertain the wounded heroes at your end. What did you think of the flat?'

'It's very nice, Robin. I recognised some of Grandma's prized possessions from the downstairs rooms.'

The flat consisted of two large bedrooms, an adequate lounge, bathroom and very small kitchenette. I doubt if my grandparents had expected to live in it, but they must have thought that one or another of us would wish to visit.

It seemed strange to be sitting down to dinner in the dining room I remembered sitting in with the family. Now I sat at one end of the long dining table with men I hadn't known until a few hours before, while around us sat other officers at small tables arranged around the room. On my right was a young pilot officer and on my left an army captain, both of them anxious to pass me tureens of vegetables, and from across the table a man wearing a kilt and all the trappings of a Scottish regiment smiled cheerfully, saying, 'We're lucky that most of the vegetables are grown on the estate. I'm going to miss this place.'

'Will you be leaving soon?' I asked curiously.

'At the weekend, my dear.'

'Are you going home?'

'Bless ye no, love, I'm rejoining my regiment.'

'Lucky you,' said the pilot officer, 'I wish I knew when I was getting back into service.'

How could I be expected to understand why men who had been wounded wanted to get back into it? Was it something to do with heroism, bravado or sheer recklessness? At the other end of the table Robin was deep in conversation with two Naval officers and I knew their talk would be about the war and only the war.

I looked round the room and found Major Carter sitting at one of the smaller tables. He was being helped with his food by one of the officers sitting with him, and as I looked away the Scotsman said gently, 'Have you met Major Carter? He was expecting his wife but once again she's not showed up.'

'Yes, I met him before dinner. He had a letter from her.'

'Oh, aye, letters is all he gets. Poor chap, he's in for a great disillusionment where that young woman's concerned.'

For a few moments there was an uncomfortable silence then they were asking questions about life in London, the bombing raids and the courage of the civilian population, before they started to satisfy their curiosity about the Albemarle family.

When I told them that my father was likely to be a prisoner of war in Japanese hands and that his sister was married to an Italian banker living in Umbria it provided us with enough conversation to take us to the end of the meal when one by one they disappeared to their individual pursuits.

'Well, that wasn't too bad, was it? Robin said with a smile. 'I suggest we go up to the flat and make ourselves comfortable. We have a lot to talk about, Joanna. Let's do it over a drink or two.'

I was delighted to see that a fire had been lit in my bedroom, and in the lounge a log fire glowed halfway up the chimney. Robin produced two glasses and a bottle of Sauternes and we sat in comfortable armchairs on either side of the fireplace.

The warmth of the fire and the wine made me drowsy but he would have none of it. 'We have to talk,' he said urgently. 'You have a lot to tell me, Joanna, about the missing letters, about your life since we last met.'

'What about your life?' I said in a mistaken attempt to defer the ordeal, but Robin would have none of it.

'My life is an open book, you know that, Joanna. Nothing unusual has happened to me except that my career has been put on hold until after the war. There are no lurid love stories. I come from a happy, well-adjusted family who never change, as you must know, so what in my life could possibly be of interest?'

For a while I sat silent, staring into the fire, while Robin came to refill my glass. I blessed him for his patience as he sat back in his chair, his bright hair gilded by the glow of the fire and lamplight, his face strangely pensive. I dreaded seeing that expression change into one of compassionate disbelief.

I started slowly with the departure of my father after our return from Italy. I tried to tell him about my helplessness to find a life of my own, my mother's clinging assumption that we were bonded together and that anything and anybody outside that bond could have no place. I did not once look at him, and it was only at the end of another silence that he said, 'Tell me about the letters, Joanna.'

This was harder. The long months of waiting for letters that didn't come, the fears of rejection and the tears that even my father seemed to have forgotten my existence, and then the despair at finding them hidden away in that old hat box at the back of a kitchen cupboard. There were tears in my eyes and in my voice, and suddenly Robin was besides me, lifting me up, holding me in his arms, cradling my head against his shoulder, and in my heart there was peace and a strange contentment.

How easy it was at that moment to transmute the love I already had for Robin into something else, something in tune with despair and longing, with shame and the need to be loved. How suddenly normal it felt to know that we were a man and a woman tormented by circumstances, living in a crumbling tottering world where only the moment was real and when yesterday and tomorrow belonged to infinity.

Passion and our joy in it was all that we had, nor did the morning find us disenchanted. They were days I believed I would remember for the rest of my life: sunshine and sea, Reckmire Marsh and Robin. Neither of us had any thought of where we would go from there, only joy in what we had had. And at the end of those days Robin went back to war and I went to Surrey to see my mother.

Fiercely I told myself that whatever life did to me, whatever she might do to me, nobody or nothing could take away those days at Reckmire with Robin. It was only when I let myself into her empty flat that I came down to earth with the realisation that this was reality and that what Robin and I had had was fairytale.

How impersonal the flat seemed. The table under the window was laid for afternoon tea for two people, and since I had not informed Mother of my arrival I suspected that she was entertaining Mr Walsh. I went into the bedroom and unpacked the small case I had with me, then I returned to the lounge to wait. I heard their voices in the corridor, Mother's bright and cheerful and the deeper sounds of his laughter, then they were in the flat and the surprise on their faces was comical.

'Why on earth didn't you tell me you were coming?' she said. 'How long are you staying?'

'Only over the weekend, Mother. I have to report on Tuesday morning.'

'Really, Joanna, I do think you could have let me know. I've all sorts of engagements planned for the next few days, I suppose I'll have to think about cancelling them.'

'There's no need for you to do anything of the kind, Mother. I shall be quite happy looking up old friends and spending a little time in familiar surroundings.'

'Which old friends?' she demanded.

'Well, the friends I made at the library. One or two girls I knew, and Mrs Prothero. I would like to see her again.'

'I don't see why. She wasn't the easiest person to get along with. One would have thought she was doing us a favour when we had her to help in the house, instead of the fact that we were employing her.'

'Do sit down, Ernest, and make yourself at home. I'll just put my coat away and perhaps Joanna will put the kettle on.'

'I'll do it, Linda, you two will want to chat,' he said quickly, and from the way he went into the kitchen and started opening cupboards I quickly gathered he was well accustomed to treating the flat like home.

'He's really very nice,' she confided to me quietly. 'Janice and Marion are a little piqued that he spends so much time here, but they were both accustomed to living alone. It was a terrible wrench when you had to go, Joanna. We hear the bombers coming over every night − it must be quite dreadful living in London. When you wanted to join the Wrens I thought you'd be well away from the city.'

'I'm quite happy at the flat, Mother, and Jill and I get along together.'

'I hope she's a nice girl. Do you go out much together?'

'Some of the time. She's friendly with an American officer at the moment.'

I don't know why I gave her that piece of information, and quickly wished I hadn't when she said, 'Mrs Goodchild has two Waafs billeted on her and they're both going around with Americans. How do those girls know whether they're married or not? Is Jill going to marry this American she's friendly with?'

'I really don't know, Mother, they come and they go.'

'Exactly. I don't want you to become involved in any wartime romance, Joanna. The entire world has turned upside down, but after the war when things get back to normal you'll be glad you kept both feet on the ground.'

'We don't any of us know what life will be like after the

war, Mother. We don't even know if we're going to survive the war.'

'I don't want you talking like that. I know Hitler is all over Europe and Japan is there in the Far East, but America is in the war and now Hitler has gone for Russia. Mr Walsh says it will be over quite quickly now.'

'Nobody knows that, Mother.'

'Ernest says ...'

She was stopped short by him coming out of the kitchen carrying the teapot, then he was shepherding us into our seats at the table and cheerfully pouring the tea.

He was a pleasant little man, the sort Mother could dominate with her little girl winsomeness so that he would never really know he was being manipulated. He delighted in waiting on us, and Mother chatted happily, her face dimpled with smiles, and she looked so pretty and pristine neat.

I wished I could take her at face value but I couldn't. They would always be there between us, those letters stowed away in the kitchen cupboard, and as the evening wore on her sweetness began to cloy and Ernest's evident devotion annoyed me. I couldn't understand why he couldn't see that other devious Linda behind that personality that was just too nice.

He left soon after eleven and Mother said sweetly, 'Now we can have our little chat, Joanna. Are you meeting some interesting people at the Admiralty?'

'I meet a great many important officers, all of them more interested in their jobs than they are in me, and all of them probably married with children.'

'Isn't Jill a driver in the Wrens then?'

'Yes, Mother.'

'But didn't you say she was involved with an American officer?'

'Yes.'

'She must meet young men then, but you've just said all the men you meet aren't interested in you.'

'That's right, Mother. They must think I'm the sort of dull girl who is guaranteed always to behave myself and never play the temptress. Perhaps that's why I get the old steady ones and Jill gets the jolly ones.'

I was intrigued by the expressions that crossed her face. She didn't want her daughter to be thought of as dull; on the other hand she wanted me to remain hers with no outside intrusions. To test my thoughts I asked idly, 'Mr Walsh is very nice, Mother. I'm glad you've found a man friend to look after you.'

'Oh, you mustn't get any wrong ideas, Joanna. He is very nice, but a friend is all he is. I've told him that I appreciate all he does for me, but when the war is over and you come home it will be very different.'

'How different, Mother?'

'Well, you know, darling. We're a pair, aren't we? We shall be going places together, doing the same sort of thing. Ernest would feel quite out of it. He understands, Joanna. He can never accuse me of misleading him.'

'And if I wanted to get married, Mother, if I met some man during the war who wants to marry me?'

'But we've talked about that, Joanna. Wartime romances are not meant to last, and if there is somebody for you in the future we'll talk about it then. It will be nice to be back in your own bedroom again and take a lie in in the morning. Do you have to be up at some ungodly hour in London?'

'Sometimes we don't go to bed, Mother. But, yes, it will be nice to spend a night in civilised Surrey without one ear attuned to the air-raid sirens.'

I had thought I would fall asleep as soon as my head touched the pillow but instead I tossed and turned for what seemed hours. It was within my power to shatter my mother's complacency forever. I could tell her about Reckmire, about Robin and me and about the letters, but I wouldn't do it.

My future was a closed book. I belonged to a generation that could remember a short golden past, a past we believed would go on uninterrupted into a narrow genteel future, but instead we had been thrown willy-nilly into a nightmare. Girls whose lives had revolved around tea dances and tennis courts, young men who had sailed boats for pleasure, ridden horses at point to point races and played games with enthusiasm and comradeship. Now the games were grimmer, the struggles were life and death ones, and the future contained only uncertainty and the possibility of death or disaster.

166

I was not afraid of life as we were living it, but I was terrified of having to return to this flat and the sort of future my mother envisaged for us.

In the few days that followed Mother's friends came to tea. They asked questions about my life in the Wrens and all assumed that I was longing for it to be over so that I could return to normality.

Miss Carson greeted me with great warmth and I understood why when I saw that she was managing the library practically single-handed since her only assistant was a very doddery old man who was also deaf.

'He's been in the library service for years and should be retired but they've brought him back to help me out. He does two afternoons and one morning and a lot of people complain because he's slow,' she informed me over a cup of tea in her office.

'Is your mother still living in the country with her sister?' I asked her.

'Yes. I'm relieved about that. Is your mother coping, Joanna?'

'Oh, yes, I think so.'

'And she does have Ernest Walsh to change her library books and generally look after her and one or two of the other ladies.'

I smiled. 'He seems an amiable little man.'

'Well, yes. I've know Ernest a long time. I knew his wife and she was an awful lot like your mother. Small, pretty, always nicely dressed. She made all the decisions and Ernest always complied.'

Her voice was even, conversational, but her views on my mother were so accurate I had difficulty in meeting her level gaze.

As we parted at the door she said gently, 'Don't be too anxious to come back here, Joanna. I'll have no difficulty in getting library assistants and there should be something better in store for you. Do you hear from your father at all?'

'No. Not for a long time.'

'That must be worrying, particularly with Japan in the war against us. Is there no nice young man in the offing?'

'Nobody special,' I answered lightly.

I could never tell anybody about Robin. Robin was special, he was part of the happiest time in my life, and he was the lover of my present. I could not begin to hope that he would be part of my future. Try as I would, Robin and my future remained a misty dream.

On New Year's Eve he came up to London for three day's leave. In the glow of candlelight we danced at the club until dawn crept slowly across the city and back at the flat we made love on the rug in front of the fire, deep sensuous love that was joy and comfort, anguish and ecstacy. Later on New Year's Day we walked through the park where a keen north-easter brought tears to our eyes and snow drifted flirtatiously through the leafless branches of the trees.

On the last night of Robin's leave the bombers were back and we disdained the air-raid shelter in favour of the flat, arrogantly assuming that we were immune from everything terrible that was happening to others.

Jill came back from spending a few days with her parents in Wiltshire and I shelved much of my own pain in comforting her after the departure of her American for the Far East.

I felt helpless in the face of her despair.

'It's over,' she told me, her face set in lines of obstinacy and anger. 'He hasn't said so, not in so many words, but he's joining his ship and after the war he'll go back to America, he won't come back here.'

'Is he going to write to you?' I asked.

'I don't know. Letters are futile even if they get through. He's not mine, Joanna, he never was. He was simply lent to me for a while and now he's gone. Aren't you lucky not to have fallen in love with some man who's in the war? There'll be somebody else, there always is.'

It was bravado. There would be somebody else but whether he would matter or be just somebody to ease the sense of loss I would probably never know.

The real Jill hid behind the brittle light-hearted girl who flirted endlessly with a stream of young men, and then at the end of March she met a young squadron leader who danced with us both and I learned he was on the same base as Robin. He too was now a squadron leader and the two men were friends. Later Jill said, 'You were very anxious to ask about Robin. I thought he was just your cousin.'

'I thought so too.'

'You mean things have changed?'

'He came up to London for New Year and we went around together. I also spent a week with him in October at Reckmire. He is my cousin, Jill, but I think I'm in love with him.'

'Oh, well, it happens,' she said blithely. 'I've asked Peter if they can get here for a long weekend soon. He said he'd let me know. I do hope they can.'

I had no communication with Robin, no telephone calls and no letters, but Peter telephoned Jill to say they could wangle a weekend at the end of April, a weekend we both looked forward to with eagerness.

'They'll go straight to the club,' Jill informed me. 'I told him we'd meet them there.'

We wore our dresses and Jill said with a laugh, 'I feel like a girl tonight. Uniform's glamorous on a man but it's too much of a leveller on a woman. Tonight I want to feel like a woman, I want to look beautiful and feminine. You're very pretty, Joanna. I hadn't really realised just how pretty until I saw you with your hair loose and that floating dress swirling round your ankles.'

The dress had been an extravagance but I had loved it on sight. A deep azure blue chiffon that seemed to have a life of its own, and brought out the colour of my eyes.

We didn't care that men were looking at us with admiration and other women with something akin to envy. Our eyes were on the door where we could see every new entrant and in the meantime we danced until Jill said in some exasperation: 'It doesn't look as if they're coming, but wouldn't you just think one of them might have let us know?'

'We don't know what's happened, Jill. All sorts of things could have cropped up.'

We could see one of the barmen pushing his way across the room through the crowd of dancers and when he reached our table he leaned across to Jill, saying, 'There's a telephone call for you, miss, you can take it in the little office over there.'

Our eyes met, and with a shrug of her shoulders Jill said, 'It looks as if they can't make it.'

169

I waited, my hands clenched under the table, my eyes straining through the smoke until I saw her returning. Quickly she gathered up her wrap, saying, 'We've got to get out of this, Joanna. Come with me.'

'But what is it? Are we meeting them somewhere else?' I cried.

She was pushing her way through the crowds that lined the floor, and helplessly I followed in her wake, ignoring the light-hearted banter, and the hands that reached out to pull me on to the dance floor.

Outside in the clear night air a pale crescent moon shone in a starry sky raked with searchlights. The dark empty streets confirmed that the air-raid sirens must have sounded and as we ran across the street an ARP warden called to us to take cover.

We ignored him. Instead we ran towards the flat and it was only when we stood staring at each other in the doorway that Jill gasped, 'Joanna, it's Robin. He didn't get back after the last raid. His plane and three others came down over Normandy. All leave has been cancelled.'

I didn't feel anything. I followed her into the flat and she pushed me into a chair, saying she would get me a drink. She came back with a glass but I couldn't hold it. My hands were trembling too much. She held it to my lips so that the sharp taste of brandy trickled down my throat and I spluttered helplessly.

I felt icy cold and my teeth were chattering. I couldn't cry. I felt like a dead thing. Jill was putting a rug over my knees before putting a match to the fire.

'Cry all you want to,' she said sharply, 'scream if you must. I know what you've lost. I loved him once, remember, I suppose I still did in a way, but your memories go back further than mine, you can't be sure if it's Robin the cousin you have lost or Robin the lover.'

I was remembering Robin the first time I had seen him, racing across the sands with the sun gleaming on his blonde hair, his face filled with consternation, and I had thought him beautiful. I was glad that I had loved him, glad that we had been lovers. It was a love that would remain locked in my heart forever.

In the days that followed I went about my duties automatically. Nothing registered. I was like an automaton, a mechanical thing, obeying orders, living each day yet uncaring about tomorrow, and still I could not cry.

I was driving a Rear Admiral back from the shipyards in Barrow and it was almost dusk on a grey miserable day chilled with fine rain. Unthinking I pulled out on to a traffic island in front of a huge army truck and it was the squealing of tyres which brought me suddenly to life. I realised only the driver's vigilance had saved us by inches. Shaking with fear, I brought the car to a sudden halt so that my passenger and I jerked forward and a sudden stream of invective from the Admiral prodded me unmercifully into the land of the living.

'Pull in here,' he commanded.

There was a layby off the main road, and I saw that the army truck had pulled in behind us. My passenger left his seat and through the driving mirror I watched him talking to the driver of the truck who appeared visibly shaken. When he returned to the car he said abruptly, 'Drive on to the hotel at the junction of the next road and pull into the car park. I've not been happy with your concentration for some time, young lady.'

The Admiral had a reputation for being tetchy, a stickler for discipline and one who didn't suffer fools gladly. As I followed him into an almost deserted hotel I was trembling at the thought of the ticking off or worse that would follow.

He led the way into a deserted room off the main hall and then pointed sternly to an empty table and two easy chairs placed near the window.

'Sit there,' he said sharply, 'I'll order tea. I think we could both do with something stronger, but if you drive like that without alcohol I don't believe in tempting providence.'

He was the one who poured the tea and added milk and sugar, then fixing me with a stern eye he demanded, 'Now, young lady, what is more important in your life than arriving back safely, or don't you care any more?'

It was the last sentence that made me look at him sharply, startled, and it was the kindness of his expression that

171

brought the stinging tears to my eyes and the relief of being able to talk.

How easy it was to talk to a stranger. I told him about my loss and Robin's presence during the happiest years of my life. I told him about my mother and the void my father had left in my life, and gradually some of the pain lifted and his bluff kindness was preferable to sentimental sympathy.

'I knew there was something bothering you right from the time we set out this morning,' he said evenly. 'And now, my girl, you've got to come to terms with the rest of your life. A great many young men, and women too, will have gone from our midst before this war ends, and I don't want to go on with the usual platitudes about life having to go on. We both know it has, and that young man would be horrified if he thought you were going to spend the rest of your life grieving for something that's gone forever. You're a young, pretty girl with all your life in front of you and you owe it to him to face it with a courage he would have understood.

'Now you have a good cry while I get myself a whisky at the bar. When you feel better come out and join me and we'll continue our journey.'

When I joined him a little later I had repaired the ravages to my face. After taking a good look at me, he said, 'That's much better. Now you look like an officer in His Majesty's Royal Navy. You could do with a few days' leave, I'll see what I can do.'

'Thank you, sir, but I'd really rather be working.'

'You need to get down to Somerset to see your grandparents. They'll appreciate it at this time, and if you ask me it's a meeting that is long overdue.'

True to his word, several days later I was told I could take four days' leave, and with his advice ringing in my ears set out on the morning train for Somerset.

This was Robin's countryside, the soft rolling hills and pretty villages, the sea lapping on long stretches of sand and country roads lined with ancient trees. Cattle grazed placidly in the meadows, and as I walked up the drive from the gates I sensed a timeless quality in the soft breeze that stirred the leaves of spring. Above in a cloudless sky a small plane droned and rooks came drifting down to settle in the top branches of the beech trees.

I remembered foolishly that Grandfather Fowler had always said it was a good omen when the rooks nested high, and for the first time in months thought about summer when so recently I had been unconcerned if the sun never shone again. Angrily I told myself, 'It's too soon, too soon to be forgetting, too soon to be looking forward to other things,' and then I saw Rusty, Robin's spaniel, running down the path, his long ears flapping in the breeze, then he was leaping up at me, yelping with excitement, and I knelt down on the grass at the side of the drive and hugged him in my arms.

Dimly I heard somebody calling his name and with a short bark he left my arms and ran back along the drive. I looked up to see Aunt Marcia walking towards me, shading her eyes from the sunlight. Rusty was running excitedly between the two of us and I saw recognition dawn in her eyes. Then she came quickly towards me and took me into her arms.

For a while she stood staring at me and my first reaction was that she looked older. Her hair was liberally sprinkled with grey and she was thinner than I remembered. She still had that gentle tranquil air that had been so different from Aunt Corallie's though. Tucking her arm through mine she said a little breathlessly, 'Mother'll be so pleased to see you, Joanna. Edward too, but he's out on the estate at the moment. He's always so busy. We lost a lot of our permanent farm hands and although we have land girls it's not the same.'

'How are my grandparents, Aunt Marcia?'

'There's so much you don't know, Joanna. Father died last month. He'd had several warnings, heart attacks, each one a little more drastic. I really think Robin was the final straw and Mother fortunately doesn't seem to know what time of day it is these days. I take it you know about Robin?'

'Yes. It was terrible.'

I didn't know if he had told his mother about me, whether we saw each other, how much we were involved. In the next moment however she was saying, 'Robin told us that he had

173

met you in London and that you were rooming with a girl he knew.'

Evidently that was all he had told them and I was glad. My grandfather was dead and there were so many times when I could have seen him, so many times I could have written to them, if only I hadn't been so convinced that they didn't want to hear from me.

'Everybody is telling me that time is a great healer, Joanna, but I can't come to terms with Robin's death. Edward keeps himself busy on the estate. I don't believe it's entirely registered with Mother. I'm the one who can't face up to it. I don't sleep, I can't eat, I keep expecting him to come in at the door, always with a smile on his lips, my beautiful son who gave us such joy. You liked him too, didn't you, Joanna?'

'Yes, Aunt Marcia, I loved him.'

She smiled. She took my statement for girlish exaggeration, and continued, 'So much seems to have happened to this family during the war. First of all it was your father. The War Office informed us he was a prisoner of war in Japanese hands and there has been nothing since. Then there was Corallie living in Italy and Italy at war with us. We haven't heard a thing from them and don't know how they have survived during these terrible years. Robin's death was the last straw so far as Father was concerned.'

'I'm sorry, Aunt Marcia,' I murmured, hating the inadequacy of my words.

'And then there was you, Joanna. We never heard from you. You never answered our letters. Surely you must know how comforting your letters would have been, if only as a substitute for Robert?'

So Robin hadn't told them about my mother's involvement. Now I would have to tell them myself, make them see that none of it was my fault, that I too had felt deserted.

I sat with Aunt Marcia in the kitchen looking out across the rolling landscape towards the purple hills beyond. She produced coffee and freshly made scones but I noticed she only pushed hers around her plate.

'Is Grandma in bed most of the time?' I asked her.

'No. She gets up quite early, but she sits in her room gazing out along the drive. It's almost as though she is waiting for those she has lost to come suddenly striding out of the morning mist. We'll go up there to see her now. No doubt she's wondering who our visitor is.'

Grandma did not turn round from her place at the window when we entered her room. She sat in her chair, a tiny figure in black, far removed from the vital, graceful woman I remembered.

Chapter Fifteen

It took me the rest of the day to recover from the realisation that my grandmother didn't recognise me.

'Mother, this is Joanna come to see us,' Aunt Marcia said, drawing me forward, but Grandma merely looked up at me with a puzzled frown on her face.

'Joanna?' she murmured vaguely.

'Yes, darling, Robert's daughter.'

'Robert isn't here.'

'No, of course not, but we're very pleased to see Joanna. Mother, surely you remember her at Reckmire, and during your holiday in Italy? I know she's grown up now, but you've talked about her often.'

'Joanna went away. Her mother took her away.'

Aunt Marcia looked at me helplessly. 'We'll leave her alone now, Joanna. Tomorrow she could remember everything. This is what happens.'

It was only when we were letting ourselves out of the room that Grandma said, 'When did she come to Reckmire? I thought it was Gabriella who came to Reckmire.'

'They both came, Mother. Don't worry your head about it, you'll remember in a little while.'

I was shown into my room overlooking the pastureland which swept down to a meandering river and Aunt Marcia said, 'I hope you'll be able to stay with us a little while, Joanna. How much leave did you get?'

'Four days.'

'Will you be wishing to visit your mother or are you content to spend it here?'

'I'd like to spend it here, Aunt Marcia, if it isn't too inconvenient?'

'Gracious, no. We'd love to have you.'

'Will she remember me, do you think?'

'I do hope so, Joanna. She was very sad when you didn't answer her letters.'

'Robin didn't tell you anything?'

'Only that he'd met you in London and that one day you would tell me.'

Uncle Edward too had aged, but he greeted me in the most friendly fashion and took me round the estate in the trap pulled by fat Daisy the Welsh pony.

In the days that followed I shopped with Aunt Marcia in Dunster and Minehead, and walked miles with Rusty, either along the meandering country lanes or the empty beaches.

I saw Robin everywhere. In the house and in the garden. I went into his room and looked at the view he'd seen most of his life from the window. I stared at photographs of him taken with his school friends and later at university, at pictures of him sailing his boat, riding his horse, wielding his cricket bat, and always the smile was familiar, warm and embracing. Lovingly I handled the things that had been dear to him, his tennis racquet, his golf clubs, and tears sprang into my eyes when I saw the photograph of me with the family standing in the gardens of Reckmire.

Gabriella's beauty shone out like a beacon beside my unremarkable schoolgirl appearance, but there was another photograph Robin had kept of me leaping along the beach, my arms spread wide as if to embrace the wind, my face alight with joy, and on the back he had written, 'Joanna at Reckmire, aged thirteen.'

Aunt Marcia found me sitting on his bed in tears and we wept together. Her memories went back much further than mine, mine were too recent, too unsure, and if she was surprised that I should feel so much grief when she believed we hadn't been close for years, she thought it merely the grief of a gentle-hearted girl for a boy she had liked.

I was never really sure if Grandma accepted me as the same Joanna she'd known at Reckmire but I often sat with her, listening to her talk of my father and his sisters and the old days.

Sometimes there was a great puzzlement in her eyes and then in the next moment it had gone and she would stare out of the windows, her smile gentle, her expression pensive.

On my last evening I sat up late with Aunt Marcia and Uncle Edward and it was then I told them about the letters. It gave me real pain to tell them, to show my mother up in a bad light, but they were both tolerant enough not to condemn her. Instead Uncle Edward said gently, 'There's no lasting harm done, love, you're back with us now and you know you'll always be welcome. Have you thought what you'll do when the war is over?'

'No. I don't seem able to think beyond the war. When we have good news it's always followed by bad, but I want my father to come home. Is there a possibility, do you think?'

I saw the look that passed between them, and Uncle Edward said, 'We would all like that, Joanna. The War Office were not hopeful and it is all happening so far away. We know the Japanese are capable of great cruelty, but although we fear the worst, we hope for the best.'

It was small comfort but I knew he was right. I could not rely on my father's homecoming to resolve the pattern of my life, it was something I had to do for myself, even if it meant hurting my mother and distancing myself from her.

I returned to London laden with new laid eggs, fresh country butter and home-made bread and scones. Jill's face lit up when she saw everything and that night over the feast we made I told her about my days in Somerset and she told me about her latest conquest, another American.

Seeing the expression on my face, she laughed, saying, 'I'm on a merry-go-round that never stops, Joanna. It's my way of getting through the war. Men come and go and I don't want to face the trauma you did each time one of them doesn't return. By the way, your mother rang up. I told her you were out of London.'

'Did she say what she wanted?'

'She asked where she could get in touch with you, but I

told her it was all very secret and she had to be content with that.'

As always her voice was plaintive. 'I've tried several times to get you, Joanna. That girl who shares the flat is never in in the evenings. Where have you been?'

'Mother, you know I can't talk about where I go.'

'Not even to your mother?'

'Not to anybody, Mother. Is something wrong?'

'I simply felt I had to talk to somebody and get a little sympathy. Mr Walsh and I have quarrelled. He's gone off in a sulk to his married daughter, completely failing to understand my point of view, and my friends are all secretly pleased that we've quarrelled. They didn't like it when he gave me all his attention.'

'Why have you quarrelled?'

'Well, he was getting very serious, dear. Starting to talk about where we would live after the war, Bexhill or somewhere like that, and when I said I had you to think about, he said, oh, you'd be all right here in the flat, that you were perfectly capable of looking after yourself. I told him I wasn't having my daughter returning from the war and finding herself alone.'

'Mother, I *am* able to look after myself. I shall be a different person after the war, we shall all be different, and I shall need to make my own life. You should try to do the same.'

For what seemed an age there was silence at the other end of the telephone then came her voice, cold and peevish. 'You're just like your father, Joanna. He accused me of holding him back, keeping him away from people, now you're doing it. I thought about you and let Mr Walsh go. This is the thanks I get apparently.'

I heard the line go dead and slowly I replaced the receiver on its stand. After one look at my face, Jill said, 'What now, Joanna?'

When I told her she simply commented, 'Well, at least it's brought matters to a head. She knows now that you're not simply going home after the war to pick up the pieces.'

The letter came several days later, many pages of it in Mother's neat schoolgirl writing with precise paragraphs and much underlining of sentences she believed I should take to heart.

It was a letter filled with recriminations, about my character, and my father's. Then perhaps she'd read it through and had doubts about it because suddenly the content changed. Now I was her darling daughter, the child she only wished to shower with affection just as her own parents had done with her.

'I loved Father and Mother so much, Joanna. All I want from you is the same kind of commitment. I told Mr Walsh that you and I were a pair and although we would both be friends with him, any thought of marriage at this time was out of the question.'

She ended her letter with the words, 'Let me hear from you soon, Joanna, and be assured that you have all my love and are constantly in my prayers.'

Without speaking I passed the letter across the table for Jill to read. I couldn't trust in my own thoughts, I needed somebody else to say if I was right or wrong.

She read it through without comment, then handing it back said, 'Thank heaven I'm never going to have that sort of trouble with my mother. We used to fall out something rotten when we were all at home. I have two sisters and two brothers, but I'm glad of them now. None of us has been smothered with affection. My parents loved us all but it was a happy-go-lucky household. If we did wrong we were chastised, if we did well we were praised. This is sick, Joanna, this clinging. Doesn't she want you to meet a nice man and marry him?'

'She would find a hundred and one excuses why I shouldn't and another hundred and one things that were wrong with him.'

'Then you're just going to have to be firm. This is your life, Joanna, and it's the only one you're going to have unless there really is a case for reincarnation. Even so, it's the only one you have now, the only one you're likely to remember this time round.'

At long last the tide turned for the Allied forces in Europe. Russia had withstood the German assault on the outskirts of Stalingrad and they were falling back against our forces on the continent. The nightly bombardment still went on but now the Germans were using flying bombs which fell indiscriminately but did not endanger the lives of German pilots.

The morale of the civilian population was high in spite of the nightly bombardment of our cities, and the glimmer of light that we could now see at the end of the tunnel told me that I would have to think seriously about the sort of future I wanted for myself.

I had men friends in plenty but nobody special. Somehow they were all of a pattern, those young men with laughter on their lips and shadows in their eyes, and then Jill announced that she intended to marry her American Naval pilot. For the first time I met members of her family who came up to London for the ceremony.

They were a friendly, happy party, her father who was a doctor and her mother who looked so incredibly young in pale peach she'd been saving for something special. Only one sister could attend, her youngest sister Diane who was a land girl, robust and country fresh with pink cheeks and laughing eyes, determined to enjoy every minute of the day, and her brother Rodney who was on three days' leave from his regiment.

None of the bridegroom's family was able to come over from the States, but the church was filled with young Americans all anxious to give the bride and her groom a good send off. Jill looked lovely in sky blue georgette and before they left for their brief honeymoon she thrust her posy of carnations and Lily of the Valley into my hands, hissing, 'Your turn next, Joanna, don't wait too long. I'll be back Thursday.'

I showed her folks round our flat and entertained them to afternoon tea, but when they had all departed the day seemed suddenly flat. I stood at the window looking down the street. A chill little wind had risen but I was thinking about something Jill's mother had said as I let them out.

'Jill told me about Robin, Joanna. She brought him to see us once. Such a handsome boy and so nice. All the girls fell in love with him.'

'Yes, he was nice,' I replied, somewhat inadequately.

'I would like Jill to have married somebody from this country, for the selfish reason that we would have seen more of her. After the war she'll be living in America.'

'You'll be able to visit and she'll come home as often as she can,' I said sympathetically.

'Well, of course, and John and I have never interfered. We've brought them up to be sensible. He's nice, don't you think?'

'Oh, yes, I do, very nice, and very much in love with her.'

She beamed. 'Yes, we thought so. Goodbye, Joanna, do come and see us if you get the chance.'

I thought about them driving home, laughing and chatting about the day, and wondered what my mother would have thought of them. Too chatty, too instantly friendly . . . and then my thoughts were halted by the sound of the telephone ringing shrilly in the hall.

My first thought was that it was Mother. I had answered her long letter without taking up the points she had raised, and I knew it would not have satisfied her. Now she was probably ringing to make me say the things I had been unable to put in a letter.

It was Aunt Marcia's voice, however, which spoke to me and I knew immediately that something was wrong by its tone.

'I'm sorry to bring you bad news, Joanna,' she said gently. 'Mother died in her sleep last night, she hasn't been well for some weeks now. The funeral is next Tuesday. Do you think you could come?'

'I'll try, Aunt Marcia, I'm sure I can find somebody to stand in for me.'

'Well, we would like you to be here, Joanna. There's only Edward and me here, and in normal times the funeral would have been at Reckmire but we can't possibly go up there now. It will be at the church in the village and later on we'll see about my parents' names being added to those on the family vault.'

There were only a handful of people in the little churchyard for my grandmother's funeral, and they were those who worked on my uncle's estate. Grandmother had lived in the area for a very short time and few local people knew her. Aunt Corallie and her family were living in a hostile land, Robin had gone and the fate of my father was precarious, yet it seemed the words spoken over my grandmother were for Robin also.

I sat in the front pew in the village church with my aunt and uncle, and it was only when we turned to walk out of the church that I saw the pew behind was occupied by Paul Cheviot and another man. They fell into step besides me with a murmured 'Good morning' and all through the committal I was aware of Paul's presence.

Later, Aunt Marcia turned to him with a warm smile, saying, 'I'm so glad you could come, Paul, it was lucky I found you at the War Office.'

'Very lucky. Another few days and I'd have been back with my regiment.'

The other man was introduced to me as Mr Allandale, my grandparents' solicitor from the North, and then we moved out to the cars. I drove with my aunt and uncle but not before I had seen the solicitor driving with Paul and heard Aunt Marcia saying, 'Robin would be glad to think Paul was here. They were friends from school although we always said they were not in the least alike. How long can you stay, Joanna?'

'I must go back in the morning, Aunt Marcia.'

'In that case I'm sure Paul will be glad to drive you. He too has to go back to London in the morning.'

'I have a return train ticket, Aunt Marcia, I really don't need to trouble Paul.'

'My dear child, I'm sure he'd feel awful if we allowed you to go back by train.'

Over lunch she raised the issue and Paul said immediately that he would be delighted to drive me back but we had to be off early as he had a meeting at the War Office later in the day.

During the afternoon we were made aware that the solicitor wished to read my grandparents' will and immediately Paul stated his intention of absenting himself from the proceedings.

183

'There's really no need,' Uncle Edward said quickly. 'You've known the family a long time, there's nothing secret about any of this.'

'Nevertheless I'll take a turn around the estate,' he said, showing more sensitivity than I had ever given him credit for.

Mr Allandale explained that my grandparents' will had been made while Robin was still alive but there would be no problems. The money left to him would automatically revert to his parents just as my father's would come to me if he failed to return. There was money left for Aunt Corallie and her family and bequests to charities and old servants. It was the last clause which left me visibly stunned however when the solicitor read, 'We leave to our granddaughter Joanna Albemarle the house known as Reckmire Hall in the County of Westmorland and sufficient money for its upkeep. Joanna loved the sea and for many years was denied it. Now she can either keep the house or sell it as she so wishes. It is our earnest wish that she will keep it.'

I could feel all eyes upon me as the solicitor brought his reading to a close, then after shaking hands with us in turn, he made his departure.

'You're surprised that Reckmire was left to you, Joanna?' Aunt Marcia asked quietly.

'Well, yes. I can't even begin to think what I will do. I shall need to find a job when the war is over and what will I do in that big house all by myself? My mother will never go there.'

'My parents took that into consideration when they left the property to you Joanna. They had no wish to separate you from your mother, but they did believe it was unhealthy for you to be denied the normal joys of womanhood by staying too closely to her. This was the only way they knew of assuring themselves you could have a life of your own.'

It was discussed again over dinner and this time Paul Cheviot was present. If the contents of my grandparents' will surprised him he gave no indication of it until much later when my uncle went out to see one of his employees on the estate and my aunt went into the kitchen to make coffee.

Then he said, 'So you are going to be the last Albemarle to live at Reckmire?'

'I'm not sure that I am going to live there. It isn't a very practical idea.'

'But a useful solution designed to get your mother off your back.'

'You don't know anything about my mother,' I said haughtily.

'Come on, Joanna. I know a great deal about her. I know who kept you away from the family and I know about the letters.'

'How? How do you know?'

'Robin told me none of the family had heard from you for ages, and later, much later, I asked him why when I knew that you and he were friends again.'

'What did he tell you?'

'That she'd hidden them.'

I said nothing more, and for a while there was silence. My aunt came back into the room and Paul said easily, 'I've been asking Joanna what she intends to do about Reckmire but she doesn't seem to know.'

'Well, of course not, Paul, it's something she needs to think very carefully about.'

'I'd know what to do with it if it had been left to me, particularly if I loved it as much as Joanna evidently does.'

'And what is that?' Aunt Marcia asked.

'I'd turn it into a country hotel. Get in some first-class staff to run it, keep the flat on for my own use, and make it so successful people would be clamouring to stay there. All it needs is a little bit of initiative.'

'What do you think about that, Joanna? I must say it's something that never even entered my head.'

'I can't even begin to think about it.'

'Then we'll talk some more on the way up to London,' said Paul.

'You need some good people to advise you. At this moment it's serving as a hospital for wounded heroes. There's nothing to say it couldn't make a top hotel.'

By the time I retired my head was buzzing with ideas. Uncle Edward had joined in enthusiastically with Paul's

185

suggestions, saying, 'It's a thought, Joanna. You'd be there to keep an eye on things, with a superb staff and the best chef you can find. It would give you a great purpose and you'd be living in the house you're so fond of. Try getting your mother interested. Who knows? She might suddenly realise that there are great possibilities.'

My eyes met Paul's across the room and I could feel the warm red blood flooding my face. He knew as I knew that my mother would hate the idea, and in the next breath Aunt Marcia said, 'Well, of course it's far too soon even to think about changing things yet. We don't know how long the war is going to last and all this is very much in the future. Anyway, you'll have a lot to think about, Joanna.'

Chapter Sixteen

We walked about nothing else on the way back to London. I had never thought to see Paul so full of enthusiasm for anything. He was discussing Reckmire as a personal dream, something he believed in. The more we talked the more I began to see the possibilities he envisaged. I could imagine the guests arriving along the drive, the conversation in the dining room, the relaxation in the beautiful drawing rooms, and the ministrations of soft-footed servants over exquisitely cooked meals and in beautifully appointed bedrooms.

'There's a good golf course within four miles, and you could have horses, Joanna, and resurface the tennis courts and perhaps add to them. In no time at all you'd have the most prestigious country hotel on the coast.'

'All I would need would be the guests,' I murmured quietly.

'Don't you think they'd come? Believe in yourself a little. See yourself as a young woman sitting on a fortune. It's not going to happen is it, Joanna? You're going to go home to Surrey and settle for mediocrity, go shopping with Mother, drink tea with Mother, be a slave to her bridge afternoons and women's gossip.'

His voice was taunting, the old Paul who had always had the power to put me down. We did not part as amicably as we had set out. I thanked him for the lift and my last impression was of his cool smile and dark cynical eyes.

Three weeks later I went home for the weekend to Surrey. I had telephoned my mother the evening before to tell her I would be arriving and across the room Jill had raised her eyebrows before saying, 'Are you going to tell her everything, Joanna?'

'Yes, I have to.'

'And what do you expect will be her reaction?'

'I'm not sure.'

'My dear girl, of course you're sure. She'll be angry. Angry that your grandparents have seen fit to leave you the house that she hates. She'll see it as a betrayal, and I can tell you there'll be tears and tantrums. Are you up to them, do you think?'

I said nothing. Instead I picked up my weekend case and with a brief smile said, 'I'll be home Sunday evening, Jill, wish me luck.'

I left the car at the side of the flats and walked through the gardens. I could see Mother standing at the window so I raised my hand to wave to her, but when I reached the front door Mother's friend Janice and Mr Walsh were just emerging.

Janice smiled then said effusively, 'Well, here you are, Joanna, your mother'll be delighted to see you. How long are you home for?'

'Only until tomorrow afternoon, Janice.'

Mr Walsh met my smile coolly but held the door open for me to pass inside the building.

Mother was still standing at the window when I entered the flat and without turning round said, 'Did they say anything, Joanna?'

'Janice asked how long I was home for. Mr Walsh didn't say a word.'

'It takes him all his time to speak to me. He's always in the flats visiting Janice or that new Mrs Wray. I think he does it deliberately.'

'Then I should ignore him, Mother, he's being very childish.'

'Well, he considers that I've hurt him. He was prepared to marry me. It isn't easy for a man to swallow that the woman he wants to marry puts her unmarried daughter first.'

'I'll put my case in the bedroom, Mother. I haven't brought much, it's only for one night, you know.'

'It's hardly worth coming for one night.'

The small pretty rooms stifled me, but I knew it wasn't really the rooms, it was the expression on my mother's face, that tight-lipped, shut-in expression which told me that she was angry: with the two people who had just left the flats, with life in general.

'After the war, Joanna, you and I are going to look around for somewhere else to live. They're building some flats out on the Guildford Road. There are notices up about them but of course they can't start the building work until the war is over.'

I didn't answer, so she said sharply, 'You surely don't expect me to stay on here if he comes to live with Janice or that other woman? They'd only be snickering and sneering behind our backs. Besides, those new flats will be more spacious than this one. We'll buy a new car and take a nice long holiday, somewhere in Scotland perhaps.'

'Have you had lunch, Mother?' I asked.

'I thought we'd go out. I so seldom go out for lunch now. I don't want to bump into them, but it doesn't matter if you're with me.'

So we went into town and had lunch at one of the cafes. The food was ordinary but she seemed to enjoy the fact that we met several of her friends who chatted amicably and all made the same sort of remarks, like, 'Perhaps the war will soon be over, Joanna, and you can come home to stay. You'll be looking forward to that, won't you?'

We looked at the shops and sauntered back to the flat in time to see Mr Walsh assisting Janice out of his car with her shopping.

'Have you been out to lunch?' she called. 'We've been to the new place at the top of the high street. It's very nice.'

Mother and I merely smiled while Mr Walsh seemed to behave too gallantly towards his companion as he carried most of her parcels into the flats.

By this time I was wishing fervently that I could avoid telling her about Grandma's death and my legacy, but there would never be a right time and she had to know.

The opportunity came later as we sat over our afternoon tea. She had gone on and on about the vagaries of Mr Walsh and the smugness of the two women he came to see. At last I could stand it no longer and blurted out, 'Mother, I have to tell you that Grandma Albemarle died last month.'

'Died! How did you get to know?'

'Aunt Marcia telephoned me.'

'How did she know where you were?'

So I told her I had seen Robin in London, but nothing of our deeper involvement. I told her about my visit to Somerset and Grandma's failing health, and that my father was a prisoner of war in Japanese hands. All the time I was dismally aware of her resentment. Cutting me off abruptly, she snapped, 'Did they ask you to go to the funeral?'

'Yes, Mother. I stayed the night at Aunt Marcia's and came home the next day.'

'What about your grandfather?'

'He died some time back, and no, I didn't go to his funeral, I didn't hear about it until later.'

'I don't suppose they asked about me?'

'As a matter of fact they did, Mother, they have always asked about you. If you'd taken the trouble to visit them they would have made you very welcome as they always made me.'

'Was it a very big funeral?'

'No. Grandma wasn't well known in the area. Only my aunt and uncle, her solicitor, Paul Cheviot and I. Some of the people who work on the estate were at the church.'

'Paul Cheviot? Wasn't he Robin's friend?'

'Yes. He's in the Army. He drove me up to London the next day.'

'I suppose she's left a great deal of money.'

'If father doesn't return after the war I am to receive his share, the rest went to Aunt Marcia and Aunt Corallie.'

'Isn't Reckmire a nursing home now? Whatever will happen to that?'

'They left Reckmire to me, Mother and sufficient money for its upkeep.'

If I had said I'd been left an estate on Mars she couldn't have been more astonished, and I waited for the astonishment to turn to anger and then to spite.

'How absolutely ridiculous to leave that lonely rambling

place to you when they must have known you didn't want it, that neither of us would ever want to live there.'

'It's a beautiful old house, Mother. To most people it would be a dream house with its lovely parkland, the sea lapping on the rocks, and within easy reach of the Lake District. I love Reckmire, Mother.'

'Surely you told them you didn't want it, or at least you're going to sell it, although that won't be easy. It will be left in a terrible mess. I can't see anybody taking it on when they realise it'll cost a fortune to restore it. It'll be a white elephant on your hands for years, Joanna. Your grandparents certainly did you no great favour leaving you that monstrosity.'

I could feel my anger mounting. I had wanted to broach the subject of what I might do with Reckmire gently and at some length; now I could hardly believe that it was my voice telling her coldly that Paul Cheviot and I had discussed its possibilities all the way back to London.

'Paul's right, Mother. It would make a beautiful hotel, not only because it's in such a good place. The rooms are large, the whole house is crying out to be lived in again, but very few people would be able to take it on as a private home. As a country hotel it's perfect.'

'Joanna, you're being ridiculous. It's frightening when the sea comes pouring along that beach, and all those long dismal marshes fill with the crying of sea birds. Who in their senses would want to stay in a place like that?'

'Well, I would for one, and other people have loved it. You've always had this thing about the sea and you won't even try to change.'

'And what's it got to do with Paul Cheviot anyway? Are you going around with him?'

'No, Mother, I'm not. I told you he was at the funeral and he drove me back to London. He was kind enough to offer his advice, and quite honestly I think he's given me a wonderful idea.'

'And what about me? I have no intention of living at Reckmire, so are you intending to leave me here where my closest friends have deserted me because of you?'

'Mother, that isn't true. How could you possibly tell your

friends how I intend to spend the rest of my life when I don't know myself? You can't live my life for me any more than I can live your life for you, I don't know what the future holds for me, I can't even think what is going to happen after the war is over, but I can't come back to coffee mornings and bridge parties, shopping and taking tea in the high street, moving into a new flat because you don't want to see your old friends. Mother, we both have a life to live. I love you, and when you need me I'll be here, but we have to be prepared to stand alone and give ourselves time to grow.'

How does one deal with a lost child who has never expected to be asked to stand alone? Her face was a mask of shocked bewilderment and I felt I had betrayed her totally.

I could hear her sobbing in her bedroom. Unable to stand it any longer I left the flat and walked briskly across the park. I was on my way back when I saw Mr Walsh walking Janice's dog along the path near the duck pond. I thought at first he was going to ignore me, then thinking better of it he muttered a brief 'good evening'.

I fell into step beside him and for some time we walked in silence, then he said sullenly, 'I suppose you're looking forward to coming home as soon as the war's over?'

'I'm looking forward to the war being over, Mr Walsh. I don't know what my plans are except that I shall only be coming home on regular visits.'

He turned to stare at me.

'I understood you'd be coming home to live permanently. At least that's what your mother told me.'

'I don't think that's a very good idea, do you, Mr Walsh? After all I made the break when I joined the Wrens, now I have to start thinking about some sort of job. Mother knows I'll always be there when she needs me but we both have to live our own lives. I'm so glad she has good friends she can rely on.'

I bent down to pat the dog, purposely not looking at him until my words had sunk in, then I was relieved to see the smile on his face and hear the warmth return to his voice.

'What does your mother think about your plans?' he asked cautiously.

'I'm sure she'll agree that they're for the best when she's got used to them. I left her alone to think it over. Perhaps I'd better get back now. Goodbye, Mr Walsh.'

He smiled. 'Goodbye, Joanna. It's been nice talking to you.'

I knew that he would think about our conversation and hoped in time they would resume their friendship. He quite obviously still thought a lot about her and he was the type of man who would spoil and cosset her. I hoped what he received in return would be enough for him.

It was raining when I arrived back in London, soft April rain that felt like a caress on my face. My heart felt strangely light, and when I looked about me it was as though my own feeling of euphoria was echoed in the faces of those around me. Shoulders were squarer, heads were uplifted, and there were smiles on faces that had known four long years of grief. Things were going well for us at last in Europe, Germany was on the verge of defeat and Hitler was holed up somewhere in his secret bunker.

I heard Jill humming when I let myself into the flat and while she made coffee I told her about the weekend I had spent in Surrey.

'So you've told her at last?' she said when the tale was told.

'Yes, and I hated myself for it. She has a chance of happiness, Jill, I hope she has the good sense to take it.'

'What will you do when the war is over?'

'Thanks to my grandparents I have enough money so I can afford to think for a while. There's Reckmire. I don't know how long it will take to make it a house again, but I shall definitely go up there if only to recapture something of the past.'

'Will you sell it, do you think?'

'Jill, I don't know. I can't bear to think of anybody else living in it, but I'm too young to stay there without a job of some sort.'

'Couldn't you do something with it?'

'Paul Cheviot suggested turning it into a country hotel

but I'd need so much advice. After all, what do I know about the hotel business?'

'But it has possibilities?'

'Perhaps.'

'Would he help you?'

'Oh, Jill, how could I ask him? We never got on, you know, and after the war he'll be going back to the family woollen mills in Yorkshire. He'll have too much to do after all this time away even to think of helping me sort Reckmire out.'

'All the same, I'd give it a thought. If not Paul, somebody else would step in, I feel sure. If the place was good enough for a nursing home then why not a country hotel?'

'Anything happened at the Admiralty while I've been in Surrey? Do you know what I'll be doing in the morning?'

'I haven't a clue. The news is good, Joanna. I'll be off to live in America pretty soon, I hope.'

'Won't you miss England terribly?'

'Well, yes, of course. The mere thought of it fills me with nostalgia, but we'll visit in happier times, I hope. My folks will come out to us and at least we speak the same language.'

I laughed. 'That is an advantage, I suppose. I wonder how my aunt and uncle in Italy have weathered the war? I hope I'll be able to visit them pretty soon.'

'And Carlo? Are you hoping to visit him?'

'He's probably married to my cousin by this time. It's so strange to think that he's been at war, probably in one of the Italian services ranged against us.'

'The enemy!' Jill said with a one-sided smile.

'I suppose so, although I still remember how kind he was, how sweet to a besotted English schoolgirl which is what I was then.'

'I don't think Italy's heart was ever in the war, I think they were dragged into it protesting. At least they've made Mussolini pay with his life for joining up with Hitler.'

I shuddered when I thought of Mussolini and his mistress captured when they had almost reached the Swiss border, and their execution on one of the hills about Lake Como. It all seemed a long way from the dreaming

194

countryside of Tuscany and Umbria and my joyous memories of Florence. Jill echoed my thoughts when she said, 'You'll all have so much to talk about when you meet again, Joanna.'

Chapter Seventeen

Weeks later I sat in the car waiting for the two senior Naval officers who were visiting Camell Laird's shipyard in Barrow-in-Furness where they were inspecting progress on the latest submarine.

A warm sun shone out of a clear blue sky and as I sat there, suddenly the entire shipyard seemed to erupt into life. Men poured out of the yards and the offices waving Union Jacks, hugging one another, shouting with joy, surrounding the car, opening the door and pulling me out to hug me with delighted smiles. The war in Europe was over.

It was 7 May, and at Rheims Germany had surrendered unconditionally to the Allies but if we rejoiced at the news we remembered too the miracle of Dunkirk, the treachery of Pearl Harbour, and the helplessness of a civilian population under nightly bombardment.

It was joy and relief unconfined. Later would come the memories of despair, vulnerability and bitterness at the cruel waste; the weeping for those men and women who would not be coming home. But for now who could begrudge us the celebration of victory?

I was seized and kissed by the two officers who had travelled with me in dignified silence and on the way back to London we drove through towns and villages alive with the sound of church bells and where flags and streamers straggled the streets and children sat at long wooden tables piled high with rations of food that had been hoarded for weeks in anticipation of today.

In London they danced in the streets. Trafalgar Square

was crowded with people and for the first time in years lights streamed down on the crowds in front of Buckingham Palace while they cheered until they were hoarse at the sight of the King and Queen on the palace balcony. Jill and I cheered with them. Tears streamed down our faces and we were kissing strangers with the same sort of affection we would have accorded brothers. The war was over, tomorrow or the day after we would think about the peace.

I went down to Surrey on a golden morning at the beginning of June on four days' leave. The trees were bursting into pale green leaf and the hedgerows were alive with May blossom. I had telephoned my mother the evening before to tell her that I was coming and her reply had been that everybody had been asking when I expected to be demobbed and that the library was very anxious to have me back on a full-time basis. I didn't expect the few days ahead to be easy ones.

She looked well. She had changed her hair style from its neat shingled shape to a flattering bob and was wearing a tweed skirt and pretty pink blouse which was a nice change from her favourite beige.

When I commented on how well she was looking, she said airily, 'Well, of course I'm relieved that the war is over and we're getting back to normal.'

Hastily I said, 'How is everybody, Mother, Janice and the others, and how is Mr Walsh?'

'They're all quite well and looking forward to seeing you,' she replied cautiously. 'I've had the car serviced and there's no reason why we shouldn't go out somewhere,' she added. 'Mr Walsh has been trying it out and he says it's taken no harm from being laid up so long.'

'Wouldn't he like to come with us this afternoon, Mother?'

'Oh, I don't think so, dear. I told him I wanted you all to myself for these next few days. He understands perfectly.'

So we drove into the country and had afternoon tea. She sat beside me with a contented look on her face, I couldn't be unkind enough to call it smug, but I was troubled. Day followed day in the same pattern. None of her friends called but I saw Janice in the hall and she greeted me with a smile and said, 'You'll soon be home for good, Joanna.'

I went one morning to see Miss Carson at the library and she was quick to inform me that Mother had asked her if there might be a permanent position for me after the war, and then she looked at me quizzically, waiting for my reply.

'I doubt if I shall be coming back here,' I told her. 'I made that very clear to Mother some time ago.'

'Then she hasn't accepted it, Joanna,' she replied. 'What are you going to do?'

So I told her about Reckmire ending with the words, 'Am I being very selfish in wanting a life of my own?'

'Well, of course you're not,' she said firmly. 'There will be a lot of girls coming back to their homes but they have mothers who don't stifle them or expect to be their sole preoccupation. My own life's been dictated by Mother's illness but your mother's a perfectly fit woman, young enough to make a whole new start. And I'm sure you don't want to end up like me, an old maid working at the library, depending on books for excitement and the joys of foreign travel. Get away, Joanna. Besides, what about the gentleman friend who fetches and carries for her, changes her library books and helps her in and out of the car as if she was a piece of Dresden china?'

I laughed. 'He hasn't been around so it's unlikely I'll see him before I go back. I think he's had explicit instructions not to call.'

'Well, he'll be in this morning around twelve to change his library books. He's a creature of habit, I can almost set the clock by him.'

'Then I'll hang around and wait,' I replied.

After coffee I wandered round the shelves. Nothing seemed to have changed, the old men still sat reading the newspapers in the corner of the room and the laughter and shouts of the children came in through the open window from the school across the way. It seemed incredible that all the years of war had left things the same and yet I knew that some of the schoolboys I remembered were now in uniform and many of them would never see their sons striding across the cricket pitch they had loved.

At a minute to twelve Mr Walsh arrived carrying three

books which he handed in at the desk and then proceeded to the shelves. I waited until he had made his selection then joined him while he waited for them to be stamped by the assistant.

He looked up and smiled and I waited for him at the door. Together we set out down the street and he said almost shyly, 'Any news about demob, Joanna?'

'No. We still have a war raging in the Far East, I don't expect anything until it is completely over.'

'And then what, back to the library?'

'I don't think so. Nothing has changed since we last talked, Mr Walsh. I'm glad you and Mother are friends again. She's told me what a help you've been with the car and many other things.'

For some time we walked in silence and then he said somewhat diffidently, 'I don't think she's really taken it in that you don't mean to come back here, Joanna. I don't discuss it with her, not even when she's going on about your coming home. I'm prepared to wait.'

'You're that fond of her, Mr Walsh?'

'Well, yes. She's the kind of woman I've always admired, sweet and gentle, shy and pretty.'

It was very evident he hadn't discovered the steel underneath that all too gentle exterior. If he spent the rest of his life talking the way she talked, liking the things she liked, no yearning after the sea, no large dogs, then perhaps life with Mother would be bliss, but would it be enough? Curiously I asked, 'Have you ever had a dog, Mr Walsh?'

'Oh, yes. I always had a dog when I was younger, but my wife wasn't all that fond of them and Linda isn't keen. Actually Linda has a lot of the same ideas as my wife Anne had. She didn't like the sea. She said her arthritis was always worse at the coast so we tended to take our holidays in Scotland or the Lake District.'

I began to feel less guilty about his affection for Mother, or that I was shelving my responsibility. I hoped Mother would see that she could have happiness with the man walking beside me. There was no doubting the sincerity of his affection for her.

'Has Mother said any more about moving into a larger flat?' I asked curiously.

'Not for some time. Of course no building could start during the war and although we've driven past the site a couple of times she's never seemed too bothered. I rather think she shelved all thoughts of them until you made up your mind what you wanted to do.'

'It doesn't rest with me, Mr Walsh. Please believe me I am not coming back to Surrey to live. She will always know where she can reach me and I shall visit her as often as possible, but I do want her to make a life for herself. Please go on being her good friend. I'm sure in time she will come to realise just how important you are to her.'

His face lit up with such a warm blushing smile that I warmed to him. I hoped and prayed that in the years ahead my mother would not disappoint him with the actions that had driven my father away and alienated me.

For the rest of my leave whenever Mother's thoughts strayed to what she expected after I returned home I quickly changed the subject, and if she appeared slightly bewildered when I refused to discuss it, the time passed without problems. It was only on my last evening that she said, as she stood in the doorway to my room watching me pack, 'Have you decided what to do about that house on the coast?'

'Do you mean Reckmire, Mother?'

'Whatever it's called. I hope you're going to sell it? You could do a lot with the money. We could buy an absolutely wonderful flat and there's no way you could hope to live there on your own.'

'I haven't any idea about it at the moment, Mother. When the time is right I'll go up there and take a look round. At the moment it's still a nursing home so there's nothing I can do.'

'You'll see, they'll have completely ruined the place. It'll want a fortune spending on it. I can't think what your grandparents were thinking about and it's not going to please Corallie or Marcia.'

'Aunt Marcia doesn't want it, they have the place in Somerset, and Aunt Corallie has lived in Italy all her married life. Why should they mind?'

'I still think it's ridiculous. And I suppose you think your father's coming home after the war and he'll want to live there? You'd rather live with him than me.'

'I'd like my father to come home, Mother, I pray for it every single night, but I can't think beyond that. Please, we have been happy together these last few days, don't let us quarrel now.'

She turned away abruptly and I heard her a few minutes later opening and closing cupboards in the kitchen.

Life in London resumed normality because now there were no nightly air-raids and yet we were all aware that in the Far East the Japanese were fighting bitterly to hang on to the territories they had taken.

On 6 August an atomic bomb was dropped on Hiroshima and three days later on 9 August, a second on Nagasaki. The Japanese had been our enemy, a cruel and treacherous one, but tempering our jubilation was horror at the population of two major cities lying dead or dying from a pestilence too horrible to contemplate.

The Japanese had had enough. On 2 September 1945, on the battleship *Missouri*, General Douglas MacArthur received the unconditional surrender of the Japanese Government. World War II was officially over.

At the beginning of November I went with Jill's family to see her depart for America. Tears were shed, but Jill eventually stood smiling from the rail of the *Queen Mary* and continued to wave until the ship became a disappearing speck on Southampton Water.

Two days later I left the London flat for the last time to drive north to Reckmire. I left the keys with the cleaners who had already moved in and did not look back as I drove my newly acquired Hillman out of the square. A chapter of my life was over, tomorrow would be a whole new start.

Book III

Chapter Eighteen

It was early evening when I let myself into the hall at Reckmire Hall. It was hard to imagine that only a few weeks before it had been a nursing home occupied by young men and a hospital staff. The hall stared back at me, stark and empty of furniture, and my footsteps echoed hollowly as I walked across the floor to stand in the centre staring round despondently.

The electricity was on, but only a single light bulb shone from the fitting in the centre of the hall. Once there had hung a brass chandelier, ornate and gleaming with at least twelve bulbs, and my heart sank when I realised every room would be the same, devoid of furniture and sparkling with hospital starkness.

My grandparents' furniture had been placed in storage when they elected to go to their daughter in Somerset and now I would have the task of bringing it out.

I could hardly believe that the last occupants had left nothing behind. As I wandered from room to room the same air of desolation met me. Only the flat at the top of the house gave any indication of warmth and I moved about quickly switching on all the lights, hunting for an electric fire which I found in the main bedroom.

This was home. This was filled with memories of Robin and those fateful few days we had spent together, but he had gone, and now it was just a flat, impersonal and vaguely sterile.

I had informed Grandpa's solicitor that I would be arriving at the flat and he had arranged for the electricity and the gas to be on, so for a while I unpacked my suitcase and put away my clothes, then I went into the kitchen to make coffee. In the cupboards were tins of salmon and fruit, biscuits and jam, enough at any rate to make a modest meal, and I had brought bread and milk with me. Tomorrow there would be time for shopping and a visit to the solicitors in Kendal.

My spirits rose as the room grew warmer and I knelt on the rug in front of the fire sipping my coffee and eating ham sandwiches.

Lamplight and the glow from the fire gave the flat a more lived in air and soon I would have to think about making up the bed, hoping against hope that I would find an electric blanket or a hot water bottle.

It was months since anybody had occupied the flat and Robin had been more aware of where everything was kept than I. I thought dismally about the large empty rooms beneath me. The undraped windows that looked out on the gardens and the sea, and then I thought about the turret room.

I was not nervous of the empty rooms, but as I opened the door of the flat I was very aware of the cold that met me. I returned for my trench coat, and ignoring the light switches made my way unerringly by the help of the bright moonlight that came through the large windows.

The turret room had always remained unchanged, and so it was now. Only one chair stayed in its place facing the door and I thought about Major Carter, sightless and waiting for a young wife, and wondered if she ever came and if they had a future together. How many silent and lonely hours he must have spent in this room. I could feel the tears pricking my eyes as I moved behind the chair towards the window.

Moonlight illuminated the long reach of Reckmire Marsh and the sea rolled in benignly across the smooth sands. I was about to turn away when from out of the shadows I saw somebody walking slowly towards the sea, and my heart missed several beats when I saw that it was a man, somebody tall, his hands thrust into the pockets of his coat, who came to stand at the edge of the surf staring out to sea, pensive and brooding.

Who was this stranger who was invading our beach at

such a late hour? Then, with my heart racing, I thought the impossible: Robin or maybe my father. Suppose my father was home in England, suffering from amnesia, wondering why he was here and unable to remember people he had loved.

Without a second's thought I ran out of the room and down the stairs, my fingers hurting in their haste to unlock the bolts on the doors, then I was scrambling across the rocks and running wildly in the wake of the tall figure strolling away from me along the shore.

I was gasping for breath, willing him to turn, and was only feet away when suddenly he must have sensed my presence. He turned. For a long moment a sense of utter desolation swept over me, then came the surprise. It was Paul Cheviot's face that looked back at me, his eyebrows raised in cynical surprise, a half smile on his chiselled lips.

I gasped, 'Paul, what are you doing here?'

'I might ask you the same question,' he answered coolly.

'This is my house,' I answered him without hesitation.

The smiled deepened. 'Yes, of course. Joanna Albemarle has come back to claim her inheritance, and have you decided what to do with it?'

He was aware that he could always make me angry, and I was angry now. With his sarcasm, so subtly patronising. He knew very well that I didn't know what to do with it. Reckmire was a white elephant hanging round my neck and this was not the time to be angry or too proud.

I fell into step beside him as we turned towards the house, and quietly I said, 'I saw you from the turret room, I hoped you might be my father. Surely we shall hear something now that the war in the Far East is over?'

'You think he would come here before anywhere else?' he asked curiously.

'I don't know. I only hoped. What are you doing here, Paul?'

'I'm due for demob in a few days now, I'm just having a quiet weekend and I decided to stay at the Flying Horse and renew my acquaintance with Reckmire. I spent some happy hours here with Robin and his family, the happiest time in my young life, now it's gone forever. This was my last goodbye to the place.'

'I see.'

'You're in the flat, I suppose?'

'Well, yes. Tomorrow I have to arrange about the return of the furniture but I can't stay here, Paul. I can't just restore the house and live here doing nothing. I'm twenty-five years old, I need a job. Do you think anybody would be interested in buying the place?'

'Unlikely. So soon after the war I doubt if there's that sort of money about, and in a place of this size you'd need staff to run it. Ask your solicitor for some advice.'

'Would you like to come back to the house for a drink? There's sherry in the cupboard or I could make coffee.'

He consulted his watch, then with a brief smile said, 'I doubt if the Flying Horse locks its doors. Perhaps for a little while.'

So we returned to the house and while I made coffee Paul sat staring into the fire and I could only guess at his thoughts. That they were not of this moment I felt sure. Most likely they were of other years when he came to this house with Robin and Gabriella was here, dark and lovely and strangely exotic.

I handed him his coffee and for a moment he sat with the cup in his hands and I waited, expecting some reference to the past, surprised when he said, 'Did you ever think about my ideas of turning this place into a country hotel?'

'How could I? I don't know the least thing about hotel management, or how to set about it. I feel sure Grandpa's solicitor would pretty soon scotch that idea.'

He shrugged his shoulders. 'You would want real advice, Joanna, not the advice of a country solicitor who probably handles very little beyond property, wills and death duties. I would know how to handle it but then Reckmire doesn't belong to me. I do suggest you give it some thought and try to get some proper advice. You say you need a job? You could make this your job. A sheltered upbringing's done little to prepare you for life in the big world, Joanna.'

I bit my lip angrily, the sharp retort quickly on my lips. 'I haven't lived in a sheltered world since I was twenty. I've lived in a capital city bombed night after night and I've done my war job to the best of my ability. I know you listened to stories about my mother but I'm not like her, I never was.'

He smiled. 'I know you were always quick to slap me down, but then your mother always made the rules, didn't she, and your father conformed?'

'They did split up.'

'And not before time.'

'I don't want to quarrel with you, Paul, but do we have to talk about all that now?'

'No, you're right and it's time I was getting back to the pub. I hope you get everything sorted out, Joanna. I can't even think that in no time at all I'll be back in the family mills doing a job I hate, quarrelling with my father, resentful of my mother. At least you've had the guts to make the break.'

'Why don't you?'

'For what? I'm an only son. One day the mills and everything that goes with them will be mine. I have a cousin who's held the fort for five long years and who won't relish taking a back seat, but I'd have too much to lose if I decided to cut and run. Besides I don't really know anything else.'

'But you have ideas?'

'Yes, I have ideas about tea planting in Ceylon, safari in Kenya and sheep farming in New Zealand, but it's all better done by people who have the know how. I'd be an amateur, Joanna. In the woollen mills of Yorkshire, I know what I'm doing.'

We walked in silence through the empty house and I let him out through the front door. We did not shake hands. Instead he looked down at me with his familiar one-sided smile before saying, 'If we don't meet again, Joanna, good luck.'

I couldn't sleep. For hours I lay tossing and turning until first light found me in the tiny kitchen making coffee with my mind in turmoil. My thoughts were all of this house as a famous hotel. Its rooms devoted to the comfort of guests who would arrive in their expensive cars, demanding first-class service, expecting luxury they were willing to pay for.

I thought about rooms filled with flowers and polished furniture, gardens tended by an army of gardeners, hot houses and vegetable gardens, and stables filled with thoroughbred hunters. I thought about expensive food exquisitely served, and bedrooms and bathrooms, delicate and beautiful, looking out on a sea which in my imagination was always blue and calm.

I imagined the staff I would have. Willing and gracious, soft-footed and softly spoken, imbued with a sense of loyalty to the hotel and its guests, and by the time the rain patterned on the windows and I saw with amazement that the time was eight o'clock, I knew what I must do.

I drove quickly through the empty village street because it was too early for the shops to open and only a solitary paperboy was pushing his bicycle from one house to the next.

I drove quickly into the car park besides the Flying Horse, looking around to see if Paul's car was still parked there and relieved to see that it was. The front door of the small inn was open and a sleepy landlord stared at me with the utmost surprise as I asked at the bar if Mr Paul Cheviot was having breakfast.

'That he is miss, and he's asked for his bill so you've only just caught 'im. Who shall I say is askin for 'im?'

'Joanna Albemarle.'

He raised his eyebrows. 'Miss Albemarle fro' Reckmire, is it?'

'Yes.'

'Wait 'ere, miss, I'll not be a minute.'

While I waited a young girl came in to remove the ashtrays of the night before overflowing with cigarette stubbs. The smell of cigarette smoke was still prominent, and she next appeared with a vacuum cleaner and proceeded to clean the floor after placing the chairs on the small tables. Then the landlord was back, saying, 'Mr Cheviot's asked me to take you to 'im, Miss Albemarle. Perhaps you'd like some breakfast?'

'Coffee would be very nice.'

'Follow me, miss.'

Paul was the only person eating in the tiny dining room, sitting at a table near the window and staring at me with the utmost surprise on his face.

He pulled up a chair for me to sit next to him, asking if I would like breakfast, and the landlord was quick to inform him that he was bringing me coffee.

'Well, well,' he said. 'What exactly merits a visit from you at this ungodly hour?'

'Paul, I have to talk to you. I've not been able to sleep, I've lain awake all night thinking about what you said last night.'

'What did I say?'

'You know very well. About turning Reckmire into a country hotel. I think you're right, it will make a marvellous hotel, but I don't know how to go about it. Where can I get advice, who will help me?'

'Talk to your solicitor when you visit him this afternoon,' he said stolidly.

'I want you to help me. You know exactly what we should do.'

'We?'

'Yes, we. You love Reckmire. You have all the ideas. You must have thought about it or you'd never have brought it up in the first place.'

'My dear girl, it was a pipe dream, nothing more. I have a job to go to, and it's miles away. How could I possibly help you here when I return to Yorkshire and the family?'

'But you hate the mills. You even hate your father.'

'Putting it a bit strong perhaps, but in a way you're right. Father and I have never seen eye to eye, but trying to get along with him secures my future. What are you offering in its place, Joanna?'

'I would make you my manager. You could help me run the hotel. If the hotel is successful you would be too.'

'My dear girl, I would want more than that. Are you aware of what I would be giving up to help you? Three woollen mills in Yorkshire with full order books. Work people who expect me to return to run those mills and a stern father who asks for nothing less. You're not even sure if this place would take off.'

'You said it would. You said that was what you would do if it had been left to you instead of me.'

'But it wasn't, Joanna. I wasn't a grandchild. It was a

vision of what might have been, nothing more.'

'Then you should have kept your opinions to yourself instead of making me think they might work. Why didn't you mind your own business?'

He raised his eyebrows maddeningly. 'Well, I must admit this is a taste of the old Joanna I didn't like, the girl who couldn't stand me.'

'I can see I've wasted your time. I'm sorry.'

The landlord appeared with my coffee which Paul poured out with a steady hand and a thoughtful expression while I sat seething and wishing I was a million miles away.

He went on calmly buttering his toast and spooning marmalade on to his plate. After I had finished my coffee I scrambled to my feet pushing back my chair.

'Going already?'

'There's nothing more to be said. I'm sorry I bothered you, Paul, you must be anxious to get back.'

'Well, it's a fair journey and not a very nice day for crossing the Pennines.'

He rose to his feet but didn't offer to take my hand. With a brief goodbye I left him to his breakfast while the landlord stared after me curiously as I let myself out of the door.

I could settle to nothing. I was angry with myself for even thinking that Paul Cheviot would help me. I felt humiliated, and yet on thinking it out, how could I really ask him to forsake an assured future for a vague prospect?

I had offered to make him my manager, but manager of what? A pipe dream, that was all. By late morning I had already talked myself into the idea that Reckmire must be restored into looking a house again and then hopefully sold.

I telephoned the storage warehouse and asked for the furniture to be brought over as soon as possible, then I telephoned the solicitor to say I would be able to keep our appointment in Kendal at three o'clock. It was still raining but I felt unable to stay in the house. I would drive into Kendal and take a look around. It was years since I had been there and surely I would be able to get some lunch there at one of Grandma's favourite restaurants.

Once more I donned my trench coat and placed a silk scarf

over my head then I ran down the stairs and crossed the hall. I heard the sound of a car outside and stood just within the door wondering who my caller might be. I heard the doorbell echoing noisily in the empty rooms and opened the door to meet Paul Cheviot's eyes with the utmost amazement.

'Going out?' he asked in surprise.

'Yes,' I said, gathering my thoughts. 'I'm going into Kendal to see the solicitor.'

'But your appointment wasn't until this afternoon, I thought I'd be sure to catch you in.'

'Well, you have, but I was restless. I couldn't stay in the house doing nothing with so many things on my mind.'

'Particularly this house and its future? We have to talk and I don't propose to do it with the rain coming down and you clutching that umbrella like a lifeline.'

For a long moment we stared at each other, then I stepped aside so that he could enter the house. We faced each other in the empty hall until Paul said, 'Well, aren't you going to invite me into the flat so that at least we can talk in comfort?'

He followed me across the hall and up the curving shallow staircase. After a moment he said, 'It's hard to think what the place looked like in the old days. I don't suppose you've done anything yet about the furniture?'

'I've asked them to bring it over as soon as possible, hopefully early next week.'

'I'm glad. It's horrible like this.'

Within the flat he took the chair in front of the hearth easily, and I stood opposite, unsure why he had come, watching him gazing critically round the flat's living room, the only sound the steady beat of the rain on the window and the distant rumbling of the sea. I was determined that he should be the first to speak, that deliberately I would not ask him why he had come, and maddeningly he made me wait, fully aware of my chagrin and impatience.

He took out his cigarette case and leisurely lit a cigarette, offering the case to me and when I refused slowly putting it back into his pocket. Then, through a haze of cigarette smoke, his eyes met mine, cool sardonic eyes that were faintly amused. Still I stayed silent.

'I suppose you're wondering why I've come?' he said at last.

'Yes. I didn't think we had anything else to say to each other.'

'I thought so too, Joanna, but you gave me something to think about, and the more I thought about it the more I came to realise its possibilities.'

I stared at him, surprised, my heart racing oddly.

'Right from the start I saw them but it all had nothing to do with me, neither this house nor you. Now when you asked for my help I still didn't think it was any of my affair, but if you spent the night wondering I've spent the rest of the morning doing the same thing. You know what you are asking of me, don't you? That I should infuriate my father who has never got along with me. Leave a job for which I have been trained all my adult life, a family business that was my grandfather's and which I knew would one day be mine. My mother will be devastated, if she can still remember what day it is, a state of mind she has adopted after years of living with a man who has neither time for her nor love. Living in her own world has been her defence against him. Now she doesn't know anything else. What, my dear Joanna, did you suggest putting in its place?'

For a minute I stared at him, then hoarsely I said, 'To make you my manager,' and he laughed derisively as I knew he would.

'Your manager. My dear girl, I am the director of a lucrative firm. It simply isn't enough to lure me away from that.'

'Then what?'

'A partnership. Two innocents embarking upon a world of which they know nothing, but a world of possibilities if they keep their heads on their shoulders. You couldn't do it alone. I could, but then Reckmire isn't mine. Once again, Joanna, what's in it for me? I'll take nothing less than a partnership. Straight down the middle. A half share in the hotel, the takings, its success or failure. But by God, if I come into it it's not going to fail. I've been brought up to discount failure. If you decide to take me on those are my terms and I will accept nothing less. I don't know how long you want to think about it, or even if you want to think about it at all, but if it doesn't appeal to you then I suggest you sort out this mess and put the house on the market as quickly as possible. In one thing your mother was right. Your grandparents did you no favour when they left this house to you.'

'Why do you say that?'

'To live here because you love it. To bury yourself here without work, without companionship. No, they didn't think too deeply when they made that decision.'

'They always hoped my father would come back.'

'But would he want to live here now if he did? Would he really want to recapture a youth that's gone forever?'

I didn't know. All I knew was that there was a bubble called hope dangling before my eyes and another called opportunity. Without Paul all I had was a pipe dream and a house that nobody might want; with him there was vigour and ruthlessness, a strong man standing beside me, even if he was one I had never really understood or even liked.

He was watching me closely, interpreting the shadows of doubt that crossed my face. Suddenly rising to his feet, he said softly, 'It's no use, is it, Joanna? You don't think it would work, and on reflection I think you're probably right.'

I watched him walk across the room towards the door and dismally I heard his footsteps retreating along the passage and down the stairs. I wanted him to turn round with some words of encouragement and gentleness but he didn't, and then something inexplicable sent me rushing after him, calling to him from the stairs, 'Paul, wait. You can have it, everything you want, a business partnership!'

He stood staring up at me.

'Half of everything we make, everything we accomplish?'

'Yes. Come with me to the solicitors, you can explain things better than I can.'

He smiled.

215

Chapter Nineteen

Three weeks passed. The furniture was back in the house and decorators had changed the rooms from clinical whiteness to softer, more livable hues. Reckmire was a home again.

The solicitor in Kendal was, if not scathing, unconvinced that the house could ever become a country hotel. He gave me a hundred and one reasons why this was not possible, all of them good ones, and as each day passed I was beginning to agree with him. Of Paul there was no sign. No telephone calls, and even if I had known where to find him pride wouldn't have allowed me to try.

My anger at his cavalier treatment prompted me to place the house in the hands of an estate agent, though always at the back of my mind was his enthusiasm for the project. But that was before he had seen his father, and now in all probability he had changed his mind and didn't quite know how to tell me.

I was very aware that the fate of Reckmire was discussed in the village. Whenever I passed Mrs Peabody was very much in evidence at her front door, usually in the company of other women who turned their heads to watch me drive past.

I did most of my shopping in Kendal or Lancaster and felt a strange reluctance to go to the baker's shop in the village. I knew that Lottie had been nursing during the war and had seen nothing of her since I returned. I was surprised therefore to see her waving to me from the dunes one morning when I walked along the beach. She had always been reluctant to venture down so I went to join her, climbing up the rocks where once Robin had pulled me after him.

She was smiling, and looked hardly any older than she had at our last meeting.

'My mother said you were down here, Joanna. I was hopin' I might see you this mornin'.

'I heard you were nursing. Is it a permanent vocation?'

'Yes. I'm in the Midlands at the moment but I'm 'opin' to transfer up here as soon as there's an opening. I'm a staff nurse now so there's a good chance.'

'I'm glad, Lottie, you've done well. Has your sister been demobbed?'

'She came out o' the army a long time ago, invalided out she was, but then when she got better she joined the Land Army and worked on local farms. I expect the army was glad to be rid of her and she's been good on the land.'

'I must say you don't seem to think much of her.'

'She's always been trouble, but she does seem to 'ave settled down a bit. Are you visitin', Joanna, or are you intendin' to live 'ere.'

'What does Mrs Peabody say I'm doing?' I couldn't resist asking, and was rewarded by seeing the deep red blush suffusing her cheeks.

'You can tell me, Lottie, I've seen the women gossiping every time I've been into the village,' I added.

'Well, she comes into the shop with all sorts of stories. My mother doesn't say anything because she doesn't know anything, but Cook left Reckmire afore the war so she's lost her main source of tittle-tattle.'

I laughed. Well able to imagine Mrs Peabody's frustration at having to guess instead of being told.

'Everything's changed, Lottie. Both my grandparents are dead and Robin was killed during the war. My father's still out in the Far East, that's if he's still alive, and although I see Aunt Marcia, none of us has heard from Italy since the war was over.'

'But you're here. What are you going to do with the house?'

'I honestly don't know. It was left to me.'

'Gracious, Joanna, are you going to live in that great place on your own?'

'I'm having all sorts of thoughts about it but up to the

moment none of them make sense.' I had already decided I would say nothing to Lottie yet. In any case there was very little I could tell her and supposition would only cause a lot of gossip.

She was walking beside me, pensive and thoughtful, and after a while she said softly, 'I'm sorry about Robin, I liked 'im. Actually I had a terrible crush on 'im. He never made me feel like a country bumpkin – not like that friend of his.'

'You didn't like Paul?'

'No, but then you didn't either.'

'He was at Robin's house for Grandma's funeral, I got along with him rather better. People change, Lottie. You've changed and so have I.'

I didn't know why I was defending Paul when I was so furious with him.

We reached the gate leading into the gardens and I said, 'Come in and take a look round. I've got the house fairly straight, at least the carpets are down now and most of the furniture in place.'

'Did the nursing home leave a terrible mess?'

'No, they were very good.'

While I made tea she wandered around the house, and when at last she joined me in the morning room I was surprised to see tears in her eyes.

'Oh, Joanna,' she said sadly 'it's like walking through a monument. No voices, no laughter, it's like a dead thing.'

I stared at her. She was voicing my own feelings every morning when I walked downstairs to pick up the morning post. The house did feel like a museum with notices for silence written large on every wall, and yet I felt fiercely protective towards it. It was my house, I had a duty towards it, how could I ever betray it?

'Are you sure it's safe to be livin' in this great house all on your own?' Lottie was saying while she sat at the table spooning sugar into her tea.

'I haven't thought about it.'

'You should tell the police you're 'ere and get them to keep an eye on things.'

'Yes, that's a good idea, Lottie. I'll do that.'

'I'm only home for the odd day or so but I'd like to see you again.'

'Well, you know where to find me. Come for coffee in the morning and we'll talk some more.'

'I'll do that. The roads are so lonely at night and there's rain coming on. Are you wanting anything from the shop?'

'Oh, yes, some of your mother's cakes. You know what I like. Here, I'll give you some money.'

'No. My treat, Joanna.'

I watched her leave the house, running along the garden paths, then turned back into the house and bolted the stout door securely behind me.

Lottie and I were drinking morning coffee in the kitchen with an array of her mothers baking before us when there was the sound of a car screeching to a halt in front of the house, followed by the loud ringing of the front door bell.

It was Sunday morning and I stared at Lottie in amazement, but she merely said. 'Like as not it's the local police. I got my father to telephone them last night to take a look round here.'

'Thank you, Lottie. I'd better go and talk to them.'

I hurried to the door, pulling back the bolts and opening it, but instead of a uniformed policeman I found Paul Cheviot standing in the courtyard looking up at the house.

I couldn't help the resentment that flashed in my eyes at the sight of his amused expression. His large tourer stood in the centre of the courtyard and before I could say anything he said evenly, 'I've left my luggage at the Flying Horse then I came straight here. You seem very surprised.'

'Well, of course I'm surprised. I haven't heard from you, no telephone calls, nothing to tell me you were coming. I thought you'd forgotten about me.'

He raised his eyebrows in maddening surprise before following me into the hall then said casually, 'I didn't see any point in ringing you until I'd something concrete to tell you. I'm staying at the pub. After all, we must observe the niceties. You don't want the village up in arms at our staying together.'

'I've just made coffee,' I told him. 'Lottie's here, we're in the kitchen.'

He followed me. On entering the kitchen Lottie looked up with surprise. Paul merely greeted her with a cool nod and observed, 'Cakes. Highly fattening. Just coffee for me, please.'

His mere presence upset Lottie. She became silent where before she'd been happy to chat, and he appeared to enjoy her discomfiture. There were so many questions I wanted to ask him, but not in front of Lottie, and he sat back in his chair calmly drinking his coffee and eyeing us both with cool detachment.

I watched Lottie gathering her handbag from the floor, her face flushed, saying quickly, 'Well, I'd better be goin', Joanna. My mother'll be expectin' some 'elp in the shop.'

'Don't you close on Sundays then?' Paul asked quietly.

'There's allus work to be done when we're closed,' she answered, jumping to her feet, spilling things out of her bag which Paul nonchalantly bent down to retrieve.

She snatched them from him and almost ran out. At the door I said urgently, 'Please come again, Lottie. Next time you're on leave.'

She nodded, and the last I saw was her running figure hurtling towards the gates. When I returned to the kitchen Paul was helping himself to a bun and in some exasperation I said, 'You make her feel inferior, you do it deliberately.'

'What nonsense. She does it to herself.'

'She's my friend and she's nice. You could try to be a little kinder to her.'

'Why? She's made up her mind I'm the devil incarnate, let her get on with it. The coffee pot's empty, is there any more?'

'I'll make some,' I said, snatching it away from him.

'Thanks. We'll talk about our plans over another cup and you shall tell me if you approve.'

While I made the coffee he sauntered out into the hall and for all I knew the rest of the house because the coffee was ready and waiting by the time he returned to the kitchen.

'I must say you've worked very hard to get it looking like this. The carpets are good, the furniture is excellent, but of

220

course we'll need to think about the dining room. Guests won't want to sit round a large dining table, they'll want individual ones, and we'll need to match up more chairs for the lounge.'

'We are going ahead with it then?' I gasped.

'Well, of course. I've burned my boats, Joanna. I've had one hell of a row with my father. My cousin's taken over from me and ...'

'Your mother?'

'She actually wept. But whether she fully understood what she was weeping about I can't tell.'

'Your father thought it was all very stupid, I suppose?'

'You suppose right. My father knows nothing outside the mills he's served since he was thirteen years old. My grandfather introduced him to them then and he doesn't see why I can't accept them as he did. My cousin will please him. He has a wife and three children, he never went to war, and now he's got what he really wanted. I wish him joy.'

'The solicitor thought the idea preposterous.'

'Well, of course, what did you expect?'

'I came away thinking he was right. Paul, how are we to start? How do we know it will ever be anything beyond a dream?'

'I can tell you what we want. We want a first-class manager who knows the business. French cooks and Italian waiters, a Scottish housekeeper, and an army of maids and cleaners. You can handle those, you must know people in the village who will be looking for work.'

'I know hardly anybody in the village.'

'Then ask your friend Lottie.'

'She's a nurse and returning to her hospital tomorrow.'

'Then talk to her mother, for heaven's sake. She's a shopkeeper, she's bound to know what goes on in the village and who's out of work.'

'But the house won't be ready for ages, there's a lot to do. How can I offer anybody employment in a year, two years?' I cried.

'My dear girl, I'm talking about months. We can't afford to linger on for a year, certainly not for two. We've got to get this thing on the road quickly and I've already made a start.

I've got a man coming to see me in the morning. He's been managing a hotel in Gloucestershire for years, an extremely posh and well-known hotel, but the owner was killed during the war and the man who took it over has let it go to seed. Bit of a womaniser and a drinker apparently, so my chap's fed up and looking around.'

'How did you know about him?'

'I have contacts, Joanna. I was with a chap in the army who knew the place well. I have to admit it was a shot in the dark but I think I've got him interested. At any rate he's coming here in the morning around eleven. You can rustle up a light lunch, I'll see that the fires are lit and the rooms look inviting, then of course there are the stables and the grounds to think about ...'

He added this last as an afterthought and I stared at him thinking that they were surely of secondary importance.

'I mentioned them before, Joanna. The tennis courts will have to be restored. We need decent horses in the stables, and when things really get moving to find room for a swimming pool.'

He was going too fast for me but at least the lethargy had gone. There was light at the end of the tunnel, the dream was taking shape.

'Why not call to see Lottie's folks this evening?' he said firmly. 'I can drop you off there when I go to the Flying Horse. There's a fetching little barmaid there who mightn't be so bad behind our bar when we get around to it,' he said blithely.

'Won't we have to get permission from some authority or other to turn Reckmire into a country hotel?'

'Well, yes. I've done some homework and I think we should change your solicitor in Kendal. He's getting on, he's one of the old school and we need somebody younger, somebody with the knowhow to handle our affairs.

'But he was Grandpa's solicitor for years.'

'Grandpa is dead, Joanna, you and I are very much alive and raring to go. I know a good firm in Manchester. Solicitors in Leeds are out of the question. I don't want my father talking about us to his cronies at the club.'

Bewildered, I couldn't keep up with his enthusiasm, but

I was grateful for it. It seemed to me that for the first time in years I had a strong man standing behind me who could cope with anxieties, heart searching and possible disasters. I sincerely trusted the latter would be few.

Lottie was amazed when I arrived at the shop door early that evening, and as I talked to her parents I saw her eyes grow round with astonishment.

I told them of our plans, the way we hoped to transfer Reckmire and that we hoped it would create work for a great many local people. When I had finished it was Lottie who said probingly, 'Will Captain Cheviot be in this with you Joanna? Are you goin' to marry him?'

For a moment I stared at her wide-eyed, then I laughed. 'Good gracious, no, Lottie, there's nothing like that between us. He's simply going to be my business partner and I do need him. I'd never have thought about all this if it hadn't been for him.'

'That's all right then,' she said seriously, and her mother said, 'None of that's any of our business, Lottie. What exactly can we help you with, love?'

'I need to know if there are people in the village who would be able to work for us? Chambermaids, cleaners, gardeners and groundsmen – stable hands too if we ever get around to the stables, although I expect Paul will handle that side of it.'

'Well, I daresay the gardeners your grandmother had would be willin' to go back there. Two of them are home from the war and haven't any work yet that I know of. Mrs Peabody knows most of the women in the village who might be willing to go into service. Could you talk to her, Joanna?'

I visualised Mrs Peabody, arms akimbo, small shrewd eyes staring at me out of her red florid face. Mrs Peabody was a gossip; in no time at all our plans would be all over the village and it was too soon. Some of my reluctance must have shown on my face because in the next moment Lottie's mother said gently, 'I know she's an awful gossip, love, but she thrives on 'avin' a role to play. She'll thoroughly relish giving you information about who you should employ and who you shouldn't, and she's straight. She'll be that thrilled at 'avin' been asked to help she'll do anythin' you say.'

After a few minutes I thanked them for their advice, saying, 'I'll call in to see her then. Will she be at home do you think?'

'Oh, yes, she rarely goes out in the evening unless it's to the Mothers' Union meeting at the church and there isn't one tonight.'

I stood at Mrs Peabody's front door where the step was polished in white donkeystone and the letterbox and the latch were of polished brass. I could hear the sound of the knocker behind the stout wooden door, and then footsteps on the linoleum-covered vestibule. The door opened, and the large buxom figure of Mrs Peabody blocked the doorway.

She stared at me standing in the dim light of the street lamp and I said haltingly, 'Good evening, Mrs Peabody, I'm Joanna Albemarle.'

'I knows who you are, lass.'

'Could I talk to you for a few minutes, please? I'm sorry if I've come at an inopportune time.'

'I'm on my own, you'd best come in.'

I followed her down the hall after closing the outside door behind me. She escorted me into a tiny living room where a fire burned brightly in the grate, its glow falling on polished brass and copper, two comfortable arm chairs on either side of the hearth, and on the rug a huge tabby cat.

She pointed to one of the chairs, saying, 'Sit there, love. I was just 'avin' forty winks, I usually do when I've 'ad my tea. Can I get you a cup, or a glass o' sherry? I allus has some in.'

'Sherry would be nice, Mrs Peabody,' I replied, after which she bustled into the kitchen and reappeared minutes later with a fairly large glass filled with light golden sherry.

I wasn't sure how to begin but she was the first to start by saying, 'It were right sad about your grandparents, and a pity they 'ad to be buried so far from 'ome. Whatever's goin' to happen to that great big place?'

'It was left to me, Mrs Peabody.' And I was rewarded by seeing her eyes open wide with surprise.

'Well, to be sure,' she said cautiously, 'and what will

224

ye do livin' there all by yerself? Isn't yer father coming 'ome then?'

Briefly I explained the position where Father was concerned, and she shook her head sadly before adding, 'And Master Robin too. It's almost as if a whole generation's been wiped out. I remember them all 'ere in the summer, the fun they 'ad, and yer aunt, Miss Corallie, allus so lovely and proud on that 'orse of 'ers. What's 'appened to her in Italy then?'

'I think Aunt Marcia and Uncle Edward are trying to get over there before long. I hope they're well.'

'Well, I allus say it's best to marry an Englishman, somebody you knows. Foreigners are all right in their place, but it's when war comes that yer all at sea.'

I sipped my sherry, feeling her eyes on me, questioning, inquisitive.

'Why does you want to see me, Miss Albermarle?'

So I told her about our thoughts and plans for Reckmire and she listened without speaking until I had finished, most unusual for Mrs Peabody, and when I had she remained staring at me for several minutes before finding her voice.

'Well,' she said at last, 'You 'ave surprised me. A country hotel, is it? Folks round 'ere might not like it, you know, cars comin' at all 'ours o' night, strangers in the village, 'orses canterin' over farmland.'

'But think of the trade it would bring to the village, Mrs Peabody, the work for some of the villagers. Besides the house is far enough away from the village not to cause any upset.'

'What sort o' people would you be wantin' to work for ye then?'

'Cooks, chambermaids, cleaners. Gardeners too but perhaps my grandparents' old gardeners will be available.'

She sat back in her chair reflectively while I sipped my sherry, excellent sherry it was too, and I had always surmised that Mrs Peabody would be a woman who liked a glass of stout in the evening.

'This is somethin' I'll just 'ave to think carefully about,' she said. 'Just you enjoy your sherry while I set my brains to work.'

225

At that moment the tabby cat stretched and yawned, then rising to his feet leapt gracefully into my lap.

'I hopes you likes cats,' she said with a smile. 'He's decided to accept you. It takes 'im a few minutes to make up 'is mind. Now 'e'll keep you company while I puts my brains to work. His name's Eustace by the way.'

Eustace purred on my lap while Mrs Peabody sat back in her chair with her eyes closed. I wasn't at all sure whether she was thinking or had decided to finish her nap.

Chapter Twenty

I left Mrs Peabody's with the distinct impression that she was pleased to have been approached. I cautioned her to keep everything to herself until something definite emerged, and at the door she said in a conspiratorial whisper. 'I'll not be sayin' a word, Miss Albermarle, and when yer ready I'll keep my eyes and ears open. You did right to come to see me, I knows everybody worth knowin' i' these parts.'

Mr Fenton stood in the doorway of the baker's shop puffing on his pipe and when I drew close he fell into step beside me.

'I'll walk up to the Hall with you. It's dark and lonely up there and you never know who's knockin' about. I take it Mrs Peabody was in?'

'Yes. She's promised to help when we receive permission to go ahead with our plans. I do hope she'll keep things to herself until then.'

'She'll do that all right, and then when you ask for her help she'll be quick to tell the rest o' the village that she's known about it from the beginnin'. I think you can rely on her to give you some help. She knows everybody, their good points and their bad ones. She'll be keepin' her eyes and ears open, you can bet yer life.'

I laughed. 'That's just what she said she would do.'

'Will there be some trade in it for us, do you think?'

'Oh, yes, I'm sure there will.'

'Well, we're only the village bakery, you know, but they do come to the shop from miles around. Our bread and cakes are second to none.'

227

'I think the village generally will benefit if everything goes to plan, Mr Fenton.'

He left me at the front door of the house after seeing me unlock the door and put on the lights. He seemed well satisfied with our conversation and I heard him go whistling down the drive before I closed the door.

I began to feel anxious about the visit from the hotel manager in the morning. A light lunch, Paul had said, and Mrs Fenton had promised to send up fresh bread in the morning. I promised myself to be up early to prepare and hoped he would think I looked like the chatelaine of Reckmire Hall.

Paul arrived early and sat drinking coffee while I told him about my interview with the Fentons and Mrs Peabody.

'Can she be trusted to keep her own counsel until the plans have been accepted?'

'Oh, yes, I'm sure she can. I know she's the village gossip but I did caution her and she will be glad to be in the secret.'

He left me to stroll around the house and I knew he was as restless as myself. Our visitor arrived just before eleven and I left it to Paul to show him round the house while I prepared our buffet lunch in the morning room. I heard the sound of their voices and later saw the visitor strolling with Paul in the gardens on their way to the stables at the rear of the house.

He was a tall slender man with well-cut silver hair and an urbane air. His attire was sombre but elegant, and I had no difficulty in picturing him in a hotel of some standing.

When they returned to the house I told them that lunch was ready and I had laid it out on a long coffee table in front of a glowing fire. We talked pleasantries when all the time I was longing to ask him what he thought about Reckmire and our dream for it. Indeed he was on the point of departure when he took my hand at the front door, and, looking down at me with a gentle smile, said, 'I have admired your home, Miss Albemarle. A family should live in this house, the sort of family you come from, but the war has altered a great many things. I would say that anything is preferable to parting with this house. Mr Cheviot has promised to keep

228

me informed. I have told him that I am very interested. It will depend of course how long I can tolerate my present position or if I am invited to take on something better in the meantime.'

'Well, what do you think?' Paul demanded as soon as our visitor had left.

'Oh, I think he's perfect, I liked him. Will he come to us, do you think?'

'Well, you heard him. It will depend on how quickly we can get things moving. Benjamin Gainsborough ... it does have rather a grand air, don't you think?' I've got a good feeling about all this, Joanna. I think it's all going to work. I'm going into Kendal this afternoon to try to chivvy these plans through as quickly as possible. I've had an architect pal of mine draw up plans from the documents you brought from the solicitor. The sooner I get them in, the sooner we can get a move on.'

His enthusiasm was contagious. I sang to myself as I cleared away the remains of our lunch and later I was donning my trench coat before walking on the beach when I heard the telephone ringing shrilly in the hall.

My first thought was that it would be Mother. I had telephoned her several times but she had showed no interest in my plans for the house and after that I had let her do most of the talking. I had always been the one to place the call. Now I hoped that she had relented and was calling me.

It was, however, Aunt Marcia's voice that came to me and there was a strange hesitancy in it. I knew in that first instant that she had no good news to impart.

'I'm so glad to have caught you, Joanna,' she began. 'I tried earlier but there was no reply.'

'I had visitors, Aunt Marcia, I didn't hear the telephone.'

'Joanna, we've had news from the Foreign Office about Robert. I'm so sorry to tell you that he died in a prisoner of war camp in Burma two years ago. Darling, he won't be coming home.'

I could feel the tightness in my throat, the pain of unshed tears, and then I was thanking her for letting me know, and she was saying, 'I've written to Corallie. One of these days we must hear from them. The war's been over some time now. I worry about them.

'Perhaps you should let your mother know about Robert, Joanna?'

'Yes, I'll ring her later. Goodbye, Aunt Marcia.'

I sat on the stairs and cried. I hadn't seen my father for years but somehow he had always been in my thoughts, somebody who was coming back, somebody who would miraculously make everything right, somebody I would love. Now I felt suddenly alone.

I telephoned my mother in the early-evening and broke the news gently, but the next moment she was saying, 'You have absolutely no excuse now, Joanna, to linger on in that Godforsaken place. You must put it on the market at once and come back home.'

'I am home, Mother.'

'How can you say that, Joanna? Mr Walsh has asked me to marry him and we're having one of those flats I told you about. You could have this one and a job at the library. I'm not asking you to live with us, but we'd be here if you wanted us. Think about it and let me know quickly so I can take this flat off the market.'

'Mother, don't you care that my father is dead? That he was dead and none of us knew?'

'Well, of course I care, you silly girl, but a lot of men died during the war, and you seem to forget that Robert went off to the Far East without a second's thought for either you or me.'

'It was his job Mother.'

'Oh, I know there's absolutely no use in arguing with you, you always took his part. That's Mr Walsh at the door. Don't forget to think about what I've said and telephone me about the flat.'

I heard the line go dead and replaced the receiver with a mixture of despair and disbelief.

When Paul returned to the house later he stared at me in surprise when I opened the door. I knew that my face was streaked with tears and my eyes were red from weeping, and with his usual directness he said, 'What's the matter with you? You look like the very devil.'

230

The tears flowed afresh and he continued to stare at me until at last I was able to blurt out the reason for my distress. I waited for his reaction, but when it came it was not what I had thought it would be.

'I know you always had the hope that he would come back, Joanna, and I didn't want to be the one to disillusion you. You would have heard long before this if there'd been a chance that he was still alive. Prisoners of war from the Far East have been pouring back, only the dead ones had still to be traced.'

'Then why didn't you say something? Why did you let me go on believing in providence?'

'I don't think providence played much part in the war in the Far East. Don't you want to hear how I've gone on in Kendal?'

'You're as bad as my mother. When I tried to tell her about Father all she could think about was my going home, living in her flat and getting back to the library.'

His face was sober, questioning. 'And what did you tell her?' he asked pointedly.

'What do you think? I said I'd be back in the morning, that I'd live in the flat and Reckmire could go to blazes. What do you think I told her?'

'That's more like the Joanna I remember. I trust you told your mother to go to blazes?'

'She thinks I'll go back, I can't make her see that it's impossible. She's just got to learn the hard way that I'm here to stay.'

'Right. Well then, let's go into the drawing room and I'll tell you what is happening. I'm sorry about your father, Joanna, I really am, but it's only what I expected. I liked him. He wouldn't want you to go to pieces over it.'

I knew he was right, but while I listened to his enthusiasm, his certainty that there was a future for us and Reckmire, the other half of me was remembering my father on that evening we had spent in London listening to Ivor Novello's music, his face filled with enjoyment, his warm applause which even Mother's remote frown was unable to quell.

In the days that followed I felt dizzy with the way matters progressed. Paul wanted the entire enterprise to be completed

231

by the summer and deplored the few days of Christmas when work stopped.

Between Mother and I was a stilted annoyance. Dutifully I telephoned her and was informed that the flat had been sold so I was far too late to do anything about that. They were intending to marry in the spring when their flat would be ready for occupation, and they would be spending a week in the Cotswolds. The marriage would be a quiet one, but she hoped I would attend, otherwise people would gossip.

They intended spending Christmas with Mr Walsh's daughter in Essex and consequently no mention was made of my going to Surrey. I didn't mind. I had visions of spending it at Reckmire and went so far as to buy a Christmas tree for the hall which I lovingly decorated with a supply of baubles I found upstairs in the old nursery.

When I had asked Paul what we should do about the nursery, he had said he hadn't made up his mind.

'It would make a very nice bedroom, Joanna, and quite honestly I don't want this to be a place for young children, even if we keep it as it is. I want it to be for older people with a great deal of money, people who play golf and like riding, people who like to go racing and sailing. Children are better in hotels where the coast is safe and they can play endlessly on the sands.'

I knew at that moment that the nursery was going, but when he started having ideas about the turret room I said adamantly that this was going to be my bedroom.

'But it's a funny shape,' he protestd, 'sticking out from the rest of the house.'

'It's the one with the view of Reckmire Marsh, and if the rest of the house is going to be changed then they can do something with this too. Anyway, I've always loved it. I'll be happy to have my bedroom here and the small room next door will make a perfectly good sitting room,' I replied stoutly.

'Miss Albemarle's private quarters set aside for her personal use and sacrosanct,' he said sarcastically.

'If you like,' I answered. 'Where do you propose to live?'

For a long minute he stared at me, then said, 'Well, here

of course. I'll live in the flat, but I suggest we eat in the dining room at our own table. We should make an effort to get to know our guests since we are the owners of the place.'

I stared at him steadily until at last he gave a little laugh and lowered his eyes, then with a mocking bow said, 'You are the owner of the place, Miss Albemarle, I am merely your business partner.'

I had the distinct impression that most of the workmen and any of the other people who came to the house thought that Paul was joint owner, and I believed it was an idea he had fostered. Men on the telephone always asked for Mr Cheviot, never Miss Albemarle, but I determined I would come into my own when female staff had to be interviewed. When I said as much to Paul he merely said, 'Well, of course. There will be the flowers to arrange, the maids to employ, although a good housekeeper won't like you interfering.'

'Nevertheless,' I rejoined, 'I would like to interview the housekeeper and the receptionists.'

He grinned. 'You shall, Joanna, but not the stable hands or the gardeners. The Lodge House is empty since old Mr Carpenter moved out with his daughter and grandchild. It will be a good incentive when we choose a head gardener.'

'You've thought of everything, haven't you, Paul?'

'I hope so. Isn't that why you wanted my help, Joanna? You might like to thank me one day.'

'I couldn't have done any of this without you,' I answered seriously.

He smiled, that faintly mocking smile that always seemed to place me at a terrible disadvantage, then to my utmost surprise he stepped forward and took my face in his hands, lightly, gently, and lowered his head and kissed my lips. It was not a lover's kiss and yet it went on in a strangely masterful way until I stepped back and he released me.

For a long moment we stood staring at each other, then with a jaunty smile he moved away, calling over his shoulder, 'I've got an interior decorator coming in the morning. I think you should be there. I want his ideas on the reception hall and the drawing room. You can take him up to the turret room and get some ideas on what he can do with it.'

I didn't answer him. That kiss had disturbed me. It had meant nothing to him, and yet it had been masterful, dominating, and had left me trembling uncertainly, one moment angry that it had happened at all, the next wanting it to happen again. I lived that kiss again and again, remembering his dark brooding eyes looking down into mine, and the singular charm of his smile. Something had happened to me during that kiss.

At the beginning of January I received a long letter from Aunt Corallie. It was warm and filled with humorous anecdotes. She said very little about the war but said that she and her husband were both well and that Gabriella was married and living in Rome. With Aunt Corallie's typical absentmindedness she failed to tell me if she was married to Carlo although I imagined she was.

She approved of what I was doing at Reckmire, congratulating me warmly on my initiative, but was surprised that I had enlisted Paul Cheviot to help me. Wasn't he destined for three large woollen mills in Yorkshire?

She ended her letter with an invitation to visit them at the earliest opportunity, saying, 'Italy is still beautiful, Joanna, in spite of the war, and now we are all the very best of friends and are going to remain so.'

Aunt Marcia told me that she had wept sorrowful tears about Father, but in her letter she made no mention of him.

When I told Paul that I had heard from her he merely shrugged his shoulders, then with a cynical smile said, 'And when are you thinking you might go?'

'Gracious me, I can't even think about going yet. I want this place to be ready before I do.'

'How is Gabriella?'

'She is married and living in Rome.'

'We expected it, didn't we? Wasn't she engaged to that fellow Carlo?'

'No. She was in love with him.'

'Don't women usually marry the men they are in love with?'

'Unless something happens to prevent it.'

'Well, apparently nothing came to prevent it with

Gabriella. Did it grieve you, Joanna? You were a little in love with him yourself.'

'It was a schoolgirl crush.'

'Oh, is that what it was?'

He grinned and left me alone, and I stared after him, sullen and resentful. Would there ever come a time, I wondered, when Paul and I could talk without jibing at each other? I had thought it was possible when we first started on the Reckmire venture. Now more and more it was the old Paul who provoked me and made me angry.

Chapter Twenty-One

My mother's wedding day was set for the third of April which was a Thursday and although I was reluctant to tear myself away from everything that was happening at Reckmire, I told myself that it was my duty to go.

'How long are you expecting to be away?' Paul asked sharply when I told him my plans.

'I shall go down one day and come back the next. I'm not sure where I can stay, they're going into the new flat when they come back from their honeymoon and the old one has been sold.'

I had been troubled about what to give them for a wedding present, and knowing Mother's passion for good porcelain I had decided to give her a large Crown Derby bowl which had been one of Grandma's proudest possessions.

I was about to wrap it when Paul said, 'That bowl looked particularly well where your grandmother displayed it. Will your mother appreciate its value, do you think?'

'Yes, I'm sure she will. She has always been fond of this sort of thing.'

'Even if it comes from Reckmire?'

'Even then.'

'Who is giving the bride away?' he asked curiously.

'Paul, you know as much as I do. I'm not looking forward to it and I'll be glad to be home.'

I was surprised therefore on the morning I was due to leave when Paul strode across the terrace to where I was putting my small case into the back of my car.

'You can put that in my car, I have to go up to London for a few days on business. I'll drive you there and drive you home after the wedding.'

I stared at him in surprise. 'Isn't this a little sudden?' I asked.

'Well, yes. I'm meeting a friend, somebody I knew during the war, somebody who has a sister who might turn out to be the sort of receptionist we're looking for.'

'Have you met her?'

'Yes, I was invited to spend a weekend at the family house in Essex and she was there. Classy sort of girl. She was on leave from the WAAFs at the time.'

'But will she be interested in working for us?'

'I'm hoping so. She'd worked before the war for some hotel on the South Coast. If she's back there she might not be willing to change. On the other hand, if we made it worth her while she might be persuaded.'

'You're always so sure, Paul, that money can buy anything,' I said wistfully, and he laughed. 'It usually can. At least, that's been my experience.

As we drove south the clouds lifted. We ate lunch at a rather upmarket hotel south of Birmingham. Paul said, 'Look around you, Joanna, it's glossy and overly new, hasn't got Reckmire's charm or its tradition. Look at the people. Pretty ordinary lot, aren't they? They've come to look the place over because it's new. Not exactly the sort of people who are looking for gracious living.'

'Why do you say that?'

'Because they're businessmen with their secretaries, family men with their noisy children, not our sort at all.'

'What are our sort?'

'Nice people. The sort of people one met abroad before the war, people who expect good service, quiet luxury and good taste.'

'And you think we can provide all that, Paul?'

'Yes I do. I have faith in Reckmire and I have faith in you. I won't let you down and I expect the same sort of commitment from you.'

He was staring into my eyes from across the table and there was so much conviction in his voice, I could feel his strength reaching out for me, as potent as the kiss he had surprised on lips that had never expected to experience it. It was at that moment that I knew I wanted him to love me, and began to love him.

After he had retrieved my luggage from the boot of his car he stood looking up at the flats for several minutes before he turned to say, 'You'll ring me as soon as you know when you're leaving? You'll find me at this number.'

I watched him scribble the number into a notebook, then he tore the page out and handed it to me.

'I hope the wedding turns out better than you expect, Joanna. Maybe you'll find things better all round.'

He smiled, and getting into his car drove swiftly out into the road.

I heard the sound of women's voices and laughter long before I entered the flat. I had long since relinquished my key so I rang the bell and waited. Miriam Heythorn answered the door. Immediately her face was wreathed in smiles and she called out, 'Joanna's here, Linda. Do come in, dear, I'm just helping to sort things out.'

Miriam had been at school with Mother and was one of her bridge friends and a pillar of St Mary's church. When I entered the flat however it seemed to be overcrowded with women since Janice was there as well as two other of Mother's bridge friends.

She came out of the bedroom and I went forward to embrace her. The living room of the flat was filled with cardboard boxes and the women were engaged in wrapping up china figurines, crockery and cutlery. Janice said, 'We're trying to get all this over to the new flat later today, Joanna. We're so glad you're here, you'll be able to take some of it.'

'I didn't come in my own car,' I explained, 'but of course I'll help in any way I can.'

'Whose car did you come in?' Mother demanded.

'Paul drove me. He had an appointment in London.'

'I hope he's not expecting to come to the wedding? You didn't ask, Joanna, and all the arrangements have been made.'

238

'He isn't coming to the wedding, Mother, he's merely picking me up to take me home.'

'I've arranged for you to stay with Janice,' she said. 'This flat was sold as soon as we put it on the market.'

'I'm glad, Mother.'

'Well, it's a very nice flat, but you will have to take a look at the new one, won't she, girls? It's perfect.'

They all agreed that it was indeed perfect, and then Janice said, 'We'll take your case into my flat, Joanna, so that you can unpack. When were you thinking of going back?'

'Tomorrow after the wedding or the next day, whichever is convenient to you, Janice.'

'Oh, the day after, dear, I'd like you to stay a little longer than just the one night. We have so much to talk about and I'm dying to hear about your plans for your hotel.'

'That is something I can't even begin to envisage,' Mother said sharply. She shivered delicately, and hurriedly I said, 'I have your wedding present here, Mother. I'll unpack it so that it can go to the new flat with the rest of the stuff.'

They gathered round while I unpacked the box containing the bowl, then in the midst of the cries of admiration Mother said sharply, 'I remember that bowl, wasn't it in the lounge at Reckmire?'

'Yes, Mother. Grandma loved it so much, and I know how much you prize good porcelain. I looked around but didn't see anything nicer than this.'

'Well, of course, dear, it's very valuable, and at Reckmire in those great lofty rooms china like this was perfect. The new flat's much bigger than this one but I'm not sure where I can find a home for this.'

Nobody spoke. In one sentence she had informed them that her wedding present had come from a large gracious house but had no place in her own. There was an uncomfortable silence, and then with a little laugh Mother said, 'Oh, well, I know you wanted to please me, darling, and you haven't seen the flat so how could you know? It's quite beautiful, of course, all Grandma Albemarle's things were beautiful. Put it back in the box, dear, and pack it well so that it won't get broken.'

I could have burst into tears. I wanted to take the bowl

239

away, to return it to the house that had nurtured it, but I had to watch Mother lay it on one side as if it was of no consequence.

Janice's flat had always had a more lived in air than Mother's. Her colour scheme was warm, her furniture more shabby, and yet there was something heartwarming in the sight of her little dog sitting on the rug wagging his tail and the bedroom she showed me into where the carpet was a little faded and the curtains didn't quite match.

'If they're happy I'm pleased for them.'

'Well, I knew Ernest's wife. She was a pretty, spoilt little thing. Her parents doted on her and so did he. It seems to me that he's always been looking for somebody just like Mary and Linda's a lot like her, in her looks and her ways.'

I smiled but offered no comment. Janice said gently, 'We were all so sorry to hear about your father, dear. He was a lovely man, so warm and friendly.'

'Yes, it was very sad.'

'And who is this young man who's helping you with Reckmire? Do I sense a romance in the offing?'

'I've known Paul a long time, Janice. He was a friend of Robin's and he spent long summer holidays at Reckmire. He knows the place better than I do.'

'And there's no romance?'

I laughed at her persistence. 'There's no romance at the moment, Janice. Tell me about tomorrow.'

The wedding's at St Mary's at eleven o'clock and the reception's at The Grange, that's the new place near the flat. It has a very good reputation.'

'Will there be many guests?'

'About seventy, I think. Ernest's sister and her husband will be there as well as his daughter and her husband. I'm not sure if they'll be bringing their children. Your grandfather's old friend Mr Sinclair, the bank manager, is giving her away.'

She laughed. 'I thought she would have asked you to be her bridesmaid, instead she's asked Ernest's unmarried sister Ella.'

For the rest of the afternoon we packed boxes into several small cars and took them over to the new flat. I drove Mother's car and she sat beside me telling me things she thought I should hear. That Ernest's family had been very kind and made her very welcome, that his daughter Angela was sweet and although she called her Linda already behaved like her daughter, and the grandchildren were sweet and terribly well behaved.

Ernest had given her all her own way with regard to the flat, and the new people coming into the old one had bought her furniture so they'd been able to have a fresh start.

She was so full of information in no time at all we were pulling into the forecourt of a very large block of flats encircled by a large garden. They looked opulent and expensive enough even for mother.

I had known what the flat would be like. I knew mother's taste, pale pastels and plain carpeting. Crystal chandeliers and pale limed oak furniture. The effect was cold on a cool April day, but she was quick to explain that when the sun shone the flat was beautiful.

I expressed my admiration for everything that I saw, and later Janice whispered, 'It makes my place look like a rabbit hutch, doesn't it, Joanna?'

'Your flat's lovely, Janice, it's so warm and homely.'

'I know. Your mother would have loved to get started on it, she was forever telling me how it could be changed. I wonder why she hasn't asked to help out at your place, she does so love anything to do with interior decorating.'

I was glad at that moment that Mother didn't like Reckmire. Not even her love for exotic surroundings and a chance to spend money would tempt her to Reckmire.

The last night we spent together in her old flat was passed looking at old photographs and I was hurt and surprised when she laid aside those of Father, saying, 'You can have all those if you want them, Joanna. If you don't I'll destroy them.'

It rained in the night but by mid-morning the sun came out and Mother was up and about, twittering about her flowers, her wedding outfit, and that Ella was late arriving.

'As soon as she comes I want you to go down to Janice and go with her to the church. There's nothing you can do here, Joanna, Mildred will help me get ready.'

241

I felt superfluous since I was not allowed to help her dress and when Ella arrived in a flurry of excuses about the morning traffic I was hastily thrust out into the passage. With a shrug of her shoulders Mother said, 'Nobody has to know what I'm wearing, Joanna. You do understand, don't you, dear?'

Janice greeted me with morning coffee and I thought she looked smart in navy blue and white while I was wearing a jade green wild silk dress and matching floppy hat.

'How pretty you look,' she said warmly. 'I wish I could wear that colour but it does nothing for my grey hair. Did you see what your mother was wearing?'

'No. She's keeping that a secret.'

'Even from her daughter, Joanna?'

'Even from me.'

'Oh, well. We're driving to the church in Joyce's car. Linda has only ordered one wedding car so she's expecting everybody else to make their own way to the church.'

I wasn't sure about Joyce's driving. she had laid her car up during the war and long before then had only driven along the high street to the shops or to local friends. She preferred to accept lifts than drive herself so I was quick to say that we could go in Mother's car and smiled inwardly at the relief on her face.

The church was crowded and Janice whispered, 'Good gracious, I didn't think it would be this busy. Your family's always been well known in the town. Linda'll be so thrilled.'

I was aware that people were staring at me, no doubt wondering at the role I might be playing, but there was none for me, I was merely a spectator. My eyes wandered across the aisle to where Ernest sat with his best man, a portly middle-aged gentleman. They sat staring in front of them, occasionally speaking to each other, and only when a small woman and two teenage girls took the pew behind them did they turn to smile.

Mother's friends sat around me dressed for the occasion, and now and again there was a rustle of interest when the pews behind Ernest filled up. A young women wearing buttercup yellow joined the older woman behind Ernest and I surmised that this must be his daughter. I also imagined that the stocky young man who had shown us to our pews was her husband. I thought she was a little older than I, and once her eyes met mine and she looked away quickly, making me wonder what she had heard about me, the girl who could have prevented this marriage but who had been selfish enough to follow her own path. Her father's happiness today was because I had chosen that path.

All these thoughts were filling my mind as the organist entertained us to a selection of Kettelby's melodies. At a signal from the vicar the choir came slowly down the centre aisle and he went forward to meet them. Ernest and his best man stepped slowly from their pew, and then when the choir had taken their places Mother arrived on the arm of Mr Sinclair, followed by Ella.

I couldn't help the tears that suddenly filled my eyes, she looked so young and pretty in pale pink, her hat a froth of chiffon roses, standing beside Ernest so small and neat, making her responses in her breathless whispering voice.

I wanted the day to be over quickly. The food at the reception stuck in my throat because it was at the hotel where I became aware that I really was the outsider. Mother greeted Ernest's daughter with affection, telling all those who cared to listen that she was a real daughter to her, that Ernest's family had taken her to their hearts and made her welcome, and all the time I stood with people I knew, only too aware that they felt as uncomfortable as I.

I was deliberately made to feel an interloper. It seemed it was only when she stood with Ernest in the hotel foyer that she suddenly remembered my existence and called out, 'Mr Sinclair will drive you and Janice back to the flats, Joanna. We're taking my car to the new flats. Write soon.'

If she had taken a pitcher of cold water and flung it it my face I couldn't have felt more chilled. I watched Ernest's daughter fidgetting with her two children who had been brought to the reception, thinking that nobody had attempted to introduce us, and Janice whispered, 'Haven't you spoken to her, Joanna?'

'No. We sat at different tables and Mother didn't introduce us.'

'Then I will,' she said stoutly, and before I knew what

was happening she had taken my hand and was pushing ahead through the throng in the foyer.

'Good morning, Marion,' she said. 'We've already met but I don't think you know Joanna.'

Marion raised her head and seemed suddenly flustered. There was unspoken hostility in her eyes even when she smiled and said stiltedly, 'How do you do?'

It was so silly. She didn't in the least care how I was and there was nothing to say beyond the fact that things had gone well, the lunch had been nice and the day had been fine. When we parted company Janice said, 'Oh dear, she's not the friendliest of girls, but then Ernest went to stay with her in a fit of pique because your mother said when you returned home she'd have little time for him.'

'Do you think we might go now, Janice? I have to let Paul know where he can pick me up tomorrow and people are beginning to drift away.' The bride and groom had already departed and Mr Sinclair was nothing loth to make his departure. I felt that a chapter of my life was irrevocably over. The day should have been happy but all it left me with was remembered pain.

Tomorrow, I told myself, is the start of the rest of my life. As I drove northward with Paul I was glad that he asked no questions about the wedding and seemed more concerned with the success of his interview with our new receptionist. I found it difficult to concentrate, and after a while he said, 'You don't seem very interested.'

'I am interested, Paul, I was thinking of something else, that's all.'

'All right, what have I been saying then?'

'You're pleased that you've talked her into coming. If you're satisfied then I suppose I must be.'

'What went wrong at that wedding then?'

'Absolutely nothing. Mother looked beautiful and happy, the church was full and the reception was brilliant.'

'And that's all you're going to say about it? Perhaps now we can forget about your mother and concentrate on this venture we're in together. I managed to get Rebecca Lester to agree to work for us. She's smart, beautiful and intelligent. You'll like her.'

'Will I like the sort of salary she's agreed to come for?'

'You get what you pay for in this life, Joanna.'

'If you say so.'

'Well, we've got our manager, our receptionist, and I heard the gardeners are coming back.'

'When? When did you hear?'

'Last week. I'd have told you sooner but all you could think about was your mother's wretched wedding. Perhaps now you'll be able to get around to seeing that Mrs Peabody. We shall need those chambermaids and cleaners. I've also advertised for a housekeeper. We can interview her together.'

I looked at him. I could have done nothing without him, and yet I felt I was being hauled along in his wake and the feeling was not always comfortable.

Chapter Twenty-Two

It was difficult to believe that in three months Reckmire Country Hotel was open and entertaining its first guests.

Gone was the old dining room with its large dining table and in its place were many smaller tables for two, four and six guests. In the entrance hall was a carved important-looking reception desk and an imposing lift to the floor above as well as the flat. A huge red turkey carpet stretched across the floor adding warmth to the pannelled oak walls and doors, the suits of dark armour and the hanging chandeliers. From the hall the shallow curving staircase ascended, and priceless pictures hung side by side with oil paintings of long dead Albemarles.

When I questioned why they should be there Paul explained patiently that it would help the guests recognise that once this had been my family home and respect it as such.

Matching furniture had been added to that already in the drawing room and morning room, and in the conservatory a fountain played and a stream rippled between exotic plants.

The library and the billiard room were unchanged from my grandfather's time but the bedrooms had all been named after flowers. The Orchid Room and the Primrose Room, the Rose Room and the Violet Room, and many others all with colour schemes to match their names.

Mr Gainsborough presided over his domain with urbane charm, always attentive, prepared to listen to appreciation as well as grievances, and behind the desk stood Rebecca, efficient, attractive, her dark violet eyes belying the severity of her navy blue suit with its snowy organdie collar.

In the realms above, Mrs Anderson, our Scottish house-keeper, ruled over an army of chambermaids and cleaners, and indeed Mrs Peabody had been as good as her word when she kept her eyes and ears open for suitable employees.

I had been amused to see the list she presented me with, containing a list of names with the fors and againsts ticked off efficiently.

'Do you know them all personally?' I had asked her.

'That I do. Jenny and Mary Hodson are farmer's daughters, both of em allus neat and tidy, but there are five sisters and three brothers. The lads and two o' the girls work at the farm. I know for a fact that Jenny and Mary are looking for work elsewhere.'

'Alice Stedbury's a flighty minx but she's a jolly sort o' girl. If there's little temptation I reckon she'll do. Then there's mi niece Violet who's leavin' school at the end o' July. She's a capable lass, and doesn't give mi any cheek. I think she'll be glad if you can take her on, and her friend Elsie'll be lookin' for work.'

'I take it you think these girls are capable of looking after bedrooms, making beds, the usual things?'

'Oh, yes, I do. The others'll make good cleaners. There's Mrs Dawson, she's cleaned up at the old Mr Stedman's for years, 'e doesn't appreciate 'er and pays 'er peanuts. She'll be glad of a change. And the other two ave 'usbands who got injured in the war and aren't likely to work again. They keeps their 'ouses like palaces, they'd be glad of jobs to go to.'

'Well, thank you, Mrs Peabody. I'll certainly see all these people and will probably be able to offer them work. Have you heard any adverse remarks passed in the village?'

'Well, you know, there's allus somebody ready to criticise and ye can never stop some folk talkin',' she said darkly.

'You mean about the traffic in the village, the cars coming and going?'

'Well, that amongst other things.'

'What other things, Mrs Peabody?'

Her face was darkly flushed and she seemed uncomfortable.

'I don't take any 'eed, Miss Albemarle, you know yer

247

own business best, and when I 'ears 'em gossipin' I just sez they know nowt about it and there's nothin to talk about anyway.'

'Mrs Peabody, I want this enterprise to be successful. If there's anything likely to prevent it I feel I should know.'

She looked down at her shuffling feet but I stood my ground. Raising her eyes, she said doubtfully, 'Well, it's mainly you and that Mr Cheviot. They wonder what's goin' on with 'im doing all the orderin', interviewin' gardeners and groundsmen, and livin' at the 'all. They seems to think you'll be marryin' 'im now that the place is open at last.'

I stared at her, seeing the narrowed eyes in her florid face, the curiosity in them, and was determined I was not going to satisfy that curiosity so that she could spread my answer around the village.

I smiled airily. 'Like you say, Mrs Peabody, they'll always have something to talk about. Mr Cheviot's been a tower of strength. Indeed none of this would have been possible without his help. I'll get around to seeing these people within the next few days. Thank you so much for your help.'

I knew that her eyes followed me along the village street and that I had left her wondering. At the same time I was angry, angry with a village that needed to poke and pry into the business arrangement that Paul and I had, and angry too about all those times when he seemed to have taken over, both Reckmire and me.

The hotel was full and we were booked solid until the end of November. Soft music played in the dining room and the tables groaned under silver and cut glass, while the French chef produced gourmet meals that were met with appreciative compliments.

Paul and I sat at our special table against the wall where we could survey the room. I was well aware of the satisfied smile on his lips as he poured the wine and I was aware also that those dining around us were curious about us, curious in the nicest possible way.

They were sophisticated people. If Paul and I were having an affair, it was none of their business. The women eyed my clothes, my jewellery my make-up and my coiffure. I had spent money lavishly on the right sort of clothes at Paul's insistence. 'You need to look the part, Joanna. Get yourself up to London, buy the best you can find, and get your hair done as well as advice on your make-up.'

The men eyed me with some speculation as well as admiration. I was pleased with my new image. I was beautiful, elegant, and I was a puzzle to them.

I felt impatient with Paul, with his complacancy, his obvious delight in our success. I know it was illogical to feel this way but the arrival of Major Gorman had had a lot to do with it.

He arrived in the company of a young woman during the early-afternoon. Paul and I were chatting in the gardens about his ideas for a croquet lawn.

'Why do we need one?' I had argued. 'The tennis courts have been finished, we're having a pool, and you're talking about improving the stables. Why a croquet lawn, for heaven's sake?'

'Some of the older ladies are long past their tennis days, but they might conceivably enjoy a game of croquet, Joanna' he had said, raising his eyebrows in surprise at my objection. 'You said you wouldn't interfere with my handling of the grounds and gardens. I hope you meant it?'

I bit my lip in some exasperation, but in the next minute a voice called out, 'So it is you, Cheviot, who's got an interest in this place. I saw your name in the brochure and wondered if you were the same Cheviot I knew during the war.'

We turned to see a man mounting the steps. He was wearing expensive country tweeds and was followed by a girl young enough to be his daughter. He was tanned, with a debonair moustache and an easy manner. The girl was pretty. A porter followed, carrying some very expensive luggage.

Introductions were performed and Major Gorman said, 'I thought you were heading for Yorkshire after demob, Paul? The woollen industry, wasn't it?'

'I changed my mind,' he said evenly.

'Well, you've got yourself quite a pile here. Is this Mrs Cheviot?'

'No, this is Miss Joanna Albemarle, my business partner.'

Major Gorman took my hand and pressed it, but when his eyes met mine I knew that he thought I was anything

249

but Paul's business partner. There was amusement in his face and, looking up quickly, I did not miss the sardonic smile that curled Paul's lips.

Now he was pouring wine for me, lifting his glass nonchalantly, saying easily, 'Here's to us, Joanna, and to Reckmire.'

When I didn't immediately take up my glass, he said drily, 'Not drinking, Joanna, or can you think of a better toast?'

I bit my lip nervously and he said softly, 'Something's bothering you. I've sensed it for days. Care to tell me what it is?'

'I shouldn't mind so much, but I can't help it,' I whispered.

'What shouldn't you mind?'

'Your living here, people thinking all sorts of things about us, the villagers talking.'

To my utmost surprise he threw back his head and laughed delightedly. Then catching sight of my hurt surprise he immediately became serious. 'Well, of course they speculate about us. A man and a woman into something like this, living under the same roof, sharing the same table night after night, and for all they know, the same bedroom.'

'But we don't. Surely they know that?'

'Why should they? The turret room is in a part of the house well away from the others and they all know I'm in the flat. I'm not going out of my way to tell anybody that dinner is usually the last I see of you, and how are you going to enlighten them? The villagers will always talk about something. Let them talk about us if it titillates them.'

'I don't want them talking about me, I don't want Major Gorman undressing me with his eyes and thinking I'm your mistress!'

'What do you propose we do about it then?'

'I don't know, but something obviously.'

'Oh, obviously. What had you in mind?'

He was sitting staring at me with maddening composure, his face a picture of bland innocence, and angrily I snapped, 'You could live somewhere else. You could make it more obvious that you're in that flat alone.'

'I can think of a better idea, Joanna.'

'What?'

'You could move into the flat with me, or I could move into the turret room. We could stop all the suppositions, all the village tongues wagging, by getting married.'

I stared at him in amazement, looking for the amusement he often reserved for me, but his expression was strangely anxious, and nervously I said, 'Oh well, if you can't be serious ...'

'I am serious, Joanna. I'll admit that never in a thousand years did I expect to be proposing to that little girl with the sand and sea in her hair. But it's years later and she's grown up and beautiful. You never thought it either, did you, Joanna?'

'No. Then you loved Gabriella. You didn't even like me.'

'That's true. But then we didn't know there was going to be a war. We didn't even dream that one day Reckmire would be yours and that together we would be changing it into something else, that Robin and your father would be gone and everybody in this wretched village would be gossiping about us.'

There was no banter in his voice, and his eyes were searching my face as his hands reached for mine across the table. I was suddenly aware that those sitting nearest to us were looking at us, and Paul said quickly, 'Come on, Joanna, let's get out of here. I can think of better places in which to ask a girl to marry me.'

He stood at the table waiting for me to walk out of the room with him, and I was aware of innumerable eyes following us. There were people everywhere, but he took hold of my hand and led me towards the conservatory at the back of the lounge, and here with the scent of orchids around us and the sound of the waterfall in our ears, he took me in his arms and asked with a strange and touching humility: 'Joanna, will you marry me?'

Our engagement was the talk of the hotel. My room was filled with flowers and cards bearing good wishes. We gave a party for the hotel staff and another for our guests and

251

the news quickly got round the village so that everywhere I went I was met with warm smiles and good wishes for our happiness.

Major Gorman stopped on his departure to say with a broad smile, 'Well, I'm very glad to see he's been bowled over at last, and by the loveliest girl I've seen in a month of Sundays. Keep him on the straight and narrow, my dear, and I hope you'll both be truly happy.'

I watched him laughing with his companion on the way to his car. He waved jauntily before getting into it and driving away.

Paul joined me as I returned to reception, saying, 'That was Gorman leaving, I suppose?'

'Yes, didn't you say goodbye to him?'

'No. I didn't want to be the recipient of one of his more lurid jokes, particularly in your presence, my dear.'

'Actually he was very circumspect.'

'With you, yes. He'd have been rather less so if I'd been there. Have you noticed anything missing in the hall, darling?'

I looked around curiously, then I stared to where the first flight of stairs divided to see that the picture of my grandmother had been taken down and the expanse of dark oak pannelling stared back unadorned.

'Why have you taken it down?' I cried. 'It was so beautiful and it's been there so long.'

'It's gone up in the dining room and I want a portrait of you there instead. You in that black dress with the sable around the neck and at the bottom of the sleeves. When I saw you in that dress I thought I'd never seen you looking more beautiful and I've commissioned a good artist to paint you. He's coming every afternoon next week, Joanna. You can chose the place you want. He'll make the backdrop to please himself anyway.'

'Don't you think our guests might think it a little ostentatious?' I asked.

'Not at all. You are after all the owner of Reckmire, it's a family place not simply a corporation. I want people to talk about us, about the hotel but mostly you.'

I was touched and ecstatically happy. I was in love, I felt

that I was loved in return, more important to another human being than I had ever been, and it was moments like this more than our moments of shared passion that made me happy.

Summer came to Reckmire and by this time the tennis courts had been resurfaced, Paul had purchased a string of decent horses for the stables and the gardens were at their best. We were fully booked up until well into the autumn. One morning Paul caught up with me as I walked through the deer park.

He was smiling, handsome and tanned, and I was joyfully aware of the rush of pride in my heart when he said, 'Not busy then, Joanna?'

'No.'

'I've nothing much on either, so I suggest we drive off somewhere. What's the point of being engaged if you can't show people your engagement ring?'

I laughed, and he said, 'People have been asking about it, haven't they?'

'Well, yes, one or two.'

'We'll drive over to York and I'll buy you the most vulgar ostentatious ring we can find, then you can flash it around the hotel and the village.'

'I'm not very sure I'm in favour of something ostentatious?'

'It's only my joke, Joanna, you can have whatever you fancy as long as it's not an emerald. My mother had an emerald and she always maintained they were unlucky. It's probably an old wives' tale though.'

'Mother used to think green was unlucky. I don't see how it can be, I've always thought of green as the colour of spring, but I won't choose an emerald if you'd rather I didn't.'

In the end I chose a sapphire surrounded by diamonds which received everybody's admiration, and we spent a happy afternoon driving across the fells to York and an even happier time wandering the streets of the ancient city.

I was about to retire for the night when the telephone rang shrilly on the table in my sitting room, and immediately my spirits sank. It could only be my mother calling me at that hour.

Instead of Mother, however, it was Janice's voice that

came to me over the 'phone, trembling and mournful, and immediately I knew something was wrong.

'Joanna, something terrible has happened. Ernest has had a heart attack and he's in intensive care.'

'When was this?'

'Yesterday at the golf club. He collapsed on one of the greens. You can imagine the sort of state your mother's in. Can you dome down?'

'Yes, Janice, I'm sure I can. I'll be there some time tomorrow.'

When I told Paul the following morning he stared at me in dismay. 'Oh God, that's all we need,' he said shortly. 'She'll want you to stay there indefinitely, just at our busiest time, and what will you do if the worst happens?'

'Paul, I don't know, but surely he'll get well? Lots of people have heart attacks and get over them. But you do see she needs me today?'

'Yes, of course. You'll keep me informed?'

'Yes, I'll telephone you this evening.'

The journey was uneventful but I was not prepared for Ernest's daughter who was staying with Mother. As I had expected Mother was distraught, tearful, more sorry for herself than Ernest, but Marion was openly hostile.

'There was really no need for you to come,' she said sharply. 'We were managing quite well, I can't think why Janice telephoned you.'

'She must have thought I could help,' I said quietly.

'I can't think why. You haven't lived at home for years. Your mother has learned to cope without you.'

'I know. I did spend five years in the WRENS, Marion. I had to find some sort of war work, surely you understand that?'

'The war's been over some time.'

'I know. You have a life with your husband and children, are you saying I shouldn't want similar?'

'Of course not. But I didn't go to live at the other end of the country with some man I wasn't married to.'

'Is that what you believe?'

'It's what's been hinted at.'

There was no way I was going to justify my actions to

Marion. Obviously she'd listened to Mother's complaints about my behaviour and made up her mind about me. With my mother I felt only exasperation and a sense of betrayal, but I was sorry for her too.

Only a week after his first heart attack Ernest had another one which proved fatal. Marion returned to her family as soon as the funeral was over and I stayed to listen to Mother's grief, her moans that she felt like a punch ball that fate was constantly assaulting, and that there was nothing to live for anymore.

I stayed for three weeks, and every time I said I must return to Reckmire she accused me of deserting her.

I begged her to return with me. I painted a glowing picture of the hotel, promising her the prettiest bedroom, the ministrations of a devoted staff, the best food the kitchens could provide, but all she said in reply was that she hated Reckmire, there were too many memories of a family who had never liked her, of Robert, and of that lonely stretch of marsh.

'I want you back here, Joanna. I want a return to our life together. We have enough money to live well and perhaps travel abroad. We have so much to give each other. I want you to go up to Reckmire and ask Paul Cheviot to buy you out, let him have the place to himself.'

It was desperation that prompted me to say, 'Mother, Paul has asked me to marry him.'

That I had stunned her with my announcement was an understatement. Her mouth opened in surprise and almost miraculously the tears stopped to be replaced by amazement, then anger.

'But you don't like him, you never liked him! How can you even think of marrying anybody at this moment when I'm all alone?'

'Do you want me to be an old maid, Mother? Have you forgotten that you've been married twice?'

'You've never been the sort of daughter I wanted, Joanna. You left me to go abroad with your father, then you left me again to go up to Reckmire. You went into the Wrens instead of getting some sort of war work round here. Well, go back to Reckmire, marry Paul Cheviot, and try to live with yourself and your conscience. Don't expect me to come up to Reckmire for your wedding and don't bring him here!'

I returned to Reckmire the next day. It was a long lonely journey on a dismal day with low-lying grey clouds and intermittent hail. The welcoming warmth of the hotel met me like a benison and the sight of glowing log fires and bowls filled with yellow and bronze chrysanthemums soothed my jangled nerves.

Mr Gainsborough came forward to meet me, attentive, smiling, asking if I had eaten. I could hear the hum of conversation in the lounges, the clatter of billiard balls, and laughter, but I went up to my bedroom.

The long lonely reach of Reckmire stretched before me and intermittent moonlight touched a stormy sea and dark scudding clouds. I felt the sharp pricking of tears, allowing them to fall unchecked down my cheeks, and then I heard a soft knock on the door and turned to find Paul staring at me from the open doorway.

Words would not come. Instead, for what seemed an eternity we stood staring at each other, then he came into the room and took me in his arms. I was sobbing, talking incoherently, and he was patient with me, waiting without interrupting until the sobs ceased and only then said, 'Tell me about it, Joanna. You haven't made a word of sense but I do understand.'

'Oh, Paul, I feel that I've deserted her. She's so alone, she lost Father, then me and now Ernest. All the way home I've been thinking about her in that new flat that's far too big for her, away from her old friends, surrounded with memories, just sitting there feeling sorry for herself. She accused me of being selfish, never being the sort of daughter I could have been.'

'But then hasn't she always accused you of that? None of this is new, Joanna, and none of it is fair.'

'But it's what she believes.'

'So what have you said to her? Come back to Reckmire with me, enjoy the hotel, be with people, learn to love it? And she refused, of course.'

I stared at him. 'Why do you know my mother so well?'

256

'Because in a different sort of way it echoes so much of my own life. My mother's affection was always cloying, and my father was too remote. My mother expected from me all the love and companionship she never got from him, and he expected adult commitment from a child. The only real childhood I ever knew was here with Robin, and when I took him home he understood why I loved Reckmire so much.'

'I think I understand better now, Paul, why you were often bitter and impatient.'

'I was impatient with you because I saw myself in you. The lonely only child buffeted between two parents who were antagonistic, no longer caring for each other. Has your mother said she will come?'

'No, she will never come. I told her you had asked me to marry you.'

'What did she say to that?'

'She said she had no intention of coming to Reckmire for the wedding, and I must live with my conscience.'

'So you would prefer to marry in Surrey?'

'No. I want to marry here in Reckmire. It's where we're going to live and we're a part of this village. My family have been part of it for a very long time and it's something they would want.'

I did not want to tell Paul that Mother had said I must not take him to Surrey. I had no means of knowing what the future would bring, and time might alter many things.

He smiled. 'We'll make it a wonderful wedding. We'll have a banquet here for our guests and give the villagers something to talk about for months. Next weekend we'll go home to Yorkshire so that you can meet my parents. I can't promise you a happy weekend. My father will be his usual remote self, my mother will be in a world of her own, but at least it might help you to understand me a little.

'We'll set our wedding for October. By then we'll have the season behind us and things will have quietened down. How do you feel about it?'

'Well, yes, and it will give me time to think about my dress.'

'The painter came with your portrait yesterday but we

haven't chosen a suitable frame. I'll get somebody to take a look at it one day next week.'

'Are you pleased with it?'

'Yes, he's done a good job. You'll be pleased with it too.'

I stood looking at it the next morning while it rested on the floor in one corner of the nursery. A portrait of a fair, rather lovely woman with a strangely ethereal smile. Candid blue eyes looked back at me and the dark sable at the neck of the black gown glowed as it seemed to emphasise my delicate throat and the slender hand resting on black velvet.

Paul was looking down at me, waiting for me to say something. After a while he said, 'You like it, don't you, Joanna?'

'Yes, it's lovely. It flatters me terribly.'

He laughed. 'Well, of course it doesn't flatter you! It's exactly like you.'

I smiled happily at the warm glow his words brought to my heart.

Chapter Twenty-Three

I stared through the windscreen at the large stone house at the end of a narrow drive flanked with rhodedendron bushes. It seemed almost like an extension of the great four-storey mills Paul had pointed out to me on the outskirts of the Yorkshire industrial town.

Below us stretched a vista of undulating moorland and distant purple hills. The wind whistled along the terrace where we had parked the car and it was bitterly cold. I looked up at the dark windows but the house stared back at me with an almost chilly disdain.

'The old man will probably be down at the mills,' Paul said casually, 'he usually gets in around five, or perhaps a little earlier as it's Friday.'

He produced a key at the front door and then I was entering a dark wood-pannelled hall and looking round me with some interest. A dark oak staircase ascended from the centre of the hall and branched out after several steps in two directions. A large oil painting took pride of place where the steps divided. It showed a man in formal clothing, a large man with a dark moustache, who seemed to be staring down at us with stern disapproval.

'My grandfather,' Paul murmured, 'the founder of the Cheviot empire.'

'Your father's father?' I asked.

'Who else?'

A clock ticked loudly in the centre of one wall, a large grandfather clock, and there were several pieces of dark furniture in the hall, a stout carved chest and several oriental stands topped by massive porcelain vases.

There seemed to me nothing tasteful about it, but there was no denying that everything in it was valuable and over-large.

Paul had walked through the hall and disappeared down a passage leading from it. I could hear him calling, 'Is anybody about?' and then I heard the opening of a door and a woman's voice. Seconds later he returned to the hall in the company of a stout woman wearing black whom he introduced as Annie, the housekeeper.

She eyed me solemnly but offered no greeting beyond a short nod of her head.

'I suppose my father's at the mills?' Paul said curtly.

'That he is, and yer mother's restin'. She 'ad a bad night, but she knows yer comin so she'll be down presently. Yer'll be stayin' the night, Mister Paul?'

'Yes, I'll have my old room. Perhaps you'll put Miss Albemarle in one of the guest rooms? Turn some heating on in there, Annie, she's not accustomed to a house built on moorland with the wind blowing through every crack.'

Annie smiled. 'I'll get Letty to light a fire. Most o' the chimneys smoke but it'll 'ave settled down afore the lady retires.'

She bustled away and Paul said, 'Come into the drawing room, Joanna, or would you like a tour of the house before we settle down?'

'Yes please, Paul. I'd like to know my way around.'

The drawing room was unremarkable for either taste or charm. It was filled with deep Chesterfields, solid mahogany tables and plant stands. Its predominent colour was fawn, and there was an expensive oriental carpet covering the floor.

The dining room boasted a long dark oak table surrounded by eight chairs and two carvers, a Welsh dresser amply supplied with willow pattern china and a huge fireplace was brightened with brass firetongs and polished hearth.

Pictures of dark Scottish lochs and others of hunting scenes covered most of the walls, and Paul said sarcastically, 'This house was my grandfather's dream when he was a struggling office worker with no taste but good brains. When he rose to affluence he bought it and furnished it from sale rooms filled with pictures and furniture other people could no longer afford. He could tell you which factory master's house they had come from, and delighted in thinking he was now the owner of so many things he'd once envied.

'Did you know your grandfather well?'

'No. I listened to him and agreed with him, that was the only way to get along with him, and my father is very much like him. Be prepared, Joanna.'

'Were your mother's family in the woollen trade?'

'Very much so. My mother was old Sir Joshua Garfield's only daughter, the mills were his and my father a mere office worker in one of them. When my mother fell in love with him he met with every opposition it's possible to meet but by sheer hard work and guts he overcame them. Then when my mother's father died, he took over the mills.'

'That must have been a tremendous undertaking?'

'Well, yes, but we Cheviots are good at rescuing lost causes. Haven't I proved it to you over recent months, Joanna?'

'I can understand why your father was hurt and angry when you rejected him in favour of Reckmire. Suppose it had been your son rejecting Reckmire for something new?'

'Yes, there would be one hell of a row, but it's history now, Joanna. We have to look forward. If we make a success of the place my father will be the first to boast of it.'

'Which is the real Yorkshire, I wonder, those endless dark moors and the valleys filled with mill chimneys, or the Yorkshire of rolling hills and beautiful rivers? My mother had always led me to believe that the north was a sad dismal place totally devoid of beauty and history, but Yorkshire and Lancashire is so full of it. Since I discovered it I feel ashamed of those years when I knew nothing beyond the niceties of Surrey lanes and gentle countryside.'

He smiled. 'I thought of you like that, Joanna. A prim little rich girl, sheltered and protected.'

'A stupid girl who put your friend's life in danger?'

'If you like.'

'And you think a little differently now I hope?'

He laughed. 'Now I think you're wonderful. Don't be

surprised if Mother doesn't enter into the conversation, I haven't had a real conversation with her in years. I can't remember exactly when she started to deteriorate, it was probably bit by bit over the years. I wasn't at home much, school and university, then I was often at Reckmire. Don't let her worry you.'

I was not looking forward to the evening ahead of me. The house was depressing, and when eventually I went to the guestroom, led by Annie, its chill met me in spite of the low fire spluttering in the hearth.

'It'll warm up,' she said laconically. 'She's only just lit it, but when it stops smokin' she'll come in to put more coal on.'

'Thank you,' I murmured.

'I'll be makin' a cup o' tea, miss, so when yer've unpacked if you'll go downstairs it'll be ready.'

Paul had said we would only be staying one night so my case contained a dress for the evening ahead and my night attire. I was glad to see that there was a small bathroom attached to the bedroom but felt disinclined to linger in the unwelcoming room.

The windows looked down the length of the drive, to the distant town over which a pall of smoke seemed to hang mournfully. This all seemed a far cry from my schooldays in the Yorkshire I had loved.

I found Paul sitting in front of the fire with an open newspaper and almost immediately Annie appeared with a tray containing our tea and a large dark fruit loaf.

Paul watched me pour the tea, cutting a slab of cake which I placed on a table near his chair. He smiled. 'Is it all exactly as you imagined it would be?'

'It's very much as you described it.'

'Now can you understand why I loved Reckmire and why I was reluctant to invite Robin back?'

'What did you and he do here?'

'We rode. We went down to the mills and I showed Robin around, we went into the towns and looked at the shops. We never stayed long, there was always Reckmire we both wanted to get back to.'

'I know.'

I shall never forget sitting down to dinner that evening with Paul and I facing each other across the width of the dining table, his father at one end and his mother at the other.

Mrs Cheviot wore a light mauve dress that had undoubtedly been expensive, but the colour had faded and there were food stains down the front of it. Once she had been pretty. Now there was an unhealthy colour in her cheeks and her soft hair was liberally sprinkled with grey.

She had greeted me with a shy absent smile and all she could say to Paul, her only son, was, 'Where have you been, Paul? I thought the war was over?'

His father meticulously carved the joint, handing the plates round, and although the meat was plentiful and succulent the vegetables were only lukewarm and the potatoes hard in the centre.

Across the table I was aware of Paul's eyes meeting mine with the unspoken words: 'Didn't I tell you this was how it would be?'

Mrs Cheviot toyed with her food, pushing it round her plate, occasionally lifting it to her mouth, and I was aware of the exasperation boiling up in the man at the head of the table. Unable to stand it any longer he barked, 'If the food isn't to your liking, Edith, I suggest you either leave it alone or eat it.'

'I'm not hungry, dear,' she said plaintively.

'Then leave it alone. The dogs will eat it.'

'How's business, Father?' Paul asked, to take the tension away from his mother.

'Business is satisfactory, but why ask? You can't have any real interest in it.'

'You've asked no questions about the hotel, Father.'

'I have no interest in that venture.'

'Perhaps I should tell you that Joanna and I are engaged to be married?'

Not a flicker of interest crossed Mr Cheviot's face, although I did not miss the tightening of his hands of his knife and fork.

'Joanna is Robin Albemarle's cousin,' Paul explained. 'We are partners in Reckmire which is enjoying considerable success.'

263

'So you are the young woman who has tempted my son away from the mills his grandfather put his heart and soul into?' he said quietly, and with a venom which stung me into retorting, 'I very much doubt if I could have tempted him away from anything he had any real interest in, Mr Cheviot.'

Maddeningly he went on with his meal, adding more potatoes, refilling his wine glass, and from across the table Paul watched with hostile narrowed eyes.

We sat in silence until suddenly I was aware that Mrs Cheviot was humming softly to herself, and looking at her I saw that she was smiling gently in my direction.

'It's so long since we went to Whitby,' she said quietly. 'Do you like Whitby, dear?'

'I've never been there, Mrs Cheviot,' I replied, and Paul said gently, 'You should go for a few days, Mother, you're always so well when you return.'

'Yes, I should go, shouldn't I? But your father never has time to take me. Did Paul meet you during the war, dear?'

'I told you, Mother, Joanna is Robin Albemarle's cousin. You remember Robin, don't you?'

'Oh, yes. Such a nice boy. He always comes in the summer.'

The meal proceeded without further conversation until the young maid who had served us at the dining table announced that she had taken coffee into the drawing room. Mr Cheviot led the way followed by his wife and Paul while I brought up the rear. A fire burned in the grate now and the room seemed rather more cheerful than it had earlier. I went to sit beside Mrs Cheviot while Paul poured the coffee and handed it round, then for the first time Mr Cheviot acknowledged our engagement by saying, 'I hope you're not expecting us to attend your wedding? Your mother isn't well and it's doubtful if I can spare the time. Where is it to be by the way?'

'We'd like it to be at Reckmire, Father,' Paul said. 'Actually, Joanna's mother lives in Surrey, but it's too far away. We live in the village, people know us there, it seems the most appropriate place to marry.'

'And it silences the gossips,' his father put in dryly.

'We've given them no reason to gossip about us, Father, everything at Reckmire has been very circumspect. We are getting married because we wish it, not because there's been gossip.'

I read in Mr Cheviot's face the same cynicism I had so often surprised in Paul, and I was glad when the conversation turned to the manufacture of woollen cloth, a subject I was ignorant about.

I doubt if I shall ever forget that evening. Rain pattered on the windows and I could hear the low moaning sound of the wind in the chimney. Paul sat morosely staring at a field magazine while his father read the financial columns in the newspaper. Mrs Cheviot sat staring into the fire, occasionally smiling at some thought or imaginary companion.

Whenever I spoke to her she smiled but offered no conversation of her own and in some exasperation Paul said, 'I shouldn't try, Joanna. Have you consulted anybody about Mother's health, Father?'

'She's happy in her private world and unlikely to be any different. She has everything she wants, private nursing homes are expensive and she'd be the same in one of those. Probably a lot worse since she wouldn't know where she was. In a strange environment she could be utterly demoralised.'

'She hasn't always been like this, there's a big deterioration.'

'The deterioration's been steady. I see your mother every day, it's been over a year since you've seen her.'

'I know, Father, it was unavoidable.'

I wished they would not discuss her when she was sitting beside me, and why had it been unavoidable? Didn't Paul care, or did it hurt too much to see her like this?

I slept badly in that large room smelling of smoke and where the fire had died down to a handful of burning embers. The wind rattled the windows and the steady staccato beating of the rain became, if anything, more intense.

I was remembering all I had learned of Paul's early life in this house and I understood the boy I had first known with his singular remoteness better as a consequence. It was still

265

dark when I awoke, but I was aware of the tears streaming down my face and then the memory of my dream came back to me, terrifyingly real. The sound of the crashing sea was in my ears and underneath my feet I could feel the cruel rocks. My hands were outstretched, reaching out for Robin's hand, always out of reach, and I could see the wind stirring his hair and the anxiety in his eyes, then I could see Paul looking down on us, stern, remote, but he made no attempt to help us.

For minutes I lay staring up at the ceiling then decided to get up. It was five o'clock and the bath water was lukewarm. I shivered as I dressed in the chilly room but the rain had ceased. I took the eiderdown off the bed and sat with it draped over me, dozing fitfully until it was light. Then I crossed to the window. Mist hung low over the encircling hills and as I peered through the misted windows I was aware of Paul riding across the parkland. He rode with shoulders hunched, his riding hat pulled down against the wind, urging the big black horse on in a fast headlong gallop, taking the low hawthorn hedges with consumate ease.

As I walked downstairs I could smell cooking. I had reached the bottom step when the same girl who had served us dinner crossed the hall carrying a loaded tray.

Wishing me a shy good morning, she said with a smile, 'Breakfast's in the mornin' room, miss, the master's already in there.'

I followed her, unhappy with the prospect of having to eat breakfast with Paul's father, and determined that I would not let him see it. He looked up when I entered the room, favouring me with a brief nod but no words of welcome.

Breakfast was laid out on a long side table and I was surprised to see how much there was of it. Ham and bacon, eggs, fried and scrambled, grilled tomatoes, even kippers. I helped myself to orange juice and scrambled eggs.

He was more interested in the morning paper than in me. Consequently I was allowed to get on with my breakfast without attempting to make conversation. I was at first too preoccupied with my own thoughts to see that he had laid the paper aside. He sat watching me with a thoughtfulness that made me suddenly uncomfortable when I became aware of it.

'Have you never thought, Miss Albemarle, that it was a strange thing for my son suddenly to escape from the thing he knew best to enter into partnership with a girl intent on turning her grandparents' home into a country hotel?'

'It was Paul's idea, Mr Cheviot. I didn't know what I would do with Reckmire. I have asked myself many times why Grandma should leave it to me.'

'My son thought the answer to that lay in your background, the fact that your parents were divorced, and in the hope that you would shape your own destiny.'

'I wasn't aware that Paul had discussed my background with you.'

'Well, obviously. He needed to explain a great many things when he left this house and the future we had hoped for behind him. Paul was at school with your cousin and even in those days all we ever heard was Reckmire. He loved that house with more intensity than he has ever loved anything. You are a lovely young woman. Does it not worry you that his love for Reckmire is prompting him to marry you, and if it does, why are you willing to put up with it?'

'Are you always so blunt, Mr Cheviot?' I gasped.

'You can put it down to my disappointment in a son who has turned his back on me. A case of sour grapes if that gives you any comfort.'

I was too angry to answer him, and at that moment the door opened and Paul came into the room, still wearing his riding clothes. His glance passed from his father to me, and with a stiff bow his father gathered up his newspaper and left the room.

'What's he been saying to you?' Paul asked as he helped himself to food from the breakfast table.

'Nothing very much, he's a man of few words.' I could not tell Paul what his father had said to me. He was understandably angry that Paul had left the family firm to throw in his lot with me.

We stayed until mid-morning and left after coffee. Mr Cheviot informed us that his wife did not come down until after lunch and although he came out into the hall he did not wait in the doorway until we drove away.

Paul saw nothing strange in this so I kept my own counsel. I was glad to be driving home even though the dark clouds hung low and the mist persisted until we reached the other side of the pennines.

Without our presence Reckmire ran on an even keel. The flowers in the rooms were as exquisite and tasteful as I could have arranged myself; indeed if we had decided to absent ourselves for weeks I felt sure matters at Reckmire would have run smoothly.

All the same, when we entered the dining room that evening we were greeted with smiling faces, and with an interest that helped to reassure me that we were necessary and had been missed.

One elderly lady with her white pekinese came to our table where I was sitting alone. This was probably her fourth visit since the hotel had been opened and I had found her very charming and easy to please. Now she smiled down at me. 'I do wish you and Mr Cheviot every happiness, my dear, I was so pleased that you had decided to marry.'

'Thank you, Mrs Eglington.'

'When is the wedding to be?'

'We're thinking about October.'

'That will be lovely. October can be a charming month and the hotel will be quieter. I intend to book in, I wouldn't miss your wedding at any price.'

I watched her reach the door which Paul held open for her, and she was smiling up at him with coy enjoyment at being the recipient of his charm. He bent down to pat the little dog, then came towards me, a broad smile on his face.

'That is one lady who is going to be here for our wedding,' he said.

I smiled.

'We have to start making plans, Joanna. You have to let your aunt and uncle know, and then there's the Italian contingent. Is there a chance they might come?'

'I don't know. I'll write to them tomorrow.'

'I suppose you'll ask Edward to give you away?'

'Yes. What about your cousin and his family, will they be here?'

'I doubt it. We've never been close. He's always been envious. I had a better education, better prospects. In his estimate I had the best of everything. Well, now he's fallen into my shoes, but it won't have altered his opinion.'

'All the same, perhaps we should invite them?'

'I'll think about it. I'll ask a chap I knew in the army to be my best man. We telephone each other now and then, he'll not miss the chance to have a weekend here. Have you had thoughts about your bridesmaids?'

'I thought I might ask Lottie.'

He stared at me for a moment before saying, 'Not a good idea, Joanna. She's a nice enough girl but she's hardly the sort who'll be at her best in this sort of atmosphere and with the sort of people who will be there.'

'That's a terribly snobbish thing to say, Paul.'

'I don't mean it that way. Look around you, and then think about Lottie. Anyway she's your bridesmaid, please yourself, but don't be surprised if she sees it my way.'

I made it my business to go down to the bakery the next morning and as soon as I asked her I was aware of the doubt on her face, the uncomfortable silence that followed my request.

'Oh, Joanna, I'm so pleased and proud that yer've asked me, but I couldn't. I couldn't walk wi' all them folk you'll be askin'. Besides, I'm goin' to Leeds and it's likely I won't be able to be here in October.'

'Leeds!'

'Yes. I've always wanted to nurse at St. Jimmys, now I've got my chance. I'll not be gettin' home very often for awhile. You do understand don't you Joanna?'

'I'm very pleased for you Lottie, I'm just so sorry that you won't be at my wedding.'

'I'll be thinkin' about you all day. I'll ask my mother if I can walk awhile with you, it'll be some time before I get back to the village.'

We walked on the fell and sat for awhile looking out across the sea. I thought about the first time I had sat here with Lottie and her thoughts too must have been similar because suddenly she said, 'It's a long time since we sat 'ere after we'd seen our Freda in the park, Joanna. I never thought that day that you'd be livin' here and ownin' Reckmire. I never thought you'd be thinkin' o' marryin' Paul Cheviot.'

'If you could get to know Paul as I have, Lottie, you'd like him, I know you always liked Robin, never Paul, but he's been wonderful to me, a rock I've been glad to lean on. He's done so much for me. It's thanks to him that Reckmire ever took off.'

'Are you sure 'e's done it for you, Joanna? Not for Reckmire?'

I stared at her in some annoyance, and the rich red blood flooded her face. She said quickly, 'I shouldn't 'ave said that, I 'ad no right to say that. I must be gettin' back. Our Freda's comin' for lunch, it's 'er 'alf day.'

She had risen to her feet and was halfway down the fell. I ran after her. 'Lottie, it doesn't matter. I felt the same way at first, now I know I was wrong. I've learned an awful lot about Paul, about his childhood, his parents, and I do know that things like that have a lot to do with the way we are. You come from a very happy home, Lottie, you can't understand.'

'No, you're right. I can never understand our Freda. She comes from the same home as me but we're not a bit alike. Maybe I'm not good at understandin'. I do want ye to be 'appy, Joanna, and ye will be. I'm just a country girl with not much education. You wouldn't be marryin' him if ye didn't think it'd work.'

Lottie's words had unsettled me so that I thought about them constantly during the next few weeks. Of course Paul loved me, no man could pretend day after day, week after week. Because she didn't like him she didn't want to believe there was any good in him. All the same I was wishing she had never said those words to me.

Several days after I spoke to her about being my bridesmaid, Paul asked one evening over dinner, 'By the way, I've been meaning to ask, did you approach your friend about being your bridesmaid?'

'Yes, but she's going to Leeds and it probably won't be possible.'

'You mean, she's seen how unwise it would be? I think Lottie probably knows her limitations better than you do.'

He stretched out his hand and covered mine, resting on the table. 'Don't worry about it, darling, you'll find somebody else without much difficulty. One of our guests perhaps who has come here many times, somebody's favourite daughter. That sort of thing could be very good for business. I take it you are not intending trying to persuade your mother again?'

'I'm going to telephone her later tonight. She won't come, Paul, but I have to try.'

He nodded, changing the subject immediately, his voice filled with confidence and enthusiasm. 'I'd thought of a large marquee on the lawn if the weather stays nice. That way the villagers can mingle with our guests and a good time can be had by all. What do you think?'

'I think the villagers would be pleased to be asked. I'm leaving all that to you.'

It was much later when I telephoned my mother and as always her voice came over the telephone like a plaintive child's, so that afterwards it was hard to imagine that that little girl voice could say such hurtful things.

'How are you, Mother?' I began as usual. 'I hope you're keeping up with all your old pursuits and seeing your friends?'

'I'm doing the best I can, Joanna, but I am some distance away now and you know I don't drive.'

'But all your friends drive, Mother.'

'I know, but they don't always want to take the trouble.'

'Have you had any thoughts of moving back there?'

'Well, of course not. This flat is infinitely superior and Ernest and I chose it together. My friends are terribly envious that I have this place.'

'Mother, Paul and I have fixed our wedding day, it is to be here in the village church at Reckmire in early-October. We both want you to be here, Mother. You'll be very comfortable, and you'll be able to see Aunt Marcia and Uncle Edward again. And we would like you to see what we've done with the place.'

'Will Corallie be there?'

'I've written to her but as yet haven't had a reply. I believe her husband isn't well and of course it's an awfully long way to come.'

271

'It's an awfully long way for me to come too, Joanna. If Reckmire and this man is what you want I hope you'll be very happy, but I shall not be there. I hated Reckmire years ago. Whatever you've done to it won't obliterate my impressions then.'

'I'm sorry, Mother.'

'Will his parents be there?'

'I don't think so. Paul's mother isn't well. But if you change your mind please let us know. We both want you there.'

'I shan't change my mind, Joanna. I have to go now, I'm expecting friends. Goodbye.'

Over the miles I felt her anger, and as I replaced the receiver I came nearer to hating her than I had ever done before.

Chapter Twenty-Four

We were fully booked for the whole of October. Grinning gleefully Paul said, 'That's because nobody's sure just when the wedding's to be, I purposely kept it a secret.' We had decided on the middle Wednesday in October because we thought Saturday might be too disruptive with guests arriving and departing.

Aunt Corallie wrote me a long rambling letter explaining that Uncle Rinaldo was much better but unable to travel so far so that they would not be coming. Several days later however a huge box arrived containing a beautiful crystal chandelier which they thought would fit nicely into the new Reckmire. They had not seen Gabriella for some time as she was living in Rome, but Italy was back to normal and English people were once more visiting.

She hoped Paul and I would be able to visit them soon and she wished us every happiness.

Paul duly admired the chandelier and gave instructions for it to be put up in the lounge, and when I showed him the letter he said it was perhaps just as well they weren't coming as the place would be bursting at the seams. My other aunt and uncle had been given one of our best rooms at the front of the hotel while Paul's best man would stay in the flat with him.

We were watching the installation of the chandelier when three small children ran into the lounge, almost knocking the electrician off his ladder, and Paul said irritably, 'Thank God we don't get many of those. Children are disruptive in a place like this. They want amusing all the time and if it isn't possible they get into mischief.'

'You don't like children, Paul?'

'I'm not the sort of chap who drools over every brat he sees so promise me you won't go all broody on me for some considerable time? As a matter of fact, I've been having serious thoughts about that nursery upstairs. It's taking the place of another large bedroom and we don't really need it, do we?'

'There have always been children at Reckmire, Paul. Don't you want a son and heir for this stately pile?'

'One day, Joanna, but for the present how can we put an embargo on other people's children if we have our own running all over the place?'

I didn't answer him, but all through lunch I was aware of his eyes constantly questioning and when we left the room the children's father came over from his table, smiling tentatively.

'I'm so awfully sorry if the children made a nuisance of themselves. It's Penny's birthday and she's excited about her presents. We're leaving in the morning so you won't have to put up with us much longer.'

'The children have been very good, Mr Reynolds,' I said quickly. 'It's impossible to keep them quiet all the time. Have you enjoyed your stay?'

'Oh, yes, very much. My wife's parents have been raving about this place since you first opened and we've enjoyed every minute. Next year Robin will be four and he's taken to riding, he's delighted that you have ponies.'

When he left us I smiled at Paul who groaned theatrically. 'That means they're coming back,' he said dourly. 'Talking about stables, I'm driving over to Colonel Wilton's place this afternoon, he has two hunters for sale. If the price is right I thought we might buy them.'

'How many horses do we need? I thought we had sufficient when you bought the last two.'

'Leave that to me, Joanna. If the price is right I think we should speculate.'

The Wiltons were our nearest neighbours since part of their estate bordered on ours. Whenever the Colonel and his wife dined here he never missed an opportunity to tell me how much I reminded him of Corallie, then he would go into raptures about the part she had played in his youth. He was quick to change the subject when his wife appeared on the scene, and he very quickly withdrew his arm from around my waist.

I was not surprised when Paul failed to appear for our evening meal but dining alone in the lofty dining room no longer troubled me.

Most of the tables were full. There were new guests arriving in the morning while others would be leaving and I noticed that there were no children in the dining room so that the three who had disturbed Paul's morning were obviously tucked up in bed.

I was almost at the end of my meal when the headwaiter ushered three newcomers to their table, and I stared at them a little curiously because I had not known that new guests were expected.

They took their places before looking round the room, then one of them jumped to her feet and came in my direction while the older woman waved. I stared in amazement as Stella Chantry took the chair opposite mine, with a bright smile on her face, saying, 'Joanna, I should have written to say we were coming but there wasn't time. Mother booked in a hurry when Dad had a few days' leave. He said she'd never manage it but she got a cancellation. You know Mother, she's been dying to come here. We've all heard so much about it from your mother.'

'My mother!'

'Well, yes. She's never stopped talking about it. Before you know where you are they'll all be here.'

'All except my mother, Stella.'

'Really? Is she still being difficult.'

'She doesn't want to come, not even to my wedding.'

'Oh, Joanna, I want to hear all about your wedding and I want to meet your fiance. Isn't he with you?'

'He's dining with friends this evening but you'll meet him, I promise.'

'We've so much to talk about. Can I meet you later? Dad's tired, he's been working too hard recently so he's here for a rest. They'll retire early, where can we meet?'

'Ask the receptionist to ring my room when you've finished dinner and I'll come down to collect you.'

I returned to her table with her to greet her parents, then when their first course arrived I excused myself and Stella said brightly, 'See you later, Joanna.'

She enthused about the turret room which was now my sitting room, and the bedroom and bathroom which led off from it. These rooms had been my baby, and when I pulled back the drapes from the window to allow her to look along the moonlit stretch of Reckmire with the sea rolling in in silver crescents, she said, 'It's beautiful, Joanna. Your mother was right, it's absolutely wonderful.'

I stared at her curiously. 'Surely my mother didn't say it was beautiful?'

'She said it was a great stone house on a tall cliff surrounded by the sea. She admitted she had always been afraid of the sea and had no desire to come here, but said it was still very beautiful.'

I busied myself pouring sherry which she accepted with a bright smile, sitting in front of a glowing fire with the flames reflecting in polished walnut and delicate chintz. She sat back appreciatively sipping her sherry and I left it to her to start the conversation.

After a while she said, 'I can hear the sea, Joanna, and the wind.'

'Yes. This is the one room you can really hear it from.'

'This is what your mother hated?'

'Mother never stayed in this part of the house.'

'Well, I think it's absolutely marvellous that you've achieved so much. If it was me doing all this my parents would be over the moon and terribly proud of me. What does Paul think about her not coming to your wedding?'

'He isn't surprised.'

'Doesn't she like him?'

'She's never met him.'

'Well, I can tell you that everybody thinks it's absolutely terrible that she's not coming. Nobody can understand her. Surely she should be happy to see what a success you've accomplished and that you've become engaged to the man who's helped so much?'

'How can anybody understand her when I never have?'

'Everybody liked your father so much, but Mother said your mother was always terribly spoiled. Do you know your granny used to spend hours asking her friends what their daughters were wearing for birthday parties, and then your mother had to have something that cost three times as much.

'We didn't really fall out with you because you didn't go swimming with us, Joanna, it was because your mother made you into something superior. Swimming was for ordinary people. You had to have ballet lessons which were too expensive for most of us with brothers and sisters.'

'I didn't know.'

'But you're getting married here in Reckmire? Surely you're not pandering to her wishes and getting married in Surrey?'

'No, we're getting married here.'

'Good for you.'

So we talked about our plans for the wedding, the marquee on the lawn, the banquet for our guests and the villagers, the tiny village church that couldn't possibly hold all our guests, and then she asked what I intended to wear.

'I don't really know. I've asked my uncle to give me away, but obviously I have to start thinking about a gown. I'm not sure about white.'

'Oh, yes, Joanna, something that'll make news, something everybody will remember.'

At that moment the door opened and Paul put his head into the room. Seeing that I had a guest he opened the door wider and came inside. He was smiling, his mood mellow, and when I introduced them Stella dimpled prettily, quite obviously impressed with his dark good looks and the charm of his smile.

They chatted animatedly together, and Paul surprised me by saying airily, 'This is the answer to all your problems, Joanna. Why not ask Stella to be your bridesmaid.'

She beamed, and Paul went on, 'You're obviously old friends. That's so, isn't it?'

'Well, yes,' Stella said. 'From the age of four. I'd love to be your bridesmaid, Joanna. I'm not standing on anybody else's corns am I?'

'No, there isn't anybody else and I would love you to be my bridesmaid. You're here for a few days, we could talk about what we're going to wear.'

It was hard to believe that in just two weeks I would be a married woman. Like every other girl I had always dreamed of floating down the aisle in a fairytale wedding dress attended by a bevy of bridesmaids. I had imagined my father smiling down at me with pride; my mother a little tearful sitting in the pews behind; the bridegroom always elusive, but never Paul Cheviot.

Paul was deeply engrossed with the perfection of the gardens and the two giant marquees he had ordered for the day. The banquet after the ceremony was entirely his concern and I could only surmise that his usual efficiency would ensure that nothing would go wrong.

Stella rang up constantly and couldn't understand why I didn't want to go up to London to choose my wedding dress. But it was too near my mother, and I had had excellent reports about a fashion house which had opened in Lancaster.

'What colour do you want me to wear?' she asked. 'As long as it's not yellow, Joanna. It simply doesn't suit me.'

'I really don't care, decide on the colour yourself.'

'But don't you mind?'

'No, really.'

'Then it's either going to be sapphire blue or jade. Some people might think green's unlucky for a wedding.'

'I'm sure it isn't although Paul did put me off having an emerald ring.'

She laughed. 'Darling, I'm longing to see you in frothy lace and a train the length of the aisle.'

'Then you're going to be disappointed,' I said firmly. 'I had that idea a long time ago. Now I think I shall settle for something less expensive and something I can wear later.'

What I chose was a cream wild silk dress that was decidedly elegant, and with it a large cream hat decorated with cream chiffon roses.

When Stella saw it she said, 'It's beautiful, Joanna, but I'm

278

surprised you didn't go for something more traditional.'

'In ten years' time the wedding photographs will look terribly dated' I mused. 'Somehow traditional bridal wear never seems to date quite so much, but I can wear this dress for other functions and I love the hat.'

'It's a dream for Ascot,' Stella said. 'Get Paul to take you next year, you'll be in all the news reels.'

The weeks leading up to my wedding were hectic, and on the day before I stood at the window of the lounge watching workmen setting up the marquees on the lawns. My aunt and uncle were expected during the afternoon and Paul's best man, Major Bruce Rand, had arrived in the early morning, a debonair military looking man with a ready smile and eyes filled with appreciation as he viewed the hotel from the terrace and was duly impressed by everything he saw.

With an engaging grin he said, 'Nothing like this ever happens to me, but you were always a lucky devil, Cheviot. The Devil looks after his own all right.'

'Get him to explain that to you, Joanna,' Paul said, smiling.

'Well, it's just that everything always seems to fall into Paul's lap. Even in the war when we were all out there battling it out he got transferred to the War Office and sat it out in comparative peace.'

'If you can call living in London during the war comparative peace, you're right,' snapped Paul. 'Ask Joanna what she thought of London during the war.'

'I'm pea green with envy, old boy, that's why I'm being tetchy. Where do I put my gear? I brought my best uniform and borrowed a morning suit. You omitted to say if it would be a military wedding or not.'

'Not, I think,' Paul said firmly. 'I'm happy to forget about the war.'

Introductions were performed when Stella joined us and we sat together in the lounge while Paul took his friend upstairs to the flat.

'Well, he seems very nice,' she said.

'Yes, he does. We'll wait until they come down then perhaps we should eat lunch.'

Stella and I got up to enter the dining room when we

saw them coming across the room, but it seemed Paul had other ideas.

'I've got something very important to show you, Joanna, there's time for us to walk across to the stables before lunch.'

'The stables!' I echoed in some surprise.

Without further explanation he led the way out through the front doors and the three of us followed. I knew he had bought two horses from Colonel Wilton but why did he have to show them to us today, unless it was for Major Rand's benefit?

Grossman, the head groom, with the help of a stable boy was unsaddling two horses when we arrived in the stable yard while two men in riding clothes crossed towards us.

'You've got two fine hacks there, Mr Cheviot,' one of them said, 'we've enjoyed a canter over the fell.'

We smiled and the other man said, 'You've got a beauty in the far corner.'

'I think so,' Paul said, striding ahead, and the three of us dutifully followed him to the centre stall where a chestnut horse stood watching our arrival with calm appraisal.

He was beautiful and after we had all admired him and I had stood for a few minutes stroking his satiny neck, Paul said, 'Well, Joanna, what do you think of him?'

'He's beautiful.'

'He's also a thoroughbred.'

'I thought you only bought two from Colonel Wilton?'

'That's right. He's called Ralston. I bought him from Sir Mark Easby. Wilton said he'd had a couple of bad years financially and was getting rid of two of his thoroughbreds to raise a bit of cash.'

'But do we really need a horse of this calibre, Paul? He must have been terribly expensive.'

'He was. He's also my wedding present to you.'

I stared at him in amazement and Major Rand said, 'Well done, old boy, and she's worth every inch of him.'

My eyes shone as I took his hand. It was so wonderful to be loved, to have this handsome man love me enough to give me this beautiful creature to treasure, and as we walked back to the hotel Stella whispered, 'Your mother's going to hear about this, Joanna. I'm going to delight in telling her how happy you are and what a wonderful husband you're going to have.'

The warm glow that filled my heart was intensified later in the afternoon when I watched my aunt and uncle getting out of their car and rushed out to meet them so that I could help with their luggage and the innumerable parcels they carried.

They stared round the reception room in amazement and Uncle Edward said, 'We knew you'd do your best with it, Joanna, but we never quite expected it would be so grand.'

'Most of it has been Paul's idea, he's been so wonderful, I could never have done it on my own. We've given you a room at the front of the hotel on the first floor, but you won't recognise that either. It was Grandma's room, but it's been completely done over.'

Together Paul and I took them round the hotel and again and again they exclaimed with delight at what we had accomplished. Flattered, Paul said, 'Well, we haven't finished yet, I still have a host of ideas. I told Joanna before we started that I aimed to have the most prestigious country hotel in the north of England, in the whole of England for that matter. This is only the beginning.'

'Well, I don't know what else you can achieve,' Aunt Marcia said. 'Every room has been changed, and there are no rooms left to alter. The gardens are beautiful and you've resurfaced the tennis courts. Isn't there a swimming pool too?'

'There is,' he agreed.

'Then what else is there?' Uncle Edward asked in some surprise.

'Pipe dreams as yet,' Paul answered. 'We've got one of the best chefs there is. You'll be able to comment on the meal later.'

'What a pity we can only stay two nights, but we'll be back later in the year. Surely your mother would have liked all this Joanna?' Aunt Marcia said.

'I can't try again, Aunt Marcia, it wouldn't do any good.'

'I suppose not. Ah, well, we're all going to enjoy ourselves and tomorrow is going to be the happiest day of your life, darling.'

There was laughter and joy at our table that night and the other guests looked across at us with smiling faces until it seemed that our joy was theirs also.

I was too excited to sleep. It was my last night alone in the room I loved and I took delight in opening the curtains wide so that I could look along the lonely reach of Reckmire. A young moon shed its light on a sea that rolled in gently towards the dunes and from somewhere in the darkness came the distant barking of farm dogs and the eerie hooting of an owl.

My thoughts went back over the years and I found myself trying to remember those times when I had been really happy. Always here at Reckmire and during my schooldays. On that last night in London when we had watched Ivor Novello's musical until Mother had spoilt it for us by her disapproving face, and during the war. I felt ashamed that the war had brought me happiness when it brought so much misery into the lives of others, and yet I had been happy then, and with Robin who had comforted that miserable tortured girl with his love.

I would be happy with Paul. He had shown me how much he loved me by all he had done for Reckmire, and only that morning when I had seen Ralston looking at us from over his stable door. There had been so much love in his gift, and with a rush of gratitude I resolved that I would be as generous with him as he had been with me. I would give him half of Reckmire and I would tell him on our wedding night. It would be something to set the seal on my love for him.

Chapter Twenty-Five

There was mist swirling along the beach on the morning of my wedding day but I had come to know the weather in these parts very well. Early-morning mist meant that by lunchtime the sun would be emerging and the day promised to be fine.

One of the maids came in with my morning tea. She smiled as she laid it down on the bedside table.

'Yer in for a fine day, Miss Albemarle, I'm right glad.'

'Oh, I do hope so, Alice. You'll be able to watch, I hope.'

'Yes. Mr Cheviot's said we can all go because there'll be caterers and staff in. We'll all be there to wish ye luck.'

'And you'll be at the party afterwards?'

'That I shall, as well as all the village.'

I bathed unhurriedly and then suddenly Stella was there with the hairdresser and Aunt Marcia was fussing round like a mother hen.

I was glad that Stella had changed her mind about the jade. Her sapphire blue gown was beautiful, and with it she wore a small tricorn the exact shade of her gown, which we giggled over when I said it reminded me of my WRENS hat.

I had chosen small identical posies for both of us made up from cream tea roses and lily of the valley. Aunt Marcia looked elegant in beige. She came to put her arms around me, saying, 'You look beautiful, Joanna, you both look beautiful. Edward will wait for you downstairs in the hall. You can come with me, Stella.'

I smiled, my throat felt too tight for words, but after they had gone I went to the window more to compose myself than to look at the scenery. The mist had gone and there was a gentle breeze blowing off the sea. Two herring gulls flew screeching above the surf and the house felt strangely quiet until I remembered that by this time they would all be at the church waiting for my arrival.

Uncle Edward came forward to meet me in the hall and he looked handsome and distinguished in his formal morning dress.

He put his arms round me, saying, 'You look lovely, Joanna,' then we were getting into the car and driving slowly down the village road leading to the church and I was aware of the pealing of bells. As we neared the lynch-gate the vicar stood waiting with the procession of choirboys who would walk before me into the church.

So many people lined the path up to the church, villagers in their Sunday best, hotel guests in morning suits carrying grey toppers, their wives in large floppy hats, and all with smiling faces. Then suddenly we were in the darkness of the tiny church and I could look over the heads of the choirboys to where the congregation stood to await my arrival.

Stella fell into step behind us and I felt my uncle's gentle pressure on my hand, then almost before I was aware of it Paul was standing at my side and voices were raised in the opening hymn.

As we left the church after the ceremony all I remember was a sea of smiling faces, the clicking of innumerable cameras and then Paul and I were sitting in the bridal car and he was saying, 'You look beautiful, Joanna, very beautiful, and the rest of the day will be one to remember.'

'I thought we could spend a few days in the lakes. There's a hotel near Derwentwater I'd like to take a look at. I've heard rumours they're not doing too well. We might be able to assess the position and pick up some of their staff if the place is in danger of folding.'

It did seem completely incongruous to me to be discussing business on the way back from our wedding but I was too bemused with events to say so. Instead we stood on the steps of the hotel to await our guests then we were all in the marquees. The champagne flowed, the laughter reverberated and the tables groaned under masses of food.

Paul suggested that we circulate together to receive the good wishes of those present, after which we should mingle separately. My wedding finery was admired, mainly by the hotel guests, and encountering Mrs Peabody surrounded by members of her family and a group of village women she was quick to tell me that she'd expected me to wear a wreath and fall.

Stella dissolved into laughter at the expression. 'What does she mean by a wreath and fall?' she asked, her eyes dancing with laughter.

'She means a wreath and veil. It's an expression I've heard before in these parts,' I explained.

Mrs Peabody's plate was piled high with fresh salmon and she made it clear to all present that she preferred it to that smoked variety. I was pleased to see Lottie and her mother. Lottie said with a smile, 'You looked that lovely, Joanna, and yer bridesmaid ... I could never 'ave looked like that in a thousand years.'

'Well, of course you could,' I replied stoutly. 'Stella is an old friend from my very early schooldays. Who is looking after the shop?'

'Our Freda, but we've got to get back pretty soon so that she can come here. Trust our Freda not to want to miss anythin'.'

Later in the afternoon I saw her sauntering amongst the guests, a good-looking girl if a trifle bold, wearing a too tight dress and towering heels. But she did not seem short of young men anxious to help her to refreshments.

The villagers went back to their homes soon after five in the afternoon and the hotel staff began to prepare for the evening ahead. The buffet tables in the dining room were adorned with garlands of leaves and flowers, and yet more food was being set out for the evening's banquet.

Joining me Paul said, 'How on earth anybody can eat anything after this afternoon's repast beats me but if we start around nine-thirty they might just be ready for it.'

'Are you going to wear your wedding dress?' Stella asked.

'I did bring an evening dress with me, but if you're not

changing then of course I won't.'

'Stella, I'm dying to change and get rid of this hat. I love it, but enough is enough.' Indeed the cornflower blue chiffon gown I changed into made me feel less like a bride and more like the chatelaine of Reckmire.

People were in the mood to enjoy themselves. None of our guests were being charged for this night and the wine and the food were of the finest.

It was Major Rand who said as we danced around the room, 'The hotel won't have made much money this week, Joanna, it's my bet you're working at a loss.'

'I'm sure you're right, but Paul maintains that the people here are our best customers and they'll come back again and again.'

'Yes, working on the assumption that this is a sprat to catch a mackerel. Trust old Paul to think of it that way.'

I felt faintly irritated by his remark, but in the next moment he said, 'I took a turn round the gardens a little while back. The wind's got up, I could even hear the sea crashing on the rocks below the gardens. You really wouldn't think it could whip up as quickly as that.'

'Yes it can. This is a particularly treacherous coast. People have the greatest respect for it.'

But the wild night was far removed from the laughter and the feasting within the house. It was only when guests were leaving to go to their cars that the wind could be heard echoing mournfully in the trees.

The room was emptying now. People were going up, still laughing, still filled with euphoria, while others were waiting in the hall for those who had gone to collect their wraps or coats. After the last one had left Paul said, 'I'll go up to the flat with Bruce, Joanna. I have some things to collect and I'll see that he's settled in all right. I think we've done our duty nobly. I'll see you in a short while.'

I nodded, then as he turned away he said, 'Who's the girl with young Saunders, she's not a guest?'

I turned to see Freda, Lottie's sister, being escorted out of the hall with Tony Saunders, the son of one of our most eminent guests, and deciding not to involve Lottie and her family I said, 'She was here this afternoon, she's rather pretty, don't you think?'

'I suppose she is in a bold sort of way,' he said before he left me to follow his friend up the stairs.

I stood looking across the lounge when Mr Gainsborough joined me, saying ruefully, 'It will take an effort to get this right. I've asked the staff to get here early in the morning. We've already started on the dining room.'

'It's a lot of extra work for you all but it has been a lovely day, hasn't it, Mr Gainsborough?'

'Yes indeed, Mrs Cheviot, a lovely day, and what I hope will be the start of a lovely life.'

I smiled. Mrs Cheviot! How strange it sounded, but the quiet charm of his good wishes touched me more than others expressed more forcibly.

I was about to mount the stairs when he came towards me, holding out a pocket book. 'This belongs to Major Rand, Mrs Cheviot. He was making one or two telephone calls from the desk earlier this evening, he left it on the desk and may not have missed it.'

'I'll see that he gets it, Mr Gainsborough. My husband is with him in the flat now.'

I had no idea how soon the major intended leaving in the morning so I decided to take it to the flat before going to my room. Most of our guests were on the first floor and only a few of the younger element had been given rooms on the second. They were separated from the self-contained flat by a dimly lit corridor and a square hall and as I walked towards it I was dimly aware of occasional laughter and snatches of conversation.

As I opened the door of the flat I could see that the tiny hall was in darkness and that the light came from the living room beyond. I could hear men's voices, laughter and the clink of glasses and my hand was on the door to push it wider when I heard Major Rand's voice saying, 'Here's to Reckmire, Paul. You're a lucky bastard. All this and heaven too. How did you manage it?'

I knew what would happen if I walked into the room. He would look embarrassed then there would be gallantry and charm but the conversation would be changed and I would never know the answer to the question he had posed.

For what seemed like an eternity there was silence and I stood with my hands clenched against my breast, waiting. Then at long last came Paul's voice, faintly musing, speaking of old half-forgotten summers now brought piercingly to mind.

'I've been coming here for years as a guest of Robin Albemarle, Joanna's cousin. God, I resented everything he had. They all thought so much of each other, there was so much affection, so much charm. I knew they only asked me because Robin had told them I had a pretty thin time of it at home. You've never met my father but I can tell you that he was an uncaring bastard and my mother was afraid of him until she learned to shut him out by living in a world of her own.

'I felt like one of them when I came here in the summer. I loved this house, felt it was as much mine as theirs, then when another summer came round I found myself wishing he wouldn't invite me, but knowing I'd be devastated if he didn't. Robin was always predictable. I thought a lot of him. It was rotten that he got killed during the war and I'd resigned myself to never seeing Reckmire again.'

'So you've known Joanna since those early days?' Major Rand asked.

'No. She didn't come here until much later. Her father was the only son of the family but her mother didn't like the sea so they never visited. It was only when her parents went to live in the Far East that Joanna made an appearance.'

He laughed, and I knew he was laughing about the trauma of our first meeting. 'She was about ten years old,' he mused. 'I can see her now standing on that beach quite oblivious to the pounding sea that was rolling in behind her. Robin dragged her up the cliffs. We were both pretty angry but I expect I showed it more than he did. Robin was nice to her, I wasn't. Besides she was just a kid and I had a soft spot for her cousin Gabriella.

'For years I'd heard members of the family going on about her mother. I've never met the woman but I know enough about her to dislike her intensely, and I thought Joanna'd grow up just like her. I'm relieved to say she hasn't and her father was a decent chap.'

'Didn't you tell me the house was left to her?'

'Yes. I was there that weekend in Somerset when the will was read after her grandmother's funeral. I couldn't believe it. I couldn't believe that the place I loved more than any other would belong to a girl who wouldn't know what to do with it and who would probably put it on the market so fast she'd be spinning from it.'

'But she didn't.'

'No. I drove her back to London and put the idea into her head. A country hotel, something to work at when she left the Navy. Then when I left her I cursed myself for being a bloody fool by not letting her stew in a place I didn't feel she had any right to.'

'How did you come to be in it with her then?'

'She asked my help. I came down here to take a last look at it. I didn't know she was here, but she was and begging me to help. I'd always hated the mills in Yorkshire. I dreaded going back to them after the war, and the more I talked to Joanna the more I wanted to be in it with her.'

'And what exactly is your position now that the place has stopped being a dream and become a reality?'

'I'm her manager, a business partnership, half the profits straight down the middle.'

'And now you've married the girl?'

'Yes.'

'And are you satisfied with being her business partner as well as her husband?'

'God, no. I want my name on the deeds. Joint ownership. I deserve it and I'll settle for nothing less.'

'And what about the lady? Suppose she doesn't see it your way?'

'She'll agree. She couldn't run this place without me. I've made myself indispensable. Joanna's good at what she does but she hasn't a business head on her shoulders. She's beautiful, she looks the part. I can safely leave it to her to dress well, talk charmingly to our guests, be gracious to the villagers and generous when generosity is needed. You have to agree, Bruce, that I deserve more than a business partnership. Joanna owes me.'

'I'm tempted to ask if that was the reason you married her?'

Paul laughed, and the sound brought deep resentment into my heart. His laughter was brittle, cynical, and in the next moment he said, 'Have some more champagne, old boy, it's too late to start analysing my feelings. For Reckmire I'd have married Medusa.'

'You're not in love with her then?'

'I know precious little about love. My father never showed me any and my mother was so afraid of him and his opinions that she never seemed to figure much in my childhood. There have been a good many girls, most of them didn't last very long, except Alison, she lasted the longest. You met her once, didn't you?'

'Yes, whatever happened to her?'

'I took her up to Yorkshire to stay one long weekend. I thought it would be amusing to see how she got along with Father. She was abrasive, a bossy brainy woman with set ideas and ambition. On the way back she told me she couldn't ever imagine herself living in Yorkshire which I thought pretty presumptuous since I'd never asked her. There was a war on, none of us knew exactly where we were going, but Alison knew we weren't going in the same direction.

'She telephoned me several times but I told her I was busy. I never saw her again. Funnily enough soon afterwards the old lady died in Somerset and I went down for the funeral. It was then I met Joanna again.'

'Just at the right moment,' said Bruce dryly.

'I suppose so. Joanna isn't complicated. She knows I'll work damned hard to make this the best country hotel anywhere in England and I'll do the best I can to be a model husband. She doesn't need my money, she has enough of her own, so I don't constantly need to be handing out gifts as expensive as Ralston. This sort of marriage works for a great many people. Why not for us? Besides a wife blessed with too many brains would bore me.'

'A marriage of convenience.'

'If you say so.'

'I get the feeling the girl is in love with you. A woman in love will soon recognise if it isn't being returned.'

'I've managed very successfully to cover my tracks so far. I'm not likely to fail now. Joanna'll give me what I want. As you say, she's in love with me. Drink up. then we'll finish the bottle.'

I fled back along the passage and into the corridors beyond. In the turret room, our bridal room, a fire burned brightly, the leaping flames casting shadows on the walls and ceiling, and I was aware of the moaning sound of the wind and the surf crashing on the rocks, sounds I had never been afraid of for they had been friends in the heart of that young girl who had come to Reckmire as a stranger.

My pale face stared back at me from the mirror, streaked with tears, my heart hammering with suppressed rage, a rage burning with a sense of betrayal, and the knowledge that it had all been a lie. The day that had started out with so much promise had ended with a night of revelry and laughter, a night when my beauty had not been enough to make Paul Cheviot want to marry me for myself, only for Reckmire.

I felt sick with humiliation. I had almost given him half of Reckmire because I believed that he loved me. His reward for loving me. Now I was only aware of a new and bitter resolve. At that moment my husband walked into the room.

Chapter Twenty-Six

His manner was jaunty. In his hands he carried a bottle of champagne and two glasses, and on his face was the look of a man who had come to fulfil his part of the bargain by making love to his wife. After a few moments, wariness came into his eyes when he saw the anger in mine.

Puzzled, he asked, 'Did you see most of our guests off, Joanna? I went downstairs to see if there were any leftovers but everything was quiet. There'll be a lot for the staff to do in the morning.'

'Yes, Mr Gainsborough said as much.'

He put the glasses and the champagne down and came nearer, saying, 'I say, Joanna, you're not annoyed about something are you? I had to go up to the flat to sort out some clothes.'

'Where are they then?'

'Bruce told me to leave them in the wardrobe. I've got everything I need here for the moment, I'll collect the others tomorrow.'

I picked up the discarded dress and went to hang it in the wardrobe. I knew that his eyes followed me and when I turned round the puzzlement was still there. 'You're angry about something, Joanna. I thought everything went splendidly. Now come on, you can tell me. What or who has annoyed you?

'I say, you're not cross that we're not going away immediately, are you? I did say we'd go up to Derwentwater when most of the guests have gone.'

'Business and pleasure I think you said?'

'Well, yes. Come on, Joanna, nowhere on earth is better than Reckmire. We'll have our Eden here, Derwentwater can wait.'

'If you say so, Paul.'

He looked at me uncertainly. 'You're in a funny mood. You're probably tired, it has been a long day, but there was never a dull moment, was there? Come on, darling, have some champagne.'

He walked to where he had left the bottle, turning to say, 'A toast to our future, Joanna.'

I watched him filling the glasses, then handing one to me he said, 'What shall we drink to? Reckmire and its continuing success, our future here together?'

'Yes, Paul, to Reckmire and the continuance of our business partnership which has been so successful.'

Across the rim of my glass I saw the doubt in his eyes, the wariness, and putting his glass down sharply on the mantlepiece he said sourly, 'Isn't it time we had done with this business partnership, Joanna, and settled for something different?'

'What had you in mind?'

'I was thinking of joint ownership. After all I am your husband, I don't want to spend the rest of my life feeling inferior.'

'I've never regarded you as inferior, Paul. I couldn't have done any of it without you. After all, I haven't got a business head on my shoulders. When it comes to that I'm inferior to you.'

'What do you mean?'

'I look the part, I know how to dress, how to talk to our guests, be gracious to the villagers.'

I was deliberately echoing his words spoken to his friend but oblivious to my sarcasm he said stoutly, 'Well, exactly. We're a good team, Joanna, me with my business acumen, you with your beauty. We can't fail. But I'd feel a lot happier if I felt I really belonged.'

'You do, Paul, as much as you belonged in all those long years when you came here with Robin and my family accepted you with great kindness and generosity.'

His face was dark with anger as he snapped, 'And is that

all, Joanna? Is that all I mean to you? A visitor to be treated with kindness and generosity when the spirit moves you?'

'My grandparents left Reckmire to me and I intend it to remain that way. I think it would have been their wish. But I can see that you are angry. Does that mean that half of Reckmire was to be your reward for marrying me? If so, try to imagine how inferior that makes me feel.'

In that moment anger and emnity throbbed between us, an obscene living thing that made my heart flutter wildly, trembling in my hands so that I put my glass down sharply on the mantelpiece besides his. His face was as stony and cold as it had been when I looked up at him on the day Robin had pulled me to safety from the boiling sea, eyes that were hostile, lips that were a cold straight line in his angry face, then before I was aware of it he reached out and grasped my arms, the strength of his hands painful as his fingers dug into the soft flesh.

'All right,' he hissed, 'if that's how you want it. It seems to me that you're the same sort of cold bitch your mother was, but if you don't want to hand over half of Reckmire, you'll give me what I'm entitled to as your husband.'

I struggled wildly as his hands tore at my skirt. I could hear the delicate silk tearing, then he was lifting me bodily in his arms, flinging me unceremoniously on the bed, then his mouth was on mine, stifling my scream of rage, and as I continued to struggle he hit me savagely, again and again, until I lost consciousness.

My head was throbbing wildly when I awoke to a room lit by the first grey tints of dawn. I was alone, lying naked on my bed, and for a while I lay still waiting for the memories of the night before to send me shaking with sobs into the bathroom. I stared at my face in the mirror. It was pale, dark circles emphasised eyes filled with pain, and when I touched my cheek gingerly it ached and I could see a dark bruise discolouring the skin.

There were bruises on my arms and legs and both my breasts. I sank down weakly on the edge of the bath, shocked with the knowledge that my husband of one day had raped me.

I stumbled back into the bedroom and looked at the clock

294

beside the bed. It was five-thirty and throughout the house there was only silence. In two hours staff would be stirring, fires would be lit, the chefs would be starting breakfast, and in just a few hours my aunt and uncle would be leaving for Somerset. How was I going to face them like this?

I dressed in a tweed skirt and twin set, making up my face carefully, trying to hide the buise by pulling my hair forward, rouging my cheeks to hide their pallor, swallowing aspirin to combat my aching head.

I joined my aunt and uncle at their table in the dining room, not missing my aunt's sharp questioning look as I endeavoured to join in their conversation normally.

The guests would be amused at my pallor, putting it down to a night of passionate love. There was no sign of Paul over breakfast. When I toyed miserably with my food my aunt said, 'Aren't you feeling well, Joanna? You don't appear to have much appetite?'

'I think it was all the recent excitement, Aunt Marcia. It's really been going on for weeks. This morning just seems a little flat, that's all.'

Stella joined us and I saw that she was dressed for travelling. As she helped herself to fruit juice she said, 'I'm off this morning, Joanna, when can we expect to see you in Surrey?'

'I'm not sure. I must visit Mother soon though.'

'Well, drop me a line when you're coming and we'll meet for lunch.'

'I will.'

She chatted on, and I was glad that she was there. Stella had always been a chatterbox, totally engrossed with conversation and never too interested in things around her. I relaxed in time to see Major Rand enter the breakfast room, smiling across at us as he ordered his breakfast. There was still no sign of Paul and I wondered if he had slept in the flat, or if not where he had spent most of the night.

After breakfast I saw my aunt and uncle and Stella to their cars, my aunt's last words being, 'Come to see us soon, Joanna, and try to visit Corallie. Why not spend a honeymoon in Italy later?'

A honeymoon! There would be no honeymoon for Paul

and me. I could not think that there would be anything for us in the years that lay ahead.

In the small bedroom in the flat our wedding presents were laid out in their profusion, many of them still wrapped, and I set about opening them.

Major Rand's luggage was stacked in the tiny hallway and I knew he would be returning for it after he had eaten his breakfast.

He knocked lightly on the door where I sat surrounded by toasters and tablecloths, fruit bowls and ornaments, all the usual array of wedding gifts that friends and acquaintances had bought in the hope that theirs was the only one of its kind. He put his head round the door and grinned.

'Hard at it, I see,' he said brightly.

I smiled. 'It's something that needs to be done.'

'I've looked around for Paul but he doesn't seem to be anywhere about. I have to get off, Joanna, it's a fair drive and I have an appointment this evening. I've had a super time. If I have any spare cash I don't know what to do with you can be sure I'll be back.'

'And we shall be very pleased to see you.'

'I say, Joanna, that's a nasty bruise on your cheek. Not been knocking you about already, I hope.'

I laughed. 'No. I drank too much champagne and walked into the bathroom door. It hurt a little at first but not now.'

'You've got quite a job on there, you should get Paul to help you.'

'I don't mind. I hope you have a good journey home, Bruce, thank you for everything. Perhaps you'll find Paul on your way down?'

'Well, if I don't, will you tell him I looked around for him?'

He took my hand in a firm grip and I did not miss the kindness and unexplained understanding in his smile.

If only I had not gone to the flat last night and heard that conversation between Paul and Bruce, if only I hadn't stood in the darkness to listen. If that had not happened I would have given Paul half of Reckmire when he came to me and today I would be happy believing that he loved me, had always loved me for myself without hint of wanting more.

I would never know now if having half of Reckmire would have changed him. Now he did not have to be kind or give me something as expensive as Ralston, he no longer had to pretend. Would I see the real Paul, the Paul that had always been there?

Leaving the wedding presents neatly stacked on the floor, I went into the sitting room with the idea of writing to all those who had sent us gifts and their good wishes. I heard footsteps in the hall and then Paul stood in the doorway. We stared at each other, and he said as though nothing had happened between us, 'I can see you're busy, I was wondering when we should get around to dealing with that lot.'

I didn't answer, and with a short rueful laugh he said, 'I'm not going to apologise, Joanna, we deserve each other. I'm staying in the flat. I'll leave some of my gear in your wardrobes so that the staff will not gossip, and none of our guests are going to know. They'll think we keep this place on as some sort of office.'

'Just as you like, Paul.'

'If it's your intention to divorce me, I'll tell the world what a cold calculating bitch you are, that I've worked my guts out for you and you've been willing to let me. It'll be a slanging match the village will be bouncing from for a very long time, and it'll do this place no good. It's either that, Joanna, or we carry on as normal.'

'Normal, Paul?'

'Well, yes. Business partners, I think you said. Neither of us will expect anything from each other. We'll look after the hotel, make it work as we planned. Beyond that you can do anything you damn' well please and you can be sure I'll do the same. In public we make an effort. Is that understood, Joanna?'

'Yes. Not because you say so, I don't have to take orders from you, but because of Reckmire. Neither of us is going to destroy Reckmire.'

'I suppose Bruce Rand's gone?'

'Yes. He looked around for you but you were nowhere about.'

'I went riding. On Ralston. He's all he's cracked up to

be, Joanna, I thought you'd like to know. I never take my gifts back.'

'Then I shall take very good care of him.'

After one long hard look he slammed petulantly out of the room.

We were polite to each other. We smiled and conversed, we chatted to our friends and our guests. Christmas was almost upon us and we were fully booked. Being busy kept me from thinking too much and my duties were confined to the hotel whilst Paul was kept busy on the estate.

I had known I was pregnant for several weeks but I could not bring myself to tell him. There were mornings when I felt ill and had to force myself to behave normally. Meals were sent back half eaten, and one morning the housekeeper asked if I was unwell, that the kitchen staff were anxious in case I was not enjoying the food they cooked.

I looked into her wise anxious eyes and I knew that she knew.

'But you're delighted of course, Mrs Cheviot, and the master too. Somebody to carry on here when you're both too old to be bothered.'

I smiled, and I knew that she stared after me, puzzled at my lack of enthusiasm.

I wrote to Aunt Marcia to tell her and telephoned my mother.

'Well, I must say, you haven't wasted much time,' was her rejoinder. 'Perhaps with a baby to look after you'll begin to have a little sympathy for me.'

'Sympathy, Mother?'

'Well, yes. You'll begin to understand perhaps what attention you need to give to a child. How it can take over your life just as you took over mine.'

'I'll come to see you as soon as I can get away. I thought I might visit Aunt Corallie in Italy. If I do I'll spend some time with you on the way. I'm afraid it won't be until after Christmas.'

'There's really no need, Joanna, I'm sure you'd prefer to spend all the time you can spare in Italy.'

Was I really as cold as my mother? Could I really ever be so unkind to my child? I had no answers. Only when

I looked across the table into Paul's eyes did I see the mockery in his, and knew that in his view there was no difference between us.

I had no feeling for my unborn child, conceived in anger and bitterness, and I knew that Paul too would be indifferent. He did not like children, he thought them noisy and disruptive, cluttering up the place with their toys, demanding attention. He was cynical about those people who professed to like them. It was in desperation that I decided I must go to Italy sooner than later.

I told him of my plans one evening as we were finishing dinner and his reply was typical.

'You'll be staying for the rest of the winter, I suppose?'

'I'm not sure how long I'm staying but Aunt Corallie wants me to go and it will be nice to see them all again.'

'You'll remember me to them, particularly to Gabriella?'

'Of course, particularly to Gabriella.'

'I suppose she's married to that chap she was engaged to and with a family by this time? The Italians are doting parents to their little bambini.'

On the day of my departure I waited in the hall while the porters put my luggage in the car. There was no sign of Paul and I had the distinct feeling that guests and staff alike were waiting around to see if he made an appearance. Something of our animosity for each other must have got through to them, but I went about with a smiling face saying my farewells.

I was at the door of my car when he appeared, walking nonchalantly across the terrace, bending dutifully to kiss my cheek.

'Well, have a good time my dear, and a safe journey,' he said quietly.

'Thank you. I'll let you know when I'm coming back.'

'Of course.'

As I sank into the driver's seat he smiled down at me. It was a smile for the spectators and did not reach his eyes. It struck at the anger in my heart and as I started the car I said casually, my eyes never leaving his face, 'By the way I'm pregnant, I thought you should know.'

Without a backward glance I drove the car out of the courtyard and along the drive.

Pain and anger lashed at me throughout that long drive to my mother's flat and the three days I spent with her did nothing to assuage that anger.

For the first time in my life her carping failed to upset me. It was only a reiteration of other hurts. She accused me of only half listening to her, of thinking more of my father's sisters than her, and of deliberately shutting her out of my life.

Once I would have argued with her, pampered her, worried about what she called my neglect, now I listened to her and did nothing.

Three days. It felt like a hundred years. It was with a feeling of acute relief that I drove to Heathrow Airport to join my flight for Florence.

'You'll be staying here when you return to London, I suppose,' she said shortly.

'No, Mother, I shall go home. I'll write to you from Italy and telephone you when I arrive home.'

I drove away quickly and with the realisation that I had left two people seething with resentment.

Paul would not be happy with the news of my pregnancy and Mother had been reluctant to discuss it. On our last evening together she had looked at herself thoughtfully in the hall mirror, saying, 'I can't begin to think of myself as a grandmother. All my friends are saying I look far too young.'

'Even when many of your friends are grandmothers themselves.' I hadn't been able to resist saying.

'Well, yes, Joanna, but you have to admit most of them are quite plump and matronly. Thank heavens I've kept my slim figure and my hair colour.'

Now as I drove towards the airport I knew that the old Joanna had gone forever. It would be a totally new Joanna that Aunt Corallie would meet at the airport in Florence and I wondered how long it would take for her to see the difference.

As I stepped down from the plane in a morning golden with sunlight I was unprepared for the changes I would find in Italy. My memories were all warm and glowing with joy. I did not think that other people and places could change too.

My first surprise came when Aunt Corallie crossed the arrivals lounge to greet me and for an instant I stared at her without recognition. I did not know this tall silver-haired woman with her sad lined face until she smiled and held out her hands, then I went forward eagerly to embrace her.

She held me away from her, looking into my eyes, then some of the laughter suddenly came back into hers. 'You're so much like the girl I used to be, Joanna, but looking so elegant and sophisticated. Do you realise the last time we met you were a schoolgirl, terribly excited about everything and thrilled to be wearing your first long frock?'

'How is Uncle Rinaldo? I do hope he's much better?'

'Yes, he is. His recovery has been slow but I think at last he's on the mend.'

'And Gabriella?'

I did not miss the sudden shadow that crossed her face, or her hesitation until she said, 'Gabriella is living in Rome, we don't see her. Although I have written to tell her you were coming to stay with us.'

'Oh, yes, I would like to see her. I suppose she's married? Does she have children?'

'What a lot we have to talk about, Joanna. We both have so many questions to ask. My car is in the car park, we'll drive straight back. Rinaldo will be waiting very impatiently.'

'I'm so looking forward to seeing Florence again and the beautiful countryside. Did it all change terribly during the war?'

'Many things changed. Of course we didn't suffer air attacks like the English cities but places did change, and people. Some more than others.

I stole a quick look at her profile but she was totally engrossed in manoeuvring the car into the stream of traffic. I felt a vague feeling of unease as we drove in silence on the first stretch of our journey. I had expected to find Aunt Corallie as volatile as ever, gay and effervescent, filled with news about Gabriella and life in Italy, a person totally unlike this darkly clad elegant woman with the sweet sad face.

It didn't seem to matter that we had little conversation. I was in love once again with Florence and the sunlight shining on warm stone, turning the river into molten gold, with the tall stately cypresses standing high on gentle rolling hills and tiny towns crowning those hills with magnificent cathedrals.

I sat back in the car with a strange contentment. 'How beautiful it all is,' I said softly. 'Suddenly at this moment I feel I've never been away.'

She only smiled, and for the rest of the journey I sat silent absorbing the scenery and the gentle peace of it all.

The huge wrought iron gates were open awaiting our arrival and then we were driving slowly through the parkland towards the house. I saw no changes in the avenue of cypresses, in the stone urns that edged the terrace, gay with flowers, and the tall windows glinting in the sunlight. My shock came minutes later when Uncle Rinaldo came through the french window to meet us, leaning heavily on his stick, his hair silver-white, his face still handsome but filled, like Aunt Corallie's, with a strange sadness.

I went forward quickly to greet him, then he was escorting us back into the house while servants came forward to take my luggage and Aunt Corallie said, 'I've put you in the same bedroom you had before, Joanna, I thought you would like that. We'll have lunch when you've had time to freshen up, and then you shall tell us all about Reckmire. I don't suppose anything's changed about the countryside or the village, and I would recognise the house, wouldn't I, even though it is now a plush hotel? It is still beautiful?'

'Yes, that's exactly how it is.'

'Well, no more now, dear. I'm sure you'd like to change into something cooler before you join us for drinks before lunch.'

I followed the servant up the shallow marble staircase and into the room which I remembered vividly. Through the window I was able to look out across the gardens to the vineyards beyond. There were people working there and as I turned away I could hear the peal of bells from the campanile on the hillside.

I changed quickly into a silk afternoon dress, glad to get out of my travelling suit, and as I touched up my makeup a young dark-haired maid came into the room. She was very pretty. Smiling, she said, 'The Signora has said I should unpack for you. My name is Maria.

I smiled, thanking her warmly, and left her to put my things away. As I ran lightly down the staircase I looked around me with eagerness. The hall was exactly as I remembered it, shining with soft marble floors and pillars, marble tables on which rested urns filled with flowers, and what I had never forgotten, the cheerful tinkling of a fountain from a courtyard.

My aunt and uncle sat outside on the terrace and a man servant was serving drinks. It was exactly as it had been all those years before except that my father and Robin were dead, so too were my grandparents, and Gabriella and Carlo were absent. Something of my thoughts must have conveyed themselves to Aunt Corallie because raising her glass she said lightly, 'We should drink to absent friends, I think, to those we loved and who are with us no more.'

I could feel the sudden pricking of tears, and as I looked towards them I saw that they were looking into each other's eyes and that something vague and unspoken hovered like a spectre between them.

Chapter Twenty-Seven

I had thought on the day of my arrival that very little had changed. The house and gardens were beautiful, the sun shone every day out of a clear blue sky, and in the fields and vineyards men and women sang as they worked, and yet as day followed day I came to see that my memories were wishes, and that there were undercurrents of bitterness and sadness in the house that I had associated with laughter and so much joy.

At first I thought it was my uncle's recent illness and the fact that he was recovering too slowly which caused it, but Aunt Corallie had changed more than he. Aunt Corallie had always been the warm impulsive one, the one who had embraced life with so much joy and laughter. Now beneath her smile I saw only a strange bewildering sadness and when I spoke of Gabriella I was aware of her desire to change the subject, particularly when her husband was present.

Three days passed and all I knew of Gabriella was that she was married and living in Rome. It was one morning when Aunt Corallie and I rode together before the sun reached its zenith that I said quietly. You haven't told me why Gabriella and Carlo are living in Rome when I understood Carlo's business interests were here?'

She reined her horse in abruptly and for several minutes we sat staring at each other before she said, 'Gabriella and Carlo did not marry, Joanna, much as we hoped they would.'

She rode on ahead of me and when I caught up with her I could see that her cheeks were wet with tears. Without looking at me she said, 'There is so much you don't know and it hurts me to speak of it. I don't talk about Gabriella when Rinaldo is present. He idolised her, Gabriella was always his princess. Now he feels that she betrayed us, and not only us – Carlo, his family, everything she had been brought up to believe in. You think everything is the same, but war did things to us too. It inflicted wounds that were punishing and cruel, wounds that will never heal.'

We rode in silence and it was not until after dinner when my uncle retired early, saying he felt particularly tired, that we were able to speak again.

Although the days were warm the nights were cold and we sat looking out on a sky glittering with stars, silently sipping our wine. I did not want to be the one to break that silence; instead I waited, knowing instinctively that she would want to talk about it. She began haltingly, searching for the right words and the story that unfolded brought a new context to the war I remembered.

'We were happy, you saw how happy we were during that time you were with us, but you also saw Mussolini's men marching in the streets, strutting through the villages, changing order into chaos.

'He promised all those eager young men an empire to rival that of Julius Caesar, a new Roman Empire stretching across a third of the world, a world divided between Germany, Japan and Italy. And how those young boys rushed to join the colours to become part of his dream!

'He took all our young men, and young women too, and then his generals came here demanding money for their master, any treasures they could lay their hands on, and one of them took Gabriella.'

I stared at her in horror. 'You mean he made her go with him, into the army?'

Her mouth twisted with bitterness. 'He took her as his wife. Oh, don't think that Gabriella was entirely blameless. She watched Carlo go away to fight and before her eyes her safe world was crumbling. She saw our money dwindling, saw that the same thing was happening to Carlo's parents, and there was no guarantee that he would return unscathed from the war. In the man she married she saw only stability.

305

He was the new Italy, the conquering Italy. The rest was over, we were over.

'Rinaldo pleaded with her not to go, I pleaded with her, but to no avail. She said she had no intention of pledging her life and her future into waiting for some wounded hero to come back to her in a period of flag waving and noble sacrifice. Living was for now. The final straw came when one by one our treasures were returned. I watched Rinaldo's pride crumble along with his health, and there were those about us who said we had been paid for Gabriella. The fascists had bought her and us as well.'

'Do you never see her?'

'No. I write to her and occasionally she answers my letters but hers tell me little. You know what happened to Mussolini and many of his closest generals. Gabriella's husband was tried for war crimes and went to prison. I don't know if he is still there or if he's been released, but she will not leave Rome. She has so much of her father's pride, my pride also. She does not say if she has any money, how she is living, but in every letter I beg her to come home. I tell her that her father has forgiven her, that it is time to put the past behind us, but you will see, she will answer my letter and that is all.'

I couldn't help it, I had to ask about Carlo. I said tentatively, strangely afraid of her answer: 'Did Carlo come back from the war? Was he angry or sad about Gabriella?'

'Oh, yes, he came back but he does not come here now. His parents died after the war was over within months of each other and he has been spending a lot of time abroad. Rinaldo is too proud to visit him because he is ashamed of what our daughter did.'

'I'm so sorry, Aunt Corallie, I thought we were the only people to be suffering. I knew that Germany was having a terrible time towards the end but somehow or other I couldn't think that the war would change Italy.'

'Lives change in the strangest way. The obvious changes in wartime are terrible but there are other ways that are far reaching and just as terrible.'

I knew what she meant. But for the war I would not

have married Paul. But for the war my father might still be alive and we could be together. Robin would be alive and Reckmire would be a family home again instead of an impersonal hotel filled with strangers.

I lay awake most of the night thinking about Gabriella. I visualised her somewhere in Rome with a man embittered by war, resentful about his prison sentence, ostracised by people who had once rushed to entertain them.

What did she remember when she received her mother's letters? Her home, her parents, the love she had discarded so lightly? Oh, Gabriella, I thought miserably, I too know what it is like to long for something sane and perfect, something only remembered from another time and place.

I drove my aunt's car into the dreaming villages of Umbria and Tuscany. I walked with the sun on my arms through ancient squares, raising my eyes to the glory of majestic cathedrals, loving the tall sad cypresses, graceful and slender against the summer sky.

The beautiful ornamental gates set at the end of the long drive leading to Carlo's villa were closed and I stopped the car only momentarily to stare along the drive, wishing I had the courage to open it and drive through. The closed gate was unwelcoming, it was as if the man who lived there had no wish to welcome visitors, and yet the desire to see him again was very strong.

I had no thoughts of returning to England. I received no word from Paul and did not write to him. If my aunt thought it strange that my new husband treated me in such a cavalier fashion she said nothing, and I was glad. My explanation to her would have been as difficult as hers had been to me.

It was market day in San Gimignano and I spent my time wandering along the stalls and through the mediaeval maze of streets and walls and gazing at its famous thirteen towers. I drove back to my aunt's house in the late-afternoon, when the sun seemed to turn everything into dazzling gold, and for the first time the gates of Carlo's villa stood open and welcoming. I pulled the car up at the gates, my eyes searching the long drive ahead, finding the pale stone villa sheltering behind its grove of cedars. With every ounce of courage I possessed I steered the car through the gateway and along the drive.

Gardeners turned to stare at me. It may have been my imagination but they seemed to have a puzzled air as if they hardly expected to see a woman disturbing the peace or the solitude that surrounded them.

For some time I sat in the car after I had brought it to a halt in an area below the terrace. I wanted to get out and climb the steps leading up to the house, but I was unsure of my welcome. It was a gardener who approached the car, smiling, taking off his battered straw hat, who made me make up my mind.

'You wish for someone, Signora?' he asked tentatively.

'I am not expected. Is Conte Varasi at home?'

He nodded, pointing with his hand towards the steps and the formal gardens beyond. 'Near pool,' he said, 'you find him there.'

I thanked him and got out of the car. I know that he watched me and when I turned to smile he smiled encouragingly in return.

I walked on, skirting the house, admiring the gardens until beyond them I saw the silver gleam of a pool. A man sat alone on the terrace overlooking it, but he sat with his back towards me and as I stood haltingly, uncertain if I should go on, a Doberman dog which had been lying beside his chair got up and came towards me.

He came with menace, his lips laid back baring his teeth, a snarl in his throat, the hackles on his neck bristling. I shrank back fearfully. The man rose from his chair and turned towards me. He was wearing dark glasses and I could see that he leaned heavily on his stick, standing stiffly to attention, calling to his dog, 'Brutus, come here.'

The dog paused, still growling, but after a second command he returned reluctantly to his master's chair. Relieved, I went forward slowly until we came face to face.

He stared at me without recognition and in those first few seconds I was only aware of the silver wings at the side of his face, accentuated by the darkness of his raven black hair. I remembered Carlo's face alive with laughter and the joy of living, but this man's face was remote, and there was pain in it. The hand on his stick was clenched tight as though it pained him to stand, and his chiselled lips were unsmiling.

I was an intruder and he was waiting for me to explain my intrusion. He did not remember me, and in those first few moments I was wishing I could turn and run from him without explanation, simply a curious traveller who had seen the gates to a castello and decided to investigate.

He was staring at me, waiting for an explanation, and in some confusion I said helplessly, 'You don't remember me?'

He raised his eyebrows. 'Should I?'

'Perhaps not. It's many years since we met. I'm Joanna, Gabriella's cousin. I was here with my father and my grandparents before the war.'

The expression remained remote, and in some confusion I said quickly, 'I'm sorry, I should not have come, but you were so kind to me that summer, I wanted to see you.'

His expression softened, and with a brief smile he said, 'Forgive me, Joanna, of course I remember you but I have very few guests these days. I must ask you to forgive my bad manners. Please, come and sit with me and I will ask the servants to bring wine.'

The Doberman eyed me cautiously as I took my place beside him, and Carlo said, 'Brutus is as unsociable as I am, I must ask you to bear with us. How is Rinaldo? I hope his health is improving.'

'Yes, rather slowly, but he is much better.'

'And Corallie?'

'She is well.'

'So you have come back to Italy. Are you finding it very changed?'

'The countryside no, the people yes.'

'Ah, well, that is inevitable. And in England too, people will have changed, that is what war does to you.'

'My aunt told me that you had been injured in the war, but you will get well again surely?'

'They tell me I am responding to treatment but it is so slow. I am hoping to have treatment in America in the summer, some new treatment that is only available there at the moment.'

'I do hope it will be successful.'

He smiled, shrugging his shoulders as if he could hardly dare to believe it.

'And what changes did the war wreak in your life, Joanna?' he asked quietly.

'My cousin Robin was killed serving with the Air Force, my father was a prisoner of war in the Far East and died out there. Both my grandparents are dead.'

'I'm sorry. I remember them, they were charming people. What happened to you during the war.'

'I joined the Royal Navy and worked as a driver in London.'

'It was not pleasant living in London when the Germans bombed it, but you survived, and what have you done with your life since then?'

'My grandparents left their house Reckmire to me and we have turned it into a country hotel. Very successfully, I think.'

'You say *we* have turned it into a country hotel?'

'My husband and I. I married Paul Cheviot. He came here too before the war, perhaps you will remember him?'

'Yes, he came with your cousin. I remember that you did not like him very much and he did not like me, because of Gabriella, I think.'

'Yes.'

'Ah, well, one should not look back, I think, and now the war is over, and we are friends again. Is your husband with you?'

I was spared from answering by the arrival of a manservant carrying a silver tray containing glasses and a bottle of Orvieto, and we both watched as he poured the clear golden wine before handing a glass to each of us.

Lightly, Carlo said, 'Orvieto is famous for its wine, I think you will like this one.'

He appeared to have forgotten that he had asked me if Paul was with me as he stared thoughtfully into the waters of the pool. Silence sat easily between us. There was a serenity about him in spite of his injuries and if the laughter had left his eyes, it had been replaced by a peacefulness which would have been alien in the old Carlo.

I did not wish to overstay my welcome and sensed he was tired. As I rose to leave I held out my hand, saying, 'I expect my aunt and uncle are wondering why I'm so late so perhaps I should get back now. I do hope your treatment will be successful, Carlo, it has been lovely meeting you again.'

When he attempted to get to his feet I said quickly, 'Please don't get up. Goodbye.'

'I was churlish, Joanna, I should not become a recluse in my remote castello. Will you dine with me one evening, you and your husband?'

'My husband is not here, I came alone.'

'Then perhaps you will dine with me and I will try very hard to be more entertaining. Shall we say Friday evening at eight?'

'Thank you, I shall look forward to it.'

He smiled. 'I too shall look forward to it.'

I left him, turning at the path leading into the gardens to wave to him and he raised his hand and waved in return.

I felt bemused by our meeting. I would have to tell my aunt and uncle about it and was unsure how they would view the thoughts of our dinner engagement. I need not have worried. Uncle Rinaldo said pleasantly, 'I hope this means that Carlo will feel free to visit us again as he did in the past. Our family and his have been friends for centuries, it grieved me when the friendship seemed to be over.'

Later I said to Aunt Corallie, 'I don't think it was Gabriella who kept Carlo away, it was something else − his injuries perhaps, maybe the things the fascists took from his family. There are probably a great many reasons.'

'Did he mention Gabriella at all?'

'Just once in passing. He did say one should never look back.'

'He knows you are married?'

'Yes, of course.'

For a moment her eyes twinkled mischievously before she said, 'You did have a schoolgirl crush on him. Are you quite certain it's gone.'

'I'm a married woman, Aunt Corallie.'

'I hadn't forgotten. A most unusual married woman who is in no hurry to return to her new husband, who doesn't write

311

or telephone. It is a situation singularly open to question, I think.'

I looked away, searching for a change of subject, and she said quietly, 'I don't want to pry but things are rather less than perfect, I think. I simply don't want you to run headlong into more trouble. Here is a man suffering physically, perhaps mentally scarred by a war he wanted no part of, and a woman alone. It is a delicate situation.'

I knew that she was right, but it did not stop me looking forward to our dinner engagement with a secret joy. I dressed for it with a pleasure I had not known for a long time, choosing a gown in dark blue wild silk that showed off my shoulders and slender waist, a gown that made Aunt Corallie's eyes light up with sly speculation. As I prepared to leave the house she said evenly, 'Take my white mink stole, Joanna, it is warm now but it could be cool later on.'

I was glad of it in the open car, but the wind was soft on my hair and brought with it the scents of the earth, herbs and clover, and the dark mysterious perfume of cypresses.

A servant admitted me into the house and in spite of the passage of time I was reminded of that other occasion when I had taken my first step into the beauties of the Castello Varasi. As I looked around me Carlo came forward to meet me, saying easily, 'Many of the paintings are new, Joanna, the old and valuable paintings were taken during the war to finance the effort. Some I recovered, but most of them I shall never see again. We are dining in the only room that remains unchanged, the morning room off the terrace.'

He limped only slightly and in the lamplight his face seemed less strained. Brutus the Doberman was lying stretched out in front of the window, only raising his head to stare at me for a fraction of an instant.

The next day I had difficulty in remembering what we had talked about the night before. Carlo set out to be charming, the meal was excellent, but I was uninterested in what we were eating. I was nervous, like a girl on her first date, and yet I was aware of his dark eyes smiling into mine, the charm of his voice, and that other feeling of half remembered joy.

After our meal he escorted me round the castello and I saw the raw pain in his eyes when he described the differences the war had wrought. Then we sat in the drawing room where the servants had put a match to the fire and listened to music, melodious Italian music that filled my heart with memories.

We did not speak of Paul or Gabriella, it was as though we had only just met, that love had not touched either of us before, and yet above us and around us were fleeting memories of that other time when I had agonised over the pains of my first love.

It was when we stood together in the doorway, with my hand resting in his, that he said, 'Shall I see you again or are you thinking of returning home?'

'I have made no plans, but I suppose I must go home soon.'

He stared at me curiously. 'You do not appear to be in any hurry to return home? I find that very strange in someone who has been married such a short time.'

'I know.'

'Perhaps it is time I made an effort to get back into the land of the living, in which case perhaps I shall see you if I call on your aunt and uncle?'

'Oh, yes, Carlo, they would be so pleased, and so would I.'

I turned to leave and impulsively he took hold of my hand. 'Joanna, why do I feel that you are unhappy, that love is something you know very little about? Why did you want so much to meet me again?'

He was staring down at me, watching the expressions chase themselves across my face. My answer should have been light-hearted, superficial, but I could not flirt with Carlo. It was as though the years in between had never been. His face was just as dear as before, the eyes that gazed down at me were just as kind, and I was a girl again, loving him, needing him to love me as I had needed him before. I could feel the sting of tears in my eyes, sense the concern in his voice as he said, 'Joanna, what is it? Why are you so unhappy?'

I could hardly believe that it was my voice saying, 'I loved you so much, Carlo. I knew you didn't love me, I was just a young girl with a crush and I had to get over you, but when I came back to Italy I couldn't simply go away without seeing you. Now it seems that I have to forget you all over again.'

I strained to draw my hand out of his clasp but he held on to it, staring down at me sombrely, then raising my hand to his lips he said, 'Come back to me, tomorrow or the next day, whenever you wish, but come back to me.'

I ran down the steps across the courtyard, tossing my aunt's white mink into the car and driving away oblivious of the chill wind rustling restlessly through the trees overhead.

Chapter Twenty-Eight

In the days that followed I agonised over what I should do. I yearned to go back to the Castello Varasi but I knew that it was pointless. Carlo had not loved me then, he did not love me now. We might talk about the past but always between us would lie Gabriella's shadow and my marriage to Paul.

What could I say to him? I don't love my husband, he doesn't love me. We married because we needed each other, because he wanted Reckmire and I wanted a prop to lean on. I have to go back to him because I'm expecting his child. And I would watch the expressions on his face, sympathy, perhaps even a little tenderness before the shutters came down, telling me none of it was important to him.

I was aware of Aunt Corallie's questioning gaze and the summer days sped by and in the end it was Carlo who came to me. I was sitting in the gardens where I had said goodbye to him before the war and watched him crossing the lawn towards me, limping a little, his eyes hidden behind his dark sunglasses. He sat down beside me, saying quietly, 'I realised you were not coming back, Joanna, so I have come to say goodbye. By the time I return from America you will have gone home.'

'You are going to America?' I cried stupidly.

'Yes. I told you I hoped to go there. It has come rather sooner than I expected.'

'How long will you be away?'

'I'm not sure. Why didn't you come back to the Castello Varasi?'

'I made a fool of myself, I must have embarrassed you dreadfully.'

'Is a man embarrassed when a beautiful woman tells him she was once in love with him?'

I didn't speak, and for some minutes he sat looking across the gardens, then he said softly, 'Would there have been a time for us, Joanna, if there had been no war? It wouldn't have been when you were a young girl because then there was Gabriella and our lives would have been different, but if we were meeting now for the first time, yes, I think there would have been a chance for us, but now you have Paul.'

He rose to his feet and stood looking down at me. 'Go home, Joanna, forget your memories of Italy potent with wine and sunshine where you found it so easy to love. Go home to your cool green land and your busy life with the man you married, that is my advice.'

I wanted him to hold me, to feel his lips on mine, but he bowed briefly and walked away from me. It felt like the desolation of our first goodbye only this time there was no Paul waiting for me in the darkness.

Two days later he telephoned me. His voice was cool, non-committal, saying in clipped accents, 'Do I take it that you want our child to be born in Italy or is there a remote chance that you might be coming home?'

Without a second's thought I said, 'I intend to come home at the beginning of next week.'

'I suppose you'll be spending some time with your mother?'

'No, I'm coming back to Reckmire.'

'As your business partner perhaps I should report that the hotel is flourishing. The winter has been successful, the men are out in the fields, the stables are thriving, the hens are laying, and the hotel is filled with people.'

'I'm very glad to hear it.'

'All achieved with the utmost effort on my part and hardly any on yours.'

'I'm aware of it.'

'Give my regards to your aunt and uncle. Haven't they thought it strange that you stayed with them so long? By the way, how is Gabriella and her handsome Italian?'

'Gabriella lives in Rome and I haven't seen her.'

I made no mention of Carlo. Let Paul think he was married to Gabriella. Neither of us would meet him again and it was unlikely we would meet Gabriella. She had written to say she was too busy to visit but sent me her best wishes, a letter entirely impersonal to a mother who wept over it.

It was mid-March when I arrived home, wearing clothes that disguised my thickening figure.

Guests sat at the windows enjoying the warm sunlight and the flowers, the sea rolled in in benign crescents across the firm golden sand and staff rushed to welcome me in the hall and to bring in my cases from the car.

There was no sign of Paul, but tea was served to me in my sitting room and from the gardens below came the sound of voices and much laughter. Indeed it was several hours before I faced Paul and then only across the dinner table. I was seeing the maddening raising of his eyebrows, and his caustic voice saying, 'So you're back, Joanna, and looking remarkably well, albeit a little plumper.'

Ignoring his remark I said, 'The hotel is fully booked for the summer?'

'The hotel is fully booked until after Christmas.'

'That's good then.'

'Very good. I've purchased a couple of horses from Colonel Stevens, both good hackers, and I've employed a new kennel maid. We have more and more guests who are interested in riding and we've got a new boathouse since many of the guests are bringing their boats here.'

'I hope you've told them this coast isn't particularly safe for sailing? The winds whip up at an alarming rate and there are rocks hidden by the sea.'

'I've told them all that. In fact I told them to ask you about the dangers of Reckmire Marsh of which you've had first hand experience.'

His sarcasm was insufferable but I made myself reply, 'I shall most certainly dissuade them from doing anything as foolish as I once did.'

'Nothing's changed in the village. Your old friend Lottie is going to be married, some lad from one of the hill farms I believe.'

317

'I must write to her then.'

'And your friend Mrs Peabody has had quite a lot to say about the absence of the new bride so soon after her marriage. It's to be hoped the child looks something like me or she'll be questioning how you came by it.'

'She would be more scandalised if I informed her,' I snapped.

In the days and weeks that followed I was subtly aware that although I might be the owner of Reckmire it was Paul who made the decisions, Paul who commanded the staff, Paul who ordained that although the hotel was booked to the hilt there should be room for more.

I watched him walking round the gardens in the company of a tall stout man who appeared to be making notes and they were deep in discussion. I had no idea who the man was and when Paul failed to mention him I asked, 'Who is the man I saw you with this morning and why was he making notes?'

'He's a director in a firm of surveyors who have recently extended a large house in the Highlands. It's incredible what they've done with it, from being a medium-sized country house it's now a castle. People will go on from here and see the difference.'

'Does a place have to be enormous to attract guests? The hotel is fully booked. Besides we have no room to extend.'

'Oh, but we have. If we get rid of the deer park at the back of the house there's room for at least six more bedrooms and a ballroom.'

'Get rid of the deer park when people travel miles simply to look at them! Besides the building will be ruined if you start adding to it.'

'Not if it's in keeping with the rest of it.'

'Why do we want a ballroom? Then we'd have to employ an orchestra. Really, Paul your ideas are running away with you.'

'On the contrary, yours have remained in a time warp of gentile obscurity. Your grandparents' portraits remain on the wall, their pictures are everywhere, the only things that have changed in this place are the people who pay the bills, our guests.'

'Isn't that what we both wanted? Isn't it a fact that you wanted Reckmire long before there was any possibility that either of us would have it?'

'It's true, but the original idea to change it was mine, and now I want to change it further.'

'You can't change it without my consent and I won't give it.'

Although his voice was even I knew that he was angry. His face was white, his lips set in a cold straight line, but before he left the dining table with his food hardly touched he muttered, 'He's gone away to draw up plans. When he returns I'll refer him to you. Pay him for his work up to date and tell him that he would do well not to take orders from underlings but go straight to the fountainhead, even if she does happen to be abroad at the time!'

I watched him walk quickly through the dining room and out through the swing doors, while those around us looked at me curiously, sensing that between us there had been words.

If the surveyor came back I never saw him, but the atmosphere between Paul and myself was even more strained than before. I did not have an easy pregnancy, I was constantly sick and felt so tired some days it was an effort to mingle with our guests. On the days when I felt reasonably well I walked round the estate and along the beach. I looked across the park land at the deer sheltering under the trees and was there one day when the vicar came striding down the drive.

He smiled, joining me at the rail. 'What a beautiful sight that is, Mrs Cheviot,' he said brightly. 'There can't be many deer herds left in this part of the country.'

I smiled. 'Were you going up to the house, Vicar?'

'Yes, I've got an old parishioner, Mrs Davies. She's a hundred at the beginning of next month and the villagers want to give her a day to remember. I was wondering if we could have something here?'

'What a lovely idea, Mr Fielding. You can have the morning room and I'll arrange for some flowers to be brought in for her.'

'Should I mention it to your husband first?'

'Why, no, I'll tell him when I get back to the house.'

His face was doubtful and when I looked at him questioningly he gave a little smile before saying, 'Well, it's just that he warned me not to ask for too many local affairs this year, they interfere too much with business.'

Completely uncontrite when I taxed him with it, Paul merely said, 'If we let them have one they want another, then another, and in no time at all we'll be doing nothing except catering for the village.'

'Oh, Paul, that's nonsense. It will do us no good whatsoever to fall out with the villagers, and Mrs Davies is a dear old lady who will enjoy spending her birthday here.'

'I'll tell the vicar he can have it on this occasion, but no more this year. You're looking decidedly peaky. Why don't you go to stay with your mother for a few days?'

His sarcasm was too obvious to expect a reply.

My son was born prematurely at the end of June, a small fretful baby who cried constantly, and a nurse was installed for two months to care for us both.

I called him Robin. On the occasion Paul came to look at him he stared down at the child unsmiling and made no effort to touch him. I was watching his face closely for any sign that the small helpless baby had invoked any feeling of paternal tenderness but there was none. Instead he turned away, shrugging his shoulders and saying, 'It's evident the child's going to take after your mother's side of the family. He screams for attention most of the night. He'll want taking in hand when he's old enough.'

He strode to the door, then almost as if he voiced an afterthought he said, 'The surveyor's coming to see us on Monday, I'll refer him to you of course.'

'You know my views on the subject, you can deal with it.'

'Oh, no, Joanna. I want him to hear it from the owner of Reckmire not the rubbing rag.'

'You're hardly that, Paul.'

'The only way I talk to the surveyor is to tell him to go ahead with the alterations. The Westermans are willing to take over the deer, they've been wanting them for years and they have the room for them. If you are still against it then you can inform the surveyor and the Westerman's that they've lost out.'

He left me, closing the door firmly behing him, and minutes later the nurse came in to find me distressed. She was a bright warm-hearted Irish girl who didn't know what to make of a situation where the child's father showed no interest in his child and very little in the child's mother.

'Ah, but it's a cold fish he is,' she said stoutly. 'Doesn't he know you've had a bad time and that the baby's suffering too? I've seen his sort before. I'll never forget that young boy who had to call his father "sir".'

'Who was this, Kathleen?'

'A family I went to, to look after the mother. The poor lady was that delicate and she'd had a nasty operation. I stayed with them two months until she was well enough to get around, but it was the young boy I was sorry for. There the poor lad was, missin' his mother, and his father was a cold fish who rarely spoke to him. Had to call his father "sir" he did, and stand up when he entered the room. I was glad to get away I was.'

'I expect you'll be glad to get away from here, Kathleen.'

'No, really. I'm very comfortable here and I loves you and the baby, but it's him, cold as charity he is. Oh, ma'am, I'm that sorry, I shouldn't be sayin' these things, it's none o' my business.'

I was dreading the day when the nurse had to leave, but two days before a letter arrived from Aunt Marcia to say she was coming north to stay with me for a few days.

When I informed Paul he merely said, 'We've had a cancellation on health grounds so she can have the room. I don't want her in the flat, she'd see and hear too much.'

I knew what he meant. Our domestic arrangements were hardly those of a devoted family.

I was feeling much stronger. On the doctor's advice I took long walks around the estate, and one morning I felt well enough to go riding. On my way to the stables I met a group of riders leaving. They were a jolly party riding healthy hacks. We passed with murmured greetings but I knew they had no idea who I was. The stable yard was empty except for a girl sitting idly on a mounting block, swinging her legs.

321

She turned to stare as I crossed the yard, and then she grinned and I recognised her instantly as Lottie's sister Freda.

'Hello, Freda,' I said, smiling, 'How long have you been working here?'

'I came when you were in Italy. Mr Cheviot said 'e wanted somebody who'd bin used to workin' with animals. I heard 'im tellin' some people one day in the village, so the next day I came up 'ere to see 'im.'

'I see. And he was impressed with your experience?'

'Well, I worked as a land girl when I got out of the army, and the farmer never 'ad any complaints. It beats servin' in the shop. I really 'ated that after our Lottie went away.'

There was something earthy and wholesome about her. She was pretty in a bold sort of way, and I was aware as I had always been of her sly amusement. It wasn't exactly insolence, but she was in no way overawed by my station in relation to her own. I might be the owner of Reckmire, but it was Paul she would take her orders from. I was dismally aware of this within minutes of talking to her.

'I thought I might ride this afternoon, Freda, I usually ride Ralston.'

'Mr Cheviot let Miss Falshaw ride him. She's gone over to see some relatives who live at Dunshaw.'

'Miss Falshaw?'

'Yes. She's stayin' at the hotel so that she can visit them. Didn't Mr Cheviot tell you then? They went over to dine at Dunshaw last night.'

'What other horses are available then. Not very many, I suppose?'

She slid down from her perch and walked with me across the yard. She walked with a boyish swagger in her velvet cords, pointing to a stall where a chestnut horse stood with his head over the stable door.

'There's Maxton. We only got him a couple of days ago so I don't know what 'e's like. Mr Cheviot seemed to think somethin' of 'im.'

'It doesn't appear as though I have much choice in the matter. Will you saddle him up for me?'

I watched while she saddled the horse, then she stood back while I mounted him.

'Are you alone here, where are the other stable hands?' I asked her curiously.

'Young Albert's off sick, snagged his hand on a nail 'e did and it's gone septic. George Riley's gone off with two teenage boys who are only just learnin' to ride. I likes bein' on my own. Albert 'asn't two words for a goose and George Riley picks on me. 'E doesn't like 'avin' a girl on the premises.'

I smiled. 'I'll try out the horse along the beach.' Then as an afterthought I said, 'I've written to your sister, Freda, will she be getting married in the village?'

'I suppose so. I'll be glad when it's all over. The livin' room's full o' weddin' dress material and presents, waitin' for her to come home.'

'When will that be?'

'Soon, I 'ope.'

I had no fault to find with Maxton. He was gentle and obedient and I couldn't see why Miss Falshaw couldn't have taken him instead of my horse. Freda had told me Paul had accompanied her the evening before with some relish. She had watched my face carefully for any sign that I was annoyed by it, but I had probably disappointed her by my air of indifference.

For mid-August it was a soft balmy morning. The sea was calm, the air filled with the scent of bracken and woodsmoke and my spirits revived as the breeze lashed my face bringing back much of its lost colour.

By the time I returned to the stable Riley was back, coming forward with a smile to take the horse after I had dismounted.

'It's nice to see ye up and about again, Mrs Cheviot,' he said. 'What do ye think about the 'orse?'

'He's a very nice horse, Riley.'

'Aye, that 'e is.'

'Who did my husband buy him from?'

''E paid a good price for 'im fro' Miss Falshaw's relatives over at Dunshaw.'

'Then I'm very surprised Miss Falshaw didn't ride him

today instead of taking Ralston.'

He grinned. 'She's 'ad 'er eye on Ralston for some days, Mrs Cheviot, and it was all right wi' the master.'

I said nothing more but my curiosity grew about the attributes of Miss Falshaw. In the background Freda smirked.

As I approached the house I was delighted to see Aunt Marcia hurrying along the path to meet me.

After she had embraced me she held me away from her, searching my face and saying finally, 'You look much better than I expected, Joanna. I've telephoned almost every day. I suppose Paul told you? He said you were far from well and resting so I said not to disturb you. Things are quiet on the farm at the moment so your uncle and I thought we should drive up to assure ourselves that all was well.'

'When did you arrive?'

'About an hour ago. I've left Edward in the lounge reading his paper. They told me you'd gone riding so I thought I'd walk across to the stables. How is the baby?'

'Becoming stronger, I think, but he's so incredibly tiny still, and fretful. This is the best day I've had since he was born.'

'And is Paul very thrilled to have a son?'

'He must be.'

'I was so thrilled when I got your letter and pleased that you want to call him Robin. He's the only Albemarle in the family even if his surname will be Cheviot.'

That was the moment when I decided to call my son Robin Albemarle Cheviot whether Paul agreed with it or not.

For the first time in weeks I ate lunch with my relatives in the hotel dining room, at the table always reserved for Paul and I and which caused some curiosity amongst the guests.

Paul did not appear for lunch and I felt I had to make some sort of excuse for him.

'I'm sure he'll be in for dinner,' I said evenly. 'He had to ride over to Dunshaw this morning, business I think.'

'What has your mother had to say about the baby?' Aunt Marcia asked, 'She must be terribly pleased?'

'I'm sure she is.'

'Isn't she dying to see him?'

'She doesn't urge me to visit, she knows how busy we are, and of course winter is just around the corner.'

She nodded. Then Uncle Edward changed the subject by asking about my time in Italy and Aunt Marcia talked sadly of Gabriella and her estrangement from her parents.

'I was so sure she would have married that nice boy Carlo, he was so handsome, he came from such a good family and it was something we all wanted. Did you see Carlo? We heard he'd been wounded during the war.'

'Yes. He was hoping to go to America for treatment. I hope it will be successful.'

'I wonder how he feels about Gabriella? Did Corallie say if they heard from her, or if her husband was out of prison?'

'She talks about her so seldom, and hardly at all if Uncle Rinaldo is present. Aunt Corallie writes to her, and she did receive a letter sending me her best wishes. They know absolutely nothing about how she is living, only that she is in Rome.'

'I can't think that any family has changed as much as ours has, and to think that once we were so happy together, and that this old house was a home, a much loved home. Oh, don't think I'm criticising, dear, you and Paul have done wonders with the place and you couldn't have lived here on your own, it's just that my memories are so different from the reality.'

We were on the dessert when Paul arrived and immediately I was aware of the change in him. He was smiling confidently, almost perkily, greeting my aunt and uncle with enthusiasm, taking his seat at the table with unaccustomed good humour.

'Well, well,' he said affably, 'this is an unexpected pleasure. Did you suddenly decide to visit us?'

'It seemed like a good idea,' Uncle Edward answered him. 'Before the summer ended.'

With a smile in my direction Paul said, 'Riley told me you'd been riding, she's been decidedly peaky since the baby was born, I'm glad to see you taking an interest again. What did you think of Maxton?'

'He's a nice horse. How did Miss Falshaw cope with Ralston?'

'Very well. She's a good horsewoman. Actually she's gone upstairs to change. She'll be down presently and you can meet her.'

'It's nice to see the hotel so full. You've had a good year, I take it?' Uncle Edward asked.

'We're booked up until after Christmas. Actually we've little competition around here and we're getting well known. We have to keep on our toes in case things change.'

'Change?' Aunt Marcia said curiously.

'Well, yes. We can't afford to sit back on our laurels. There are one or two large properties on the market. It only needs somebody to come up with a similar idea and we're competing.'

'I suppose so. Which properties are you thinking of?'

'Well, there are one or two around Coniston and Windermere, and one or two in the Dales. I've heard of another one this morning, one that could be a real headache if they get the go ahead.'

'In this area?' Uncle Edward asked.

'Beyond Dunshaw. Old Sir Alec's place. The family haven't lived in it for years. Like this place it was a nursing home and when the war finished the daughter and her husband came back for a few years. They're living in Provence now, got fed up with the place, couldn't get good staff and the place has now gone to seed. It has great possibilities, all it needs is somebody with some know how and money, a good deal of money.'

'Well, let's hope for your sake that it takes some time before anybody's interested,' Uncle Edward said evenly. At that moment however Paul rose to his feet and signalled to a woman entering the dining room to join us.

She was introduced to us all as Miss Lena Falshaw and quickly dispelled any picture I had had of her in my mind. She was a large-boned young woman with a broad ruddy face and short dark hair sprinkled with grey. I put her age at around thirty and she gripped my hand with the firm pressure of a man.

She was wearing a serviceable navy blue skirt and white

shirt blouse and set about ordering her midday meal with
gusto.

'I hope you didn't mind my riding your horse, Mrs
Cheviot?' she said bluntly. 'Mr Cheviot said you were
ill and wouldn't be riding. I felt pretty awful about it
when we got back and Riley said you'd been out on
Maxton.'

'I'm a little out of practice, Miss Falshaw, please don't
worry, I enjoyed my ride on Maxton. You have relatives in
the area, I believe?'

'Yes, over at Dunshaw. My uncle Horace. He bought the
Gantry House.'

'Really? I didn't know,' I answered, and Aunt Marcia
said curiously, 'What happened to old Mrs Gantry then,
did she die?'

'No, she's in a nursing home. She was terribly senile and
the house was far too big. My uncle got it cheaply but it
wanted the earth spending on it.'

'And has he the idea of doing the same with Gantry that
Paul and Joanna have done here?' Uncle Edward asked
blandly.

'Gracious no, it's not nearly big enough, but he does have
other ideas. He's a great go-getter, I'm sure he'll think of
something.'

Watching Paul I could see the half smile on his face as
he listened to her. It made me feel uneasy, it was like the
smile on the face of the tiger, and catching my eyes upon
him he raised his glass in a salute before drinking. Then,
with a broad smile, he said to Aunt Marcia, 'And what do
you think of our son and heir?'

'I haven't seen him yet. Joanna hurried upstairs to change
and we're going to see him this afternoon. He hasn't been
too well, I hear?'

'He screams his head off, and is decidedly puny. I suppose
he's coming on.'

'Well, he was premature. You'll find him far more
interesting in a short while.'

'I'll find him more interesting when he's eighteen. I've
never been the sort of chap to drool over infants.'

Nobody spoke, and after a few minutes Lena Falshaw

said diplomatically, 'I had a sister who was premature, we all thought she wouldn't make it but you should see her now, she's a great sportswoman, plays golf and tennis and rides to hounds. Last year she joined a climbing expedition to tackle the Eiger.'

We were all impressed, and I managed to flash her a grateful smile.

Later in the afternoon Aunt Marcia held the baby, looking down into his puny pallid face with gentle compassion. 'Poor little scrap,' she said. 'He's had a rotten start. You're not looking well, Joanna. It's a pity the nurse couldn't stay on. Can't you get a replacement?'

'I've asked Alice, one of the chambermaids, if she'd like to take care of Robin. She adores him and she's very good, I think it will work very well. We can get somebody else to take her place upstairs.'

'You never did have a proper honeymoon,' she persisted.

'I did have those weeks in Italy, Aunt Marcia.'

I often wondered just how much Paul and I fooled her by our show of unity. There were many times when I caught her watching me keenly and it was so hard to pretend. At those times I longed to be able to tell her how deep was my unhappiness but some misguided sense of loyalty prevented it. I knew in my heart that Paul deserved half of Reckmire, then I remembered how contemptuously he had dismissed me when he told his friend how little I mattered in his scheme of things.

'When is your mother going to see the baby?' Aunt Marcia asked.

'When he's able to travel. She won't come here so obviously I shall have to take him down there.'

Her glance spoke volumes, and changing the subject she said, 'I hope our sudden visit didn't put you out too much, Joanna? We would have been prepared to stay in the flat, we really didn't expect a room in the hotel.'

'There was a cancellation, Aunt Marcia, and we wanted you to be comfortable. The baby cries a lot.'

I couldn't be sure that my explanation was accepted, but

how could I expect her to understand a situation where two people who had not been married a year slept apart, and where the father of the child could not be bothered to call in to see him?

Chapter Twenty-Nine

Paul's good humour persisted for the rest of their stay, but when Uncle Edward said that perhaps they could extend their visit for a further week he was quick to say that unfortunately their room was booked and there was no other.

They could quite easily have been accommodated in one of the rooms on the upper storey but when he made no mention of them I kept quiet.

On the morning they left Aunt Marcia said gently, 'We're so glad everything is going well for you, Joanna. Paul is quite evidently pleased with life, and don't worry about Robin. He's getting stronger every day and looking bonnier.'

Paul sent his excuses on the day they left that he would not be in for dinner, that he had a business engagement, so I dined alone. I saw that Lena Falshaw was also absent from her table and I couldn't help thinking that she was the business engagement he had referred to.

I was not left long in doubt. I was writing letters in my room when he came in just before ten o'clock and I looked up in surprise since he seldom visited me in my sitting room and never in my bedroom.

My surprise must have shown on my face because he said lightly, 'Perhaps I should have made an appointment, Joanna?'

'Don't be silly, Paul.'

'Well, I have to talk to you very urgently, matters are moving all too quickly.'

I stared at him doubtfully, and with a little smile he said,

'I'll pour you a sherry. I don't want what I have to say to come as too much of a shock.'

I watched while he went over to the sideboard and started to pour the sherry, then he came back to me, handing me a glass before he took his seat opposite mine, staring at me enigmatically over the rim of his glass.

I had the strangest feeling that what he had to tell me was not conducive to my welfare, and I waited, watching him twirl the stem of his glass slowly in his fingers while his eyes met mine, filled with cynical humour.

'Your patience demands my full admiration,' he said at last. 'Most women would be urging me to get on with it.'

He laughed when I didn't answer him, and I realised anew how little mirth there was in his laughter.

'I take it you're entirely happy with events here, Joanna? That you don't see any need to change anything and that we should go on ad infinitum exactly as things are today?'

'I don't see anything wrong with the way things are. The hotel is successful, guests continue to arrive and rebook. I think the venture has been entirely successful, thanks largely to you.'

He bowed his head in mock humility, then in the same level voice continued, 'So you're happy, and this is how it stays?'

'I don't understand what you're getting at, Paul.'

'I intend to make it clear to you, just answer my question.'

'All right then, yes, I'm happy with Reckmire as it is.'

'That's what I thought. Unfortunately, Joanna, I am not. I'm ambitious, I've got my teeth into this business and I want to go on. I've been having serious talks with Horace Falshaw over the last few weeks and he's made me an offer I'm more than tempted to accept.'

'What sort of offer?'

'He's got his eyes on a large property near Kirby Lonsdale. It's been empty for a few years now, nobody wants to buy a house of that size, it's much larger than Reckmire and at the moment I'd say it's a bit of a monstrosity, but it does have possibilities.'

'What sort of possibilities?'

'It's on the bank of a river with good salmon fishing. It has extensive grounds that could harbour a golf course, the tennis courts could be relaid and there's room for a ballroom. We could get the same people in to update it who worked on updating this place and as it's only about twenty miles from here it would hardly be a threat.'

'You know it would be, Paul!'

He smiled. 'Not with the guests you prefer. The sort of people who like peace and quiet, soft lights and sweet music, gentle pursuits and intelligent conversation. The other place would cater for the living, younger people, people who like parties and dancing, squash courts and hunting. You're not afraid of a little competition, surely, Joanna?'

'What are you really trying to tell me, Paul?'

'I'm saying I want out. I want to expand and that's something I can't do here. These last few weeks have proved that. There's to be no tampering with what remains of the old Reckmire, no getting rid of the deer park, no extending the house in case the ghosts of your grandparents are affronted.'

'And what would Mr Falshaw be offering you if you decided to go in with him?'

'Half of everything, the profits, the acclaim, a straight split down the middle.'

'Which is everything you have here?'

'Not quite, Joanna. Here I'm a partner in everything except the ownership of the house. There I would have that also.'

'Doesn't it matter to you that the success we make of this place will ultimately be for Robin's benefit?'

'It matters very much, Joanna. Everything, like you say, will one day belong to Robin whether I'm alive or not. I can sweat my guts out to make it work, but in the end he'll be in a position to order me out. A business partnership can be dissolved. I'm not a believer in gratitude. I never felt any for my father, I'm not expecting any from my son.'

'Gratitude, like love, has to be earned. Did that never occur to you?'

'Love, my dear girl, is as transient as a summer storm.'

332

'I'm not talking about the love between a man and a woman.'

'Neither am I. I'm talking about any kind of love. Maybe I never knew any, maybe I've never given any, but something in black and white with everything legal and above board, that's different. I've promised to let Falshaw know if he has the go ahead by next weekend. In the meantime, Joanna, I suggest you think seriously how you're going to run this place without me. You do have a good staff. Unfortunately they can be poached for more money, it goes on all the time.'

'Doesn't it worry you in the least that you can do this to your wife and child?'

'Hasn't it worried you that you shut me out, Joanna? That however much I helped you, worked for you, I wasn't considered worthy enough to be asked to join you in owning Reckmire?'

'You had half of everything else!'

'It wasn't enough. Go ahead and divorce me, but if you do I warn you I'll take your staff and your customers so that in the end all you and that child will have will be a house as lonely and empty as those marshes outside the window.'

We stared at each other in silence, then with a brief smile he walked to the door. Before he closed it behind him he said quietly, 'One week, Joanna. I'm sorry it's not longer, but it's all the time there is.'

The sharp closing of the door was like the severing of the rest of my life. Feelings of betrayal, anger and despair chased themselves across my heart. There was hatred too, hatred for the man who was my husband and the father of my child, but never had he seemed more omnipotent.

His threats were not vain ones. He had meant every word he had said and I had no doubt that he would systematically set about ruining me if only to show me that I could have prevented it.

He did not love me, or our child. Feelings of love would never sway him, and I should have known. Memories of the first day we met tortured me now, that boy who had looked down on me with contemptuous resentment as I scrambled up the rocks behind Robin, had looked at me with the same

333

contempt a few minutes ago. He knew that he could defeat me if I did not give way to his request, and I found myself remembering his mother, living in her shadowy world, devoid of love and compassion from the two men she had a right to expect it from.

Defeated and desolate, I knew that Paul had won.

He insisted that his half ownership of Reckmire be made entirely legal, that there should be no loopholes, no word of mouth. He wanted it in black and white — and before the ink had dried on the page he informed me that he intended to close the hotel for the months of January and February so that work could go ahead on the extension.

I watched with tears streaming down my face while the deer were rounded up, beautiful gentle creatures who had come to me shyly to take titbits out of my fingers, gazing at me with large eyes sheltering behind incredibly long lashes. Now, terrified and bewildered, they were caught and hustled into trucks to be released later into their new environment.

The villagers stood in silent groups watching the procedure, standing with grim faces and then turning away to walk muttering angrily back to the village.

Only Paul seemed unaware that his decision to extend Reckmire was causing anger in the vicinity, and I knew the anger would increase when the lorries started to arrive, causing havoc on that long rambling high street, scattering dirt and dust, creating furrows in the road, filling the peace with the sounds of a builders' yard.

Mrs Peabody was their spokeswoman as she accosted me one morning while I walked along the drive. She had been waiting for me and my heart sank when I beheld her standing stoutly near the gatehouse, oblivious of the wind that swept in from the sea and the freezing rain.

Her large red face was wet with rain but more than that I was aware of her indignation as she snapped, 'I've bin waitin' for ya, Mrs Cheviot. We want to know what's 'appen'n now the deer've gone? Yer grandparents would 'ave bin 'orrified to see them go.'

'We're extending the hotel, Mrs Peabody, and creating a nine hole golf course. It will bring trade into the village and probably find work for a good number of you.'

'We 'as work, Mrs Cheviot. We'd rather be without work than see things changin' like they are changin'.'

'Yer've not thought to say a word to us about what you intend to do. Oh, I know you think it's none of our business, but most of us 'ave lived round 'ere as long as the Albemarles and anythin' you does to the house'll not be worth much if all the village is against you.'

'And is all the village against us, Mrs Peabody?'

'Aye, it is. Some o' the men 'ave been to see the vicar and asked him to see yer 'usband, but much good that'll do, I'm sure.'

'What do you mean by that, Mrs Peabody?'

'It's you 'e should be comin' to see, Mrs Cheviot. You're the owner of Reckmire.'

'I'll tell my husband how you all feel about the changes. Perhaps he will decide to speak to you if the vicar arranges a meeting.'

'Aye well, that's the least 'e can do.'

She stalked away from me without a backward glance, leaving me filled with disquiet. Paul would sweep their complaints aside like autumn leaves. He would regard it as none of their business and he was arrogant enough to disregard their efforts to ostracise us from the community.

When I told him of my conversation with Mrs Peabody he shook his head irritably. 'None of this is any of their business, Joanna. They're not paying for it, and if they haven't the sense to see that it could be an asset to the village then that's their affair.'

'At least you should make an attempt to mollify them,' I persisted.

'I don't see why. I don't tell them how to spend their money, how to decorate their homes or object when they build monstrosities in their gardens. Why should they interfere with us?'

'My grandmother always got along with the villagers and I want to do the same. If the vicar telephones, please try to be patient and at least make them understand what you're doing.'

'That will be difficult when my wife understands none of

it. I suppose you told the Peabody woman it had nothing to do with you?'

'You know I don't agree with it, that is sufficient.'

The village hall was full and as we walked down the centre aisle to take our place besides the vicar on the dais, I was aware of the antagonistic silence and that hostile eyes followed our every movement.

My eyes swept over the room but not a single person present smiled and my heart sank at the sight of a truculent Mrs Peabody in the company of two of her sons who were local farmers. I knew most of them, housewives and shopkeepers, farm labourers and school teachers. Whatever their calling not a single one of them was going to stand up and say they were in agreement with Pauls's proposals for changing Reckmire.

He listened in grim silence while one after the other they stood to their feet to condemn his proposals, then when they had all had their say he rose to his feet. He already knew that charm would have no effect on his audience, so he dispensed with it. Instead he used the sort of forthright behaviour they would understand.

'I've listened to you all with a great deal of patience,' he began, 'and in many ways I can understand how you feel. I can only tell you that you are crossing your bridges before you come to them. When these alterations are complete you will have one of the finest country hotels in England in your area, a place that will attract people from abroad as well as from this country, people who would bring a great deal of money into the area.

'All right, all right, money isn't everything, but in this day and age it's very essential. I'm ambitious for Reckmire, I want it to be the best, for my wife and myself and for our son who one day will take over from us. I don't interfere with your homes or your livelihood, I don't expect you to interfere with mine. I can only tell you that I am employing the very best workmen both for the outside work and the interior decoration, there will be nothing shoddy about Reckmire, nothing to let the village down ...'

'Yer've already let the village down by gettin' rid o' the

deer,' a red-faced man interrupted angrily.

'Do I tell you when to take the cows to market, Marshall, or send your pigs for slaughter? Do I tell you how to paint your house or dig your garden? I do not, and I will not allow you to tell me how to run either my house or my business.'

'Why doesn't the lady who owns the 'ouse 'ave somethin' to say about it?' the same man said truculently.

'We own the house together and the business. Do you allow your wife to speak for you or are you competent enough to speak for yourself?'

'I never thowt a granddaughter of Sir Robert would 'ave signed away 'er birthright, but if that's the case I've no more to say.'

He sat down heavily in his chair, his eyes staring into mine accusingly, and for the first time the villagers looked less than confident. They had expected me to be their ally. Now I was as much their enemy as Paul. In tones meant to pacify them he was saying, 'Please bear with me. All I am asking is a few months between Christmas and Easter when the workmen will be busy, and unfortunately there will be more traffic coming and going along the high street. After Easter it will all be over, you will be invited to a grand opening ceremony, and anything you care to organise in the summer, I will do my best to encourage our guests here to patronise.'

It was over. The villagers shuffled out of the hall muttering together, the vicar shuffled his papers and endeavoured to appear unconcerned while Paul was all geniality in the knowledge that he had won.

We drove back to Reckmire in silence and it was only when we drove to the forecourt that Paul exclaimed with delight at the sight of a Ferrari in all its shining elegance. He walked round it, admiring its beauty, exclaiming with delight that we evidently had a foreign guest of some note.

As we walked into the hotel he said evenly, 'Do you think Corallie has taken to driving a Ferrari, Joanna? If the car belongs to her I can anticipate some objections to what I intend to do here.'

I didn't answer. My eyes were on a tall dark man standing

at the reception desk. The receptionist said something to him and he turned to greet us.

Carlo was quick to inform us that he was on the way to Scotland to stay with friends and had remembered that he had to pass close by to Reckmire. He had booked in for only one evening and Paul was quick to invite him to dine with us.

He informed me that his treatment in America had worked remarkably well, but all Paul wished to talk about was the Ferrari, its speed and its petrol consumption. Then he embarrassed me by saying flippantly, 'What happened to Gabriella then? I hear you missed out on that one.'

Carlo permitted himself a small tight-lipped smile, but undeterred Paul went on, 'Marriage to a fascist will have taken some living down in Corallie's exclusive society. I must say I fancied Gabriella myself once, she was beautiful and there was an air about her that was pretty captivating. I expect you were absolutely floored when you came back from the war to be told what had happened?'

'The war altered a great many things for most people,' was all Carlo permitted himself to say.

'Well, yes, here are Joanna and I, married and owning Reckmire when once we hated the sight of each other.'

Carlo smiled. 'It is said that hatred and love can be very close.'

Paul grinned. 'You bet your life,' he said easily. 'I have to go over to Yorkshire this afternoon. You don't mind if I leave Joanna to entertain you, I hope?'

'Not at all, I shall be charmed.'

'Well, don't work too hard at it, I know Italians are noted for their charm. I haven't enough of it, I don't want her thinking too much about the difference in us.'

That afternoon we rode our horses across the fell and although it was cold it was exhilarating in the keen wind that blew straight off the sea and the distant Cumbrian hills covered by their first snow stood out entrancingly.

Although it was Saturday the only people we met were a group of fell walkers and later after we had stabled our horses we walked along the beach. Looking back at the house, Carlo said gently, 'I can understand why you loved it when you were a child. It has great character, Even now when it is a hotel the character is still there.'

In sudden anguish I blurted out Paul's plans for it and how it would be changed. There was anger as well as anguish in my voice, and he stood looking down at me, his expression concerned, until I said quickly, 'I'm sorry to burden you with all this, Carlo, it's just that I've sat all morning listening to the villagers' complaints. They were my complaints too but Paul rode roughshod over all of us.'

We retraced our steps, walking in silence. We had only just reached the house when I said anxiously, 'I've done nothing but talk about my troubles, Carlo, I haven't even asked about Aunt Corallie or my uncle.'

'Your aunt is very well, Rinaldo has had two heart attacks and is looking very frail. He worries your aunt but she is keeping a brave face in spite of her troubles.'

'Doesn't Gabriella go to see her father?'

'No. Perhaps it is his bitterness that keeps her away, but he would forgive her, I'm sure, if she went to see him.'

'Did Aunt Corallie tell you that I had a son?'

'Yes. You must be very proud of him.'

'He's beautiful now. Italy would be so wonderful for him with its sunshine. All we can look forward to is the winter and Robin was born prematurely so he had a very bad start.'

'Then you should bring him to Italy, your aunt and uncle would be delighted.'

I smiled but offered no comment.

Paul did not return that evening to dine with us, and I was aware of Carlo's dark eyes surveying me across the table, his face sculptured in candlelight, chiselled lips smiling as in silence his eyes met mine.

By the time Paul arrived we were sitting in the lounge sharing a bottle of wine and immediately I knew that he had been well pleased with his mission into Yorkshire.

He sat down at the table with us, ordering Scotch, and immediately saying, 'Well, it's all settled, Joanna. We'll get Christmas over and close in the New Year until Easter. That should see everything completed and in working order.'

'What about the weather?' I asked.

339

'Oh, we'll get by. The roads will be well gritted so that the lorries can get through, I'll put the planners up here and the men can find room in the village. The pubs'll be glad to fill their rooms in the worst months of the year. Has Joanna told you what we're doing with the place, Carlo?'

'Something about it.'

'She's not exactly enthusiastic but she will be when the money starts rolling in. Pity you can only stay the one night, you could have had a look round the place. You're the first Italian we've had. We get French and Germans often. It's funny to think that just a few years ago we were hell bent on destroying each other, and now all is forgiven. Tell me about your car? It's my ambition to own one of those.'

'I've had it about nine months, I'm well pleased with it.'

'Well, I should think so. If you ever feel like getting rid of it, how about giving me the first refusal?'

Carlo merely smiled and looked at his watch. 'Perhaps I'll retire now,' he said evenly. 'I have a long drive tomorrow and the weather looks to be changing.'

'What makes an Italian want to go to Scotland at this time of year?' Paul asked curiously.

'Old friends I thought I should see.'

'Don't you mean an old love affair? Only a woman would get me to Scotland at this time of year.'

Carlo did not enlighten him, and I cringed inwardly at the crude gibe. When Carlo rose to his feet to leave us I decided it was time for me to retire also. The three of us shook hands formally and Paul said, 'There's a chap over there I want to talk to. If I don't see you at breakfast, Varasi, I hope to see you some other time. When you want to dispose of the Ferrari, I hope.'

Chapter Thirty

Christmas and the weeks leading up to it were hectic. The hotel was full and I left it to Paul to organise entertainment for our guests while I spent hours arranging flowers, decorating the giant tree in the hall and seeing to it that chocolates and fruit were ordered for every bedroom.

I had a willing team to help me and my son was growing stronger now and slept longer and more peacefully.

Alice proved to be a first-class nursemaid. She was a jolly girl, young at heart, and I knew that when I was away she would be a considerable help in the hotel. I firmly believed her to be loyal and not much of a gossip.

Paul showed little interest in his son, but surprised me by saying, 'This'll be no place for you when the workmen move in. Why not go stay with your mother? The baby's too young to be got at.'

'What exactly do you mean by that?'

'Well, she got at you and your father, or else I've been listening to untruths all these years.'

I telephoned Mother that night and was surprised to hear the doubt in her voice, particularly as she was always telling me on the telephone and in her letters that she was Robin's grandmother and hadn't even seen him.

'Well, you did say he was fretful, Joanna, and my nerves have been bad recently. The doctor gives me tablets for them, and a baby crying all the time can be very disturbing.'

'Mother, Robin doesn't cry very much at all now. He's a lovely baby, I thought you wanted to see him?'

'Oh, I do, I do, but isn't it the wrong time of year to be bringing him such a long way?'

'It isn't the best time, I agree, but it's chaos here. If you don't want us at this time, Mother I'll ask Aunt Marcia.'

'And have her say I'm difficult as usual? No, Joanna, I shall expect you in the New Year for a few days.'

A few days, and then what?

What a difference a baby made to Mother's smart flat and ordered existence. I was glad he was only a tiny baby and not a toddler who would cause chaos amongst her many ornaments and pastel furnishings.

'I'm not surprised he looks so delicate, being born in that awful place. He must be quite terrified by the sound of the sea all the time,' she said.

Her friends were invited to view and they brought gifts and thought him sweet. She carried on with her bridge parties as usual so on those afternoons I wrapped him up warmly and endeavoured to visit the people I knew.

I didn't want to overstay my welcome and was unsure about when I should state my intention of returning home. The decision was taken out of my hands when Mother indicated that she and three friends had decided to go on a bridge holiday to Interlaken at the end of January.

'They wanted to go on a cruise, Joanna, with absolutely no thought that I hated sailing. And I ask you, sailing in January, however large the ship! It would have taken a week at least to reach calmer waters. I suggested the bridge holiday, it's being organised from the club so it should be very good. Anyway they all agreed. I hope it doesn't put you out, darling, but I'm sure you're anxious to get back to Reckmire if only to see how the builders are getting on.'

She made no mention of my staying on at the flat in her absence, I don't even think it occurred to her, so on a cold fine day we left Surrey only to arrive at Reckmire with the hills obscured by flurries of powdery snow where it mingled flirtatiously with spume blown inland from the sea.

The place looked dreary and there was a fine coating of dust everywhere. The staff had taken extended paid holidays and were not expected to return until two weeks before Easter. There were no flowers on the reception desk, and no smiling manager to come forward to receive me or obliging porter to help with my luggage.

An empty house would have looked unwelcoming but it could soon be brought to light with blazing fires and the glow of lamplight. But an empty hotel made me think of failure, a dream that had gone wrong.

Robin was fretful but after I had fed him and the room became warm from the two bars of an electic fire I had turned on, he fell asleep.

From behind the house came the insistent sounds of hammering mingling with other noises that told me there were workmen at work.

From the windows at the back of the hotel I could see parked lorries and building material piled up everywhere. Deep furrows where the lorries had driven over the parkland were frozen into ridges of solid ice and I shuddered to think of the state the village roads might be in.

Disconsolately I wandered through the empty rooms. There was no sign of Paul, and after reassuring myself that Robin was still sleeping peacefully in some exasperation I pushed my feet into boots and my arms into the warmth of my sheepskin jacket before leaving the house to walk to the stables. There must be some sign of life there since the horses would need attention and somebody there would know where I could find my husband.

I called out on entering the stable yard and to my relief I heard somebody answering me, then Riley was there, smiling amicably, though somewhat surprised.

'I thought you'd be away some time, Mrs Cheviot. 'Ave ye just got back?'

'Yes. The place is deserted. I knew the staff had been given leave but surely the local cleaners are coming in as usual?'

'Well, I saw two of 'em comin' up the drive this mornin', but when the cat's away I suppose the mice'll play.'

'What do you mean by that, Riley?'

'Well, Mr Cheviot's away for a few days. Gone up to Scotland, I believe.'

'I didn't know. Are you all alone here, Riley?'

'I can manage, ma'am. In fact I manages a lot better

without 'er. She's a good opinion of 'erself and doesn't take kindly to advice. I'd 'ave preferred to bring my niece in fro' Ilkley. Bin used to 'orses all 'er life she 'as, and I could 'ave relied on 'er.'

'You can't rely on Freda, Riley?'

'Oh, she's right enough, but I gets two words for one back when she needs to be chastised. The boss is amused by 'er instead o' backin' me up.'

I nodded. I'd had experience of Freda's insolence but I was surprised Paul was prepared to condone it.

'Can you manage here on your own, Riley?'

'That I can, ma'm.'

I had the strangest feeling that there was something more he could have said but whatever it was he decided to ask ''Ow's the baby, Mrs Cheviot? I expect 'is grandmother's bin glad to see 'im?'

'Oh, yes, Riley. Yes, she has. He's very well, getting stronger all the time.'

'That's good, ma'am. I think the master said 'e'd be back next Wednesday, 'e'll be glad to find ye at 'ome.'

I smiled and turned away. My husband would be completely indifferent to find us at home. He had got what he wanted. That Robin and I went with it would hardly matter.

Paul returned and seemed surprised to find me there. He was cynical about my mother as I knew he would be, but apart from that he asked no questions and I told him nothing of our visit to Surrey. By the same token I asked no questions about his stay in Scotland and received no information in return.

The weather was awful. Driving rain and sleet, crashing seas mingled with the sounds of lorries crunching across the parkland and hammers and other tools used by an army of workmen. I felt sorry for them sheltering under tarpaulins, the rain dripping from sodden souwesters, their feet slipping and sliding in mud and clay.

With my return the cleaners set about cleaning and polishing and gradually something of its old sparkle returned to the deserted rooms. In the kitchens I produced huge pans of soup which were taken down to the builders' huts for the workmen and Paul grinned, saying that they'd never had such molly-coddling.

In early February on a day when a pale watery sun shone fitfully on frozen fields and smouldering grey seas, Aunt Corallie arrived. She swept into the house smothered in furs, her fine grey eyes wide with surprise, ready to do battle with the man who was destroying Reckmire.

Paul listened to her tirade without speaking until she had finished, then without raising his voice he said irritably, 'Reckmire is our place Corallie, and it's up to us to do what we want with it. It's no longer a house, it's a business enterprise, and we've got to be one step ahead of any competition. Why don't you reserve your judgement until it's finished?'

'How can you expect your wife and child to sleep with the sound of building going on night and day? And when the electricity is turned off and the water? How can you expect a baby to live in this environment?'

'I don't. Joanna went to her mother's, I didn't expect her home.'

'If you expected Linda to have her and the baby for four months, you don't know very much about your mother-in-law!'

'Only what you told me, Corallie, what all of you told me long before I met her daughter.'

'Then you must have known she'd not stay very long. You're hard and ruthless, Paul, you don't care about anything or anybody outside your ambitions. I would have thought at least you'd care something about your son's welfare?'

'If you're so concerned, what suggestions can you offer? The nursery is comfortable enough. If she wants another nurse for the baby she knows she's only to ask.'

'She doesn't have to ask, Paul. This is her house, her money. All she wants from you is consideration. A little tenderness wouldn't come amiss either.'

'This is our house, Corallie, our money, and all I'm doing is turning a small country hotel, charming, pleasant, comfortable enough, into the best there is anywhere in the country. If she can't stand it for another six or seven weeks then I suggest she moves out. As you've just said, she can afford it.'

'You're cold, Paul,' she stormed, 'cold and hard. Joanna's only just getting over the birth of the baby and he's only five months old. I intend to take her back with me when I go at the end of the week, and she won't be back until you've accomplished what you've set out to do.'

'Well, I think that's a splendid suggestion,' he said with a satisfied smile. 'I'll be sure to let her know when the place is habitable again, and the staff have returned and she can once more become the lady of the manor.'

In some desperation I cried, 'Really, Aunt Corallie, I can manage very well. I can't possibly go to Italy for seven or eight weeks.'

'Indeed you can, Joanna, and think of the baby. He'll be far better off there than lying in that room upstairs with mayhem going on outside the window. You can be ready to travel in a couple of days and I'll telephone Rinaldo and ask him to arrange for us to be met in Florence.'

Paul smiled across at me. 'There you are, my dear, you're off to Italy. This is a good example of the way the Albemarles have always had of rearranging people's lives. You might find the weather unpredictable in February but at least you'll be cossetted. Spare me a thought now and again while I'm trying to resurrect Reckmire.'

Aunt Corallie merely favoured him with a look of pure dislike and I realised going to Italy was the best solution open to me. I could not exist or expect my baby to exist in the present circumstances, but in Italy there was danger to my heart and as I met Paul's amused gaze I became afraid.

The following day I drove with Aunt Corallie into Kendal. 'We shan't be away long,' she said cheerfully, 'and you've got that nice village girl to look after Robin.'

Indeed Alice had said, 'I'm that glad yer goin' out, Mrs Cheviot. You've bin lookin' ever so peeky and it's a nice day.'

'Thank you, Alice, we shan't be away long but I'm going to spend a few weeks in Italy and there are some things we'll need.'

She stared at me doubtfully and I was quick to say, 'We

shall still need you. You'll have work in the hotel, and when we get back I'll be glad to have you look after Robin again.'

'I thought p'raps you didn't think I was up to it, Mrs Cheviot?'

'Alice, I'm delighted with the way you've been coping, but this stay in Italy is my aunt's idea. Now I'm looking forward to it.'

Kendal was only a small country town and Aunt Corallie was quick to say, 'Don't worry if you can't get everything you want, Joanna, you can always shop in Italy. We'll have coffee in that little cafe we've just passed, it'll help to keep the cold out.'

The cafe was warm and cosy and we had only just sat down when a cheerful voice hailed us, saying, 'Mrs Cheviot, how nice to see you.'

I looked up to see Lena Falshaw looking down at us, smiling affably, and before I could answer she had pulled one of the empty chairs out and taken her place at the table.

I performed introductions and she said breathlessly, 'I've been rushing round like mad shopping for Aunt Josie. They're off tomorrow on a cruise to the Med and she's a hopeless packer. She always forgets something.'

She chatted on about one thing after another until she said, 'I see the workmen have started on Reckmire. It's going to be quite something when they've finished.'

I smiled. 'Was your uncle very disappointed that Paul decided to stay with Reckmire instead of joining him in that other enterprise?'

'Which enterprise was that then?' she asked in some surprise.

'Why, Sir Alec's place. Paul said it was on the market and he and your uncle were interested.'

'Oh, my uncle's always dreaming up things he's interested in but the hotel business isn't one of them. I'm sure you're mistaken, Mrs Cheviot, I've heard nothing about it.'

'But I'm sure when you and my husband were visiting Dunshaw earlier on they were talking about doing something together.'

'Yes that's right. My uncle sold him a horse, Maxton.

You rode him that afternoon when I rode yours. They were haggling about the price. My uncle wanted his pound of flesh but in the end he capitulated and your husband got him at the price he offered. Gracious me, Uncle George would never be interested in the hotel business, he's far too indolent.'

Once again Paul had lied to me to get his own way and the sense of betrayal was so acute I felt like screaming with the pain of it. The conversation at the table flowed over my head while my aunt and Lena talked casually, and now and again I was aware of Aunt Corallie's eyes searching my face curiously.

At last Lena Falshaw went, and I made myself smile and answer her words of farewell, then Aunt Corallie leaned forward, asking anxiously, 'Is something wrong, Joanna? You don't look well.'

'Can we go home now, Aunt Corallie? We've finished our shopping.'

'Well, of course, dear. Did that woman say anything to bother you?'

'No. I misunderstood Paul about something, I'll sort it out when we get back.'

Without another word we rose from the table and made our way out of the cafe, hurrying to where we had parked the car while all the time I was aware of her anxiety and my own blinding anger.

I didn't want Aunt Corallie there when I spoke to him, so immediately we arrived back at the house I left her opening her parcels while I marched across the churned up parkland towards the building office where I thought he might be. He was in conversation with two other men when I entered and they all stared at me curiously.

'I need to talk to you, Paul,' I said urgently. With annoyance he said testily, 'I'm busy right now, Joanna, can't it wait?'

'No.'

He looked at his companions with a resigned smile. 'The lady of the house has spoken. Can you give me a few minutes?'

348

They went, and raising his eyebrows he said, 'Really, Joanna, is this necessary? Couldn't it have waited until I got back to the house?'

'You've lied to me for the last time, Paul. You never had any intention of going into business with Lena Falshaw's uncle. All you wanted was your half of Reckmire and you didn't much mind how you got it. You can't deny it.'

'Have I tried to deny it?'

His effrontery made me suddenly speechless, and taking advantage of it he said evenly, 'I work better when I'm in command, Joanna. I don't like being subordinate to anybody, least of all my own wife. If lying to you meant that I won, then I was prepared to lie to you.'

'Even if it was dishonest?' I snapped.

'Even then. Don't you realise even now that I did it for us? I'm prepared to put everything I have into this venture. You were not even willing to put my name on the deeds. How did you find out, by the way?'

'We met Lena Falshaw in Kendal. She told me it was Maxton you were haggling about, and only Maxton.'

'Oh, well, it's done now so there's no point in arguing about it.'

He was brushing me aside, picking up the plans he'd been looking at with the two men, indicating that my anger was too trivial to interrupt his work, and with as much contempt as he would have brushed away a bothersome insect.

'Can we get on with what we were doing now, Joanna?' he asked calmly.

'Paul, that is the last time you will ever lie to me.'

'I doubt if I'll ever need to lie to you again, my dear. I'm eminently satisfied with the way things are going.'

I turned on my heel and left him with as much dignity as I could summon up. It was hopeless, our marriage was hopeless and the future was sterile and joyless. He had half of Reckmire, I had my son and the other half, that was the sum total of it.

I was relieved that my Aunt was tactful enough to ask no questions although she knew my anger concerned Paul.

The day before we left for Italy I went into the village with flowers for the church. The two women arranging them

349

thanked me shortly and then disappeared with them to the other end of the church. It was left to Mrs Peabody who I met walking along the path outside to say, 'The vicar's sick visitin', Mrs Cheviot. I've just seen 'im goin' into old Mrs Haslam's.'

'I didn't come to see the vicar, Mrs Peabody, I brought flowers for the church.'

'You'll 'ave come along the main street then. What did ye think about the state of it?'

'I thought it was quite dreadful but it will be put right as soon as the workmen have finished at Reckmire.'

'We only 'as your word for that,' she said truculently.

'My word is all you need, Mrs Peabody. The road will be put right if I have to pay for it myself.'

'Eh, Mrs Cheviot, but it's a shame what's happenin' to that lovely old house. Doesn't it make yer heart break to see it, or don't yer mind what he does?'

'Good morning, Mrs Peabody. You have my word that the road will be repaired.'

I left her staring after me, her large florid face sorrowful, and the next morning as Paul watched us leave for the airport I asked him for his assurance that repairs to the road would be carried out.

'Well, of course they will,' he said testily. 'I don't want any of our guests to see the village looking as though a bomb had hit it. They'll have to be patient. If I have any hassle from Mrs Peabody, she'll have to deal with my solicitors.'

I turned my head away sharply as he bent to kiss me, so that his lips found contact with the side of my head, and if Aunt Corallie saw she kept her thoughts to herself.

As the plane took off into a cold grey sky my spirits lifted. Easter was late this year. There would be eight weeks when I would try to forget the trauma of the last few weeks, eight weeks without the sound of hammering disturbing the early morning and the sight of Paul's uncaring face across the dining table.

Eight weeks to absorb the peace of the Italian countryside. I was unafraid of the danger to my heart.

Chapter Thirty-One

I was remembering Italy in the beauty of her summertime and the golden splendour of her rolling hills and blue blue sea. I was unprepared for the chill wind and the showers that blotted out the distant views of cathedral towers.

Although Aunt Corallie reassured me that Uncle Rinaldo was much improved in health I could not believe it since he looked increasingly frail and he seemed to spend every day sitting besides the window looking out across the parkland.

Occasionally he would pick up a book but nothing seemed to interest him for very long, and when I tried to engage him in conversation I would see his eyes close and knew he was sleeping.

My aunt refused to admit that his health was deteriorating and it was Carlo who voiced his fears to me one evening after dinner while we strolled along the gallery looking at old family portraits.

'I'm worried about him,' Carlo said seriously. 'Corallie says the doctors are satisfied with his condition, but there is no life in him. I think she should send for Gabriella.'

'You think it is so serious?' I asked.

'Yes, I do. Corallie is afraid Gabriella's presence would upset him, but if she doesn't come soon she may not see her father alive.'

His words were brought back forcibly when during the next night I heard a scream and, rushing out of my room into the corridor, saw Aunt Corallie running along it, her nightgown floating ethereally, her face distraught, eyes wild with tears. Uncle Rinaldo had died in his sleep.

I had always thought that my aunt would be able to cope with everything, she had always seemed so sure of herself. Now she was a bewildered shadow of the Aunt Corallie I had known and it was left to Carlo to arrange my uncle's funeral and inform Gabriella that her father was dead. We did not hear from her and until the day before the funeral we did not know if she would come.

She arrived that evening. It was late and the servants had locked up for the night when we heard the sound of a car stopping in the courtyard. Aunt Corallie, who was sitting huddled in her chair, looked at me with surprise in her reddened eyes.

'Who on earth is it at this hour?' she whispered. Then we heard the clamour of the doorbell sounding in the stillness of the house.

'I'll go, Aunt Corallie,' I said quickly, and by this time we heard the sound of the butler's measured tread crossing the hall, and the creak of bolts being drawn back.

I hurried out into the hall in time to see the manservant taking a small suitcase out of the hand of a woman standing staring round the hall, then her eyes met mine and although I knew her immediately there was no sign of recognition in hers.

I smiled, stepping forward to meet her, saying, 'I'm so glad you've come, Gabriella, your mother is in the salon.'

'Who are you?' she asked haughtily.

'Joanna, your cousin. Have I changed so much?'

She stared at me for several moments before her face relaxed into a smile, then she came forward to embrace me.

'I wouldn't have known you, Joanna, but then you were just a schoolgirl when we were last together.'

At that moment Aunt Corallie came out into the hall, and immediately with a little cry ran forward to take her daughter into her arms.

We talked long into the night and by that time I had begun to realise that this was not the old Gabriella. This was a woman who had learned to survive in a world where old values were forgotten. She smoked constantly, lighting one cigarette from another she was discarding, and I could see that the glowing beauty of her youth had been replaced by a lean sophistication. When she talked her hands gesticulated to emphasise her words and in those few hours before the dawn I learned about a life totally alien from my own.

She had waited for her husband to come out of prison but he had not gone to her but to his mistress, some woman she had not known existed. Too proud to ask her parents for help she had found work in an art gallery but the pay had been poor. She was not a professional woman, all she had was an old and honourable name, but now questions were being asked about her marriage to a fascist who had been tried and found guilty of wartime offences.

With some bravado she glossed over the trauma of her existence in those early years after the war, and tearfully Aunt Corallie asked: 'Why didn't you come home, Gabriella? Your father was bitter but he would have forgiven you. Why don't you come home now?'

She shook her head. 'It wouldn't be the same, Mother. I've made a new life for myself, I have new friends, I'm living with a man. Oh, we haven't any money, he's a musician, a good one, there isn't always work − but we are happy. There are times when we are poor, then we quarrel and fight, but at other times we are so happy together. We have fun, we drink wine in the little squares in the hills above Rome, and we have friends who are like us.'

Corallie was staring at her, trying hard to reconcile this newfound daughter with the one she remembred, and with pain in her voice she cried, 'Oh, Gabriella, none of this should have happened. You should have been here with us, waiting for Carlo to come back from the war. We did so want you to be the Contessa Varasi.'

'Try to understand, Mother, that I was already flawed. I didn't want to wait for some wounded hero to come home to me. I thought after the war the old order would change. Didn't they tell us it would? Didn't you and father believe that the old families would count for nothing? I believed if I was part of the new order, at least you and father would not suffer.'

'Then how can you say you were flawed when you did it for us?' Aunt Corallie cried.

'Because I should have been too proud to want to be one of them. I should have stayed with you, defiant, unyielding, waiting for them to do their worst, watching them take our possessions, waiting for the day when there would be no contes and contessas, only comrades. I understand why my father was too proud to forgive me, why Carlo won't forgive me.'

'Carlo does not mention you, Gabriella. He has been very kind, has taken all the burden of the funeral arrangements off my shoulders, but you will see him tomorrow. I hope at least that you can be friends.'

Gabriella shrugged her shoulders with a small tight-lipped smile and my heart sank. Would Carlo look at her and remember that he had loved her, could love her again? Could I bear to see that happening?

I had never seen an Italian cemetery before and was unprepared for the intricate masonry of tombs for prominent noblemen and less pretentious ones showing pictures of the deceased and bearing offerings of flowers and garlands.

The Flamouri tomb was a large white marble edifice in a prominent position and when we arrived the cemetery paths were lined with black-clad women wearing veils on their heads and men standing bare-headed in the cold. They stood with bent heads as our procession moved slowly forward to the tomb and the bell tolled dismally from the high campanile.

Gabriella walked in front, holding her mother's arm. They were both heavily veiled. I walked behind with Uncle Rinaldo's nephew, and behind us Carlo walked alone. I had watched earlier when he bowed without smiling over Gabriella's hand, not offering to kiss her cheek, and I wondered how much pain there was in their meeting.

It was over at last, the prayers and the committal, and we were driving away down the long hill and along the quiet road towards the castello in the distance. I was wishing Aunt Marcia could have been there but she was in bed with influenza and Aunt Corallie had said neither of them should think of coming.

A repast had been laid out for us in the hall and I

354

admired Aunt Corallie's composure as she circulated among her guests, encouraging them to eat although she ate nothing herself.

Across the room Gabriella chatted to Carlo, his handsome dark head bent slightly to hear her words, interested but expressionless, and as she talked her hands gesticulated nervously as they had the evening before in the salon.

I was left to observe the proceedings alone since my Italian was practically non-existent and the people present had known each other for years. Aunt Corallie joined me, saying, 'This is difficult for you, Joanna. Most of them speak only a little English. I shall be glad when it is all over and they begin to leave.'

'Has Gabriella said how long she can stay?' I asked curiously.

'She is going back to Rome in the morning.'

I stared at her dismayed. 'So soon? But I thought she would have stayed on now that you are alone.'

'I hoped so, but there must be pressing reasons for her to return. I have been foolish. I thought she would stay to rediscover the life she once knew, even the love she once knew. Instead Gabriella will go back to Rome and her musician and Carlo will go back to his lonely castello and his regrets.'

'It is hard to go back, Aunt Corallie, to expect things to stay the same.'

'And she is nervous when she speaks to him, and he is polite. Hardly the attitudes of two people wishing to rekindle a lost love.'

We remained silent, both of us aware of the two people across the room, his polite bow as she sauntered away, her easy careless smile, and my aunt murmured sadly, 'Nothing is left, Joanna, only ashes. Tomorrow she will return to Rome but this time I can't lose her. She is my daughter and she's already been too long out of my life.'

One by one and in groups the people began to drift away, and then Carlo was there, raising Corallie's hand to his lips, assuring her of his help should she need it. Then he was bowing over my hand, saying evenly, 'I shall see you soon, Joanna. I'm glad that you are here at this time.'

His words were casual, hardly burdened with deep feeling, and yet his dark eyes gazing into mine said so much more. Or so I believed. Bemused and uncertain, I watched him walk away from us across the room and then Aunt Corallie's voice brought the treacherous colour into my cheeks.

'You love him, Joanna. I have known for some time. Oh, I know that you loved him once when you didn't know anything about love, but this is different. Now you exist in that soulless, joyless marriage with your heart crying out for love, and whatever the outcome, I will not blame you.'

I stared at her helplessly. 'He is kind, Aunt Corallie. That is not love.'

'I am aware of it, but Carlo is a man who is adept at hiding his thoughts. You are a married woman with a child. You will have to be the one to tell him that your marriage is as empty as your life.'

'And then?'

'Then you might see the real Carlo emerge from that cloak of reserve he has cocooned himself in since he came back after the war. Rinaldo and I waited for the Carlo we knew for so long but all we had was a cold remote stranger. All too slowly he is returning. Perhaps you will be the one to bring him back to us.'

'He may not love me. The trauma of my marriage may only embarrass him.'

'Perhaps, but it would be so awful if you never knew.'

Her smile was gentle before she turned away, then she was joining Gabriella in the doorway to say goodnight to their guests.

I went into Robin's room before I retired, and the young Italian girl who had been looking after him smiled prettily, saying, 'Your baby has been good, Signora. I took him into the park, not once did he cry.'

'I'm so glad, thank you for looking after him. Your English is very good.'

'I would like to be English nanny, work in England when my training is finished.'

'When will that be?'

'I have permission to stay until you go home, this is practice for me. If you give me good report at the end it will be helpful.'

'I shall be glad to. Is your home in Tuscany?'

'In Orvieto. My name is Teresa.'

'Thank you for all your help, Teresa. I'm so glad my aunt knew how to find you.'

'It is honour to work for the Contessa Flamouri. My father work in the vineyards, my mother too when she was younger.'

I smiled at her enthusiasm and bade her goodnight.

It had been a sad day and a long one. I had thought I would be ready for bed long before midnight but I was not tired. I felt suddenly very wide awake, and when there was a knock on my bedroom door while I sat at my dressing table brushing my hair I was glad to see Gabriella.

She came into the room, perching unceremoniously on my bed, smoking a cigarette held in a long amber cigarette holder.

'I hope you don't mind if I finish my cigarette, Joanna? I smoke far too much. Would you like one?'

'No, thank you, I've never enjoyed them.'

'I suppose Mother's told you I'm going home to Rome tomorrow?'

'Yes. I was surprised. I hoped you'd stay on for a while.'

'That's what Mother hoped too. I promised Stefano I'd get back as soon as the funeral was over. He's a baby when I'm not there. Very insecure, God knows how he'll cope when I'm out of his life for good.'

I stared at her. 'You intend to go out of his life?' I asked curiously.

'There's nothing permanent about us. He's amusing, talented too, but filled with frustrations when his talent isn't harnessed.'

'Don't you love him?'

Her laughter was altogether cynical. 'He came into my life at the right time, when I needed somebody, when I thought I'd suffered so much I couldn't suffer any more. Like I said before, we're happy together. We laugh a lot, drink a lot, surround ourselves with people like us. But love is something else.'

'Your mother would like to visit you in Rome.'

'I know, she would like to come back with me, but I can't allow her to see where we live, how we live. My mother loves Rome, the fountains and the shops, the life that strolls and saunters through the Borghese Gardens, the museums and galleries, the limousines on Vittorio Veneto, the Christmas market in Navona Square and the array of flowers on the Spanish steps. She has no concept of the back streets of Rome, the poverty, the pent up anger of a generation of men and women who were promised the earth and received nothing.

'My father punished me for years because I married Andrae Amerigo without remembering that he'd brought me up to want the best and be satisfied with nothing less. While Carlo's treasures went my father retained his, thanks to my marriage to Andrae. After the war it was to be a new order. Andrae would be somebody, I would be somebody, Italy would own a third of the world. You can't even begin to imagine how desolate life was when it fell to pieces around our ears.

'Andrae was sent to prison and for five long years I was ostracsised by my parents, spat upon by the newfound lords of creation who had believed in that same fascism they now spurned.

'I waited for them to release him, then he turned on me, cursing me for being my father's daughter, part of the old order he had hated and rejected. He went to Maria Capprionelli. I didn't know it but she had been his mistress for years.'

'Where are they now?'

'South America. Italy was too hot to hold him. You will never understand a hatred strong enough to make you want to kill. Even now, when I think about him I could kill him, without mercy or pity, not because I ever loved him but because he took me away from a life I can never return to. He took away my girlhood, my faith in innocence, my belief in values that mattered. You'll never understand, Joanna.'

I didn't speak, but I did understand an anger at the

betrayal of trust, a blind fury that a man could use her without either love or understanding, and in that moment I knew that an anger like that could make me kill too. Her voice faded into the background, the room I was in became nothing but a shadow and I was staring into Paul's face: arrogant, amused eyes that were narrowed into tantilising indifference, his mouth cold, etched with a cynical smile, and I could have killed then. With a weapon in my hands I could have watched that smiling face disintegrate into bloody insignificance.

'Joanna, what is it? Why are you looking at me like that?'

With a mighty effort I pulled myself together, staring at her face, wide-eyed with surprise.

'It's nothing. I understand how you felt, that's all.'

She got up from the bed and started to pace around the room.

'My mother has told me that my father left me nothing in his will but she will change it now since all his money was left to her. He would have expected it anyway, he knew that she would never let it stand. When everything has been sorted out she will see that I am financially catered for, then I must think about leaving Stefano.'

'He means so little to you?'

'We were never destined to spend the rest of our lives together. I shall give him money which will be quickly spent. For a while he will live well, his friends will be invited to join in his newfound prosperity, and then when the money is spent he will hope one of the women who have helped him to spend it will stay with him. I have no illusions about Stefano. Do you know the worst thing he can say to me when he is angry with me? That I'm a high-class bitch with a body and no heart.'

'Is that when you will come home?' I asked quietly.

'Here to Tuscany? Heavens no, I'd stagnate. My mother would like me to come home, she'd like to think that Carlo would love me again and that one day I'd be the Contessa Varasi. It's a forlorn hope. I shan't come back and Carlo will never love me.'

'So, what will you do?'

'I'm not sure. For a while I'll get out of Italy, somewhere where Stefano won't come looking for me hoping for hand-outs. France perhaps, maybe America. Somewhere where money talks, somewhere where I can find a man richer than me so that I'll know he isn't marrying me for my money. I suppose that strikes you as being entirely mercenary but I'm not looking for a lame duck, I've already had a surfeit of those.'

'I'm only surprised that you should be looking for a man at all,' I murmured.

She laughed. 'Not ostensibly perhaps. A rich man who would adore me, shower me with jewels, escort me to all the right places. With my sort of luck I'll probably fall in love with a handsome artist starving in a garret somewhere, a man who would be desperate for admiration, somebody to bolster up his shattered ego, buy his wretched pictures to make sure he stayed with me.'

She laughed, then suddenly her expression changed. 'Gracious me, Joanna, I've spent all this time talking about me and I haven't said a word about you. You married Paul Cheviot. I must say I was surprised.'

'Why?'

'Well, I seem to remember you were rather less than good friends. You didn't like him and he could be pretty moody and difficult. He chased after me at one time, but it was when I was at Reckmire and I suppose I was different and there was never anything in it. I always thought he was ruthless, totally unlike Robin, and yet they were friends.'

'Yes, they were different.'

'And you're happy, Joanna? Mother told me about the hotel.'

'You wouldn't recognise Reckmire. It's been very successful and now he's tearing some of it to pieces to make a ballroom. The deer have gone.'

'That's terrible. People came to see the deer. And why does he have such a big say anyway? Didn't they leave the place to you?'

'Yes, but I had no idea what I'd do with it. Making it into a hotel has been Paul's idea.'

'Well, don't be so grateful that you allow him to ride

roughshod over you. I've gone through that and it doesn't work. One day, Joanna, I might just pay you a visit, see how the old place has changed, scandalise the village with my Italian car, Italian clothes, and foreign flamboyance.'

I laughed, Mrs Peabody's face coming instantly to mind.

'I wish Mother would get away for a while, there are so many memories here,' she said sadly. 'Would you be willing to go with her, Joanna?'

'Well, yes, if she doesn't mind about having a young baby in tow.'

'Carlo was talking about it earlier this evening. He has a villa near Positano. I wouldn't be surprised if he didn't offer it to her for a few weeks. It's very beautiful, the most beautiful coastline in the world. You'd love it.'

My heart was racing. The Gulf of Solerno had always been a dream in my heart but I had only ever seen pictures of it. Slides in the schoolroom of Vesuvius overlooking the bay of Naples, the island of Capri and the tiny villages clinging to the rocks on that glorious drive from Sorrento to Amalfi. We had listened entranced while a besotted teacher had kept us enthralled with her stories of the holiday she had just spent there, and now here was Gabriella linking that long-lost moment with the present.

Chapter Thirty-Two

We drove to the south on a morning golden with sunlight, when the Mediterranean lay placid and blue below us. My baby son slept in my arms for most of the journey, but before we reached Naples his Italian nurse took him from me, saying gently, 'So that you can see how beautiful it is, Signora. I have seen it before, many times.'

We ate in the early-afternoon at a small taverna overlooking the Bay of Naples with Vesuvius dreaming in the background and I found it hard to remember that this tired old volcano had created so much havoc in the past and not so very long ago. As if he guessed my thoughts Carlo said, 'You should see Pompeii, Joanna. It is hard to imagine how those poor people on a golden day such as this could have died so tragically.'

We drove onwards past olive groves sleeping in the sun's warmth, through towns and villages of warm red stone, and Carlo pointed to where Capri lay sheltering in the early-evening mist. The tortuous winding road led onwards, but always round every curve there was a new vista to delight our senses, and at last, above Positano, we came to the villa.

It was almost too beautiful. Sheltering amid pine groves, fountains tinkled deliciously over marble steps and from the terrace we could see the gardens tumbling down the hillside to where lights were strung out along the shore, glittering and gleaming like a jewelled necklace. In the scented dark we sat listening to the cicadas and from somewhere below the haunting tune of an old Neapolitan love song only added to the magic.

After two weeks Aunt Corallie said that it was imperative she returned to Florence. She looked happier and assured us she felt better but there were many things she needed to attend to in Florence, particularly where her lawyers were concerned. Immediately Carlo said we would all return, but she quickly said, 'I want Joanna to stay here. Both she and the baby are looking so well now and she's happy here. Please let me have my way about this. I shall be very sad if you leave Positano because of me.'

Later that evening she came into my room with a selection of sun hats and sun lotions. 'You might as well make use of these, Joanna. I shall not want them again, and the sun is getting stronger every day.'

'Must you go back, Aunt Corallie? You'll be all alone in the castello.'

'I have a lot to do. I want to sort out my money. Rinaldo left everything to me but I intend Gabriella to have her share. Do you know she did not want me to go to Rome, and I can only think it's because she is ashamed of the way she lives. I am not happy about her living with this musician and don't want her to squander her money on people like him. I have to make sure about a great many things.'

'I think you will find that Gabriella knows exactly what she wants from life, Aunt Corallie.'

'I think you're probably right, but what do you want, Joanna? Will you go back to Reckmire to linger on in that loveless, sterile marriage or will you snatch at the happiness that waits for you here?'

'Why are you so sure that Carlo loves me?'

She smiled. 'How does a proud man tell a woman he is in love with her when she is of a different race, is married to somebody else and has a child to care for?'

'I don't know.'

'In five weeks, Joanna, you may find out. That is another reason why I am going home. To give you time together. There are many barriers to break down: pride, reserve, on his part, on yours all the inhibitions your mother placed around you, and the courage it takes to end your cold joyless marriage. How much courage do you have?'

I didn't answer her. There had been so many times when I

had had to call upon my courage, but did I have the courage for this? Not the courage to leave Paul, or Reckmire, but the courage to find out if Carlo wanted me, if he could love me, and that it was not some immature echo of the past that had stayed with me.

Aunt Corallie left us together, polite friends, Carlo in his role as host and travelling guide, me appreciative of his kindness and generosity but burdened with a world of doubt and uncertainty.

Carlo was the perfect host. Togther we went to Pompeii and wandered her ancient streets. We looked down into the crater of Vesuvius until the smell of sulphur became too much for us. In Carlo's yacht we sailed to the Island of Capri and spent an enchanting day wandering through the narrow thoroughfares, drinking wine in sunlit squares and exploring the villa of Tiberius where I received from an Italian who loved his country my first real history lesson on Ancient Rome.

The sunlit days fled by and I came no nearer to reaching behind his reserve and began to despair. It was on the morning I declined his invitation to go with him to Naples, saying that I would prefer to sit in the gardens with my son, that he said with a brief smile, 'You should have told me you were tired of sight-seeing, Joanna.'

'Oh, but I'm not, I've loved it, but today it will be so beautiful just to sit here and absorb the scenery and Naples is so terribly busy.'

He smiled again, then turning away he said briefly, 'I shall see you at dinner then.'

'Yes. You really don't mind?'

'Not in the least.'

I stood on the terrace watching his car weave its way along the tortuous bends in the road above the sea until I could see it no longer, then I returned to where my son lay sleeping under the sun canopy.

No longer the puny sickly baby I had fretted over in England, but a baby robust with health, his rounded limbs firm and glowing. And unbidden came the memory of Paul's indifference to the child.

I heard Carlo returning to the villa while I dressed for

dinner, and felt strangely nervous in case he had been annoyed that I had declined to accompany him into Naples. I need not have worried. His smile was as friendly as always, and as he passed over a glass of wine he chatted easily about the turmoil in the city streets, saying I had been sensible to stay away.

After dinner he excused himself on the grounds of having certain telephone calls to make and I wandered out on to the terrace to stand in the scented darkness looking down on a vista of lights twinkling around the bay, and on the hillside from innumerable villas and rambling streets.

I heard the sound of his footsteps crossing the terrace and then he was standing beside me, leaning on the terrace rail, looking out towards the sea, and there was a tightness in my throat like the sting of unshed tears.

I was unprepared for his voice, low and saying sadly, 'I dreamed about this place during the war. I couldn't think that when it was all over it would remain unchanged when everything else was changing so dramatically. You must surely have felt the same about Reckmire?'

'Yes. We were living in a time of limbo, but never for a single moment did I think we would lose the war. I never even realised that the people we were at war with might feel the same way.'

His expression was bitter, infinitely sad. 'I would like to have felt like that, Joanna, but I had no faith in our ultimate victory. There was no heart in it, and no reason for it. The war was destroying so much beauty and culture in our country. War is a destroyer and only a destroyer. They have healed my body but there are other scars they could never heal.'

'Are you thinking about your possessions, your parents or Gabriella?'

He stared at me intently. 'Possessions can be replaced in time, my parents died when I was far away, but I was not thinking of Gabriella. A young foolish love affair is not something a man thinks of when he stares death in the face.'

'Is that all she meant to you?'

'That is all.'

I was staring up at him, his dark hair etched in moonlight. I could not see the expression in his eyes but like a lost child I went naturally into his arms. I could feel his heart thudding against mine as we clung together in that soft scented night and I had no thoughts beyond the towering passion our first kiss aroused in me. When at last he put me away from him to stand looking down at me, his hands on my shoulders, the old sickening doubts hit me like a knife. Was it the proximity of man and woman that had brought us together or was it something more? For my peace of mind I had to know. I could feel myself trembling and gently he said, 'You're cold, Joanna. Perhaps we should go inside.'

We moved back into the light from the window and seeing him calm and distant again, I cried urgently, 'I'm not tired, Carlo, I'm afraid. I love you, I've loved you for a very long time, but it was always so hopeless, don't you see?'

'Hopeless for you, do you mean, or for me?' he asked softly.

'For me. I thought you loved Gabriella.'

'But you are the one with a husband and a child. I at least am free to love where I choose.'

I felt as though he had slapped me, I felt wanton and ashamed, and without another word I went running into the villa, the tears streaming down my face, needing somewhere where I could hide. I threw myself on my bed in an agony of tears but he did not follow me. I cried alone, and it was during the long sleepless night that I realised that passion was not love and I had to know or go home.

I breakfasted alone and was told that the master had gone down to the harbour early and was on his boat. I finished my breakfast quickly, and snatching up a cotton jacket I made my way down the hillside to the harbour. I looked out at the array of yachts and power boats anchored there, finding Carlo's easily and seeing that the dinghy lay alongside and that he was on board in the company of two other men. I stood there uncertainly and then he saw me, holding up his arm in recognition, much as he might have done if there had been no night before.

One of the men jumped into the dinghy and began to head for the harbour wall where he invited me to clamber aboard, then we were heading back to the yacht and Carlo was reaching down to help me aboard. He introduced his companions but I never remembered their names. With easy camaraderie Carlo explained that they were involved in a regatta of sorts in the Bay of Solerno and as we left the shelter of the harbour I could see that we were in a procession of other yachts with similar intent.

I was handed a life jacket and from that moment I was part of a crew until later in the afternoon we swept past the finishing post in the lead. We were fêted by the others, champagne was drunk in large quantities, and then as the sun was setting in a blaze of glory I was shaking hands with our two companions whose names I still did not remember, and we were driving up the steep road towards the villa.

'We'll celebrate this evening,' Carlo said easily, 'There's a trattoria up in the hills that I'm particularly fond of. The food is excellent. Did you intend to come sailing with us?'

'I didn't even know there was a regatta. I wanted to talk to you.'

Not in the least disconcerted, he said evenly, 'We can talk up there in the hills just as well as we can talk here.'

On the way to my bedroom I called in to see my son who was fast asleep. His nurse looked up at me, smiling, 'You enjoyed today, Signora?'

'Yes, very much, Teresa. I'm sorry I didn't let you know, I didn't know myself that I would be going out in the yacht. Is everything all right?'

'Oh, yes. We sat in the garden, and he slept most of the afternoon. Tomorrow is Sunday. I must go to church in the morning.'

'Of course, Teresa, I will stay with him. And please, you must ask if you want time to yourself.'

'I am happy with things as they are. I go to church always, but I have no family here, I do not pay visits.'

I smiled and wished her goodnight.

Teresa had leapt at the chance to act as Robin's nursemaid, we were her work experience and she told me constantly how lucky she was to have found such work with a lovely baby and a nice English lady.

I was realising anew how precariously the houses clung

to the mountainside as we climbed ever upwards so that even the power of the Ferrari was taxed until at last we came to a trattoria lit with tiny twinkling bulbs, and where candlelight gleamed across table tops.

Carlo explained that in the summertime it would have been crowded but at this time of year only local people who knew its reputation would be dining. We were welcomed warmly by the proprieter and I felt that Carlo had been here many times, perhaps with other women to dine in intimate candlelight while below the Mediterannean lapped in gentle solitude around the bay.

We dined off tender roast lamb flavoured with rosemary, and vegetables that could only have been gathered that morning, cooked to perfection. We ate wild strawberries smothered in a delicate strawberry-flavoured liqueur and thick cream, then out on the terrace coffee and brandy were served to us and Carlo's eyes smiled into mine over the glass he was warming in his hands.

'It's so beautiful,' I murmured appreciatively. 'The Italians should be a happy people. They have this beautiful country and the sunshine, how can they not be happy in this laughing land?'

He shrugged his shoulders, answering slowly, 'Alas, Joanna, beauty and sunshine are not always enough. In many of our cities there is great poverty, the Mafia creates danger where there should be only peace, and yet under it all there is the strong heart of Italy beating under a land burdened with history. Once the world was ruled from the city of Rome. Britain had an empire on which the sun never set. In the end I think we must learn to accept that nothing is forever.'

'I learned that simple truth a long time ago.'

'Indeed. You learned not to reach for the moon, perhaps, but to take what was on offer on the way.'

I stared at him doubtfully. 'I'm not sure I understand you?'

You came looking for me after the war, Joanna, at a time when I shunned both people and life. You came bringing memories of happier times, and with the promise of a new and rare tenderness. I believed in you, I believed in your honesty and I came to feel that the time was right for us, but then you went home to England and had his child.'

I stared at him in shocked surprise.

'Carlo, you have to believe me, I was having his child when I came to Italy. My husband raped me on our wedding night, a night when there should have been love and tenderness. There are so many things to explain but one thing is very sure — Paul never loved me and I will never love him.'

'Why did you marry him?'

'You've told me that the war changed your life, don't you think it changed mine too? The hurt that made you turn away from your friends, made you want to be alone, was part of that change. For me it was other things: the need to get away from my mother. Then my grandparents died leaving Reckmire to me. I didn't know what I could do with it but I loved it and desperately wanted to keep it. Paul came to me with his advice and his ambitions. I owed him everything, his ideas for the hotel, all the work that went in to it, and I knew how much I needed him. I knew he loved Reckmire, I thought he had come to love me but learned that he didn't. He doesn't even love his son. He can't be bothered to look at him and that, I think, hurts the most.'

'But you'll go back to him?'

'I don't want to go back to him. I don't care if I never see him again.'

'And Reckmire?'

'There are so many things I could tell you about Reckmire. It would take a long time, but if there had been no war my life and yours, Paul's too, would have been very different.'

'And we would not be here on a warm scented night drinking brandy together in the moonlight,' he said with a gentle smile on his face.

'Now you're laughing at me.'

'No, Joanna, I'm not laughing at you. Before the war when you came here with your father I guessed you were in love with me, but you were so very young, only just on the threshold of life, and at that time there was Gabriella. I liked you, I listened to your aunts talking about your mother, talking about the end of your parents' marriage, and it seemed to me that you had so much growing up to do.

'When you came back here after the war I felt that seeking, wide-eyed little girl had gone forever. The woman who came towards me through the gardens was different. The growing up had been painful, sometimes sad, and you were still searching. When you said you had to forget me all over again you left me wondering if something of what you felt before was still there. Is that what you think, Joanna, do you still love me?'

'Yes, I do. I think I must love you all my life.'

My lips were trembling and tears were not very far away when he covered my hands with his. 'Come on,' he said hoarsely, 'we're going home.'

I rose and followed him, waiting while he paid the bill, then taking my arm he led me to the car. Within the darkness he took me in his arms and held me trembling against him. As we drove quickly down the hillside my heart felt like a singing bird.

I did not count the days, filled with sunshine and laughter, or the nights when I lay in his arms warm and tender after love, endless nights with nothing beyond.

I was totally unprepared for the telephone call from Aunt Corallie which informed me that the alterations to Reckmire were now complete and I should think of returning for the grand opening at Easter.

'How do you know all this?' I asked her fearfully.

'Paul telephoned. I told him you were shopping in Florence and he said it wasn't necessary for him to speak to you, he would tell me why he'd telephoned.'

'But you're back in Tuscany!' I exclaimed.

'Yes. Gabriella is with me. I can't tell you everything on the telephone but one day you'll hear all about it. Are you returning here, Joanna, or do you intend to go back from Naples?'

'Oh, Aunt Corallie, I don't know ...'

'I take it you and Carlo are in love and you don't really want to go back at all? But you have to go back, Joanna, you have to tell Paul what has happened, ask him for a divorce.'

'Yes, that's what I must do. I can't think that Paul will

be accommodating. He'll create difficulties. He doesn't love me but he'll never let me go.'

'Well, of course he will, dear, he'll not want to hang on to a wife who doesn't love him. You're not thinking of Reckmire, I hope? If the worst comes to the worst tell him he can have it. You can do that now, can't you?'

'Yes. Yes, I'm sure I can.'

'Well then, there's nothing to be afraid of. As soon as you've got things sorted out, do let me know. Good luck, Joanna.'

Carlo too was convinced that Paul would let me go. Why should he remain tied to a woman he didn't love and who didn't love him? Besides wasn't it Reckmire he'd always wanted?

I couldn't rid myself of the thought that nothing could be that easy. Paul was unpredictable, and as the plane winged its way back to England I made myself remember Carlo's tender smile as he held me in his arms at the airport.

'Don't worry, darling,' he'd said gently. 'When it's all over you'll both be coming back. We'll get married here in Italy. In the meantime remember that I love you, that I'm counting the days until you return.'

They were the words that sustained me on that long journey back to the marshes.

I had given Paul no information about when I intended to travel and he had asked for none. We arrived in London on a cold early-April day in the afternoon. Robin was fretful, and I decided to stay in London for the evening and travel north the next morning. I found a small comfortable hotel in Kensington and was glad to retire to my bedroom immediately after dinner. Next morning we were on the train for Lancaster where I had no trouble in getting a taxi to take us home.

It was market day in the village and the street was crowded with shoppers as the taxi wound its way towards the coast. They came from surrounding villages to the market and none of those busy shoppers spared us a second glance.

I stared across the parkway at the unfamiliar sight of the stone extension at the back of the house with its ornate domed room and the huge car park behind it. The character of Reckmire had gone, now it was just another hotel. As we turned in at the lodge gate and drove up the drive I felt that in some subtle way I was not going to like what was waiting for me.

A porter hurried down to the taxi to see to my luggage, and then the manager was there smiling his welcome and another porter to help me alight with my son from the car.

'Welcome home, Mrs Cheviot,' the manager said. 'Mr Cheviot said you were coming back but didn't say when.'

'He didn't know, Mr Gainsborough. I'm glad to see that you're still with us.'

He smiled but didn't speak, yet I had the distinct impression that he would have liked to have said something, something he'd decided to keep to himself.

Robin was sleeping so I laid him down on a settee in the reception area before looking around. I gasped with dismay. This was not the Reckmire I loved, the Reckmire that had been a home, it was not even the Reckmire that had been a country hotel.

Gone was the curved beautifully carved oak staircase that everybody had openly admired, to be replaced by a gilt ornate affair that matched the tall gilt standard lamps in the lounge and the gilt tables with their marble and onyx tops. Once a rich turkey red carpet had been fitted down the centre leaving an expanse of richly stained oak, but now from either side stretched a thick carpet in shades of jade and russet, the same carpet that covered the hall. My portrait had gone, and in its place hung an impressionist painting of some unrecognisable objects although I had no doubt it had been expensive.

My eyes met the manager's who was quite obviously watching my face for its reaction.

Urbane as always, he said nothing, and then looking upwards I saw a large portly man slowly descending the stairs. I stared at him. I felt I must know him, but he came towards me unsmiling and with a little bow Mr Gainsborough moved way, leaving us together. His eyes were familiar, cold pale blue eyes in a face that seemed to be etched in granite, then when his grim mouth relaxed I recognised him. Paul's father.

To say that I was surprised to see him was an understatement. Before I could say anything, he commented easily, 'You're surprised. I arrived yesterday evening. I had sosme business in Lancaster so I thought it was time to take a look at this enterprise. Paul told me his wife and son were in Italy but you were expected back today. I suppose you got out while the alterations were going on?'

'Yes. Are you staying for a few days?'

'I have to get back in the morning. Paul's away for the day so perhaps you'll allow me to be your guide to the transformation?'

'I'll order tea for you, Mr Cheviot. I'll join you in the lounge just as soon as I've changed out of these travelling clothes.'

He was Robin's grandfather but I didn't wish him to see Robin at that moment. We had written to tell him of the baby's birth but received nothing in reply and I could only feel he was as indifferent to the child as Paul himself. I asked for tea to be served to us in the lounge then hurried upstairs to change my clothes, leaving Robin in the care of Alice who had come running down the stairs to meet us.

Mr Cheviot sat with his open newspaper and I went to him immediately and started to pour the tea. Conversation did not come easily and I was glad when he suggested we look over the hotel.

We walked through the rooms in silence. My companion's face was expressionless but I had never been more angry in my life. The paintings my grandfather had collected and loved had gone and in their place were modern prints that would have screamed at the old Reckmire but which were adequate for what the house had become.

Polished walnut and mahogany had given way to teak, onyx and marble, and the lushness was degenerate instead of tasteful. The new ballroom had a dais at one end to accommodate a group or an orchestra and at the side was another room with gaming tables and a bar. Small tables and chairs edged the dance floor and overhead hung intricate modern chandeliers.

Still we didn't speak, but as we walked back to the hall Mr

373

Cheviot said dryly, 'I wonder what he'd have accomplished in the weaving sheds if I'd have given him a free hand? You hate it, don't you?'

'Yes, it's horrible.'

'Then why did you allow it. It belongs to you, doesn't it?'

'It belongs to both of us.'

'So he got it out of you, did he?'

I didn't answer.

'Well, he'll be back this evening expecting to find you enthusiastic, he doesn't take kindly to adverse criticism, so if you'll excuse me, as soon as dinner's over I'll go to my room.'

'There's no need for that, Mr Cheviot. What I have to say to Paul will keep until tomorrow, I wouldn't dream of spoiling your last evening here.'

'My dear girl, nothing you could say will spoil things for me. I didn't come here expecting to be entertained, I came out of curiosity and I've seen all I want to see. He had me to reckon with at the mills. I curbed his ambitions because I regarded them as unnecessary. I tried to get him to see things my way because they'd worked for me, but he wanted me off the board. In twelve months everything I'd ever achieved and worked for would have been history. I'm speaking the truth, Joanna.'

'Yes, Mr Cheviot, I know you are.'

We had already started dinner when Paul arrived at the table, raising his eyebrows maddeningly at the sight of me, taking his place opposite with the words, 'So my wife has decided to return to us? Looking, if I may say so, in pristine condition. More beautiful than I have ever seen her. Italy seems to have agreed with you, my dear. And talking about condition, I have to ask how mother is these days, Father?'

'I had to put your mother in a nursing home. I see her when I can but she was becoming an embarrassment, her memory had completely gone and it became impossible to entertain business associates at the house.'

'My mother hasn't acted as your hostess for years, Father, who does the honours now?'

'I do the honours. If you're insinuating that I've got some

woman living with me, you're barking up the wrong tree.'

'Actually I wasn't, I simply thought my cousin's wife might have come to your rescue.'

'She has enough to do bringing up their children. Your cousin's a good help at the mills. He's little imagination but he's a competent and loyal worker. Outside the mill I'm my own man, I don't want help from him or his wife.'

'How has my mother settled in the nursing home?'

'Well enough. She eats the food that's put in front of her, she sits for hours looking into space, and when I visit I doubt if she knows me. Occasionally she smiles and asks about some person I thought she'd forgotten about. The bills are extortionate, but it's the most I can do for her.'

'She never mentions me?'

'Not to my knowledge, why should she?'

'Only that I'm the only son she has. I thought in her rare moments of lucidity she might remember that.'

'She's in Harrogate at the Sleepy Hollow. Damned ridiculous name, but its in a sort of dale between Harrogate and Knaresborough. The gardens are nice, the food's wholesome and the nursing staff adequate. I can't do any more.'

'I take it you've had a good look around the hotel?'

'Yes, Joanna came with me this afternoon,'

'And what did you think of it?'

'It's not to my taste, nor Joanna's either I'm thinking. No doubt she'll be embroidering on her point of view before long.'

'Oh, undoubtedly. Joanna is steeped in bourgeois respectability. I prefer to live in the real world, the world where people are going places, making money they're prepared to spend on stays here. In no time at all we'll be bursting at the seams with people on the make, who want to be seen hobnobbing with those who've arrived. They'll be glad to pay for the privilege of staying at Reckmire.'

I didn't speak but every word was engraved on my heart.

'I'd like to take a look at my grandson before I leave, if that's all right with you, Joanna?'

'Well, of course, Mr Cheviot. He's a fine little boy now.'

'I'm glad about that,' Paul said. 'He was a puny little thing when he went away. If he's a fine boy now then it would seem the holiday in Italy has worked wonders for both the boy and his mother.'

His father was regarding him with a cynical amused gaze but when his eyes met mine he smiled. He understood far better than his own son that there was no defeat in my silence, only contempt.

Chapter Thirty-Three

I was angry when I reached the breakfast table the next morning. Paul's father sat alone saying that he had already wished his son good morning as he intended to leave immediately breakfast was over.

It had been Mr Gainsborough who had informed me that our housekeeper had gone, she had not liked the new decor or my husbands ideas on the hotel's future. Only a handful of the old staff remained. The receptionist had decided not to return after her holiday abroad and Mr Gainsborough believed he was on borrowed time since he was a part of that same bourgeois respectability which Paul was so anxious to eliminate.

All I wanted was fruit juice and coffee. Afterwards I went with my father-in-law to the front of the hotel where his car was waiting for him.

'I shan't be coming back here,' he said, taking my hand. 'I've satisfied my curiosity. I'm happier about the mills too. If he can do this to Reckmire, I shudder to think what he would have done there. Goodbye, Joanna.'

'Goodbye, Mr Cheviot. Sometimes I drive into Harrogate. I was at school there so I go to recapture something of the past. If there is time I'll call in to see Mrs Cheviot.'

For the first time there was a gleam of kindness in his hooded eyes, and I knew he thought I meant if there was time during my visit whereas I had really meant if there was time before I returned to Italy.

I stood in the doorway until his car disappeared through the gates then I went back into the hotel. Mr Gainsborough was at the desk so I said, 'Do you know when my husband will be in, Mr Gainsborough?'

'He's at the stables, I can't think he'll be long.'

'Are there changes at the stables too?'

I did not miss the sudden shifting of his eyes before he said evenly, 'Mr Riley retired in the new year. There are one or two new grooms.'

'Who is in charge there?'

'I do not concern myself with the stables, Mrs Cheviot. I'm sure Mr Cheviot will tell you.'

He smiled, in case I felt rebuffed by his answer, but I was convinced that whatever went on at the stables and in the hotel did not meet with his approval. My supposition was proved to be right when he said evenly, 'I doubt if I shall be here for the grand opening, Mrs Cheviot. I've had a very good offer from a small hotel in Eastbourne. The owner is a man I've worked for many years ago. We're the same age, hold the same viewpoints and I'm getting on, too old to cater for the young and the brash. I thought I should tell you myself. Mr Cheviot is already aware of my decision.'

I stared at him in dismay. 'Oh, Mr Gainsborough, I am so sorry. There's going to be none of the old people left. The receptionist and the housekeeper have gone, and now you. I don't like it.'

He didn't reply, and in some exasperation I said, 'I shouldn't have to make an appointment to see my own husband, where is he?'

'Standing in the drive, I think, Mrs Cheviot,' he replied. 'He's on his way back.'

I went to the window in time to see Paul chatting earnestly with Freda. I turned to say, 'I see that Freda is still here, Mr Gainsborough? It would seem that some of our old staff are staying on.'

'Yes, madam, I think that Miss Felton has been put in charge at the stables.'

'In place of Riley?'

'Well, there are some young grooms who can do the rough work.'

'I see.'

I didn't see. I couldn't think that Paul would put the

Freda I remembered in charge of stables and horses which he expected his guests to use. She was a firebrand, hardly the type of girl who could handle other girls or young men since she was cocky and unconventional. It would seem I had a lot to learn about the events which had taken place during my absence.

Paul appeared in the hall a few minutes later and immediately said, 'I have to go out, Joanna. I'll see you at dinner, you can tell me about Italy then.'

'I need to talk to you now, Paul, it's very important.'

He was walking away from me towards his office and I followed determinedly. He was not going to put me off. If he could talk to Freda Felton he could surely talk to his wife.

He went to his desk and started to shuffle through some letters, a frown of impatience on his face, but I stood my ground, and after a few seconds he looked up, saying, 'If it's about the hotel, Joanna, I'm aware you don't like it. Neither did my father. I didn't expect him to, but I thought you would see the advantages, appreciate the money we shall make.'

'What have you done with my grandmother's portrait and the paintings you've had taken down to make room for inferior ones?'

He laughed. 'Surely you don't think your grandmother's portrait was appropriate to the new decor? My dear girl, it belonged to the past, to the place that has gone forever. I haven't disposed of them, they're in one of the storerooms upstairs. I thought one of your aunts might care to look them over or we can send them to the sale room. Corallie won't want them, she's enough stuff in that Italian castello to fill a museum as it is. By the way, I was sorry to hear about your uncle. Quite a nice chap I seem to remember.'

'My grandparents loved those paintings. What you have put in their place is trash.'

He frowned. 'Well, of course, you would know about all that, wouldn't you? One half of the partnership is high-principled, peerless and genteel. My half on the other hand is cheap, vulgar and in bad taste. You would rather welcome the fuddy-duddys instead of the enterprising, the

379

old ladies with their bridge afternoons and knitting needles, the men with their footling memories of India under the white Raj, their obsession with the old days, their fears about how the world is going.'

'You were pleased enough to have their patronage, you welcomed them with every appearance of pleasure, and they were nice people, unpretentious, who came back to us again and again.'

'Well, of course, where else would they find a mausoleum with deft servants waiting to minister to all their needs.'

'Servants that you are now getting rid of! The housekeeper has gone, Mr Gainsborough is going, the receptionist has gone, and it would appear Freda Felton is replacing Mr Riley.'

'Gainsborough is going at his own wish. The housekeeper was all right for the old place. I wanted somebody younger for the sort of guests who will be coming now. And Freda Felton is younger and prettier than old Riley. She'll attract the young men. She's sassy enough to give them as good as she gets and it's my decision. You gave me the right to decide a long time ago, Joanna, or had you forgotten?'

'And have you managed to fill the hotel for your grand opening?'

'It'll be bursting at the seams, my girl. There'll be a buffet meal, fireworks in the gardens at the edge of the cliff ... I'll get somebody in, some good modern artist, to paint another portrait of you. Something eyecatching and extremely beautiful to hang in the most prominent position.'

'You needn't bother, Paul, I'm not staying.'

'Not staying?'

'No. I want a divorce. We don't love each other, you don't even love our son. You never loved me. All you really cared about was your dream for Reckmire. Now I feel trapped in this loveless marriage and have no feeling for what Reckmire has become. You can have it all. I'm prepared to sign over my half, the place will be yours to do with as you want. I have to leave.'

'But not because you have fallen out with Reckmire. What other reason do you have, apart from not loving me, that is?'

'I love somebody else.'

'Somebody you met in Italy?'

'Yes.'

He stared at me, his eyes narrow and glittering strangely, then in a hoarse strangled voice he barked, 'It's Carlo, isn't it? Carlo with his Castello and his Ferrari. The Contessa Varasi sounds altogether better than plain Mrs Cheviot, and I remember you were besotted with him when he was in love with Gabriella. I must say you've made the most of your stay in Italy, no doubt with your aunt's connivance.'

'Why are you so angry? It's not as though you loved me.'

'No, I don't love you. I don't know why women are so obsessed with love. It's an emotion I don't know very much about, thank God. It isn't important that I don't love you, Joanna, but you are my wife, you belong to me, and no man has ever taken from me anything that belonged to me. I will not divorce you, you will not go to Italy.'

'You can't prevent me.'

'Can't I? Are you proposing to take our son with you?'

'Yes, of course, you don't love him.'

'There you go again. Love, always love. He is mine, Joanna, and if you take me to law I shall win. There was I working hard for our future, yours and mine, and for our son who would one day reap the benefit, and there were you in Italy with your Italian lover, without even a thought for me toiling here through the long winter months.

'The courts will not allow you to take my child out of the country, particularly to a country that was so recently at war with us. If you wish to leave me I shan't stop you, but I shall prevent you taking our son. You know as well as I do that you can't win. Tell the courts that I don't love you or the child and I shall tell them that my entire life is dedicated to your happiness and securing your future.'

'Why? Why do you want us to stay? You would be happier without us.'

'Joanna, I am not prepared to discuss this any further. I have told you that I will fight you every inch of the way and you know you can't win. You can't even take the risk. Now you will remain here as my wife, you will

381

be the gracious hostess of Reckmire, you will entertain our guests and make an effort to appear to be enjoying their company, and together we will watch our son grow up. I'm not interested in babies but I shall be interested in making a man of him, the sort of man who can be as ruthless and determined as I am.'

'An arrogant tyrant, you mean?'

'If you say so, Joanna. I'm late for my appointment, I'll see you this evening.'

He left me without another word, closing the door with a sharp click, and I sank weakly down on a chair, unable to believe that this was to be the end of love, of tenderness, and all the dear normalities of life.

I knew he would do all that he had threatened and I knew that he would win. At some future time perhaps the courts would listen to a woman's pleadings but not now, men had the monopoly on their sympathy and I was the one who had transgressed. I was the one who had taken a lover. That I had received no love in my marriage would be totally discounted and Paul would be convincing.

I did not think at that moment of his ambitions for Robin. All I knew at that moment was that I had to write to Carlo who would be waiting for my news. For us it was over. As I crossed the hall to go to my room Mr Gainsborough paused to say, 'Is something wrong, Mrs Cheviot, you don't look well.'

I stared at him dully for several minutes before I said, 'I'm perfectly well, Mr Gainsborough.' Then slowly I entered the lift and pressed the button. My room was luxurious but it was my prison. Paul would put no constraints on me, I would be able to move freely as if my life had not changed at all, but this was the room I would come back to until either one of us was dead.

I sat in the chair at the window looking out over the long reach of Reckmire. The sunny morning had given way to dark clouds sweeping in from the sea and it was raining. The sea and the sky were grey, a greyness that matched my mood, and in some strange way my thoughts turned to the acrimony of my parents' divorce.

My mother had divorced my father on the grounds of

his desertion and he had allowed her to do it, that dear good kind man who was incapable of deserting anybody, not even bothering to defend it when there was so much he could have said. All the long years of her tantrums and sulks, her narrow-mindedness and her limitations. She had made my father out to be a monster. In the court's eyes she had been the injured party, a sweet gentle little woman with a young child whose husband had taken himself off to the Far East and innumerable love affairs. My mother had got what she wanted, but then she had not had a lover.

Paul would have the same sort of advantages my mother had had, and he would use them just as my mother had used hers.

I couldn't sit in my room staring into space, I couldn't bear to look at my son who had been made the threat hanging over my head. Instead I put on my trench coat and with a scarf thrown over my head went out into the rain, walking quickly along the beach, oblivious of the wet drizzle running down my cheeks so that soon the silk scarf was a wet rag over my hair and I felt chilled to the marrow.

I didn't want to see Paul again that day but I made myself dry my hair and turn it into something respectable. I took a hot bath and started to look in my wardrobe for something to wear. He would not see me looking pale and dejected, a woman who was afraid and had bowed too easily to his masculinity. As he took his place opposite me at the dinner table, for one brief moment I saw the gleam of admiration in his eyes before the shutters came down. Smiling briefly he handed over the wine list, saying briefly, 'Choose the wine you want, my dear. I can recommend the Chablis.'

On Easter Saturday the caterers moved in as well as the flower arrangers and cleaners. They came before it was properly light and by breakfast time tables covered with snowy cloths and adorned with garlands of artificial leaves and flowers were in place.

There were urns filled with lilies and orchids and everywhere were men and women polishing balustrades and furniture, vacuuming carpets. Before lunchtime the group

383

arrived who were to provide music in the ballroom. They came in a large white van complete with their instruments and were all of a pattern, clad in black leather, wearing expensive jewellery, staring up at the building with wide grins on their faces.

In the middle of the afternoon the guests began to arrive. They came in chauffeur-driven limousines or expensive cars. Married couples looking slightly superior, greeting others they recognised with shrill cries of welcome and much embracing. There were elderly men with girls hardly out of the schoolroom, elegant matrons toting young boys, and one exceedingly fat man brought a cynical smile to my lips as he emerged from his rolls assisted by his chauffeur, puffing on a huge cigar, trotting on ridiculously small legs towards the entrance where he was enthusiastically greeted by a bevy of young women.

I wondered idly what the villagers would think of the procession of cars and if the night of revelry and the fireworks that would follow would distance us further.

I walked with Paul among our guests. Conversation was almost impossible because everybody seemed to be talking at once. Cheeks were being kissed, dresses admired, the champagne flowed and plates were being piled high from the long tables which groaned under the food.

When they had eaten their fill they made their way to the ballroom and strident music filled the air. The younger element danced, the older ones stood in groups around the floor or in the foyer, but from everywhere there was noise and then at midnight came the fireworks and people went out into the night to watch, taking their drinks with them.

Our guests had paid an extortionate price to mingle with the rich and successful and Paul had stinted on nothing, neither the food, drink nor the fireworks. There were squeals of delight as the rockets flew up into the night sky to descend seconds later in a myriad of tiny stars. In their glow the parkland was bathed in light and looking down the drive I could see clusters of villagers near the gates.

Paul's face wore a self-satisfied smile. Turning towards me, he said, 'I'd say this has been a night to remember, wouldn't you, Joanna?'

'By whom, are you thinking?' I answered shortly.

'By everybody, I would think. Even the villagers have come to see the fireworks.'

'And will these people come back, do you think?'

'A great many of them will. The others are fill-ins, people who go the rounds from one occasion to the next, but I'm not interested in them. The people I'm interested in are those who have arrived, not those on the make.'

'And you think they'll come?'

'Well, of course, I've already taken bookings. None of this is your cup of tea, Joanna, you've made that very plain. At the same time I'm glad to see you made an effort – not unnoticed I can assure you by a good many of the men here, particularly the one standing with his wife on the terrace.'

I looked over to where he indicated with a nod of his head and found that a man was staring at me, a tall thick-set man accompanied by a woman who was watching the fireworks. He smiled and lifted his glass, and Paul said, well pleased, 'There, what did I tell you? He's very interested in you, my dear.'

'Who is he?'

'You mean you don't recognise him?'

'No. Should I have?'

'Gerald Lamont. Probably the best film producer in the country. Haven't you noticed all the dollies trying to catch his eye?'

'No, I can't say I have.'

He was looking down at me with a cynical smile on his face. Angrily I said, 'You make me sick, Paul. You wouldn't care if I encouraged that man who evidently wouldn't need much encouragement, or any of the others for that matter. You'd take it as a compliment to yourself that a man like that should find your wife attractive, yet you refused to let me go to the only man I have ever loved.'

'Well, of course. I don't care how many affairs you have, Joanna, I know that's all they'd ever be. Your Italian lover was something else.'

I turned away from him in disgust, but before I could leave him he took my arm in his hand, holding it in a grip of steel. 'Where are you going?' he hissed.

385

'I've had enough of your party, Paul, I'm going to my room.'

'Oh, no, Joanna, you and I are going to circulate among our guests, you are going to smile graciously at their compliments, and you will instruct the waiters to take whatever food is left to the villagers in the park. The old fuddy-duddys are going to complain about the noise, the ones who eat our food are not going to take too much notice of them. Look over there. I'm glad to see our friend Freda is making herself amenable to one of our guests.'

I stared across the terrace to see that she was wrapped in the arms of a very inebriated young man. Paul grinned, saying, 'I invited her and introduced her around as my top groom. She's a pretty girl. There'll be a few of them at the stables in the morning.'

He kept hold of my arm while we circulated. His grip did not relax and by the time we all returned to the hotel, the fireworks over, I was beginning to feel sick from the pain in my arm. When he finally released me there was a red angry bruise on it and I knew in the morning it would be dark blue.

I escaped at last but the noise went on, laughter and music, car engines and screams of farewell, then as dawn crept silently over the frosted parkland silence descended on Reckmire.

Chapter Thirty-Four

Many months passed before I felt part of the village again. When I took flowers to the church they smiled politely but immediately went on with what they were doing, whether it was sweeping the aisles or arranging flowers for the altar.

The hotel patronised the newsagent and bakery, and Mrs Felton, like the good shopkeeper that she was, received me with a polite smile and an enquiry after Robin's wellbeing. The size of our order was nothing like what it had been in the old days. Now a large baker's van from Lancaster delivered quantities of bread and pastries, but I had insisted that we should still take Mrs Felton's fruit loaves and other of her cakes and pastries which I said were far superior to the mass produced sort we were getting from the wholesalers.

I always enquired about Lottie and was pleased to learn that she was happy in her marriage and living in a stone farmhouse not too far away. I never saw her in the village. When I mentioned Freda I saw her mother's quick blush and she quickly busied herself writing out my order.

'Is she happy in her job at the stables?' I enquired politely.

'Oh, yes, Mrs Cheviot, very 'appy. She doesn't live 'ere now, you know, she's bought one o' them terraced stone 'ouses at the top o' the rise.'

'Really? I didn't know.'

'Well, she never liked the shop. She 'ated it after the war.'

'No, Lottie was always the one who helped out. Do tell her I've been asking about her. Does she have children?'

'No. It's a big disappointment to both of 'em but I doubt she'll 'ave any. She 'ad German measles when she were little, and they do say it changes a lot o' things, don't they?'

'Oh, I am sorry.'

'Oh, well, they're 'appy enough, an' what ye never 'ave ye never miss they say.'

I smiled at her across the counter before I left the shop.

Aunt Marcia and Uncle Edward came up to collect the portrait of Grandma and others they particularly wanted. I selected two pretty water colours for my sitting room and another for Robin's room, but we walked around the hotel in silence. Neither of them was impressed with the new decor, but then I hadn't expected that they would be.

My new portrait hung where Grandma's had hung in the dining room and they thought it was different and interesting but that was all, and only echoed my own thoughts on it. The artist had painted it with a palette knife so it lacked the gentleness of brush stokes. He had captured my pale hair under the glow of lamplight which gave it a reddish glow and had painted my dark blue eyes so intricately they seemed to be the only thing distinguishable in a pale ethereal face. I had worn a pastel silk dress for the sitting but he had decided to pattern it, using a great many colours, most of them with a shimmering effect.

The picture was clever. Paul thought it was good, and it certainly blended well with the rest of the decor.

Aunt Corallie's letters were newsy. She made no mention of Carlo but informed me that Gabriella was now living with her at the castello in Tuscany and they were travelling a great deal. Invariably I put her letters aside with a feeling of despair that Gabriella was back in the environment where she and Carlo had once been in love.

My son was now a beautiful toddler, healthy and full of life, and although Paul paid him scant interest I was determined to turn him into the sort of boy my father would have approved of. I tried to visit my mother as often as possible but I never looked forward to my visits. She invariably complained about the flat. It was too far away from most of her friends, none of whom came as often, but when I suggested that she move nearer the town she made the excuse that there was so much of Ernest in the flat she couldn't bear to leave it.

I was amused that every ornament in the flat had been put out of reach of Robin, even when I told her that he wouldn't have touched anything.

'Well, I like to be sure, dear,' she replied. 'You know how much I love my treasures, a lot of them were Granny's and Ernest was always buying me things. You don't say much about your husband, Joanna. He's never once been to see me.'

'You did tell me not to bring him here, Mother.'

'Oh, well, it doesn't really bother me that he doesn't come, I'm set in my ways, a strange man about the flat would be awful. By the way, your friend Stella is getting married in the autumn. I know she intends to invite you.'

'Oh, I'm so glad. Who is she marrying?' I asked.

'None of us knows him, but some man she's met in Paris.

'Her mother seems delighted but I'm not in favour of holiday romances. They invariably fizzle out. This one seems to have survived.'

'I'm so glad for Stella. I won't have time to call this visit but I'll certainly go to her wedding if she invites me.'

I was surprised when Robin said on the way home, 'Don't you like going to Granny's, Mother. I don't.'

We had the compartment to ourselves. I looked across to where he sat in the other corner, staring through the window. Children could be far-seeing and disconcerting. Turning, he smiled, that angelic smile that was so beautiful, and I said gently, 'I always thought you liked going to Granny's. You like the train and you like going to the park and visiting Auntie Janice and the other ladies.'

'But Granny doesn't like us going, does she, Mother?' he said with wide-eyed innocence.

'Well, of course she does. Why do you say that?'

He thought a moment then in a small voice said, 'I don't know, I just feel it.'

I understood it. I hadn't always known when she disapproved of something but I had always felt it.

'What had your mother to say about the alterations to Reckmire?' Paul surprised me by asking.

'She's not in the least interested in Reckmire,' I replied shortly.

He grinned. 'And the boy? I hope she doesn't mollycoddle him like she mollycoddled you?'

I didn't think that remark deserved an answer. My mother had never mollycoddled me.

Changing the subject I said, 'Have we got a suitable pony for Robin to ride? The younger he starts the better, and he's very anxious to have a pony of his own.'

'There are one or two docile mounts the younger children ride, you'll have to go along to the stables and find out.'

'I'll do that in the morning. I suppose Freda will know?'

'She's on leave at the moment, she won't be there.'

'During the busiest time of the year when the hotel is full!'

'She's worked hard and I gave her permission for her to take time off. I look after the stables, Joanna, I thought you understood that.'

'I do. There's no need to be so defensive. I'd much rather deal with one of the other girls anyway.'

'Why is that? You were always so friendly with her sister, and Freda'd make two of her.'

'She's certainly more sure of herself — and more insolent.'

'Speak to Saunders about the pony.'

'A man?'

'No, a woman.'

'A woman who is Saunders, while Freda is Freda?'

'What's got into you, Joanna? There's nothing to make a song and dance about. Saunders is new. I've told you what to do.'

So I spoke to Saunders who turned out to be a young woman slightly older than Freda, I thought, but efficient and helpful. The pony was the smallest in the stables, a sturdy Welsh pony called Gwynn whom Robin loved on sight.

There was little for me to do at Reckmire. We had staff to do everything which left me with every opportunity to go riding with Robin, or walking along the beach with him.

When the schoolchildren arrived in August I began to have thoughts about school for him.

When I broached the subject to Paul, he said irritably, 'He can go away when he's seven like I did. In the meantime what's wrong with the village school?'

'Nothing at all. I wasn't sure you'd want him to go there.'

'What's the alternative?'

'The private school at Millbank.'

'No. We'll keep in with the vicar and the villagers. Most of the kids go to the school in the village. We don't know at this stage if he's going to be intelligent.'

'He's very intelligent.'

'Clever then. I always understood there to be a difference.'

'Will you go to the school with me?'

'Can't you do it on your own, Joanna? It's only baby school, for heaven's sake, and I've a lot on here. When he's ready for Eton I'll take over.'

Talk of Eton was sarcasm. If Robin was clever enough no doubt he'd go to Paul's old school, but I stalked away from him with deep anger in my heart.

At the end of August I decided I would visit Paul's mother in her nursing home. I'd been thinking about it for weeks, but didn't say a word to Paul about my plans, dreading the sarcasm that would belittle my proposed visit, turning it into something that it wasn't.

There was a long drive lined with rhododendron bushes leading to a large stone house built on terraces where summer flowers bloomed profusely. Paul's father had said it was expensive, but it was also in a most beautiful setting so why had I been so troubled with thoughts of a dark old house with narrow passages and cinders in the grates?

People were sitting out on the terraces where a young servant was busy serving them with drinks. As I crossed to enter the house a young woman carrying a large vase filled with roses smiled at me, saying, 'Are you visiting, madam?'

'Is it possible to see Mrs Cheviot?'

Her smile broadened. 'Why, of course. She's in her room.

I was hoping somebody would come today, she doesn't have many visitors.'

'Why particularly today?' I asked curiously.

'It's her birthday.'

'Oh dear, I didn't know. I've brought her some chocolates and fruit but I haven't brought a card, I wish I'd known.'

'It doesn't matter, madam, she'd forgotten herself until a card came from her nephew this morning. She won't have much conversation, you know, but she's a very nice lady. She'll be glad you've come even if you can't get her to say very much.'

The room she showed me into was on the first floor overlooking the terraces, a large airy room decorated in pastel colours containing a double bed covered with a pretty bedspread to match the chintz curtains at the windows where Mrs Cheviot sat in an easy chair staring out into the gardens.

'You have a visitor, dear,' my companion said brightly. Turning round, my mother-in-law favoured me with a gentle smile as empty as her eyes.

A chair was pulled forward for me to sit on. Smiling, I placed my offerings on her knee, saying softly, 'Happy birthday.'

'Thank you, dear,' she murmured, then there was silence.

During it I looked around the room. It was beautiful and impersonal. There were no photographs, nothing of a personal nature at all unless it was the dress she was wearing and the slippers on her feet. A birthday card stood on the mantelpiece and her thin fingers were engaged in twisting and turning her rings.

'You have a beautiful view from your room,' I ventured at last.

She smiled and nodded.

'I've brought you some photographs to look at, Mrs Cheviot,' I said reaching into my handbag. They were photographs of Robin taken in the gardens at Reckmire and she took them from me, staring down at them with a sad puzzled frown on her face.

'He reminds me of my little boy,' she said at last. 'He'll be coming soon, after school.'

Such a wave of pity washed over me I reached out and squeezed her hand and she stared at me in surprise.

'I know you now,' she said, 'We have met before, haven't we?'

'Yes, Mrs Cheviot. I met you at your house just before my marriage.'

'You're Paul's schoolteacher, now what did he call you? Oh, dear, my memory is so terrible these days, but I do remember you. Tell me your name.'

'Joanna.'

'Oh no, dear, that wasn't the name I was thinking of. I know, Miss Marriott. Yes, that's who you are. My little boy likes you.'

'I'm so glad, Mrs Cheviot. Would you like me to put your fruit in the bowl.'

'Yes, thank you. You'll wait until Paul comes back, won't you? Why didn't he come with you?'

I stared at her uncertainly, unsure whether he was to be with me as a man with his wife, or a child with his schoolteacher, and in answer to my doubtful expression she said, 'If you see Paul will you tell him I'm waiting for him? We used to have such fun together. That was before his father found other things for him to do.'

'What sort of things, Mrs Cheviot?' I asked in the hope of learning something, anything that would make me understand Paul better.

'Oh, just things that men like to do,' she answered. A puzzled frown appeared on her face, and plucking nervously at her dress she muttered, 'There was a boy in the gardens yesterday. I thought it was Paul, but he went away.'

'Does Mr Cheviot come to see you often?'

'He came last week, or was it the week before? Like I said, my dear, my memory is so awful. Shouldn't you be back at the school?'

'In a little while.'

She began to look at the photographs again and I said hurriedly, 'Would you like to keep them?'

She smiled. 'Oh, yes, that would be nice, and when Paul comes I'll show him. Are you sure this isn't Paul?'

'No. His name is Robin.'

Again the puzzlement, then she said brightly, 'I knew a Robin once, a very nice boy who came with Paul.' The puzzlement was back on her face and tearfully she said, 'But it couldn't have been with my Paul, they were too old. My Paul is only a little boy.'

At that moment there was a knock on the door and a maid came in carrying a tray of tea and biscuits.'

'P'raps you'll do the 'onours, miss?' she said with a smile. 'I've brought your favourite biscuits, Mrs Cheviot, them chocolate ones you liked yesterday.'

Mrs Cheviot smiled, I poured the tea, and the girl plumped up the cushions on Mrs Cheviot's chair. Before she went she whispered, 'She remembers everythin' from the past and nothin' that 'appened yesterday.'

I carried the tea over to her chair and placed it on a small table I had drawn up beside it, then I offered the biscuits which she took with evident enjoyment.

I was glad of the tea but felt I couldn't have swallowed a crumb. Instead I watched her eating like a child, savouring the chocolate and chasing every crumb around her plate. There was no conversation. After enquiring if she would like more tea I collected the crockery on to the tray and placed it on a side table to be collected later.

She was looking once more at the photographs of Robin, and when she looked up she said, 'Is he your little boy? He doesn't look like you.'

'No, he doesn't. He's very much like his father.'

She placed the photographs in two rows on the table near her chair, looking at them closely, then she selected one of them. 'I'd like this one, I can think that this one is Paul.'

'Don't you have any photographs of your son, Mrs Cheviot?'

'I did have once.' A spasm of pain crossed her face and she said in a small hurt voice, 'I kept them all in my sewing box, right from the day he was a baby, and looked at them every day ...'

Her voice trailed off and urgently I said, 'Why don't you have them here so that you can look at them now?'

'He took them and threw them away. He was so angry — with Paul, not really with me at all — and I can't remember why. He said Paul wasn't coming home again but of course he is, Paul will always come home.'

Her anguish was my anguish. There were so many terrible things one human being could do to another, and I was looking at a human being who had been destroyed, a woman who had not been strong enough to get away, the sort of woman I might have become if I hadn't had the strength to leave my mother. And now I was caught up in another sort of bondage, even more cruel.

As I drove home that afternoon across the Pennines there was in my heart such a mixture of pity and anger I couldn't think which emotion was the stronger, but they were all still there that night when I faced Paul across the dinner table.

He seemed preoccupied, only picking at his food, and when he caught me watching him curiously, said brightly, 'I saw the boy out on his pony this afternoon. I must say he handles the creature very well. That young girl's good with him.'

'Yes, she's a treasure.'

'Where were you?'

'I drove into Yorkshire and went to see your mother.'

He stared at me in surprise. 'Whatever for?' he snapped. 'She wouldn't know you, what on earth did you talk about?'

'She talked about you when you were a little boy. She was expecting you home from school.'

He threw back his head and laughed. It was not laughter filled with joy but laughter filled with bitterness, and those sitting nearby looked at us, startled.

'I told you my mother was ga-ga, that's why my father's had to put her away. If I went there tomorrow she wouldn't recognise me. Like you said, she's expecting her little boy, not the son who grew up.'

'Who grew up to be cold and bitter, who uses people without either charity or love.'

'There you go again, my dear, so obsessed with love.' He was leaning across the table, his dark eyes burning into mine, and with his voice hardly above a whisper but tinged with so much anger it was as menacing as the hissing of a cobra: 'I raped you once. Most men would have done it again and again, but I find no joy in making love to a cold-hearted little bitch as soulless as her mother.'

'Why are you so angry? Is it just because I went to see your mother?' I said evenly, and my calmness only made his eyes darken and his hands clench on the table top so that the knuckles showed white.

'I don't want you analysing my life, delving into a past that belongs to me and has nothing to do with you.'

'Not even if it helps me to understand you?'

'There's nothing to understand. I am what you see and I like my women warm and passionate. They say Italians are great lovers. I can't understand how your Italian enjoyed making love to a dead thing, a thing fashioned by her mother into being a piece of marble.'

He got up from the table, threw his napkin on it and marched out of the room. All around us I met staring eyes blandly until, embarrassed, they looked away.

Chapter Thirty-Five

Our next battle concerned Freda Felton. Every day I took Robin riding. The long summer days were warm and sunny and he revelled in the long stretch of beach although I was teaching him to have respect for the tide and the way it could suddenly change.

Freda's extended leave seemed never ending and when I enquired from one of the other girls when she was expected back, she merely shrugged her shoulders and said she didn't know.

Paul had always been impatient with staff who asked for sick leave, or indeed leave of any sort unless it was their annual holiday, but now he was condoning Freda's absence without comment. Her mother was uncommunicative also when I enquired about her in the shop.

'She's away somewhere, Mrs Cheviot. I've learned never to ask Freda anythin', she tells us what she wants us to know.'

Life at the stables was hectic and the young girls employed there could hardly cope. After I returned Robin to the house I went down to help them and one of the girls, more forthcoming than the others, said sharply, 'We've 'ad no word from Freda, Mrs Cheviot, and when we asked the master 'e just said she'd be comin' back when she could. This is our busiest time, an' it's doubtful if we'd 'ave bin allowed so much time off.'

'I'll speak to my husband,' I promised, 'ask him to get extra help for you.'

'It's right good of ye to 'elp out, Mrs Cheviot. No doubt

she'll come back throwin' 'er weight about as if she owns the place.'

I went straight to Paul's office when I returned from the stables and he lifted his eyebrows in surprise at my dishevelled state.

'What happened to you then?' he said sarcastically. 'Fall off your horse?'

'No. I've just spent most of the afternoon helping out at the stables. They're overworked down there and there are not enough of them. Is it too much to hope that Freda Felton is on her way back?'

'She's answerable to me. I know when she's coming back,' he replied shortly.

'Well, for your information the rest of them are angry. If you want to keep them I suggest you get in touch with Freda wherever she is and find out when she intends to return. In your position you shouldn't have favourites.'

'Are you suggesting that Freda is a favourite?'

'No, I'm telling you she is. You wouldn't have stood for any of the others behaving like she's behaving. She's been gone six weeks. Even her mother doesn't know where she is.'

'Is that a fact?'

I stared at him in angry silence, then nonchalantly he said, 'It'll do you good to help out at the stables, Joanna, it's probably the first bit of real hard work you've done since the war ended.'

'Oh, I'll work all right. I'll work for Freda's salary. I believe it's considerably more than any of the other girls is earning?'

He threw back his head and laughed. 'You don't much like her, do you?' he sneered.

'No. I never liked her. She's brash and cocky. She's had a bad name in the village as long as I can remember and anything that happened to her wouldn't surprise me.'

'Then I might as well tell you that I gave her leave because she was pregnant. Don't ask me who the father is, she wouldn't tell me. It's probably one of the young blades she's been hob-nobbing with these last few weeks.'

'So she's likely to be away some months?'

398

'It would seem so.'

'Is he going to marry her?'

'He's not going to know. I was sorry for the girl, I've given her an advance on her wages and she's gone somewhere to have the baby. She's having it adopted so she'll not be bringing it back to Reckmire.'

'I hadn't given you credit for so much compassion, I've never seen it before. It would be nice to think I could see it again.'

'I can be compassionate when the occasion calls for it. I seldom show it to spoilt little rich girls who don't know when they're well off, but I can feel sorry for girls who land themselves in trouble, haven't any money, and nowhere to go.'

'You have a son you seldom acknowledge and a mother who would benefit from your compassion. It seems to me your loyalty to Freda is misplaced and should be given elsewhere.'

'My mother is being cared for at great expense, she wouldn't benefit from a visit from me and she'd forget about you as soon as you'd turned your back. As for my son, I'll take him in hand when he's older. Don't think I haven't watched his progress. He rides well and is getting to be more and more like the son I expect him to be. Now, Joanna, let's have done with Freda and allow me to get on with my work.'

'You're insufferable, Paul. I didn't think I could ever dislike anybody so much,' I snapped.

He threw back his head and laughed, then as I left the room he started to open the file on his desk.

That night over dinner he set himself out to be attentive but it was a cynical and derisive attention, a front laid on for our guests. I felt irritated by him as he gave a performance of pouring the wine, handing me the dishes, consulting me about the menu, saying in a voice audible to those at the tables nearest to us, 'You're looking very beautiful tonight, my dear, a stint at the stables has obviously agreed with you.'

Then to those nearest to us, 'My wife's being helping out at the stables in the absence of our head groom. What would I do without her?'

There were smiles all round, and raising his glass he said, 'To you, my dear, with a very big thank you.'

He knew that I was annoyed by the falseness and was amused by it. Never in a thousand years would I understand the man I had married, but I wouldn't let him defeat me as his father had defeated his mother.

Calmly I went on with my meal trying to ignore the pantomine.

Several days later I went down to the bakery and was surprised to see Lottie serving in the shop. She smiled at me, and I waited while she finished serving two other women who were in the shop before me.

When they left I handed over my order, saying, 'I'm surprised to see you here Lottie. Isn't your mother well?'

'No. My dad came for me last night to see if I could help out. She's got a bad cold. My mother's not one to complain but you can't serve in the shop when yer sneezin' all the time.'

'No, of course not. I hope she'll soon feel better.'

Her manner was strangely defensive and I guessed Freda was at the back of it. Her eyes refused to meet mine and I made myself say, 'I've heard about Freda, Lottie, I'm very sorry.'

She looked up, startled. 'You know then?'

'Yes, my husband told me when I asked if she might be coming back soon. I've been helping out in the stables they're so busy there. When is the baby expected?'

'She's told us nothin', and my mother says if she can't tell 'er family about it we're not goin' to ask any questions.'

'So you don't know who the father is?'

'No. We think it's some man she's met at the hotel. She's bin seen around the village with a great many o' the men she went ridin' with. Our Freda's allus been like that, we'll never know the truth of it.'

'And the baby? Is she having it adopted?'

'I'm goin' to talk to her. I'm willing to bring it up as ours. We'll never have any children of our own and we've got a nice little farm and a decent way o' life. The baby'll want for nothin'. Of course, knowing' our Freda she might not agree to it.'

'Oh, surely she will? It sounds a perfect solution to me.'

'Well, we hopes so. Of course all the village is talkin' but Freda won't care. She never has, 'owever much talk there's bin about her.'

'No, I don't suppose she will.'

'Your little boy's right bonny. I sees him trottin' down the street on his pony. Like his father 'e is, not like you at all.'

'No. He has his father's colouring, but he's like me in other ways. Tell your mother I hope she'll soon be better, Lottie. I'll see you again, I hope, before you leave?'

'I hopes so, Mrs Cheviot.'

'You used to call me Joanna. We're old friends, Lottie.'

She blushed and with a little smile said, 'Yes, we were, weren't we? I'll tell my mother you've bin askin' about her, Joanna.'

It was the beginning of November when Freda returned to Reckmire and I was in Surrey attending Stella's wedding.

Robin was now attending the village school and enjoying it. At first the village children seemed to resent him, but he was a friendly child and one by one they became his friends. He brought them to Reckmire to look at the horses, and they played in what was left of the parkland until Paul said testily, 'Must you encourage the children to play near the ballroom, Joanna? We're running a country hotel not a kindergarten.'

'They don't play there in the evening, only for a short while in the afternoons,' I retorted.

'All the same, we shouldn't encourage them.'

'It will soon be too cold to play in the park after school anyway,' I said shortly.

I decided to take Robin with me when I went to Surrey for Stella's wedding. It would only be for a matter of days, and the school didn't object.

I was more than surprised when Mother said, 'I told Stella's mother I wouldn't be going to the wedding, I'd look after Robin instead. After all, young children can be very disruptive at such a time and I thought you'd prefer to leave him with me.'

I suddenly warmed to her. I was not accustomed to her making welcome suggestions and hoped even that at this late stage her disposition was changing.

'Everybody says the man's years older than her,' she said in the next moment however, and while I made tea in the kitchen she filled me in on the usual gossip.

'He's not from round here. Somebody she met on holiday in Paris apparently.'

'Are they intending to live locally?'

'Oh no, they're going out to the Far East. He's a foreigner, you know.'

'No, I didn't. What nationality.'

'American, I think.'

'Oh, Mother, I never really think of the Americans as foreign.'

'Well, I only listen to the ladies when they come to play bridge. Stella's mother's dining out on his job, his money and the good life they're going to have. She's not wearing white by the way, but then why should she? She's certainly played the field and if he's so much older than her ...'

'Do you intend to watch the wedding, Mother?'

'Oh, no. You can tell me all I need to know, and by the time it takes place I'll be bored with it anyway. What are you giving her for a wedding present?'

'I telephoned to ask what she would like but she said I should please myself. Anything as long as it wasn't functional.'

'What did she mean by that?'

'Oh, something unusual or pretty.'

'And what did you decide on.'

'I've brought her a jade figure she admired when she came to Reckmire. It belonged to Grandma. I'll show you when I've unpacked.'

Later that evening she sat holding the jade figure in her hands, stroking its smooth lines, saying softly, 'How cold it is. I saw a lot of jade in the Far East, ivory too, but never wanted any of it. I much prefer good china.'

She watched me wrapping the jade figure in decorative paper, then surprised me by saying, 'I hope she puts the presents on display at the reception. She's not likely to receive jade from anybody else.'

Her remark made my gift seem ostentatious, vulgar perhaps, but seeing my expression she said quickly, 'Oh, if it's something she admired you can always explain why you brought it. At both my marriages I asked people who didn't know what to give us for china and I've managed to keep it all. It'll be yours one day, Joanna, all my Wedgwood and Royal Doulton. I've always looked after it.'

'Yes, Mother.'

'You like it, don't you?'

'Yes, of course.'

'But I expect your grandmother left plenty at Reckmire?'

'Some, Mother.'

I didn't tell her that there was no room for Grandma's beautiful china in the public rooms at Reckmire and that most of it resided in cupboards in the flat.

I slept badly that night, waking early to a cold grey November dawn. I felt strangely uneasy without being able to say why. The disquiet continued through breakfast when Mother said cosily, 'Robin and I are going to spend a lovely day getting to know one another. I don't suppose you'll be back much before dark.'

'I don't know, Mother. I suppose they'll be going away somewhere.'

'Her mother said she didn't know when I saw her in the hairdresser's just a few days ago.'

The disquiet continued as I dressed for the wedding. I was well supplied with clothes and had bought nothing new, but the navy and white suit was flattering and with it I had chosen a large navy blue hat, its sweeping brim edged with white silk. Mother eyed me up and down as I bent to embrace Robin, saying finally, 'You look very nice, Joanna, is that new?'

'No. I bought it for a function at Reckmire.'

'I suppose you've had plenty of those?'

'Well, yes, it's inevitable in the sort of business we're running.'

'You'd better get off then. Don't worry about Robin, we're going to be very happy together.'

She offered her cheek for me to kiss, then I embraced Robin, cautioning him to be good for Granny before letting myself out of the flat.

I drove straight to Stella's house so that I could leave my gift and her mother pressed me to drink coffee, saying, 'There's heaps of time, dear. Why isn't your mother with you?'

'She's looking after Robin.'

'I thought she'd want to watch. She could have brought Robin with her, there'll be other children watching.'

'Well, she wouldn't have the car and it is rather cold this morning.'

'All her friends will be watching.'

'Then she'll no doubt receive a full report at some future time,' I said, smiling.

'Well, yes.'

Stella enthused over the jade figure, hugging me closely, her face wreathed in smiles, saying, 'Oh, Joanna, it's beautiful. Look, Mother, this is the figure I told you about, and now it's mine.'

Her mother duly admired it and over coffee I learned a little more about the man Stella intended to marry.

'I've known him for years,' she said happily. 'I knew him before the war when he was married to a girl friend of mine. Unfortunately Susy died and I met up with him in Paris a few months ago. He has a boy called Martin, he's twelve now, and fortunately we get on like a house on fire. Did your mother tell you we're going to live in Thailand?'

'Not exactly. She said in the Far East somewhere.'

'Well, John's Canadian but he works for an American oil company. Mark's at boarding school here in England, but it'll all work out, Joanna. He's nice, isn't he, Mother?'

'Oh, yes, indeed, very nice.'

While we chatted I thought about mother's assertion that John was foreign, but then anybody north of London was foreign to Mother.

She had also said that the bridegroom was considerably older than the bride but when I met him I found him charming, extremely youthful in looks and demeanour, and when I saw how happy they were together I spared a desolate thought for the state of my own loveless marriage.

Mother's old friends were there in force, throwing confetti, greeting the newly married pair with smiles and good wishes, and again the old uneasy thoughts came back to spoil my joy in the day.

Stella and John drove off in the late-afternoon for the few days they were spending in the West Country and then I felt I could conveniently say my farewells.

The evening traffic was building up as I drove back and it had started to rain. I couldn't believe how desperately anxious I was to reach my destination. It was illogical. What had I to be afraid of?

I stood in the hall, closing the door softly behind me, and could hear Mother's voice. There seemed to me to be an urgency about it, a relentlessness, and for a moment I stood with my hand on the doorknob listening, and in that short time my heart flamed with anger at her words, uttered softly and with sibilant menace.

'Now you do understand, don't you, darling, all that I've been telling you about the sea? You must not go near it, not even along the beach, because the sea eats little boys just like it ate up my little cousin. Robin, do you understand?'

'Mummy takes me to the sea,' came his childish treble. 'It's nice, I paddle and find shells.'

'No, Robin, never again. If you do, one day the sea will eat you. Granny knows better than Mummy. You must not go near the sea again, do you understand?'

There was silence and in that moment I threw open the door and confronted her. I knew that my face was flaming with anger and she recoiled against her cushions, straining Robin against her.

'Mother, what do you think you're doing? You're terrifying him just as you used to terrify me.'

'I'm warning him, Joanna. I know what the sea can do and he's there near that terrible beach. I would be failing in my duty if I didn't warn him.'

'He's been taught to have respect for the sea, Mother, he knows to stay away from it when it's angry and to enjoy it when it's calm. All you're doing is putting unnatural fears into his mind when he's too young to understand otherwise.

405

Is this why you wanted him to yourself for a whole day, so that you could terrify him, tell him that story about your cousin?'

'It was a terrible thing to happen,' she cried tearfully.

'I know, but children are in danger from a great many things. All we can ever do is warn them and teach them to be careful. To frighten them about something as natural as the sea is dreadful. You are frightening him about the very environment he has to live in.'

'I've done my duty and I'm not sorry to have done it. It's you who fails the child by allowing him access to the beach and the sea. I kept you safe all your young life. It was your decision to go running back to Reckmire.'

I stared at her helplessly. I knew the steel behind her fragility, the colossal assurance that she was right even if the rest of the world disagreed with her. In this small tight-lipped woman I had an adversary who would not admit defeat if it stared her in the face.

Without another word I went into my bedroom and started to remove my wedding finery, then I started to pack. I knew that she had come into the room and stood in the doorway to watch me, then in a small, surprised voice she said, 'Why are you packing? I thought you were staying until the weekend.'

'No, Mother, we're going home tomorrow. I don't know how much damage you've done, but you are not going to do any more.'

'You were always an ungrateful girl, Joanna, but if that's how you feel you'd better go. I've learned to live without you, and if you can't see the sense in what I've tried to tell Robin, there's nothing more I can say.'

She retired early and in tears as she had always done after any argument either with me or my father, and after Robin had gone to sleep I looked at the photographs spread out across the long coffee table.

I had been shown them when I was a child. Photographs of the small boy who had been drowned when Mother herself was a child, a fair-haired charming little boy with a sweet gentle smile. Then there were the newspaper reports of the incident, the obituary notices, pictures of the funeral with the tiny white coffin being carried by grieving relatives.

All this she had shown to Robin and my anger against her grew.

Chapter Thirty-Six

I returned home to find Paul in high good humour. Bookings for the festive season were good, Freda had returned to the stables, and when I enquired about the child she'd been expecting I was told curtly that her sister had taken it, a boy he believed.

'I haven't mentioned it to her since the day she came back,' he said, 'and I'd rather you didn't. After all, we don't know how badly she feels about it.'

His sensitivity surprised me, but I had had no intention of discussing her child with her at any time. When I took Robin to the stables if the weather was fine she invariably was busy somewhere else, and if I met her in the grounds she merely treated me to a small smile and a murmured greeting.

We never walked along the beach. I thought I would give Robin time to forget the day he had spent with my mother, but I was uneasy when he never suggested it himself, not even when the sea was calm on one of the better days.

At the beginning of December he started to have nightmares. I could hear him screaming and when I went into his room he was thrashing about in his bed with the tears rolling down his face. When I held him in my arms I could feel him trembling, his body wet with perspiration. Even when he woke up and realised he had only been dreaming, the sense of terror remained.

The nightmare recurred frequently and in the new year he didn't want to go back to school.

'But I thought you liked school, darling?' I prompted
him.

He shook his head defiantly and gently I asked, 'But why?
You like Miss Allenby, and you have so many friends at
school. It's too cold to play in the gardens now but there
will be other things to look forward to. Why don't you
invite some of your friends for tea?'

'They won't come,' he said in a small voice.

'Why won't they come?'

'They don't like me any more.'

'Oh, darling, of course they like you. Why do you think
they don't like you?'

'They won't play with me.'

I said nothing more but resolved to speak to his teacher
at the first opportunity. I invariably met him at the school
gates because none of the other children walked farther than
the village, and when I saw the teacher leaving the school I
went forward to meet her.

Some of the children stared at us curiously. Their mothers
smiled, and one child naughtier than the others put out his
tongue at us.

The teacher frowned. 'He's got the makings of a bully,
Mrs Cheviot. He's bigger than most of the others and likes
to throw his weight about. I'll speak to him in the morning
about that episode.'

'Does he bully Robin?' I asked curiously.

'He tries it on with all the children. Robin used to stand
up to him, but these days he tends to shrink within himself.
He's still riding his pony, Mrs Cheviot?'

'Yes, when the weather is good.'

'So he's not afraid of that then?'

'Are you telling me my son is afraid of other things?'

'Well, yes. He was always the first to rush into the
playground, he loved the nature walks and never seemed
to mind how grubby he got. Last week he refused to cross
the stepping stones over that very shallow little brook near
the church. The stones are level and quite large, normally
Robin would run across them with the rest of the children,
but last week he adamantly refused to cross which gave our
little bully a lot of ammunition.'

'I'm so glad you've told me, Miss Allenby. I'll speak to Robin and try to find out what's wrong.'

I knew what was wrong. My mother had got through to an impressionable child and he was desperately afraid of water.

The nightmares continued and one night Paul heard him screaming and came into the room to find me cradling Robin in my arms.

He stood in the doorway, eyeing us coldly. 'What's the matter with the boy? This is the third time in two weeks he's been screaming his head off. If any of our guests hear him, they'll swear we're beating him.'

'It's a nightmare he's had, he'll be all right presently.'

'Get the doctor in, Joanna, we can't have this. We'll have the police here accusing us of ill treating the boy.'

I had Robin's bed moved into my room in the hope that it was only for a short period, but when Paul found out he commanded that the bed be removed.

'You're making the same sort of namby-pamby out of him your mother would have approved of. What ails the lad? I told you to consult the doctor.'

He prescribed mild sedatives but the nightmares continued, and now whenever the sea crashed against the rocks and the fog horn sounded eerily in the night, the nightmares grew worse.

It was the middle of February when Paul strode into my sitting room where I was looking at catalogues of household linen. I knew immediately that he was angry.

'I've just driven along the drive and met a crowd of village urchins screaming abuse at Robin who's out with the other children on the ponies. He rode off on his own back to the stables and Freda tells me it's happening most weekends now. For some reason the village kids don't like him, he's terrified of them, and I want you to find out why. I know bullying goes on, it did at every school I went to. Some big head, all brawn and no brain, thinks he can run things. Nobody ever ran me and nobody's going to run my son. Now what's it all about?'

'I don't know. Children often suffer from unreasonable fears.'

'Well, I know you did, but they'd been put there deliberately. Did you allow your mother to get at Robin?'

I didn't need to answer him, he knew from the expression on my face, and with all the venom in his voice that I had come to dread he said, 'It's time I took him in hand. In future, Joanna, he will ride with the other children who are staying here and will leave the village school. He's not one of them, and the sooner he realises it the better.'

'He's younger than any of the other children, we enjoy our rides together. I don't mind about the school. He's been bullied by an older boy there,' I said hoping for some compromise but there was to be none.

'No dice, Joanna. He'll ride with the other children and he'll make friends with them. There's to be no more treating him like a baby if he cries in the night. He has to learn that crying gets him nowhere.'

'I suppose this is the sort of upbringing you had?' I cried angrily. 'You must be very satisfied with the finished product.'

'I'm not dissatisfied. It made a good soldier of me, it showed me how to put this place on its feet and it made me ruthless enough to know what I want out of life and with the ability to stand on my own two feet and not expect others to do it for me. Now I intend to do the same for my son.'

'And what about me, will he be the sort of son I want?'

'Probably not, Joanna. You'd prefer him to be more like your cousin Robin, always the charmer, born with a silver spoon in his mouth and it always showed. Robin's dead, Joanna, and my Robin isn't going to emulate him.'

Stung to retort I cried, 'I thought Robin was your friend? Where is your sense of loyalty whether he's dead or not?'

'I liked him well enough and it's true we were friends, but I envied what he had, I couldn't help it. Now it's all mine and our son is going to know how to handle it when he's old enough to take over. There's another thing too, Joanna. I want you to be amenable to one of our guests, very amenable if you know what I mean.'

'No, I don't know what you mean. How amenable, and who are you talking about?'

411

'John Cavendish. He arrived last night. You must have seen him giving you the once over in the dining room?'

'No, I did not.'

'He's probably one of the richest men in the country, I've no idea how he's made his money but I'm telling you he has plenty. I've known him a long time. You can look after yourself.'

'Is he married?'

'Not at the moment. He's going through a particularly messy divorce right now from some silly woman he married. It's been said she's taking him to the cleaners where money is concerned. You have it in you to cheer him up.'

'Sympathise with his matrimonial problems or help him to spend his money?'

'I don't care about his divorce, obviously I mean his money.'

'And when you say make myself amenable, do you want me to sleep with him?'

For the first time my words stung him, and with a long stare, he said, 'That's up to you, my dear. You had no compunction in sleeping with your Italian, you're hardly a novice in that quarter.'

He strode away from me and at that moment my hatred for him was so intense I would willingly have killed him. In a blind rage I turned and would have fallen if a firm hand had not steadied me. I was looking up into a dark saturnine face and eyes that appraised me with keen appreciation.

Apologising swiftly, I turned away, but I knew that those eyes followed me across the hall.

There was no sign of Robin in my apartment on the top floor and hurrying along the corridor to the lift one of the servants said, 'If you're lookin' for Master Robin, Mrs Cheviot, 'e's with the boy from room fourteen. The boy and 'is sister came lookin' for 'im.'

I thanked her. Already it would seem Paul's plans for Robin had taken effect, and at that moment I earnestly believed that I had lost my son.

The rooms of the hotel suffocated me with their scented opulence and although it was cold and with a stiff wind blowing right off the sea, I needed to get outside into the air. I donned a sheepskin coat, and with a scarf over my hair set out briskly to walk along the beach.

I could hear the sea boiling beyond the point, feel the salt on my lips even though the tide was out. I stood watching the waves rolling in. I knew now how long it was safe to linger there.

The wind brought the tears into my eyes, miserably mingling with salt spray as I turned at last to walk back to the house. It was then I saw the solitary figure of a man walking slowly towards me and at first I thought it was Paul. Then I saw that it was somebody else, and as he grew nearer I recognised the man I had seen in the hall.

He smiled and waited, then quite naturally fell into step beside me. 'Do you often walk on the beach on days like this?' he asked evenly.

'Yes, the weather doesn't deter me,' I answered him.

He was looking down at me with a curiosity I found embarrassing. With a brief smile he said, 'I'm one of your hotel guests, Mrs Cheviot. The name is John Cavendish.'

I could feel the hot colour flooding my face and looked down quickly in case he should see it. His voice was bland however as he went on, 'I've known your husband a great many years and heard a lot about this place before it became the Reckmire Country Hotel. I came to see what it was like.'

'I hope you're very comfortable, Mr Cavendish? Do you intend to stay over Christmas?'

'I'm not sure. I've booked but I may have to leave earlier than expected.'

I didn't speak, and he didn't elaborate. We climbed the rocks that led into the gardens and then I saw Paul standing in the doorway watching us. As we entered the hotel he came forward with a welcoming smile.

'It's nice to see hardy souls venturing along the beach on a day such as this,' he said amicably.

'I saw your wife walking alone, thought a little company might not come amiss,' John Cavendish said evenly.

'If you'll excuse me?' I murmured. 'I'd like to get out of these damp clothes.'

'Before you go, Mrs Cheviot, I'd like to invite you and

your husband to have dinner with me this evening in Kendal. No disrespect to the excellent fare we have here but I get claustrophobic staying in one place and I've had excellent reports of the Mardi Gras in Kendal. It's new, and a friend of mine owns it.'

I looked at Paul, waiting for his reply.

'Well, that's very civil of you, John,' he replied urbanely. 'Unfortunately I've got a chap coming here tonight on business and it's too short notice to put him off. He'll be on the way already. But there's nothing to stop Joanna going with you. You wouldn't like our guest to dine in Kendal alone, would you, dear?'

John Cavendish was waiting for my reply, his expression difficult to read. Calmly I said, 'Thank you, Mr Cavendish. I shall be pleased to dine with you.'

I turned and left them, but all the way across the hall I was seething with resentment. There was no man coming to see Paul and John Cavendish knew it. I was being handed to him as a sop to ensure his future patronage and Paul would already be congratulating himself that I was a willing partner in his plans.

Robin was back in his room. He had changed out of his riding clothes and was sitting curled in a chair with a book on his knees but he wasn't reading. When I asked if he had enjoyed his ride, he replied, 'Yes, Mother,' in a voice that showed neither pleasure nor interest, and if this was to be the new Robin, I thought miserably, then his father's takeover was beginning to take its toll.

'Wasn't it terribly cold out there on the fell?' I asked cheerfully.

'It was all right.'

'You don't sound very sure, Robin.'

'Do I always have to go with them?' he asked anxiously.

'Well, they're very nice children. You like them, don't you?'

'They're all a lot older than me, even Cedric. He's nine.'

'I know, darling, but there will be younger children coming, and after Christmas you're going to a new school. You'll like that, won't you?'

'I suppose so.'

My heart ached for him. He was too young for changes

in every sphere of his life and angrily I thought that my mother had done this to him. If she hadn't terrified him about the sea on that day she had had him to herself he would not have had the nightmares and Paul would not have heard him screaming in the night. He would still be my little boy, enjoying our rides together, his face bright with expectation, his voice filled with laughter.

That night in the foyer Paul appraised me with quiet approval. I was wearing a simple but beautifully cut black dress, my only jewellry a gold brooch on the shoulder of my gown and long gold earrings.

Black suited my colouring and the simplicity of my gown gave me a sophistication that was not always apparent. I was immediately aware of the admiration in John Cavendish's eyes as he bowed over my hand, then he was escorting me across the hall and out of the hotel where his car waited for us.

In the main we drove in silence along the dark country roads, the glow from the car's headlights shining on branches covered with frost, and my companion said softly, 'The roads will be slippy later, the frost is keen, I hope the gritters are out.'

'I'm sure they will be, they are always prepared for icy roads in this part of the world.'

'I'm not a countryman, Mrs Cheviot. City people get spoiled.'

Indeed the gritters were already coping with the major road ahead and the big car ate up the miles driving north to Kendal.

The restaurant was charming: alcoves in intimate corners, candles glowing on every table, and although small, and the winter's night cold, most of the tables were occupied.

The owner came to greet us, and when I was introduced said with a smile, 'Your hotel has brought a lot of business into the area, Mrs Cheviot.'

'That's what we hoped for,' I replied.

The food and service were excellent and although our conversation was minimal we ate in a companionable silence that was not oppressive.

It was when we were sipping our brandy that he astonished

me by saying, 'Tell me, Mrs Cheviot, why did you marry Paul Cheviot? I know why he married you.'

I stared at him without answering and he was quick to say, 'The question was impertinent I know, but I've had time to observe you while I've been a guest at Reckmire and the question bothers me.'

'Why should it bother you? Why should it concern you at all, Mr Cavendish?'

'I've known Paul Cheviot since we were kids. I was a scholarship boy at the school where Paul was paid for. My father started to make money and we moved on to a better school. This time we were both paid for and a certain haphazard friendship developed.'

'Then you must have known my cousin Robin?'

'Yes. That too was a friendship I could never understand. Robin was a good chap, one of the nicest I met, but suddenly there was this friendship with Paul Cheviot. Paul shut everybody else out, he was possessive about Robin, and I think in the beginning Robin was sorry for him. Sorry because Paul was a loner. His parents didn't always come to founder's or sports days, I only ever saw his mother once, and if his father came he left before everybody else. That was when Robin started inviting Paul to Reckmire for holidays, and to hear him talk, Reckmire was as much his as Robin's.'

'It was my grandparents' home.'

'I know. Then came the opportunity for Paul to get his hands on it.

'I was in his company in London. The war hadn't been over very long and he'd been there on business. I knew Robin had been killed during the war and he told me about Reckmire, what he was doing to make it into a country hotel, and in some amazement I said, "What's it got to do with you? You're not an Albemarle."

'He smiled that self-satisfied smile of his and said, "I'm going into partnership with Robin's cousin. I've known her since she was a schoolgirl and she hasn't a notion of what to do with the place. I can't think why they left it to her unless it's because they didn't see much of her when she was a child. Her mother was a silly woman and wouldn't allow

416

her to go to Reckmire because it was close to the sea."

'I asked him if you were willing to allow him so much say so, and he said since you were engaged to be married there were no problems.

'I asked him what you were like, and his reply was that you were a nice enough girl, rich, spoiled and pretty helpless. When the opportunity came I thought it might be interesting to find out for myself.'

'And are you convinced that he was right, Mr Cavendish?' I asked stonily.

'No, Mrs Cheviot, I am not. I've watched you very carefully and I have seen a woman who is bitterly unhappy, a gracious beautiful lady who is out of her depth.'

I could feel my mouth trembling and across the table he covered my hand with his own. 'Perhaps it was wrong of me to speak as I've spoken, my dear, but problems between a man and a women are often impossible to resolve. I married a girl because she was beautiful, even when I knew she was marrying me for my money. Now she's in the process of taking me to the cleaners, wants to get her greedy little hands on most of it, and I'm fighting her tooth and nail. Why don't you leave him?'

Then came the relief of telling him about Carlo and about Robin. About my mother, and that if there hadn't been Robin I would have left him long ago.

He nodded grimly, surprising me by saying, 'And you're here with me tonight, Joanna, because that bastard told you to make yourself agreeable to a chap who is likely to put business his way. Believe me, my dear girl, I wouldn't be averse to that, I'm a man and admire a beautiful woman, but I'm astute enough to know that you are not for sale.'

For the first time in months I looked into his eyes and knew I had found a friend. I could make this man love me, but it wasn't a lover I was looking for, it was a friend, a champion, and the strength of his hands gripping mine made me suddenly strong.

I would fight Paul for Robin, and I would win.

How was I to know then that it was all too late?

Chapter Thirty-Seven

All over Christmas my husband was pleased with me, with the way things were going and the hotel bursting at the seams. Every room was booked and there was an overflow staying at the village inn and coming to Reckmire for meals and entertainment.

He talked about having the hotel enlarged in the near future and I wondered in annoyance what else he would sacrifice to carry out his ambitions.

I spent most of the Christmas period with John Cavendish. We danced together and rode together, we sat in the lounge drinking wine and chatting amicably, and Paul left us alone. He thought I was merely carrying out his suggestions, that I was making myself available, but there was no intimacy between John and me. We were friends, nothing more, and I derived a great deal of satisfaction from keeping it that way.

He left before New Year's Eve and a new crowd moved in for the festivities. I went to the watch night service at the village church and on leaving was accosted by Mrs Peabody who said sourly, 'I expect we can look forward to a lot o' noise fro' the crowd you've got at Reckmire in the early 'ours, Mrs Cheviot?'

'I hope not, Mrs Peabody, I hope they'll have used up their surplus energy in the hotel ballroom.'

'Yer grandparents would 'ave bin turnin' in their grave if they knew what was goin' on,' she said firmly.

'I'm sure they would.'

Just then another woman joined her, and wishing them

418

both a happy new year I made my escape.

Back at the hotel the festivities were in full flow. Couples sat on the stairs in groups drinking champagne, the ballroom was full and overflowing into the other rooms. There was no sign of Paul. I went upstairs to get out of my outdoor clothing and saw that further along the corridor in his private sitting room a light burned and from it came the sound of laughter and the voices of men and women. The sound of the festivities below came only dimly to the upstairs rooms so it was doubtful if it had kept Robin awake. I changed into a long dinner gown and after reassuring myself that Robin was sleeping soundly, left my room and made to go to the lift.

The sound of my door closing had been heard in Paul's sitting room, however, and he called out, 'Is that you, Joanna?'

I wasn't interested in finding out who he was entertaining and would have preferred to go downstairs but he was standing in the doorway, a glass in his hands and a confident smile on his face, saying, 'Come along in, my dear, I'm entertaining a few of the staff before we join the revelry downstairs.'

On a couch pulled up in front of the fire sat the hotel receptionist and Freda Felton, while standing at the cocktail cabinet was the golf professional and the head gardener. I wished them good evening but although the men came forward gallantly to shake my hand only the receptionist smiled. In Freda's eyes I recognised the old resentment.

'Drink, my dear?' Paul asked.

'Thank you. A gin and tonic, please.'

'My wife seldom drank spirits,' he said with a smile, 'but since Cavendish was here she's changed her drinking habits. I've begun to ask myself if I was wise to allow you to see so much of him, my dear.'

Ignoring his sarcasm, I asked evenly, 'Are you enjoying the festivities?'

All except Freda assured me that they were, and pointedly I said to her, 'You're not saying anything, Freda.'

She had the grace to blush, then in a hard voice replied, 'I enjoy everything, Mrs Cheviot, I'm that sort of girl.'

'Yes, I remember.'

I finished my drink and putting the empty glass down on a small table said, 'I really think we should go down, Paul. It seems very remiss of us to be distancing ourselves from our guests.'

Paul gave a mocking smile, saying, 'My wife is right to be teaching me that I'm failing in my duty as a host. Drink up then and be prepared to be assaulted by noise and a host of inebriates anxious to wish all and sundry a happy new year.'

It was just after one but men and women were asleep on the stairs and others in a state of undress were locked in each other's arms in the rooms we walked through. I felt angry to see the bowls of flowers lying wrecked on the floor, their petals crushed under heedless feet, and glasses lying on their sides on small tables, their content dripping on to the carpets with the stains spreading. Angrily I said, 'It's going to take weeks to put the place to rights. This never happened before.'

'Well, we're closed for a couple of weeks after this. We can get cleaners in, have a professional job done. What did you expect, Joanna? It is New Year's Eve.'

There was a small cheer as we entered the ballroom, and immediately Paul invited me to dance.

'It's a pity John had to leave before tonight,' he said smoothly. 'Missing him, are you?'

I didn't answer, and he grinned. 'You did very well, Joanna, he was completely bowled over. I thought you'd probably let me down but I was wrong. He's booked in for early-March you'll be glad to hear. By that time I expect his divorce will be out of the way. Did he tell you about his divorce?'

'Some.'

'Well, if he has any thoughts of inviting you to be the second Mrs Cavendish, he'll need to make it worth my while.'

'Doesn't it bother you that I think you're contemptible? Doesn't it even bother you that John Cavendish thinks you're contemptible?'

He threw back his head and laughed. 'My dear girl, John

420

Cavendish and I go back a long way. He has my measure and I have his, like two jungle cats stalking our territory.'

'You threatened to take Robin away from me when I wanted a divorce to marry a man I was in love with. Now it seems you're prepared to hand me to John Cavendish on a plate.'

'Oh, no, Joanna, not on a plate. He implied that his wife was after half his fortune. If he wants you, it'll cost him the other half.'

'You're very sure of yourself, Paul. I think you'll find John Cavendish a worthy adversary.'

'You're probably right. In any case I'm going to hang on to you, Joanna. Our marriage suits me very well. You don't put chains around me and it's given me Reckmire.'

'Half of Reckmire.'

'I stand corrected, my dear, half of Reckmire.'

Others of our guests invited me to dance with them. Men who were unsteady on their feet, others who breathed affectionate nonsense in my ears, and I hated every moment of it. There was another day of festivity left and then they would be departing with screams of farewell and promises before their cars screeched along the straggling village street on their way to the main highway.

They left behind them a place badly in need of professional care but the peace was like a benison as I stood with Paul on the terrace steps watching the last car drive out through the gates.

'Well, that's that,' he said with satisfaction. 'A great success, Joanna, and we've made a bomb. More to the point they'll all be back. Most of them have already booked in. I'm wanted down at the stables, one of the horses has gone lame apparently.'

'Which horse?'

'Not yours,' he replied airily, hurrying away across the terrace in the direction of the stables.

Robin sat at a table in the window colouring one of his books and I went to sit with him.

'Everybody's gone home now, Robin. Would you like to walk on the beach? It isn't terribly cold and we can wrap up well.'

'No, Mummy, I don't want to go on the beach.'

'But you used to love it, darling, and the sea is very calm.'

He shook his head adamantly, and trying to keep my voice cheerful, I said, 'Well, how about walking to the point where the lighthouse is? We could see if there are any fishing boats.'

'No, I don't want to go out.'

'Come along, Robin, we'll walk in the gardens for a while, then when we come inside we'll have hot buttered crumpets. You'd like that, wouldn't you?'

Reluctantly he allowed me to button him into his thick winter coat but his face was mutinous as he pulled on his woollen gloves and wrapped the scarf around his neck.

I was the one who chattered as we walked through the gardens in the direction of the village. The January day was grey but there was little wind and the leaves that still clung to the trees hung dejectedly in a colourless scene.

We walked as far as the churchgate and I could see down the road to where a perambulator stood outside the baker's shop and wondered if Lottie was visiting with Freda's child. We took a different route back to the house and without Robin noticing I skirted the gardens and came at last to the little path leading down to the point. The tide was out, a dismal grey line, and the lighthouse towered over an expanse of sand and shingle, but I felt his hand clutch mine tightly and he pulled me back towards the gardens.

'No, Mummy, no, not the sea! I don't want to walk near the sea,' he cried.

'But the sea is a long way out, Robin. Why don't you want to be near the sea?'

'Granny said it would eat me like it ate that other little boy,' he murmured miserably.

'Robin, the sea will not eat you. You must learn to have respect for it, to know when the tide is coming in and how it curves along the sand. Granny should not have frightened you with that old story.'

He was too young, and I did not know what words she had used on that long afternoon to bring such terror to his eyes. He would grow older, he would come to see

422

that the sea would never harm him if he understood it, and reluctantly I drew him away, only too aware of his tear-stained face, and the sudden relief when we saw the hotel beyond the gardens.

John Cavendish came to Reckmire at the beginning of March, bringing with him three business associates. They occupied the best rooms, ordered the choicest wines, and tipped extravagantly. The hotel was only half full because it was too early in the year for many visitors, but those that were there were more the sort I liked, people who were there for a few days to be cossetted, happy and contented with simple pleasures.

'It's a great pity that he's here to talk business.' Paul said cynically. 'He'll not have much time for you on this occasion, my dear.'

'It seems to be worrying you far more that it does me,' I answered calmly.

'Oh, well, he's booked in for Easter and the hotel will be pretty full then.'

Easter brought parents with children and once more Robin was told he must ride with them and again he was the youngest member of the group.

The weather was fine but the spring tides were unnaturally high so that from my sitting room I could hear the great waves pounding along the beach. Robin would sit with his hands pressed over his ears, his expression a pinched pitiable grimace, and I constantly had to reassure him that summer was on the way and soon the sea would be calm.

It was Easter Monday and I was kneeling on the floor in the act of removing Robin's riding boots when the door was flung open and Paul strode into the room, his eyes blazing.

I stared at him in amazement and Robin shrank back in his chair, his face a mask of fear.

'What's this I hear about your refusing to go riding this morning?' barked Paul.

The child shrank back further and his father's hand reached out and brought him unwillingly out of the chair to stand shivering before him.

'Answer me, Robin. Why did you come back to the hotel?' Paul snapped.

'I didn't want to ride on the beach,' he answered in a small trembling voice.

'Why, for heaven's sake? The tide was out, the other children were not afraid.'

Robin stood before him with bowed head, and Paul reached down and lifted his chin. 'Are you telling me you're afraid of the sea?'

The tears flowed down his face, but he nodded miserably.

'Why are you afraid?'

'Granny said it wwwould eat mmmme.'

For a long time there was silence. Paul's face was white with fury while the boy before him had sunk to the floor and I had gathered him into my arms.

'Did you know about this, Joanna?' he demanded. 'What were you doing to let your mother get at the boy?'

'It was on the day of Stella's wedding. I heard her talking to Robin. I was angry with her and as soon as I could I took him away. The damage was done. Now all I can do is talk to him, tell him not to be afraid, show him that the sea can be calm and benign.'

'No, Joanna, that's not all you can do. This afternoon he is coming with me. I'll make him walk along that beach. I'll not have him blubbering out his fears in front of the other children ever again.'

'Who told you about it?'

'Freda told me. She was there, she heard the other children laughing about it, thought I ought to know.'

'Did she indeed? Well, after today Freda Felton no longer works here.'

'I employ the stable hands, Joanna, you have no power to dismiss them, that was part of the bargain, remember. This afternoon, Robin, when the tide is out, you and I are going to walk along Reckmire.'

He left us, slamming the door behind him, and I stayed with Robin, talking to him calmly about his fears, telling him stories of a summer sea and the joys of a golden beach and sea shells and sea creatures left there for his enjoyment.

I stood on the path above the rocks watching his tiny figure trotting at Paul's side. I knew that he was crying

424

and Paul took a tighter hold of him and as they reached the line of the sea forced him to look at it before they walked on along the beach. It was cold and there was salt spray lashing my face, and the wind in my hair sent it in a wild damp strand across my face.

How small they became in the distance, but still Paul walked on, and then I was remembering that other time when I had thought I was safe, loving the tumbling waves, the taste of salt on my lips, and Robin running to me across the sands. With sudden fear I started to clamber down the rocks until I felt a firm hand reach out to pull me back.

I looked up startled, to see John Cavendish looking down at me. 'Where are you going, Joanna? The tide's coming in,' he cried.

I pointed to the figures in the distance and he stared at me incredulously. 'It's Paul.' I cried. 'He's taken Robin to the sea, and I'm so afraid.'

He stared after them. 'The bloody idiot! What in heaven's name is he playing at?' he cried.

They had turned and were coming back. I could see as they drew nearer that Robin was struggling in terror, and then Paul shook him off and walked on angrily alone.

Robin lay on the sands, struggling against the wind to rise, and then like that other time I saw the sea, curving and towering, covering the sands with giant waves in the wake of the tiny figure. Screaming in terror, I started to climb down the rocks and John came after me, both of us waving our hands, our shouts of terror lost on the wind. Then suddenly Paul saw us, and turning saw Robin's tiny figure struggling behind him. He went back, reaching out for the boy, but it was too late, the sea took him, and as Paul rushed into it in search of his son, the sea took him too.

All around me were shouts of despair and John's hands held me like a vice as, like Robin had done before him, he dragged me up the rocks towards the safety of the cliff top.

Behind us the sea came on relentlessly, mercilessly, and I remembered nothing more.

For days I lived in limbo and it was John Cavendish who

spoke to the police, arranged the funeral after their bodies were found washed ashore along the coast.

My aunt and uncle came to stay with me, appalled at the way I looked, totally bewildered that my husband and son had been walking on the beach on such a day. My mother telephoned.

I heard her voice accusing me of not heeding the warnings she had issued over the years and replaced the receiver. I couldn't believe it when three days later she came to Reckmire for the funeral.

The hotel was closed and I had no thoughts of reopening it. On the day of the funeral villagers lined the street leading to the church and from the distance the bell tolled dismally across the marshes. I was aware of Mother sitting besides me in the funeral car, her face tight-lipped as I remembered it, her hands in their pale grey suede clenched tightly in her lap.

That night John Cavendish came to my sitting room to say goodbye, he had to return to London on business. He gripped my hand so that I felt as though he was trying to instil some of his strength into my shattered life. 'Get away from here, Joanna,' he advised sternly. 'Sell the place, it holds too many memories. Never come back.'

I nodded wordlessly. It was too soon. Later I heard the same sort of advice from my mother. 'There's no need for you to stay here, Joanna,' she said, 'haven't I always warned you? I hated it, I couldn't understand why you loved it so. Now get rid of it, come back to Surrey. You don't have to live with me if you don't want to, but you can stay with me until you find something of your own. Let me know when you are coming.'

I owed so much to John Cavendish. He found a buyer for Reckmire. 'The buyer's not interested in keeping it as it is now, Joanna,' he told me. 'He fell in love with the old place and is prepared to change it back. You'd like that wouldn't you?'

'Yes,' I murmured.

'And have you thought what you'll do? You're surely not contemplating living with your mother.'

'No, I could never do that. There are so many things

I need to sort out so it will be some time before I can get away.'

I did not tell John about the debts that had piled up after Paul's grandiose schemes. Every day they came to see me, shuffling their feet in embarrassment at having to trouble me in this time of grief, but needing their money desperately.

Paul had planned to pay them from the profits he hoped to make on successful seasons, but the most hurtful thing of all was when I was asked for the money for Ralston. I loved him but couldn't bear to keep him. Instead I sold him, and seeing him walk calmly into his horsebox was like another knife twisting in my heart.

John came with the new owner whom I immediately recognised as being one of our guests soon after the hotel opened. I listened to his ideas for Reckmire, and although the staff had already left he told me he had persuaded many of our old workforce to work for him. Now only the gardeners and the grooms remained, but it was the sight of Robin's pony that brought the treacherous tears into my eyes.

Summer came to Reckmire and now the sea rolled in on crested waves and the coarse grass blew gently on the sweeping dunes. They told me that Freda had left on the night of the tragedy and that she had also left the village. I stayed away from there because I couldn't bear to see the compassion in faces that had always greeted me with smiles until Paul had made them angry.

It was one evening when the sky blazed with the setting sun that I ventured once more on to the beach at Reckmire. The tide was out and I walked slowly, standing at last to look out into the far distance to where the sea gleamed like molten gold and at a sky aflame with orange and shades of tragic crimson.

I felt a sudden peace wash over me. Not the peace of forgetfulness, but the peace of a strange understanding. I felt that I was not alone, that out of the mists of time old memories surrounded me, and those I had loved were near to sustain me. If it was an illusion it was a dear and wonderful illusion and as the sun sank lower in the evening sky I turned away with my bruised heart strangely at peace.

I started to walk back along the beach towards the house

and then across the sands I saw a man walking towards me. He was tall, and walked with a slight limp. I stared at the setting sun gilding his hair, then as he came nearer I saw his smile, and with a little cry of joy ran into his outstretched arms.

As I wept and clung to him a wild and sudden joy seemed to expel the pain that I had lived with in the months since Robin's death and the warmth and promise in his kiss brought solace to my heart.

Somehow on that long golden beach aflame with the setting sun I had experienced something magical, and now as if to assure me that it was real was the joy of knowing that Carlo had come back into my life.

Epilogue

Memories of other years engulfed me as I drove northward from the airport. Memories of Robin in his brash two-seater, and the low discreet voices of important Naval commanders in the dark anonymity of the staff car I was driving, then as the dark sun-splashed hills drew closer, memories of my grandparents and my father.

Nostalgia tugged at my heart as I drove along the narrow country roads towards the sea, where the trees were stunted, leaning away as if they were afraid of it, and where the brackish scent of the marshes was overpowering.

Late-summer roses bloomed in cottage gardens and already the trees were turning, their russet leaves falling. As I drove at last along the village street the years dropped away and I could have been a schoolgirl staring with delighted anticipation at the baker's display of confectionery.

There were few people on the village street and I guessed they would be in their homes preparing to sit down to their evening meal. I saw that it was almost six o'clock by the church clock, and then I was driving up the hill towards the stone gates of Reckmire. The park stretched before me and I stared with surprise to see that horses grazed where once there had been deer, and that instead of the ballroom there was now a vast conservatory.

The formal gardens were well tended and as I drove at last into a vacant parking space I could feel my heart pounding relentlessly and for several minutes remained in the car waiting for the courage to walk into the hotel.

It was like walking into a past I thought had gone forever.

As I stood in the entrance staring at the transformation a man walked across the foyer to greet me. He was smiling, holding out his hand in greeting. Clasping mine, he said, 'Welcome to Reckmire, Contessa. You shall tell me later if you approve of what I have done to it.'

'Are all the rooms restored?' I asked curiously.

'As nearly as possible. I came here with my wife as a guest shortly after it was opened and fell in love with the place. It had so much character and I was horrified when Gainsborough said it was being altered. I couldn't believe it had your approval.'

'No. Not entirely.'

'But it brought a different sort of clientele, I suppose.'

'Yes.'

'It has taken a special sort of courage to come back, Contessa. I admire you for it, without quite knowing why you have come.'

'Curiosity, nostalgia, the desire to recapture something that has been irretrievably lost, to lay my ghosts. I'm not even very sure myself.'

'We have given you a room at the front of the house overlooking the gardens and the point. The family occupy the flat upstairs but in any case we didn't think you would want to stay in it.'

'No. I shall be quite happy wherever you have put me.'

'A friend of yours is visiting us, Contessa. I took the liberty of telling him that you were coming here and he is very anxious to meet you again. Mr John Cavendish.'

I smiled. 'Thank you, I shall be pleased to see him again.'

The room he had given me was on the first floor and had been my grandparents' room. It was entirely charming and once again I marvelled at how faithfully the new owner had copied the taste of the original decor.

The dining room too had been restored and I stared around me curiously from my table near the window. It was there that John Cavendish joined me, smiling down at me with all his old audacity, taking my hand and saying, 'You're looking very beautiful, Joanna. If you'd been my wife I doubt if I'd have allowed you to come here alone.'

'I insisted. It was something I had to do.'

'What do you think of the place?'

'I'm impressed. I can't think it attracts the younger element.'

'The old guests have come back. It is select and expensive. Something you would have wanted, Joanna.'

I nodded.

'And you're happy with your Italian Count in enchanting Tuscany. I can see that without having to ask.'

'Yes, very happy. And you, have you remarried?'

'No. I've nothing against marriage but I'm biding my time. I don't want to make a mistake the second time. Do you have a family, Joanna?'

'Yes, I have a son, Alexander, and a daughter, Gina.'

'I'm glad. I never thought you'd come back. For months I couldn't get that terrible day out of my mind. I think about it even now. But why are you doing this to yourself, Joanna? Why now when life is so good for you?'

So I told him about the picture and the shop in Genoa, and found myself telling him about the anguish of guilt that at times poisoned my happiness.

'Why should you feel guilty?' he said in amazement. 'None of it was your fault.'

'But could I have understood Paul more? His parents must have been to blame for the way he was. Were my grandparents responsible for the way my mother was, and could I have understood and even tried to change either of them?'

'You'd never have changed Cheviot, Joanna, never think it. I don't know your mother, but people don't change. Cheviot was the product of his early life. You could never have changed him. Do you hear from your mother?'

'I write to her. One can't go on year after year bearing grudges and she's rather a sad, pitiable figure. I can tell from her letters that she hasn't changed. They're filled with reproaches, against me, her friends, her life.'

'So what is there here? Paul has gone, Robin too.'

'I know. Robin will always be in my heart, but Paul . . . I watched him go back. He was trying to save Robin's life when the sea took them both.'

431

'The boy wouldn't have been there but for Paul. You owe him nothing, Joanna, neither love nor understanding, so why torture yourself with regret now?'

How could I explain it to him when I couldn't explain it to myself? Instead I started to talk of other things before he suggested we did a tour of the hotel so that I could see what I thought of it.

Everything delighted me. Seeing the large gracious rooms restored so lovingly brought such a sense of peace and pride to my heart that alone would have made my visit worthwhile.

As John parted with me outside my room, he said, 'Care for a drive into the Lake District tomorrow, Joanna? You'd be taking pity on a lonely soul.'

'When are you returning to London?'

'I have to get back on Monday, so there's really only tomorrow.'

'Then I'll come since you've made the effort to come here to see me.'

I had always known that the weather in the Lake District could be unpredictable and it rained all day. The mountains were hidden under dark mist-laden clouds and the long stretches of water shone glassily grey, and yet it was a day I would remember. A day peculiar to England, a day so different from the sunshine of Tuscany that it would stand out in isolation whenever I thought back on it.

On parting that evening John said apologetically, 'What a pity it rained all day. You can't have enjoyed it, Joanna?'

'Oh, but I did, immensely. I do think about home a great deal, and today has been so essentially English. The soft rain lying on the wind, those grey beautiful lakes and the dark dismal conifers rising into the mist. I'll remember today when I'm basking in Italian sunshine. And I'll remember you, John, and your kindness.'

He bent his head and lightly brushed my lips with his own. 'Don't torture yourself unnecessarily, Joanna. Don't look for decency where none existed. Don't try to blame yourself for anything that happened that day.'

Many of the guests left next morning and the hotel was relatively quiet. After breakfast I went up to my room and

432

got out my trench coat and a scarf for my head. I put stout walking shoes on my feet and set out along the drive, then before I reached the gates took the narrow path that led across the marshes towards the beach.

I clambered down the rocks and made myself walk along the length of Reckmire, my footsteps followed the shingle left by the tide, and I could taste the salt and hear the rumble of the incoming tide.

It was sweet and terrible punishment, but in my heart was the picture of Robin trotting sobbing beside his father, his small hand clenched in Paul's tenacious fingers, and I could feel Paul's exasperation as he left him behind while he strode back towards the house.

I could see the waves rolling inland relentlessly and hear Robin's plaintive cries of terror lost on the wind, then they were struggling in the water and in minutes they were lost.

Nothing was left. I stood looking out to where it had happened, my cheeks wet with tears, the ache in my heart so terrible I pressed my fists hard against my chest in an endeavour to ease it, then helplessly I turned away. Was this what I had come back for, to live again the anguish of that afternoon, and if so what had I achieved?

I stumbled back along the beach, the wind tearing at my scarf until it was wrenched from my head and my hair floated wildly round my face. I saw the house and the rocks through a blur of tears but then as I looked upward I saw the figure of a woman standing on the cliff path and I paused, aware that she was watching me. At that moment she held up her arm and waved and surprised I walked towards her thinking it was a fellow guest because nobody in the village knew I was here.

I started to climb upwards, and she came to look down on me, then I recognised her. It was Lottie and it was only when I reached her side that I realised she was not alone. Standing on the path with his bicycle was a boy, and as she looked gravely into my eyes I said breathlessly, 'How did you know I was here, Lottie?'

'I saw you take the path through the marsh, Joanna. I knew where you were goin'. Ye shouldn't 'ave come down on to the beach.'

433

'I had to. I'll never come here again, but just once before I go home I had to see where Robin died.

'This is your son, Lottie?' I asked smiling at the boy who stood grave and awkwardly shy.

'We took 'im when he was born. Ye know 'e's our Freda's boy?'

'Yes. What did you call him?'

For a moment she stood silent, then she whispered softly, 'We called 'im Paul, it was what she wanted.'

I stared at her, and she said quickly, 'Come and meet 'im.'

I went with her. I felt that in the next few minutes there would be things I would discover that were important to me, and as I looked into the boy's dark sombre eyes I knew what they were. This boy was Paul's son, his eyes and the contour of his face so like Robin's I could have gathered him into my arms. Instead I took his extended hand and met his grave smile with my own.

'Get off 'ome now, love,' Lottie said. 'Tell your granny I'll not be long.'

We watched him cycling away from us along the path and meeting my anguished gaze at last Lottie said, 'She'd never tell us who the boy's father was, but I knew almost as soon as 'e was born. All those months when you were in Italy she was with 'im, sleepin' at Reckmire, never comin' 'ome and tellin' my mother she had too much to do at the stables.'

In those moments I hated Paul anew. He had refused to give me a divorce to marry the man I loved, threatened to separate me from Robin if I left him, while all the time he had been having an affair with Freda Felton. I felt so sickened by his perfidy I could have screamed in anger, and Lottie said quickly, 'It's over, Joanna, and there's nothin' any of us can do about it. We don't know where our Freda is, she doesn't write and she doesn't come 'ome. The boy's ours, we love him, and we'll bring 'im up the best we can.

'I always 'oped that someday I'd be able to tell you about 'im, just so that you'd stop thinking things could ever 'ave bin any different. They couldn't. 'E never cared for anybody except 'imself. 'E wanted you because through you 'e could get 'is hands on Reckmire, 'e never cared for our Freda, or that boy. 'E was a taker, Joanna, 'e took your family and 'e took from you and your son, then 'e took from Freda and 'er son. It's the truth. I cried about your little boy, Joanna, but I never cried for 'im.'

'You hate him more than I do, Lottie.'

'Yes, I do. I'm strict with the boy, too strict, and I'm constantly lookin' for any sign of 'is father in 'im. My sister was no angel. She 'ated it that your boy was accepted and 'ers wasn't.'

'Freda told Paul that the village children had been taunting Robin because he was afraid of the sea. It made Paul so angry he dragged Robin along the beach to his death.'

'I thought she might 'ave had something to do with it. She was like a wild thing when she went back to my mother's that night, hatin' herself, hatin' him. She wouldn't look at the child, and at night my parents could 'ear her pacin', always pacin' about her room, and my father knocked on 'er door to tell her to go to bed and let them get some sleep. Three days later she'd gone. She simply packed a small suitcase and walked out without sayin' anythin' to either of them, no letter, nothin'. None of us 'ave heard anythin' since. We don't know where she is, we've had no word.'

'That must have hurt your parents, Lottie.'

'My 'usband says good riddance to bad rubbish, but she was my sister. I'd like to know what's become of 'er.'

'The boy's been lucky to have you and your husband, Lottie. Have you told him anything about his mother?'

'When he was sixteen we talked to him. He knows about Freda and his father, he knows about your little boy and that terrible day, but he knows we love 'im. 'E's had the best we could give 'im and 'e's never given us any trouble. 'E's clever too. Won a scholarship when he was nine for the grammar school and 'is reports are good. We've lived every day as it came, Joanna, you'll understand that.'

'Yes, Lottie, I do.'

'I was so angry with myself that day on the fell when I 'inted that he might 'ave been more interested in Reckmire than you. You'd just asked me to be your bridesmaid and you were so happy, so much in love with 'im. I prayed that night that it'd work out real well for you, Joanna, that e'd

435

'ave loved you if you'd gone to him with nothin'. And you were so happy on your weddin' day when we all went up to the Hall and had the weddin' party in the marquee. I would 'ave been glad to be wrong about him, Joanna, but I wasn't, was I?'

'No, Lottie. He loved the girl who could give him Reckmire, he never loved me.'

'How long before you found out?'

'That night, a conversation I wasn't meant to hear. I couldn't believe the man I loved was saying those things about me, mean hurtful things, but now looking back I think perhaps fate intended me to hear. If I hadn't I'd have gone on living in a fool's paradise, for as long as Paul could pretend anyway.'

'I'm not tryin' to make excuses for our Freda and I'm not askin' you to forgive 'er but she loved Paul Cheviot long afore you did. She used to stand in the lane just waitin' to see 'im ridin' down from the big house with the rest of them when she was only a girl. I used to tell 'er that he wasn't a patch on the other one, yer cousin Robin, but she wouldn't 'ave it. Not that either of 'em would ever 'ave given either of us a second look then.

'She allus wanted to be somebody better than she was. She resented you because you were Joanna Albemarle and that you knew 'im, even when I told 'er that you did nothin' but squabble in them days. When she went to work at Reckmire and 'e started to take notice of 'er she never stopped to think. She said 'e wasn't happy in his marriage and one day' e'd turn to her. Nobody could 'ave convinced her otherwise.'

'Perhaps she'll come back one day, Lottie, when all this has become a nine days' wonder and people have stopped talking about it.'

'They'll never stop talkin' about it in the village. It'll be a tale that's passed on as long as they tell their children to keep away fro' Reckmire Marsh. They still talks about a girl and 'er horse racin' along that beach tryin' to beat the waves many years back. They both drowned in the sea, and that was a tale I 'eard when I was only a toddler. Now they'll talk about Robin and 'is father.'

'I haven't been into the village, Lottie. Even after all

these years I couldn't bear to see the compassion in faces I knew.'

'A friend of my mother's works in the kitchens. She said they had an Italian Contessa visitin', and I somehow 'oped it was you. I allus 'ad a feelin' that one day you might come back and I knew I had an answer to one o' the questions you might 'ave bin askin' yourself all these years.'

'This is the last time I shall come here so I don't think we shall see each other again. Thank you for bringing your son to see me, it took a lot of courage, he's a fine boy.'

''Ave ye been 'appy in Italy, Joanna? Life's funny, isn't it. I remember you tellin' me about that Italian boy you'd met there and I'd guessed you'd fallen in love with him. You said 'e was goin' to marry your cousin, but neither of us would ever 'ave guessed that one day he'd marry you.'

'No. The paths of life are often very strange.'

'And you're 'appy?'

'Yes. I am very happy. I have two children and we live in a lovely old castle in one of the most beautiful parts of Italy. It would be wonderful if you could see it.'

She smiled. 'I doubt if my 'usband'll ever set foot out o' this country, Joanna. 'E's allus said 'e had enough o' foreign travel to last him a lifetime during the war.'

Suddenly her plain honest face was lit by a bright smile and she reached out and hugged me in her arms. I watched her walking away from me and waited until she reached the bend in the lane where she turned and looked back. She waved then walked on and I could see her no more.

I had asked myself many times over the years why my grandparents left the house to me. It never brought me happiness, only a sad and tragic bewilderment, but they had not meant it to be that way. They had thought it would be a home for me with my husband and children, a place of joy and laughter as it had been in the old days, and a place for my father to come home to after years of imprisonment in the Far East. But fate had cheated us all and now I was leaving Reckmire again, never to return.

I had made up my mind that I would drive into Surrey to see my mother before returning to Italy but there was no sense of pleasure in my decision. I wrote to her often but her answering letters were always filled with complaints about people and a life which she believed had never played fair. My visit would be a duty, because she was my mother, because I pitied her, and because it could all have been so very different.

I begged her to visit us, to spend long months in the sunshine of Italy where she could have watched her grandchildren grow up, but she always had an excuse, trivial and meaningless. My poor mother who had always been her own worst enemy.

A waiter came to serve me afternoon tea with smiles and efficiency and I sank down gratefully in the warmth of the hotel lounge and began to look around me.

The room was filled with groups of people enjoying afternoon tea, conversation mingled with the sound of music, and for a moment I felt singularly alone. The room stared back at me impersonally, then in that brief moment it seemed to me that the years dropped away and I was a schoolgirl sitting with my grandmother in front of the huge stone fireplace, a box filled with photographs between us. Gabriella was there, dark and lovely, tantalising Paul with her dimpled smiles and flashing Italian eyes, and Robin was walking across the room towards us, his face warm with laughter so that my young foolish heart forgot to be afraid.

'Is there anything more, Contessa?' a voice asked, and I looked up startled to see a waiter bending over me, his smile as polite as his question, and all around me was the murmur of voices, music and laughter.

'Nothing thank you,' I replied. He smiled and walked away.

THE NEW HARTFORD MEMORIAL LIBRARY
P.O. Box 247
Central Avenue at Town Hill Road
New Hartford, Connecticut 06057

F
HYL

Hylton, Sara.

Reckmire Marsh.

$24.95

DATE			

BAKER & TAYLOR